Storm of Passion

Susannah could only stare up at Rhys, at the hawklike features that had such cold strength. There was no tenderness in them now, no gentleness, only a harsh reality.

She wanted that reality. Almost without realizing it, she rose up on her tiptoes, her face nearing his, her hand reaching upward to soothe the frown that burrowed between his eyes.

"Don't," he said, but it wasn't denial so much as surrender. His lips went down and took hers, just the way she had dreamed they would. There was anger in the kiss—cold, hard anger—and she wished she knew where it came from. But there was also life, a sudden surge of passion that ripped through both of them as a tornado rips through air, taking everything in its path: every caution, every fear, every inhibition. . . .

Renegade

Patricia Potter

BANTAM BOOKS
NEW YORK • TORONTO • LONDON • SYDNEY • AUCKLAND

RENEGADE
A Bantam Book / May 1993

ISBN 0-553-56199-5

Published simultaneously in the United States and Canada

Bantam Books are published by Bantam Books, a division of Bantam Doubleday
Dell Publishing Group, Inc. Its trademark, consisting of the words "Bantam Books"
and the portrayal of a rooster, is Registered in U.S. Patent and Trademark Office
and in other countries. Marca Registrada. Bantam Books, 1540 Broadway, New
York, New York 10036.

PRINTED IN THE UNITED STATES OF AMERICA
RAD   0 9 8 7 6 5 4 3 2 1

Renegade

Prologue

The ultimate joke!

He knew the cannonball was going to hit his ship. It seemed to move uncommonly slowly, but very accurately, as it arched through a suddenly clear night. The fog that had shrouded the ship's movements lifted, leaving only a few damp patches floating in the air like steam from a teapot.

And the *Specter II*, the ship he had so unwisely taken in a very bad bargain, lay off the Carolina waters like a crippled fox waiting to be torn to pieces by the hounds.

The first mate and pilot had taken charge of the ship. He, Rhys Redding, had just been along for the ride, to learn, to adventure, to try to forget the moment of weakness that made him lose what he'd always thought he wanted most.

The ship suddenly jerked as the first mate tried to avoid the incoming fire, and Rhys balanced himself against a keg of nails tied down to the deck. Coffin nails. He'd been told they were in great demand by the Confederacy. Bloody fitting, he thought irreverently.

His fabled luck had run out. He knew that, as the cannonball hit the stern of the ship, sending a hail of flaming wood splinters and metal raining down on the crew. He heard screams and felt the sting of pain in several places, and then the familiar sticky flow of blood.

He saw two crewmen try to hoist a white flag, but another shot sent both of them flying, and then there were more fireballs in the sky. He closed his eyes. He'd always heard a man saw his life pass before him when he died.

He wasn't particularly eager to see his own. . . .

He kept hearing the hated word: bastard.

His mother's words. The whore's words. A mistake, she'd told him over and over again. She'd sneered, "Ye be a lord's bastard. Because of you, he threw me out." She'd tried to rid herself of him, she'd told him, but the usual means had not worked. She'd hated him for being too strong, for refusing to die even in the womb.

Another shot hit the ship, and it started to roll to the left, or leeward or whatever it was. He should know after his many months at sea, but everything was a bit fuzzy now. Even the years as they passed in his mind.

The stable. Lying bleeding from the whip of an impatient lord. After his prostitute mother died, he had taken refuge there, currying horses in exchange for shelter and bread. But one time he had not been fast enough, and he'd tasted the sting of a horsewhip. He'd been eight years old, but he could still feel the pain of that whip, the humiliation. He had vowed then that no one would touch him again. No one.

The streets of London. He'd survived there nearly seven years any way he could: picking pockets, shilling for crooked games. Anything for a pence. Anything at all to fill a hungry stomach.

And then Nathan Carruthers had come along, the black sheep son of an earl. Even now, Rhys remembered his grin, the grin that defied even death. Nathan had been a charmer. A thief. And a gambler. And he'd taught Rhys to excel at all three. . . .

They had met in a London street when Rhys threw out a foot in front of a Bow Street Runner chasing Nathan, and Nathan had immediately seen a disciple in the young street tough. Nathan had to leave London, and Africa seemed a likely place in which to get lost—and make a great deal of money.

Africa . . . a sun-drenched dangerous land where Rhys had honed his natural abilities, where he had learned the ways of a chameleon, where he had learned to kill—

"Abandon ship!"

The shout could barely be heard as the ship groaned and creaked its last gasps for life. The deck slanted, and Rhys had to hold on to the rope that served as a railing. Goods, destined for the dying Confederacy, were sliding into the water. A fortune in goods. A fortune Rhys had paid for. Or traded for.

Because of a pair of hazel eyes . . .

Rhys had returned to London a rich man. And he'd come alone. Nathan lay in a grave back in Africa, thousands of miles from his home. His last legacy to Rhys had been a diamond, a perfect stone he'd found someplace. Nathan died of fever before he could tell Rhys where. He probably wouldn't have, anyway. Nathan had never been a sharing man, unless he wanted something.

Rhys already had considerable savings of his own. He'd learned well from Nathan. So many things: reading and writing, manners, ways of the gentry. Gambling. Confidence games. Even safecracking, which had precipitated his partner's flight from England.

The unrelenting hunger in Rhys for security, for the means to make himself invulnerable to others, closeted what little conscience he had after surviving on the streets, and Nathan simply hadn't had one. Rhys soon

*discovered Nathan had not paid his way to Africa out
of gratitude, nor had the disgraced lord provided hours
of impatient instruction out of the goodness of his
heart. Nathan, instead, had apparently seen in Rhys's
unique ability with languages and dialects a needed
partner in his various schemes. In the beginning, they
had been soldiers of fortune, shepherding settlers
across dangerous plains, winning their money during
the long, lonely evenings. And then Nathan had
schemes. He'd always had schemes.*

*When Nathan died, Rhys knew it was time to re-
turn to England. Although he had liked Africa, the vast
plains and vivid colors, he'd never felt as if he really
belonged there. He had a deep gnawing hunger for
something else, something he didn't entirely understand. His mother had once told him he was the son of
nobility. Perhaps now it was time to take his place
among those he'd always envied. With the diamond, he
had enough financial resources to buy his way.*

*But he didn't. His money bought him entrance into
gambling dens, and his dark reputation in the boudoirs
of the adventurous ladies of the town, but he soon
found he could go no further, not even after winning
one of the oldest estates in England.*

*And then he had met Lauren Bradley and Adrian
Cabot, the brother of the man whose estate Rhys had
won. For the first time in his life, he saw unselfishness
and sacrifice as Lauren fought to regain the property
for her beloved, even when she thought she'd lost him
forever.*

*In a rare moment of weakness, in the only moment
of weakness in his adult life, Rhys Redding did the un-
thinkable: He indulged in a spontaneous act of
generosity—*

Rhys heard the crackle of fire, then felt a tug at his
arm. It was the ship's pilot.

"Mr. Redding, you have to jump now. For God's
sake, jump."

Bloody hell, it was February. Still, he was a survivor.

He jumped, his body coiling from the agonizing shock of icy water. He fought his way back to the surface, thinking his lungs might burst from lack of air if he didn't freeze to death first. And he vowed that if he survived this, he would never do anything impulsive again, especially for anyone else. Never!

Chapter 1

Libby Prison,
Richmond, Virginia, 1865

For a moment, Rhys Redding thought he must be in heaven and the woman an angel.

But his coldly analytical mind quickly disabused him of such a notion. He certainly had done nothing to qualify himself for such an exalted place. Just the opposite, in fact, and if he believed in hell he surely must be in one. This place had everything but brimstone, and that was being stoked within his body.

If there was an angel here, by God, it was certainly by some monumental joke.

He groaned involuntarily, his body on fire, the pain in his side almost unbearable. He tried to think back, but all that came to him were shouts and the flash of guns and the terrible ripping agony that continued for days as he slipped in and out of consciousness. He remembered snatches of being aboard a jolting wagon, of gray uniforms, of curses, of being half dragged, half carried into this place.

Most of all he remembered pain. He couldn't think of when he was last free of it.

The angel moved closer to him, a bowl of water in

her hands. Through glazed eyes, he watched as she dipped a cloth in it and wiped the sweat from his face with hands that were more tender, more gentle than he'd ever felt before.

She'd done it before, he now recalled. Her fragrance was familiar, light and flowery, and memorable among the other smells of dirt and blood and death.

He tried to move, but only a gasp of pain came. Bloody hell, but his whole body was afire. He'd had wounds before, but nothing like this, nothing like this terrible burning that was consuming his whole left side.

"Water," he managed to croak through parched lips.

She nodded, and he had a glimpse of very dark hair under a bonnet, and vivid violet eyes. No, she wasn't an angel; no one that beautiful could possibly be an angel, he assured himself cynically. His experience with women left no doubt about that.

He would take what was being offered, even if there might be a subsequent price. Then he found he didn't even care about that possible price when she put a hand under his head and lifted it slightly so he could take in the water from the cup she held. He knew not to drink quickly; this was not the first time he had awakened to burning thirst, but it was difficult not to gulp greedily.

Sip by sip, he relieved some of his thirst, only slightly wondering at the patience of the woman. He could smell himself, and he winced. Why didn't it seem to bother her?

The water was gone then, and he resented that, for he didn't want her to leave him yet. With the greatest of effort, he raised his arm from under the stinking blanket that covered him, and noticed what was left of the blue uniform blouse he wore.

He sought to throw off the blanket, but the woman

put her hand on his arm. "You'll get ill," she said. Her voice was soft and drawling.

Rhys thought that was an extraordinary thing for her to say. He couldn't imagine feeling any worse than he did. But he made his body relax, and he tried to smile. "Get ill?"

A flash of humor illuminated her extraordinary eyes. "More ill, then," she replied. "You're really much better than you were yesterday, and the day before."

Rhys tried to sit a little, to obtain a tiny bit of dignity, of independence, but he was weak as a mewing kitten. "Where in the bloody hell . . .?"

She tipped her head, an amazingly appealing gesture, he observed. At least he'd lost none of his famed lust, even in his abysmal condition.

"You're not Yankee-bred," she said, a question in her voice.

Rhys tried to move again, but new waves of pain rolled over him and he closed his eyes to contain it, to keep from moaning, from showing any weakness. He hated that, showing weakness. He'd always hated it. He'd learned a long time ago how to bottle pain and humiliation, and to paint the container with indifference. "No," he finally managed.

"English?"

"Welsh," he answered, trying to figure out where he was, and why. But then on the other hand, he wasn't sure he really wanted to know. He had a very bad feeling about this.

"Fighting for the Yanks?"

Her voice was so soft that he had to strain to hear above the moaning and thrashing in this room.

He closed his eyes again, thinking of the past few weeks.

A good deed. That's how it all happened. One good deed in a life totally designed to advance one Rhys Redding.

One good deed and look what happened!

Well, never again. Weakness bred disaster. He knew that. He had always known that. Damn his hide for violating his own principles.

But he still didn't have the answer to his question. "Where am I?"

"Libby Prison," the woman said.

"What's Libby Prison?"

Her eyebrows, silky black fringes that shaded those glorious violet eyes, rose. "A Confederate prison for Yank officers, Major. Surely you must be familiar with the name."

"But I'm not . . ."

Flashes came to him then. An escape. An escape in an officer's uniform. He groaned with the irony of it. Christ, he'd been a prisoner of the Yanks. Now, apparently, he was a prisoner of the Confederates.

"You're not what?"

Who in the hell would believe him? In the middle of a war, dressed as an enemy. His gaze dropped to the soiled blue shirt he wore. It was dark and stiff with caked blood. A major's uniform, for God's sake. He remembered the man now; but even to him, the explanations for his predicament were ridiculous.

His lips stiff with self-disgust, he turned his eyes back to the woman. "Who are you?"

"Susannah Fallon," she said. She looked toward the cot next to his. "Wesley is my brother. Colonel Wesley Carr."

So her brother was a prisoner too. But how did *she* get here? Why was she helping him? He knew she had. For days. He had images in his head, images of gentle hands, an insistent voice calling him when he wanted to surrender to the sweet darkness.

He heard moans, and he looked around him, as much as he could. Men moved restlessly on cots, some moaning, some very still. The room was filled, every cot occupied and more men lying on the floor. There was only one window, high and barred. The walls were dingy, and the terrible stench, a sickly sweet smell of disease and death, was breath-robbing.

He tried to concentrate on what she'd just said. The brother. "How . . . is he?"

"He lost a leg. And . . . his will to live." Some of the light left those remarkable eyes.

Live. He remembered her saying that to him. *Live.* He remembered when the pain was so bad, he had wanted to sink into oblivion. But the woman wouldn't let him.

A moan came from her brother, and the woman moved away, her attention now absorbed elsewhere. Rhys felt an inexplicable loss. Just her presence beside him had somehow cut the pain.

He heard her offering water in a barely audible voice. The words were soothing, encouraging. Like a sweet song or the comforting ripple of water in a slow-moving stream. Rhys closed his eyes and just listened, concentrating on her, using that concentration to dull the fire in his body.

Snatches of words, of phrases. "Wes . . . think of the ranch, of Erin."

And the agonized reply. Broken. Defeated. "I am, dammit. I'm not any . . . good for either now."

"And me? *I* need you. You're all I have left." There was incredible sadness in her voice, and Rhys wanted to do something violent to the man causing it.

Strange. He'd never felt protective before, except . . . maybe . . . but that wasn't protection. That was for his own amusement, he assured himself.

"You have Mark." Rhys heard both bitterness and resignation in the almost snarled words.

A long silence followed. "I don't know . . . I haven't heard anything. . . ."

Rhys opened his eyes and looked over at the woman. Her shoulders sagged slightly, conveying weariness and grief, but still he sensed something strong, a will akin to his own. And he had another flash of her pulling him back from an abyss of some kind.

That sudden image dismayed him. He didn't like debts. He didn't want to owe anyone. Well, bloody hell, he hadn't asked her for anything; therefore, he didn't owe a bloody thing.

He clenched his teeth, trying to ignore the conversation next to him, but he couldn't turn off his ears or his eyes or his mind. And he found he didn't want to, even as warning flares went off in his head. He reminded himself of the last time he'd gone soft over a woman.

Bloody hell, he didn't even want to think about it, about the trail of mishaps that led him here. He turned his attention once more to the man and woman beside him.

"Go away, Susannah. Leave me alone."

"I can't."

"Your loyalty belongs to the other side."

"Damn you, Wes." It was incongruous, that curse coming from her, like thunder in a clear sky. Steel underlaced the silk.

So he had been right, Rhys thought, wishing like hell it didn't make her even more appealing.

A new sound came to him then, the rasp of a key unlocking a nearby door and the creaking sound of a door opening. The harsh sound of boots crunching against a stone floor echoed in the cavernous room. He turned to look, and it felt as if all the devils in hell were sticking him with pitchforks!

"Mrs. Fallon, you have to leave now." The voice was rough, and came from a man in a tattered butternut wool uniform.

"Thank you for so much time, Sergeant," the woman said, standing up. "I'll be back tomorrow."

"Yes, ma'am," he said.

"And can you ask the doctor to look at this man?" She turned toward Rhys. "He's still very feverish."

"You know we ain't got no medicines."

"But you do have water," she challenged, with that surprising undertone of confidence.

"I'll mention it," the sergeant mumbled.

Her voice changed, became all sweetness, like pure molasses. "Thank you," she said. "You've been very kind, Sergeant."

Everything in Rhys tensed, and he wondered whether it was because of the obvious lust in the sergeant's eyes. Forget it, Redding, he told himself. Susannah Fallon and her brother had talked about a man named Mark. The guard had called her "Mrs." She's trouble. He'd figured that out during the past few minutes; he had always been good at sizing up people.

She had the same combination of softness and strength that had led him astray before. He wondered if those traits were peculiar to American women. Whatever, he wasn't going to get trapped by them again.

But, despite his resolutions, his eyes didn't leave her as she pulled on a pair of gloves. She returned his gaze, a wistful smile on her face, before she followed the guard out the door. Rhys heard the grate of the lock, and all the light left the dark, airless room.

He tried to move again, now that she wasn't here to see his weakness. He felt sweat running down his face as the pain stabbed his side with renewed fury. Nonetheless, he managed to lean on his hand and look about him.

The brother, Wes, was lying still now, but his eyes were open, staring listlessly at the filthy ceiling above. Almost as if sensing Rhys's attention, he turned his face toward him. It was pale and thin; dark brown hair, lank and dirty, fell over his forehead.

"Welcome back to hell," Wes said, his mouth twisting in a grimace. "You were better off unconscious."

Rhys's stomach rumbled. He wasn't sure he could

eat, but he also knew he wouldn't get better if he didn't. "Do they feed us?"

Wes laughed mirthlessly. "Damned little. Until my sister found me here, there was even less. Not that I care much."

The declaration was said as a matter of fact, without self-pity, and Rhys suddenly understood what the woman had said about losing will. He wondered how he would feel if he had lost a leg. He couldn't imagine it.

He asked a question instead. "How did your sister get in here?"

"She's married to a Reb hero." The bitterness in his voice was back. "She's tolerated."

So she *was* married. To a Reb. And her brother was a Yank. That was . . . intriguing. And so was she, she and those depthless violet eyes that seemed to penetrate inside him. He cursed under his breath. It didn't matter anyway. He'd find someone in charge, explain what had happened, and be gone from here soon enough.

He lowered himself back onto the cot, feeling the pain flood his body, running like rivers of fire through his side. He closed his eyes against it and saw her again. Leaning over him. Washing his face. Touching with a tenderness he'd never known before.

A tenderness that hurt because it was so new. So unexpected. So totally inexplicable.

He tried to tell himself it was because she wanted something from him. But what? What did he have?

He turned over on the side that was still whole and blanked out his mind, as he'd learned to do so long ago.

Susannah managed to reach the outer gate of the prison before the tears came.

She tried to blink them back. She had to be strong for Wes. For herself.

They were the only two left. The war had taken almost everything.

She stumbled slightly as emotions threatened to overwhelm the control she'd tried so hard to maintain. Her husband, Mark, had died in a Yankee prison hospital months ago but, for some reason, the information didn't reach Richmond until the previous week. She had suspected it, of course. His men, who escaped a Yank ambush in northern Virginia, had seen him go down, had known he had been shot several times. They had not been able to go back after him, not with a passel of Yanks on their tail.

Before she had learned all this in a letter, she had made several queries, all of which had come to naught. So, hoping against hope, she had traveled from Texas to Richmond, via ship from Galveston to the Bahamas and then aboard one of the last blockade runners into Charleston, and finally by train to Richmond. She had to know. She had to try to help him if there was the slightest chance of his being alive. She had owed him that. And so much more.

She hadn't found him, but she had found a desperately ill Wes.

She angrily wiped the tears away. She hadn't been able to tell Wes yet. He and Mark had been like brothers since they were crawling. Only in this war had they separated, each going the way of their conscience. But before he had gone off to serve as a scout for General Lee, Mark had done everything he could to help Wes and herself, even marrying her when he knew he didn't have her whole heart. He gave her his protection as a Confederate officer in a county that reviled her family for its northern loyalties.

He'd wanted her to have his ranch, to have his name. Almost as if he knew he wouldn't be coming back, he'd told her he wanted his land left in the hands of one who loved it. He knew how much she cared for the land, the ranch, the horses. His older brother had already died in the war, and there were no other other Fallons left. Although Mark had never tried to push her, she knew he had loved her with all his heart, and she lived with a terrible guilt now that she had not loved him in the same way.

She had wanted to, because he was everything good and fine, but he'd been too much like a brother to her. There had been no excitement, no passion in her for him, and she'd known he hurt because of that. But she had married him because he had wanted it badly, had trusted her with his land and his life. Perhaps, she'd thought, friendship would grow into the kind of love he wanted. Everyone said it would.

Now, there would never be that chance.

She didn't even know where his body was. The thought was a constant ache in her heart. She couldn't even take him back to Land's End, the ranch he'd loved so much. And she couldn't let Wes know, not when he was so weak and discouraged. He couldn't take another blow. So she bore her grief alone, just as she had the death of her father three years ago.

Susannah walked slowly back to the boarding-house where she was staying. The bottom floor, like those of so many other homes, had been turned into a hospital, and she helped whenever she could. With a husband on one side, and a brother on the other, her loyalties had been so torn that she saw every man now as just that: a man, a person. Not a Yank, not a Confederate.

Her stomach growled, but she had no appetite. Libby Prison always robbed her of that. She ate only what she could afford—food was enormously expensive now that Richmond was encircled on three sides—and still her money was almost gone and she had yet to get herself and Wes home.

Her thoughts turned to the enigmatic man on the

cot next to Wesley's. He had been so badly wounded she thought he would die. But there had been something about him, something compelling even during the first days when he was unconscious. When he had been carried in, he had looked like a hawk she'd once found near death. Dark and predatory, yet touchingly vulnerable in its unfamiliar weakness. She had tried to nurse the young bird, but it had died. Yet deep in the dark eyes of the stranger was a flame she sensed was even stronger than the hawk's.

In the past months she had learned a little medicine and she had made her own poultices for the prisoner's wound. Infection had ravaged his body; his wound didn't heal. But then he had rallied, his spirit refusing to give up. If only he could give some of that invincible spirit to Wes.

She had found herself washing the sweat from the stranger's face, urging him to fight even harder, as if she could, in some way, give him what Wes refused to accept. She didn't really understand why she started to care so much about the Yank officer, why something about him, about those dark unfathomable eyes, stirred odd, indefinable feelings deep inside her. Why was she so attracted by the dark, harsh face, made even more dangerous looking by the dark bristle that covered part of it? She wondered how she could think of someone being dangerous when he was so ill. Yet she instinctively knew he was. She felt it deep in her bones, and she was dismayed to realize he intrigued her so, more deeply than she wanted to admit, because that deepened her guilt over Mark. She had been rewarded today. Her . . . nighthawk would live.

If only Wes would accept what had happened to his body and regain that wonderful zest for life he once had. Perhaps the major could help, could give her brother some of his own tenacity for life.

She closed her eyes. She couldn't think of that now. She wouldn't think of a future that seemed increasingly bleak.

She turned up the walk to her rooming house. There were others who needed her at the moment.

Chapter 2

It was a beautiful morning, dimmed only by the sound of cannon in the distance. The bitterly cold winter rains were gone, and the late March sun was gentle, the clouds lacy and playful like those on a bright spring Texas morning. Susannah could almost see the bluebells and the goldenrod spreading out over the fields back home, the place she loved with her heart and soul. The place she knew would heal Wes.

If only she could get him there. While they still had land left.

Susannah allowed herself a kernel of optimism. The major with the attractive Welsh accent had been so much better yesterday, the second day since he had regained consciousness. Though it was obvious he was still in much pain, he was rapidly gaining strength, the deep flame in those dark eyes growing more intense.

There was more about him than a tenacity to survive. She had tried to cipher it: a strangely detached interest in the world, and in his own dilemma as a wounded prisoner far from home. He seemed to observe everything with a dispassionate, even slightly amused, acceptance, as if life were some kind of secret joke.

He held no bitterness, which so many of the other

prisoners had, about his treatment. Only a guarded attention. But then, when he wasn't aware of being watched, she would see that his eyes, like the hawk she'd nursed, were alert, glittering, awaiting opportunity. Even in his weakened condition, that quality was obvious.

That budding kernel of optimism sprouted as an idea grew. A wild idea, perhaps, but still . . . possible. It filled her with the same hope that had sped her journey across the country to this war-torn corner—and that, she prayed, would speed her and Wes back to the land they both loved. Land that was endangered, coveted by men who would do anything to take it from them, and who were close to success.

It was land her family had defended through three wars, had died and been born on. It was her roots, her soul. And Wes's. All he'd ever wanted was that land.

She had to keep their heritage, hers and Mark's and Wes's. She had to get Wes home to it. And perhaps now she had the means to do it.

The shroud that had dampened her natural belief that good eventually triumphed over evil lifted as a stream of light, illuminated by the dark visage of a stranger, filtered through her.

Rhys Redding. Major Rhys Redding. The name itself seemed to have a strength of its own, and perhaps, since he had come all this way to fight in a war that wasn't his, he had honor to boot. He had said nothing about family, had mentioned no names in his illness, had indicated no attachments. Perhaps he didn't have a home to return to, perhaps . . .

She needed the physical strength she knew he would soon have again. She needed the will she saw in him. She needed them for Wes.

In a way, her needing him galled her. For the last four years, she had taken over control of two ranches: Mark's, which was now hers, and the Carr homestead, which had been left to Wes. She had donned pants and ridden like a man; she had defied the Martin brothers who had tried over and over again to get her to sell; she had grown in ways she'd never thought possible five years earlier. She had confidence in her abilities, but she simply didn't have the physical strength to get Wes home, not in his present condition.

Rhys Redding would have that strength in another week or so. She had never seen anyone improve so rapidly. Perhaps he would agree to help her and Wes.

But why should he? she argued with herself. Why? Her whole idea was ridiculous, yet she couldn't let go of it. She, too, could be very tenacious. And she *had* helped him. Perhaps he would feel the smallest bit obligated. She wasn't above using that when Wes was involved. And her land. She would use anything.

Anything at all.

She started planning a strategy that would honor a general.

Rhys woke from a restless sleep. It was dark. Cold. Disoriented, he tried to remember what had happened, tried to bring all the blurry images into focus.

Hands grabbed him. Rough hands.

"Move along, you damn Limey." Rage started to build in Rhys as he was manhandled by the clue-clad officer. No one touched Rhys. Not anymore.

He tried to shrug off the hands, but his own wrists were bound by handcuffs in front of him, and he felt as he had years ago when as a young boy he'd been felled by the whip of an impatient lord.

Rhys had sworn then no one would touch him that way again. And no one had. Not and lived to tell about it.

He turned his head to look at his captor. The Union major was glaring at him, as he had during the long ride to Washington. Rhys would not have been surprised at any time to feel a bullet in his back.

They couldn't hold him, not for long. That's what he'd been told. He was British, a neutral, even if he was carrying goods through the Union blockade to the Confederacy. But his ship had been chased and blown out of the water off the southeastern coast of the United States, and after swimming for shore he found himself in the hands of Union sailors, who delivered him to federal troops before returning to blockade duty. He didn't know what had happened to the rest of the crew of the Specter.

His escort to Washington included the major, who apparently was being disciplined for some reason, and two troopers. It had been a day and night already, and this morning he'd been given a hard biscuit and told to mount the fleabag horse they'd provided for him.

"I told you to move," the major said, and Rhys felt a sharp pain as the officer used his gun to hit him in the small of the back.

Rhys's reaction was immediate. No one hit Rhys Redding without paying for it. Paying triple. He had survived seven years in the London streets and ten years in Africa as a mercenary, and he knew every trick there was. He whirled suddenly; his bound hands went up and around the major's neck and with one movement broke it. Immediately, he reached down and picked up the major's fallen gun, pointing it at the two startled troopers who were saddling their horses.

"Drop your sidearms."

"The major—" one of the men began to say as they obeyed the order.

"Keys," he interrupted, holding up his handcuffed wrists.

One trooper approached very carefully, his eyes never leaving the gun.

"Quickly," Rhys said with quiet menace.

The trooper took one look at those obsidian eyes

and reached down into the major's pocket, coming up with a key. "He's . . . dead."

"Of course," Rhys said in a voice that chilled both men. "You will be, too, if you don't do exactly as I say."

They did, unlocking his handcuffs, locking their own wrists together. Rhys then backed them up to a tree and tied their free hands so they encircled the tree. They were close enough to a trail, he figured, to be able to attract attention before too much time went by. He changed into the major's uniform, then unsaddled his own horse and those of the two troopers and slapped their rumps, sending them running through the woods. He swung up on the major's horse, the best of the lot.

He grinned at the two troopers, then kicked his horse into a gallop.

Two hours later he rode right into the middle of a Confederate troop that wasn't supposed to be there. Before he could speak, a bullet ripped through his side, and a red haze filled his eyes as he fell from his horse.

Now he felt that pain again as he moved. He heard himself groan, felt the waves of agony crash through his body. His entire memory was back; he wished it wasn't. He didn't like anything about his immediate prospects. But he had confidence in himself. He had always managed to wriggle out of tight spots. As his eyes grew accustomed to the dark, his gaze moved around the room, studying the sturdy brick walls and barred windows. Low moans filtered through the thick gloom. Then he decided such intent investigation was an exercise in futility. He couldn't even crawl across the room. Depression settled over him.

And then the specter of a face floated over him. He felt cool sweet breath and smelled the slightest scent of roses, saw the lovely violet eyes. The pain started to drain away.

Until he realized it was all in his mind.

He cursed himself. He didn't need this kind of distraction. He didn't need her. He didn't need anyone. Only the weak needed people.

And he'd never been weak.

Except once. And he regretted that. Bloody hell, he really regretted it now.

She came again that afternoon, bringing sunshine into the gloom. He hadn't known it was possible that a person could bring her own light with her. But she did; and despite his vow of the night before, he felt a peculiar warmth inside, a fierce, yet poignant, hunger not only for a female body but simply for the touch of those hands. The thought would have amused him greatly if he hadn't been so bloody concerned about it. He neither needed nor wanted those capricious, unproductive emotions.

She smiled at him approvingly, and he could only guess it was because he was sitting up. A rush of pleasure teased him, and he chided himself and fought not to return the smile, to keep it to himself, as he kept most things. Smiles were meant as masks, not revelations. Remember, he told himself, she had to want something from him, a thought that he grew more certain of as he noticed an almost speculative look in her eyes.

She was carrying a pair of obviously handmade crutches, as well as a basket. A Confederate guard was trailing behind with a bowl of water. It was amazing the way she seemed to tame the usually rough guards.

Now that she had greeted Rhys with a smile, she turned all her attention to her brother. She seemed tired and worried, sad even, but there was also determination in her actions.

Wes regarded the crutches with disinterest.

Susannah—that was the way he thought of her

now—sat on the end of his cot. "Will you try them, Wes?"

"No."

"Please." There was anguish in her voice, even urgency.

Rhys tried to block out the conversation, but couldn't. He found himself listening avidly instead.

"Dammit, I'm not ready to start depending on a pair of sticks."

"Do you plan to stay here forever, then?"

"Leave me alone, Sue. Goddammit, just leave me alone."

Susannah turned around, her eyes glazed with a film of tears that nearly blinded her, and she saw Rhys's saturnine face. Their gazes caught for one seemingly endless moment, and Rhys felt as if the bottom had suddenly fallen from his existence. Jolts of awareness radiated between them, and even in his weakened condition, he felt the sensitive parts of his body glow with a shimmering heat that had nothing to do with pain.

He had the oddest sense of recognition, of something very strong binding them, like an invisible chain. Destiny? He didn't believe in destiny. One decided his own future by whatever means were available. Still, strange, unfamiliar feelings washed over him, making him feel awkward and unsure, two characteristics he despised. He unaccountably wanted to take her, to hold her, to protect her in a way he'd never protected before. He wanted to wipe away that grief shadowing such remarkably expressive eyes. Before he could help himself, his hand started to reach for her, to comfort. She stared at it before looking at his face with astonishment, then with the same kind of recognition he had felt.

She held out her hand, and their fingers met, burned. The spark deep in his groin glowed brightly, seeming to encompass both of them in one incandescent cloak, like a halo of emotional intensity and brilliance. His hand jerked away. He had known fierce hate, fierce ambition, but nothing like this wild assault of emotions, as if a cannonball had hit and blew to pieces his protective walls. He hastily tried to reassemble them, reining in feelings that were so new and unexpected he didn't know how to halter them.

Lust, he explained to himself again. Simple lust. Well, maybe not so simple. But lust just the same. He didn't know anything else, didn't believe in anything more.

Her gaze was filled with wonder and disbelief as she stood there unmoving, her hand still outstretched. Then her eyes widened and her hand fell to her side. She whirled around and walked out, leaving the basket and crutches behind.

Silently cursing himself, Rhys closed his eyes against the violent emotions still rocking him. Bloody Christ, he was discovering feelings he had never dreamed existed in him. A need to touch, to hold, to comfort that was painful in its intensity. And that was certainly, quite definitely, unprecedented.

He chuckled ruefully to himself. Rhys Redding feeling like a schoolboy! He had always scorned the weaknesses visited on those afflicted by what they called love. Women were for amusement, nothing more. Even Lauren Bradley had been only that; it had amused him to help her. Perhaps, he reasoned, this sudden, inexplicable aberration occurred only because of his injury, which must have impaired his usual defenses and good common sense.

With anger, he turned to Wes, who was staring at the door through which Susannah had left. Rhys's gaze moved contemptuously from the colonel's face to the crutches that lay next to the cot. "Bloody hell, how did you two come from the same family?"

Wes glared at him.

"Seems she has the backbone of both of you."

"Go to hell, Redding."

Rhys shrugged contemptuously. "Do you always give up so easily?" he taunted. "I thought Americans had more mettle."

Wes's jaw clenched. He sat up and reached for the crutches, swinging his left leg to the floor. One hand grabbed the handle of a crutch, and he slowly, painfully, raised his body. The crutch slipped and he fell back on the bed, sweat beading on his forehead.

He looked over at Rhys, contempt still in those dark, mocking eyes. He reached for the crutch again, and this time he managed to stand and grab the other crutch with success. He took one step, then another, his natural grace substituting for the lost lower leg. Several more steps. The pain was excruciating, the extent of his weakness unanticipated. His missing right foot ached as if it were still there, and he tried to put it on the ground. The movement threw off his rhythm, and he fell crashing to the floor, pain arcing through him. He hated the man on the cot next to him, hated him as he'd never hated before.

Wes felt a steady hand grasp his arm, forcing him up. He realized immediately whose it was, and knowing the major had been as ill as he, if not more so, he resented the strength in that grip. He shrugged off the assistance and, ignoring the pain, used the crutch to struggle to his feet and get back to the cot.

Totally exhausted, he sank down, furious at himself, furious at the man next to him. Still, he felt the smallest thrill of victory.

Rhys blandly observed the man's open anger. He grinned to himself, feeling a perverse sense of satisfaction.

Why had she run like that? She had never done anything like that before.

She hesitated outside the prison, completely befuddled by her reaction. She had meant to start her campaign to recruit the major, but then her gaze had met his, and the floor seemed to fall out from under her. She'd felt a burning inside, a rush of warm blood that drowned all sensibilities. She lost herself in those eyes, those dark eyes that seemed to reach into her very soul and extract its essence. She had felt herself tremble, losing the words she'd meant to say, consumed in the blaze that had streaked between them.

She'd run for her life.

And now she stood outside and trembled as she had never trembled before. How could she possibly ask him to accompany her across country?

She'd never reacted to a man like that before. She leaned against the brick wall for a moment, oblivious to the guards glancing at her curiously. She knew it wasn't loneliness. The good lord knew she'd seen other men in the years since Mark had been gone. The engaging captain on the blockade runner, the officers here in Richmond.

Why the dark Welshman? Wounded. Dirty. A dark, bristly beard covering a harsh face, eyes that watched rather than felt. He looked like a brigand, a renegade, not like any officer she'd ever met. She swallowed deep and hard. Did she dare go further? Did she dare ask him to help them return to Texas? Or was that fraction of a second just some momentary oddity caused by his illness, her weariness? A figment, even, of imagination?

Need overwhelmed her fear. In her mind, she had decided that Rhys Redding was her one solution, the answer to getting Wes home soon enough to have a home left. She would simply control her feelings, as she had been forced to control them over the past few years.

She could.

She would.

She ignored the fact that her legs were still unsteady as she straightened, that heat still curled somewhere deep inside, that a thoroughly unfamiliar thrill still crawled up and down her spine.

Rhys Redding found himself waiting for her the next day. He'd tried to smother that anticipation, telling himself it was only the boredom of the prison that prompted it. Any diversion would be welcome. Along with the food she usually brought.

Yet his muscles tensed every time the door opened. He found himself imagining her pleasure when she saw her brother on the crutches. And he felt the slightest sense of accomplishment, regardless of the less than entirely honorable motive behind his goading of the man, principally the exercise of his own self-anger.

Still, it had worked, and Colonel Wesley Carr had tried the crutches again this morning, and now this afternoon. Five steps yesterday, ten this morning. And now again. He had managed a few more steps and was returning to the cot when the iron door creaked open, and Susannah entered the room, trailed by a guard.

She'd always had a pretty smile, but until now it had been shadowed with worry. Today's smile suddenly turned spontaneous. Relieved. Delighted.

Blinding, dammit. Rhys felt it ripple through to the heart he wasn't aware he had. Until now. He didn't think he liked the knowledge that one was really there, lurking in the shadows, just waiting to spring forward when he was least resistant. Bloody hell, but he'd banish it back to where it came from.

"Wes," she said delightedly, obviously totally unaware of the havoc she created in the man watching her, Rhys thought bitterly. She dropped her sack of the latest offerings on Rhys's cot and clapped her hands together like a child as she watched her brother make a faltering movement. "You're doing it."

Wes grimaced. "A few steps," he admitted, frowning and darting an angry look at Rhys, a look Susannah caught.

She gazed at Rhys with a sudden comprehension and gratitude that surprised him. He'd done nothing but taunt a man he scorned. Wesley Carr was everything Rhys had always mocked: A man who, according to the conversations he'd overheard, fought for principle. Rhys didn't believe in principle. You couldn't eat principle. You couldn't build a fortune on principle.

Rhys recognized Wes's type. Damnably honorable, and physically courageous to a fault. Rhys didn't particularly care for that, either. Especially not on behalf of the aforementioned principle. To save your own skin, yes. For money, yes. But for principle? And now, the man's courage had seemed to fade when he had to face another kind of challenge.

Still, Rhys accepted Susannah's blinding smile with an appraising glance of his own, one that made her flush. She returned it, though, and this time he thought he saw that curious flash of speculation again. Before he could be sure, however, she'd turned back to her brother and watched as he took several more steps before falling gratefully back down on the cot.

She reached in her sack like Father Christmas and triumphantly pulled out an apple. "It's like gold," she said.

Wes looked around at the others in the room. Envious, hungry eyes fixed on the apple. "I . . . can't."

She went back into the sack and brought out several more and a small knife. "There's enough for a bite for everyone."

Heads turned and words passed down the cots.

"Who did you kill?" Wes asked. Susannah smiled at

this glimpse of humor, the first in a long time from her brother, who used to be so very facile with it.

"I lied," she admitted. "Just a little. I said it was for the wounded."

"And everyone thought it was Confederate wounded?" Wes probed wryly.

"They could think what they wanted," she said, not adding the fact she had also sold her mother's necklace for the apples. A necklace was not worth much today on the streets of Richmond, but the store owner had commented on it, and Susannah thought the apples would help Wes's spirits. Anything would be worth that. A necklace was only a thing. Wes was the only person left to her. She would sell her soul to extract even an echo of the brother she had worshiped.

He suddenly grinned at her. "My devious little sister." He took a piece she cut from the apple and savored its sweet tangy taste.

She then cut more pieces, which she passed down the rows of cots. Rhys was the last to receive his. She hesitated as their hands touched. Her eyes met his again, just as they had the day before, but this time she didn't run. "Thank you," she whispered.

Rhys shook his head slowly, denying anything, everything, but her gaze didn't move from his and he felt it searching, probing. "I didn't do anything."

"Yes, you did," she said, and she leaned down and brushed a kiss across his forehead. He felt the burning heat at the point where her lips touched his skin, and then it flooded through his body. One fist curled into a tight ball to keep from reaching up and pulling her down to him. That attraction between them sparked again, so strongly he could almost feel it crackle. He saw her hand tremble as her fingers passed the slice of apple into his.

Then she moved quickly away, as if she felt—and feared—that potent cry between them. She went down the rows of men, speaking to each, asking if she could do anything, write a letter or try to get more water from the guards.

Rhys watched her graceful movements, listened to her soft voice, remembered the challenge she'd thrown at her brother yesterday. A rare, fetching combination of steel and silk, indeed. Dangerous as bloody hell. He closed his eyes and didn't open them until he knew she was gone.

Chapter 3

The sound rumbled through the dirty brick walls of Libby Prison like continuous thunder. Day and night.

For the prisoners, the sound was like the sweet call of a bird. It meant the Union troops were approaching with their cannons, moving closer every day.

Rhys didn't feel the same euphoria. Union troops meant danger to him, meant that they might discover that he, a civilian, had killed a Union officer. In his delirium of the first few days, he had apparently given his real name to his captors, and it wouldn't take Union officials long to discover they had no Rhys Redding in their military ranks. But they probably had a Rhys Redding on WANTED posters.

And there was something else. He relished the visits of Susannah Fallon. They made up for the surliness of the guards, the lack of food, of sanitation, of water.

Of freedom.

Until now, freedom hadn't been that important. He couldn't have gone anyplace if he'd wanted. He'd simply been too weak. His wound was finally beginning to heal after days of suppurating, and he knew he owed that to the poultices she had brought. But it was still raw and painful. The infection had been deep.

She had also shaved him. The day after Wes had walked on the crutches, she had shaved Wesley, and then had turned to him, a tentative smile on her lips and asked if he would like to be next.

He had put his fingers to his face. Bloody hell, but it was all bristles. He must look like the very devil, and he wasn't sure he was steady enough to shave himself. He hesitated, then nodded, knowing it would feel damn good to be clean again.

He hadn't suspected the impact of her fingers on his skin. They hesitated after using a cloth to dampen his cheek and soap it, and he felt a hot rippling of his nerves, starting where she touched and reaching to his groin. He felt her hands shake, and he wasn't quite sure he really wanted her to continue.

But then they firmed. "I've never done this before except to my father and brother," she said. Then she smiled a quick impish grin. "But I promise not to inflict any more physical damage."

His body tensed, even as he felt a sense of relief. Why in the hell did he care that she hadn't shaved anyone else? And why did he like that smile very much? Devoid of sadness and worry, fitting her mobile mouth so naturally, it seemed more suited to her than the wistful one. He guessed it had once come more easily to her.

He couldn't help but give her a smile back, though it was a little guarded since something in her eyes warned him to be careful. They were usually so open, but now it was almost as if—

Rhys shook the thought away as being merely the reflection of his own dubious character. She was using the razor now, under the eye of a Confederate guard. He felt the firm strokes strike away the bristles, and he had to keep himself from moving. The strokes seemed so . . . intimate, sending heat careening through his body. He wanted to reach up and take that hand and pull her down on the cot. He closed his eyes, willing the urge to disappear.

And then she was through. He took the cloth she

was holding and wiped his face. If she touched him again, he might explode.

It was just, he told himself, that no woman had ever done that to him before, had shaved him, had touched him with such gentle efficiency. It had been a curiously intimate experience that had achingly affected him in more than one place.

Since then he had shaved himself, unwilling to subject his body and mind to the reactions she initiated. And her smile now seemed speculative, sending warning signals through him.

But still he found himself waiting impatiently for each visit, and he resented that, too . . . until he saw her and heard her soft voice.

He still hadn't told anyone he was not a Yankee major, but, for God's sake, a blockade runner. For one reason: he really doubted he would be believed. But that was a minor consideration. To be honest with himself, and he usually was, he didn't want to lose those hours with Susannah, even in this damnable place. He was fascinated with her, with the different facets he saw in her. Like that diamond of Nathan's, she was nice to look at, even valuable. But certainly nothing to keep. Not for him.

He stirred restlessly on his cot. He had moved around this morning as he had for the past several days. Every step was painful, the wound just barely closed. But he forced himself, knowing it was the only way to regain strength. And each time he moved, he seemed to bait Carr into doing the same.

By now, Susannah's brother could walk all the way to the end of the room. But upon his return he would always collapse with a curse onto his cot, then stare blindly up at the ceiling, a hopeless, frustrated look in his eyes.

Part of Rhys understood. But another part of him knew he wouldn't feel the same. He was a survivor. He'd find a way to defeat the odds, just as he always had. A bastard and stable brat, the son of a prostitute, he'd made a fortune and had tweaked the noses—and pockets—of so-called nobles.

The iron door into the hospital area opened, and he tensed, waiting with his usual expectation.

His breath seemed to stop when he saw her. She was covered, from wrists to ankles, in a plain dark blue dress. The material was thin and faded in some places, but the shade made her coloring that much more vivid, brought out the striking violet of those eyes.

She did not have a basket or sack of food. Only a small cloth bag. Her face was as grim as Rhys had ever seen it as she went over to her brother.

She received no greeting, only desolate silence.

She knelt next to Wes's cot. "They say the government is fleeing Richmond. Just a few more days, Wes. You'll be free."

"Dammit," he replied in a low bitter voice. "You think I care? What in the hell does freedom mean to a man with one leg? A man who's no longer a man?"

"I'd take Mark any way I could get him," she said.

Rhys tensed at her words. Mark. Her husband. He kept forgetting about that.

"I'm . . . sorry, Sue. About Mark," Wes said in a ragged voice. "Is there any more news?"

"Yes," she said. It was time to tell him. She couldn't avoid it any longer. She needed his strength to do what had to be done. "He's dead. In a Yank hospital." No matter how hard she tried she couldn't keep a tremor from her voice. "I knew weeks ago, but I . . . didn't want to tell you."

Rhys felt his gut tighten. He wondered if anyone would ever feel that way about him, whether a woman's voice would tremble with feeling as she spoke about him. A laughable thought. The black Welshman, he'd been called by those from whom he'd once craved acceptance. Only one person had ever looked at him differently. Another woman, a little like Susannah in some ways. She'd not feared him either.

Bloody hell. He turned on his side, away from Susannah and her brother, trying to ignore the whispered words next to him. But he couldn't.

A long silence followed the admission. And then an "Oh, God," from Wes.

Rhys turned back again at the raw emotion in Wes's voice, and saw him reach for his sister's hand, holding it tight.

"I wish you'd told me." Wes's words vibrated with bitter remorse. "You've had everything on your shoulders, haven't you? Our father. Mark. Me. Christ, you didn't need me too." For the first time Rhys felt sympathy for Wes Carr as well as anger.

"You didn't need . . . any more bad news," Susannah said.

"So you had to grieve alone. Again. God, I'm sorry, Susannah."

Wes's obvious pain for the unknown Mark caused a current of jealousy to streak through Rhys. Mark Fallon apparently had been important to both of them. Rhys hated the sudden wave of desolation, of loneliness, that washed over him, and he ruthlessly tried to banish it from his mind. He had no stake in these people's lives. He wanted none. A few more days, and he would be strong enough to try to leave here. Strong enough to convince the Confederate authorities as to who he really was.

And then what? Back to England. Back to those who paid lip service to his wealth but snickered at his heritage behind his back? To civilized England, which he'd grown to hate?

The talk faded, and there was silence. He didn't know how long it was before he heard her voice. "Major Redding?"

Rhys turned, his eyes finally meeting her worried ones.

"Mrs. Fallon," he acknowledged slowly.

"Wes is asleep. How are you?"

He moved slowly, not allowing any emotion to reflect on his face. He was very good at that, at not showing anything. He chose to raise his eyebrows in reply, a gesture that ridiculed her question.

"I shouldn't ask?" The understanding words came softly, like the gentle falling stream of water down a mountain waterfall. Cool. Refreshing. She appeared to have controlled her own pain to soothe his.

He shrugged, surrendering momentarily. It was difficult not to when she looked at him with those damnably concerned eyes of hers. "I'm a great deal better," he said. "I believe I owe that to you."

She flushed a little. "I think you would have done well, regardless."

"No," Rhys said with certainty as his gaze roamed the curve of her breasts under the dress. He wanted to touch them, to touch her. The intensity of that need was stunning. "I don't think so," he said with a smile that he was afraid was more lecherous than grateful. Or maybe he wasn't afraid; maybe she would run like bloody hell.

She fidgeted with the cloth bag. It was the first uncertainty he had seen in her, and she was suddenly even more appealing, more vulnerable. "The . . . Yanks will be here soon, perhaps by morning."

He looked at her, at the eyes made larger by the shadows of weariness, at the lips that were slightly trembling. "Your husband was with the Confederate Army?"

"Yes."

"Your loyalty . . .?"

"Is to those who are still living," she said bitterly. "I just want the war over."

Rhys watched her bite her lip, try gallantly to hold back the tears he saw hovering behind the eyes. One of her hands went up, as if to restrain them that way, and he winced inwardly. Uncertainty was out of character for the strong woman who had been coping with her brother for the last two weeks, as well as dealing with the death of a husband and a city under siege.

"And you, Major. You should be happy . . ."

To fall back into Yankee hands? Not bloody likely. Not when he had killed a Yank major and was masquerading under his uniform and rank. He could be shot for one offense or another. The last thing he wanted was an inquiry into a Major Redding who had never existed, or a dead Major Howard, who had until he escorted a particular Welshman.

Christ. He had to get out of here. He had delayed much too long.

His mind worked logically as it always did, confronting a problem and weighing possibilities. He had no documents, no proof of who he was. But she—Mrs. Fallon—was the wife of a Confederate officer, a hero, Carr had said. An idea began to form in his mind.

He was well enough to move. With pain, certainly. But when his hide was at stake, he could endure a great deal.

Susannah Fallon moved next to his cot and dropped the cloth bag. Her hand, so incredibly cool, touched his forehead, and then she smiled. "No more fever." She pushed aside the rough blanket to look at the stained bandages hugging his side. The touch of her hand against his skin ran through him like lightning. His body tensed, and he knew that under the blanket his manhood was reacting immediately.

She gently pulled the bandage from his side, and his jaw set as cloth stuck to the wound before coming off. She washed the wound and bandaged it with clean cloth she'd brought in the bag.

Rhys watched her expressive eyes as she made every move. She must have nursed before, probably frequently. She was too good, too steady for it to be otherwise. She'd never winced at his ugly wound, nor her brother's even uglier stump.

"Major?" she started, and then hesitated.

He raised an eyebrow inquisitively.

"I . . . I need help."

Anticipation tore through Rhys like a summer storm, and all his senses snapped to alert. He waited.

"Are you . . . do you . . . have any place to go?"

Once more Rhys's eyebrows arched in question.

"I mean the war is almost over . . . surely the Yanks won't want to keep you. Now." Her eyes went to the heavy bandage on his side.

If only she knew. They *would* want to keep him, but not for the reasons she thought. But she certainly was holding his interest. He suspected that what she had in mind, and what he had in mind, might well coincide.

He shrugged, still waiting.

"I have to go home," she said slowly. "To Texas. There's trouble, and we might lose everything we own if we don't. But I need help with Wes." She hesitated. "I can't leave him here, not the way he feels. And . . . and home . . . he needs to go home. He'll get better there." Anxiety and hope edged her voice.

"What kind of trouble?"

"Some men want our land. They've killed our foreman. I received word yesterday." She swallowed, obviously wondering whether she was doing the right thing, the safe thing, in asking for his help.

He measured his words slowly, carefully. "When do you want to leave?"

"As soon as possible. I know Wes isn't well, or you either, but when . . ." Her words faltered.

"How do you propose to travel?"

"A wagon," she said, now eager. "I've already bought one. And a team of horses."

Rhys thought about it. A wagon? Both he and Wes could travel that way. Horseback? That might be difficult. "Perhaps . . . since the Yanks are so close, you can get us released early. Neither of us is a threat now."

Susannah bit her lip. "I've . . . tried with Wes." She didn't have to say she had failed. That was quite obvious.

"Mrs. Fallon," he said slowly, his voice even, "I don't particularly want to be here when the Union Army comes." He watched her eyes widen.

"Why?"

He debated telling her. Her brother was a Yank; her husband had been a Reb. Her own loyalties were obviously to her family rather than a cause. And he was in a position to help that family. Just as she might be in a position to help him.

"I'm not exactly what I seem," he answered.

"What are you, Major?" Her voice had dropped to a whisper, uncertainty in the words.

An opportunist. A gambler. A soldier of fortune. All that and more. A man you should have nothing to do with. But he didn't want to scare her. He needed her. As much as she apparently needed him.

"Let's just say the Yanks would probably be happy to see me, and not for the reasons you think. Can you get me out?"

Her gaze was steady as she searched his face, his eyes. "Will you go with us to Texas?"

Texas. That was the end of the earth, for God's sake. It seemed almost as far as Africa. Rhys remembered the last time he'd done something for someone. He'd vowed never again.

But this wouldn't be for someone else. This was for him. A bargain in which both sides received something they needed: he an escape, she his temporary assistance.

He wondered whether it was a devil's bargain. But he sure as bloody hell didn't have any other place to go at the moment. No one waited in England, or anyplace else. No one cared one way or another.

He nodded his assent. But as he did, his instincts warned him that he might very well be jumping from the pot into the fire.

He wasn't comforted by the fact he had damned little choice.

Chapter 4

The streets of Richmond were roiling with crowds and emotion. Panic and grief were openly displayed on this Sunday, April 2, 1865. Lee was abandoning Richmond, and everyone in the city knew that move sounded the death knell for the Confederacy.

As Susannah hurried down the street to the government offices to make her plea, to fulfill her part of the bargain with Major Redding, she wondered why she did trust the major. Especially after he admitted to being not exactly what he seemed. Why did she go ahead and make such a bargain with so little information on him? Because she had decided days ago that he was her only hope? Because she rarely changed her mind once it was set? No, it was because she had no other option, she told herself.

And instinctively, she did trust the major, whom she now thought of as her nighthawk, and her instincts had always been reliable. She believed in them enough to put herself and her brother into the major's hands. The Welshman radiated the assurance that came from competence. She just prayed she wasn't responding to factors other than her concern for Wes, for the land she loved and that Mark had loved and had left in her care.

I will take care of it, she promised him. *I can at least do that for you.*

And Rhys Redding? If that was even his name. She would be careful, very careful. And Wes would be with them, demanding all her attention. She knew him. If she played upon his inherent protectiveness, she was certain he would become the strong big brother he once had been. A helpless female would be a difficult role to play because she was no longer helpless, no longer dependent on a man, nor had she any wish to be. But for Wes, she would become what she once was to make him whole in spirit again.

She owed him that.

Despite all her conflicting emotions—guilt, hope, even fear of the Welshman—she couldn't prevent the warm tremor that rumbled through her, a wayward flash of anticipation. She tried to suffocate them, but she couldn't. She was going home, and *he* was going with them.

It seemed right in some way, almost destined. But then she dismissed the fanciful thought as she remembered the letter from Texas that came two days ago.

It was apparently one of several sent by different routes. She was urgently needed back. Although there had been trouble during the past years—fences cut, horses and cattle rustled—it hadn't been anything she and the foreman, Stan Green, couldn't withstand. Now she learned Stan had been killed, and the rustling had increased. The Martin family, who had been trying to buy her land for the last two years, had obtained a bank note that was due in five months. There would be no renewal this time.

She bit her lip, a practice she had learned to substitute for tears. Major Redding, or whoever he was, seemed the answer to a prayer. She sensed that, in some way, he had been responsible for Wes's attempts to walk. Wes had said nothing, but there was something in the glances between the two men that led her to that conclusion. There was certainly no liking. Hostility and challenge sparked between them, but that was exactly what Wes had needed, what he still needed.

And so she had made this bargain. When he made his own astounding condition, she had no time to consider the implications of what he said. If she had any sense, she would have rejected the idea out of hand. But there was something about him, about his intensity, about his own need to leave, despite the emotionless, almost indifferent, way he had expressed it. And now she realized she had no idea who or what she had hired.

Nonetheless, she was determined. She fought against a maddened, terrified crowd that was clogging the streets of Richmond. Snippets of news traveled quickly from group to group, spreading terror as the rumors were magnified. Confederate troops were pulling out, filling the streets as they headed for the one still-open route. The city was to be surrendered at three the next morning.

If the streets were in chaos, the government buildings were worse as she went from office to office, asking for names she had learned, for officers who had been helping her, for anyone who had known Mark. Finally, she located Colonel Evan Carey, one of Mark's fellow officers, who scanned prisoner-of-war lists for her and discovered Wes in one.

As busy as he was, he listened sympathetically to her request to release Wes and another prisoner, and wrote two sets of release papers.

"I don't know if it will work, Mrs. Fallon, but you can try," he said. "Hell, why not? A day or two won't make any difference." He stood. "It's over," he added, a bitter admission of defeat. "God knows what's going to happen to the South now." He handed her the papers. "I'm damned sorry about Mark—"

"Thank you," she said, and she grabbed the papers before he could change his mind.

The precious papers clutched in her hand, Susannah fought through the crowd toward the stable where her wagon and horses were boarded. She heard a conversation between two men staving in heads of barrels, kegs, and hogsheads of whiskey. Government orders. A terrible waste, but orders were orders. Even now. As the whiskey ran down the streets, men and women, black and white, scooped it up in dippers or drank from their dipped hands.

Susannah heard an explosion, then another. The world suddenly seemed full of explosions. In the distance, she saw fire.

Somehow she finally made it to the stable. A group of men were outside, practically throwing worthless Confederate money at the owner.

"I have no more horses," he said. "They're all sold." He saw Susannah and hurried her in. "You'd better get out of here, missus. The whole city's going crazy."

He told a boy to hitch the team to the wagon and took her over to a corner, offering her a pistol. "You better take this, missus." He looked at her cautiously. "Do you know how to use it?"

Susannah nodded. Most Texas-bred women did. They had to. For varmints, both human and animal. She was an excellent shot.

"You be careful, missus. Riffraff all over the place. Looting, stealing."

Susannah looked at the gun. "Don't you need this?"

"I have another, and I doubt the Yanks will let us keep arms. You go ahead."

She nodded, then carefully tucked it under the bench of the wagon.

She had two more stops to make. She needed other clothes for Wes and the mysterious major. They wouldn't get far in those filthy and bloodstained Yank uniforms. And she had to pick up her belongings at the boardinghouse.

Fear snaked through her as she drove the wagon through the teeming streets. She was pinning all her hopes on one man, the one man she couldn't be certain of.

Why did Major Redding need to get out of the city? Why did he say he was not what he seemed? Who and what was he? She shivered slightly in the warmth of a spring day. There was something almost frightening about those dark watchful eyes. But everything else about him suggested confidence and strength. And that was what she needed so badly.

Still, he sent shivers up and down her spine, dangerous shivers. Yesterday, he had reminded her more than ever of a hawk with his unblinking gaze, calculation in them even as his mouth smiled.

Was she making a terrible mistake in trusting him? Did she have a choice?

She had to get home, and she couldn't leave Wes behind. And she knew she couldn't manage with him alone.

The prison authorities cast only a quick eye at the papers Susannah presented. Half of the prison guards had already left, joining the retreating Confederate troops; only a handful of volunteers were staying.

"If you can get them out of here, they're yours," said the lieutenant in charge.

She hesitated about leaving the wagon and horses alone. No one could be trusted now. The lieutenant saw her glance worriedly toward the dilapidated wagon. "I'll watch it for you, Mrs. Fallon."

She nodded thankfully and picked up the satchel of clothing she had obtained, then followed a private to the hospital area of the prison. Her hands clenched together, she prayed that Wes and the major would be able to travel. It had been a month since the amputation of Wes's leg, weeks since the major was injured.

The major. Who may not be a major at all.

The two men were awake when she was ushered into the dirty room.

The major's dark eyes were wary, her brother's dull, and she longed to see the blue in them sparkle with the humor he'd had before four years of war.

She went over to Wes first. "Do you think you can travel?"

"Why?"

Susannah was quiet for a moment. She hadn't told him anything before; she hadn't wanted to worry him, not while he was a prisoner. But now she had to.

"The ranch," she said. "I received a letter, dated two months ago. Stan's been killed, and horses and cattle are disappearing from both ranches. Jaime's taken over as foreman, but he's scared. The whole county's scared."

"The Martin family?"

She nodded. "They think so."

Wes swore, then said bitterly, "What can we do? A woman and a cripple."

"You should have some influence," Susannah said.

"My blue uniform in Texas? You're crazy, Sis."

"Who do you think will be controlling Texas now?" she asked impatiently. "The Union."

"Damn it. Our—your—neighbors are going to resent me. I was almost tarred and feathered that day I left. I'll never be accepted there. You would be better off without me."

Susannah didn't tell him that neither had she been accepted despite Mark's attempts, nor how isolated their ranch had become. Or, for that matter, how much the county had changed, how many men had been lost to the war. "I need you, Wes," she said. It wasn't a lie;

she would always need her brother. "Besides, Dad left his ranch to you. You can't lose it."

There was a strained silence. "How in the hell do you plan to get us there? I don't even know if I can ride."

"Major Redding said he would help us."

Wes turned around and stared at Rhys, who was sitting up. It was obvious the Welshman heard every word. "Why?" Wes asked suspiciously.

Rhys shrugged and caught the warning in Susannah's eye. "Your sister offered me a job. The war's apparently over. I don't particularly want to wait around in a hospital, and your sister needs help."

"You sure as hell don't look like a cowhand," Wes said.

Rhys shrugged again. "Is that a requirement? Besides, I don't think I said I planned to be a cowhand, just to help along the way. Always wanted to see your American West. This seems as good a chance as any."

"I just want to know—" Wes continued stubbornly.

Susannah interrupted. "We don't have time, Wes. Richmond's in chaos. If we don't get out now, we may not be able to."

"Why do we have to go now?"

"Maybe you don't care about the ranches, yours and mine, but I do," Susannah said. "I want something . . . left of Mark. I owe him that. So do you."

"But why now? Why not wait until our troops come?"

Susannah hesitated. She felt Major Redding's eyes on her. "They may . . . want to keep you. Or Major Redding. Medical reasons or something."

"It's desertion," he protested.

"It's escape, escape from captivity," she reasoned desperately. "It's going home because the war is over now." Her voice pleaded with him as she sat wearily on his cot. "Wes . . . it *is* over. Everyone will be going home, and neither of you can fight right now. You've done more than your share. Please help me." She widened her eyes pitifully as she said the words. It was, she defended herself, for a good cause.

"I'm not fit to help anyone," he persisted bitterly, his mind returning to his original objection.

"Not if you keep feeling sorry for yourself," Susannah snapped. "I've always been able to depend on you."

She suddenly sensed Major Redding's gaze on her. She turned, and his eyes were probing while holding their own counsel. Susannah suddenly thought that this was a man who lived a life of secrets, secrets he wouldn't give up easily.

He gave her a twisted smile, one full of dare and even a hint of mockery, as if he wondered whether she was really capable of doing what they had so marginally discussed. His eyes told her little else. They just did what he seemed to do so well: wait patiently, like a hawk, for the next move of his prey. No one could know that Wes's decision was of any importance to him. Except her. She knew. She felt it.

"We must go," she said, facing Wes once more. "But first you'd better change out of those uniforms. People are going crazy in Richmond now." She handed sets of clothes to both Rhys and Wes, not giving her brother any more time to demur, making the decision for him. *Please*, she begged him silently.

Rhys looked at Wes, saw the man surrender to the potent plea in her face, then stared back at her as her worried frown eased with the scent of victory. "I'll wait outside," she said. Without giving them a chance to respond, she turned.

"Is she always that bossy?" Rhys asked conversationally, but Wes just glared at him as he started taking off his shirt.

Rhys wondered if the wagon would last more than a dozen miles, much less the horses. The wheels wobbled, and the wood strained and groaned whenever they moved. The horses' ribs showed through dull, lifeless coats.

Rhys took the seat alongside Susannah, and then the reins from her hands. Wes sat back on a thin mattress. He'd barely made it on crutches through the prison corridors and had collapsed on the bed of the wagon without comment.

"I'll drive," Rhys said. It was more a command than a request and he felt her straighten, like a cat arching its back in indignation.

"I'm perfectly capable, Major." Susannah's reply was unexpectedly stony. Now that she was sitting so near to him, she felt so many things she shouldn't. Like ripples of heat up and down her back every time they accidentally touched or their eyes met. She had been in control, up until now. Or had she? "Or is it Major?"

Rhys shrugged noncommittally. It was not the time for his very complicated, convoluted story. "Major will do well enough for now, Mrs. Fallon, and I don't doubt for a moment you can drive, or anything else you set your mind on, but I'm bloody tired of just sitting."

"But your wound—?"

"Is going to hurt like bloody hell in any case," he said curtly. He made it very clear there would be no more discussion, though he was certain handling the reins was going to pull against the wound. But he knew even this sad team of horses might be hard to control amid the commotion.

The lieutenant in charge of the prison eyed their civilian clothes with suspicion, but Susannah, with that smile Rhys imagined could break a dozen hearts at once, apparently reassured him with just a few words. "We're just going home, Lieutenant. Good luck to you."

"And you, ma'am. You be careful, now." Rhys noted he didn't include the two men in his warning.

As the wagon jolted out of the prison yard and into the streets, Rhys looked back. Faces appeared against the bars of the window, but the gray-clad guards beneath paid no attention. Behind the prison, the orange glow of fire spread across the sky. He heard the roar of cannon, louder now that no walls separated him from the sound. There were other loud noises as he turned into a crowded street. Gunfire. Shouts. The cries of frightened horses. Tramping of hundreds, thousands of feet as the Confederates retreated through the city.

As they turned onto a main road, he saw them, those thousands of soldiers, and wondered how they had survived as long as they had. Many had no shoes, and their tattered gray uniforms were brown with dirt and sweat. Among them were wagons like the one Rhys and his companions occupied, each piled high with belongings. There were also wheelbarrows being pushed by men and women, apparently trying to save whatever possessions they could. They were all on the one road out of the doomed city. More explosions sounded in the distance, and the horses' ears flattened in fear. The orange-colored sky grew red as the bright afternoon turned dull with smoke.

Rhys steered the horses around a wagon with a broken wheel, and the movement stoked the pain in his side. He felt a wetness there, but he ignored it, trying to keep the horses moving, afraid that if he didn't they would stop and refuse to go on, or that some of the dull-eyed men would grab the harness and confiscate the wagon and animals.

A troop of cavalry pounded over the road, scattering the civilians as the weary Confederate troops trudged to the side.

As day turned into night, the road grew more and more crowded and the wagon crept on, inch by inch.

Not far outside the city they had to pull over as another cavalry troop and its artillery pieces moved by.

Susannah was thoroughly jolted by the lack of springs in the wagon, the incessant starting and stopping, the juts in the road from the caissons. She started to turn, to stretch sore muscles, when she spied the four men. None was in uniform and all looked thoroughly disreputable. She looked toward the road, but the group of cavalry was too far ahead, their eyes on nothing but the road in front of them. A long, empty distance stretched behind them . . . then a group of barely walking wounded. No help there.

One of the two men who were on foot had a rifle in his hand. The other two sat astride a mule, pistols tucked in their belts. Their eyes, she noticed, were intent on the wagon and horses. Feeling the first rumblings of fear, she slid a glance at Major Redding and her brother.

Her brother's eyes were closed, and he looked paler. Redding was slumped in his seat, his lips stretched thinly, and she knew that he, too, must be in pain, if not totally exhausted.

She leaned down and quietly slipped the pistol from beneath the bench. She realized how sick the major must be when he didn't seem to notice. He usually noticed everything.

Susannah clenched the gun in the folds of her skirt. She wasn't sure whether she wanted Redding to know she had the gun . . . if it wasn't necessary. The cautious part of her kept reminding her how little she knew about him, even though the other part had decided to trust him. The pistol was her edge, her one protection for herself and Wes.

She looked over at Redding and noticed that he, too, was aware of the men coming toward them. His body had lost its slump, and Susannah suddenly caught the impression of a coiled snake.

The man with the gun balanced in his hands

reached within five feet of the wagon. His eyes were greedy as they ran over the wagon, and then Susannah. "Wouldn't have any food for some starving soldiers, wouldja?"

Susannah's fist tightened around the butt of the pistol as she raised an eyebrow the way Redding occasionally did. "Soldiers?"

Although she felt the tension in Redding's body, his face had seemed to change in the past few seconds, almost to that of a dullard. The four men didn't know, as she did, that *dullard* was one word that would never fit him.

He was planning something. She could almost feel his muscles bunching up within the mismatched clothes, feel danger radiating from him.

The rifle in the leader's hands swung toward them. "If you don't have no food, we'll jest take that wagon," he said.

In that moment, she knew Rhys Redding planned to jump them, despite the fact that he had no chance at all against four men, not in his current condition. Her left hand went out to his arm as her right hand went up, her fingers steadily holding the pistol.

"I don't think so," she said softly, disregarding the sudden stare the major sent toward her.

The man with the rifle hesitated a moment and then sneered, "You won't shoot that." His hand tightened on the trigger of the rifle.

Susannah aimed at the fleshy part of his leg and fired. The man swore loudly, dropping to his knees and clutching his leg. The shot apparently alerted several of the cavalry, and a man in an officer's uniform turned his horse and headed to the wagon.

The two men on the mule kicked the animal into a trot, while the other man on foot started running toward a clump of trees. The wounded thief moaned as the Confederate officer approached.

His tired eyes took in the scene, settling on

Susannah, who was still holding the smoking gun. "Ma'am?"

"He—they were trying to steal our wagon."

Rhys turned to look at her. She was sitting, apparently calm, the gun at her side. Her face seemed pale, but her hands were steady. He didn't allow his own surprise to show. He had seen her determination, but this still came as a surprise. He'd never seen a woman handle a gun like that before, not even in Africa where dangers were many and constant.

His angel with the gentle touch!

A flash of satisfaction, even exhilaration, ran through him. He was getting another glimpse of this side to this particular angel. It was captivating, the fine steel that ran through her and made her so complex, so different from other women he'd known. He felt a familiar reaction to her, a stirring of male parts that was becoming as painful as his wound.

The officer looked at Rhys, then Wes, who was struggling to sit up. "These men—"

"Wounded," Susannah said, and Rhys noted that her voice was more accented than usual. On purpose? "My brother . . . and my cousin."

"Where are you heading, ma'am?"

"Texas."

"Good God," he said. "Do you know there's three or four Union armies between here and Texas?"

She nodded. "But I got through a few months ago." She hesitated. "My husband was with General Lee."

"Was?"

"He's dead," she said softly, and Rhys saw the officer's weary features fill with sympathy.

"His name," ma'am?"

"Mark Fallon, Colonel Fallon."

"I've heard of him," the officer said. "Captured a Yank general, didn't he?"

Susannah nodded. "I heard he was missing, so I came here to try to find out something. I learned of his death just weeks ago. And there's trouble at home."

"There's trouble everywhere, ma'am. I don't think you should be traveling like this, not with two wounded men." He eyed the wagon. "We have orders to take whatever vehicles and animals we might need."

Rhys might have interceded but Susannah was doing well on her own. He watched with interest as her eyes started to fill with tears. He knew enough about her to wonder about their authenticity. Susannah Fallon, he was learning, was not above a lie now and then. He liked that about her. He liked it very much.

She was probably the most complex and determined woman he'd ever met. The journey ahead looked infinitely more interesting and filled with possibilities.

"Now, ma'am, please don't do that," the officer said soothingly. "I'll write out a safe conduct for you. That should help. But I still don't think—"

"You're very kind," Susannah said. "But I think I—and the major here—can take care of anything."

The officer looked at the man on the ground and the gun still in her hand. "I can see. Looter, I suppose. They're all over Richmond now. Damned vultures."

He hesitated, then reached into his saddlebags for a piece of paper to scribble on. He handed it to Rhys. "I'll assign two of my men to you for the next few hours. They can catch up with me later."

He gave Susannah a salute and then galloped off. When he reached his waiting troops, he spoke briefly with someone, and then two other cavalry riders rode toward them. "Ma'am," one said. "We'll ride along with you a way."

Susannah looked at the moaning man on the ground. "What about him?"

"We'll leave him here for his friends to pick up. We

don't have time to patch up looters and deserters." He turned to Rhys. "Sir, I think we can get moving now."

Rhys cocked an eyebrow at Susannah in admiration. "Cousin," he said, his voice full of amusement, "shall we move on?" Not only was she accomplished with a gun, she was equally as talented at stretching the truth.

She nodded and he snapped the reins, and the wagon jolted forward, the cavalry men following at a short distance. Rhys turned and gave her a slow, appraising stare. He had seen a gentle side, and a determined side, but now he saw perhaps even a ruthless side.

She put the pistol back under the seat and gave him a slight, almost hesitant smile, as if she was unsure of his reaction. "I won't be a burden to you," she said. "I can help defend us."

"You could have given me the gun."

"I didn't know how good you were with one."

He chuckled. "Is that really the reason, Mrs. Fallon? Or did you not want me to know about it?" There was no offense in his question, only more amusement.

Susannah realized her explanation was weak. He was in the army, after all; of course he would know how to use a gun. And, she suspected, extremely well. She thought about lying, making up another reason, but she also sensed he would read that equally well. She knew he wouldn't accept that she'd merely forgotten about it. So she gave him a sheepish look and half an explanation. "I was raised in Texas. There's a lot of varmints there."

"I've had some experience with varmints myself," he said.

"You'll have to tell me about them. About a great many things." The retort was challenging, and Rhys was again reminded not to underestimate Mrs. Susannah Fallon.

He simply nodded.

"Who are you, Major . . .?"

"Redding. It *is* Redding," he said easily.

"What else is it?"

"It's pretty late to be asking, Mrs. Fallon."

"And you aren't going to tell me?"

He turned and faced her, his eyes so dark and deep that Susannah wondered if anyone, or anything, could ever penetrate their mystery. They sometimes glittered, as the hawk's eyes glittered at the sight of prey, but they never, ever, revealed anything more. Her body shivered, and she knew it was a shiver of warm expectancy rather than fear. That in itself was enough to make any sound person afraid.

"Only that I usually keep my word. And my bargains."

"Usually?"

"I don't believe in absolutes, Mrs. Fallon. Except maybe death. I never have."

"Where does that leave us?"

He gave her that slight twist of his lips that could mean anything. It was infuriating. "Fairly safe," he replied. "No absolutes, remember."

"Then we can rest easily?" Susannah didn't quite keep the sarcasm from her voice.

The twist turned into a smile that taunted, as if saying, "Rest easily if you can." Susannah felt another shiver, this time of ice, run up her spine . . . and a coil of heat snaking in the most private place of herself. Heat and ice. Somehow they were both a part of him, two sides of a coin.

She met his gaze, hoping that her feelings showed no more than his. "I'd better see about Wes," she said.

He arched an eyebrow, his eyes glittering, and she knew she'd failed miserably. What had she done in asking him along? Dear heavens, no one had ever affected her this way before, this ridiculously foolish, infatuated, girlish way. No, she amended, not girlish.

There was nothing childish about her feelings or the growing yearning inside her. *That* was the problem!

She swallowed deeply, trembling and physically wanting without knowing exactly what or why. She willed herself to move, but still her body hesitated before obeying, as if his silent forcefulness was greater than hers, and he was exercising it. She found her throat choked by a thickness she couldn't swallow, and her stomach was churning. It would take weeks, perhaps even months, to get back to Texas. What in God's name had she been thinking of when she'd asked him to accompany them?

Somehow, finally, she forced her gaze away from his and climbed into the bed of the wagon, taking the pistol with her.

Hours passed slowly as they inched down the clogged road. They were often ordered to the side by retreating troops. Night fell. The road was still visible though, faintly lit by the dull glare of the burning city. Rhys could still hear explosions coming from that direction. In addition, there were the sounds of cannon dragged over the road, of ambulances and their moaning cargoes. It could be a scene, he thought, from Dante's *Inferno*, a book he had particularly admired. It had appealed to his dark side.

No one seemed to care who they were, especially since they had two cavalry escorts. No one stopped to ask questions. That was what he had feared, but the retreating troops didn't even look at them.

Gradually the glow and the sounds from the city faded, although the noise from the rolling artillery and the steady but weary tramp of feet continued to shatter the peace of the night.

Susannah joined him again on the driver's bench of the wagon. After looking at his face, she took the reins from him without a word, and he didn't even try to protest. At the moment, there was nothing left in him to protest with.

He was weak, weaker than he'd thought. He was glad Susannah couldn't see his wound. He felt the wet sticky blood soaking through the bandages and knew it was sapping whatever strength he had left. He had been ignoring it for the past few hours through sheer strength of will, by mentally closing off the pain as he had learned to do years ago. But now, he wondered whether he had waited too long. He fought to remain conscious, but it became more and more difficult. He felt his body sliding, sliding . . .

Chapter 5

Susannah's hands trembled as they caught Rhys and kept him from falling off the wagon. With Wes's help, she eased the major into the wagon bed, then she pulled the clotted bandage from his wound. She fretted over her judgment in moving both him and her brother from Libby, but the major's own quiet but intense urgency to escape the prison had prompted her. He had, in fact, made it a condition of helping her with Wes. She still didn't want to wonder why.

He had seemed to be doing so well. She should have realized, however, that he *would* appear that way; that face with the slight mocking smile never revealed what he really thought or felt. She had proof now that neither she nor anyone else would have the slightest hint from him if he were in pain, or even if he were dying.

He had obviously been bleeding for a long time. She should have known, but he had appeared so relaxed when he had baited her earlier.

She should have known. The thought kept pounding at her. She should have remembered that nighthawk years ago. It, too, had spit its defiance almost to the moment it had died.

Rhys Redding. Even the name **was** stark, fitting for the dark, mysterious man, who reminded her of that bird. *Her* nighthawk. It was strange that she always thought of him that way now. Hers. But she did, even as she knew it was unwise, dangerous. It had happened almost from the moment he'd first opened his eyes in the hospital and, even as sick as he was, regarded her with amused astonishment. As much as that expression unsettled her, she would sell her soul to see that mocking smile again, those raised eyebrows over eyes that viewed the world with such cynicism.

But then she might not even have a soul left to sell. She certainly had done heavy bartering with it lately. She had played very liberally with the truth during the past few weeks, and especially the past few hours. She had never realized how easy it could be, or how productive. She had never considered herself a manipulator, but she had been doing her share of that too. With Confederate officials, with Wes, and with the major, although part of her wondered who was manipulating whom the most, where *he* was concerned.

How far *would* she go? Pretty damned far, she knew now, to get home, to get Wes back where he belonged.

Her sense of honor had apparently gone to hell in a hand basket. But the war had changed her forever. Her illusions had dimmed, and she questioned whether the meek inherited the earth. The meek, in the past four years, had been destroyed. She refused to be among them, no matter what she had to do.

Her mother would have been horrified by Susannah's transformation. But her mother was dead, along with so many others. There was nothing important now except those she loved, and the land she loved. And she would do anything, anything at all, to make them safe.

The thoughts had flashed through her mind rapidly as she tried to pull away the sticking bandages, and now she saw the open wound, the rough stitches of a too busy doctor ripped away. When had Redding re-opened the wound?

She would need to restitch it, and she winced. The skin was puffy, still red, so sore. His naturally dark skin was pale. She couldn't resist running her hand over the thick dark hair, and she felt its dampness.

Why had he insisted on driving the team?

"Anything we can do, ma'am?" The words came un-expectedly from a drawling voice. Their escorts had left them, but she had pulled over alongside a troop of Confederate infantry that had stopped for the night. She hadn't had any choice after she barely caught Major Redding as he started to slide down. A couple of soldiers had run over to help. She was grateful for their assistance, but inwardly she sighed. More lies. More and more lies.

She shook her head. "Whiskey?" she asked.

" 'Fraid not, ma'am. We could hold him for you," one said as the other helped Wes down from the wagon.

Susannah shuddered. "You don't have a doctor with you?"

"No, ma'am."

"Then a fire," she said, hoping that Major Redding would remain unconscious for the next few minutes. While the two men carried and placed him beside a tree, she searched her portmanteau for the precious needle and thread she had brought along.

She returned to Major Redding's side, barely aware of the activity around her as her patient moved slightly and opened his eyes. A new ache crawled around inside her as his gaze found her face and his lips twisted into a sef-derisive smile. "This seems to . . . be a habit," he said slowly, as if each word was an effort. "What in the bloody hell happened?"

"You insisted on driving."

"Isn't that why you . . . hired me?"

"Is that what I did?" She was not sure now as to who led whom on this expedition, at what point things seemed to have been taken from her hands and put into his.

He grinned weakly, and she knew that he read her mind again. He was so uncanny. "What else?" he asked mockingly.

"I wish I knew," she said, the slightest quaver in her voice. She wished he didn't do that to her, but he did, with those challenging eyes and rakish brows. "I still don't know why . . ."

"Ah," he goaded through clenched teeth that told her he was barely hanging on to consciousness, "but you're taking me on faith. Did anyone ever tell you that you're a most unusual woman?"

"Did anyone ever tell you that you're a very exasperating man?"

"Quite often, but usually they don't put it so delicately." He tried to sit up. His body felt heavier than usual, his head lighter. He felt her hands on him, restraining him.

"Don't," she whispered. "We—I—have to repair that wound."

The dark brows drew together.

"It'll keep breaking open if I don't," she added.

He considered the words for a moment, then nodded.

"I don't have anything . . . not even whiskey."

That half-smile appeared, the one that intrigued her with the mysteries it seemed to hold. "I'm not sure I would want you to have any whiskey," he said with a devilish gleam in his eyes.

She had to smile back at the black humor, and her hand trembled a little less. Still, she hesitated a moment.

"Believe me, Mrs. Fallon," he said, "worse things have happened. A few stitches are nothing."

Susannah wished she could believe him. They may be nothing to him, but they were a great deal to her.

She didn't know whether she could bear to hurt him, and she had never sewn a wound before.

It seemed he read her mind again. "Think of going home, Mrs. Fallon. That's what you want so badly, isn't it?"

She also wanted not to hurt him. *Think of something else.* "And what do you want, Major?"

The half-smile changed slightly, from mystery to mockery. "I don't think you want the answer to that, Mrs. Fallon," he said.

The implication was clear. Susannah bit her lip as a sizzling wave of heat swept through her. He was baiting her again, challenging with those dark eyes, with that sensuous twist of his lips. She suddenly realized she was probably hurting more than he.

She leaned down, willing her hands to be steady, and plunged the needle into the wound. He didn't even flinch. She wished she had that kind of control. She wished she could shut off feelings, shut off this combination of . . . lust combined with empathy.

She tried to make herself think of nothing but the stitches, not the supple skin that stretched over the hard body, not the control that kept it still. In and out.

I don't think you want the answer to that. His words remained in her mind. Dear God, they were so provocative.

And then she was finished. She looked at his eyes and found them watching her with that hawklike gleam. For a second, she wanted to see pain there, some kind of emotion that would tell her he was human.

Instead, he merely looked down at the repaired wound. "My thanks," he said lightly as if she had given him a penny rather than done something that ripped through her soul.

He leaned on his arm and glanced around. Wes sat on the ground, leaning against a tree, looking drawn and exhausted. Three men in tattered gray uniforms were building a fire while sneaking glances at Susannah. Rhys didn't blame them. As the fire ignited into flames, her tall slender body was outlined against the horizon, and even now when she must be exhausted, there was indomitable vitality in her every movement.

Indomitable. That was a good word for her, he thought as he remembered the determined way she'd just stitched his wound. He'd been partly amused by her concentration, and used that amusement to dull the pain. But then, as he had told her, he'd been through worse, much worse.

He looked up at the sky. A dull orange was barely visible to the north. Dust and smoke created a fog that made it almost impossible to judge the time. It had to be early morning though, and Mrs. Susannah Fallon was still functioning, keeping everything together. *She* needed *him?* That's what she'd said at the prison, but it seemed the other way around at the moment.

He'd needed her from the beginning. She had kept him alive, and then helped him escape before the Yanks came. He didn't like the situation. He'd never been on the receiving end of anything good before. For that matter, he'd never been on the giving end, either. Except once. And he sure as hell didn't want to repeat that experience.

Neither did he like the way she made him feel, that rush of exhilaration whenever he was with her, the odd, not totally physical need in him that grew instead of diminished with time. He didn't like it at all. Not even the weakness had dented it, nor the pain in his side. He'd even felt it when she had threaded her needle through his skin, when her fingers brushed the burning soreness of it.

Bloody hell, but those feelings made him feel unarmed, almost naked. Destructible. Bloody hell, it made him doubt his own reasoning, and he hadn't done that in a long time. He decided to voice his reservations.

"Mrs. Fallon, I really don't think you need me. You're bloody damned good with a pistol . . . and a little fabrication here and there. You might even be better than me," he admitted wryly.

Susannah didn't think he meant it as a compliment. Or did he? "Trying to squirm out of your—" She stopped, hesitated, then continued with a suddenly teasing, very infectious, grin, "—not absolute promise?"

That was exactly what he was trying to do, and he wasn't particularly pleased that she recognized his tactics so readily, that she'd turned his words around on him in such a provocative manner. She was learning fast. Too fast. He shrugged. "I seem to be more trouble—"

"You will be, if you don't stop trying to take charge and do too much," she said, worry erasing her self-satisfied expression at temporarily besting him at his own game. "And *I* don't need you. Wes does. No, I'm not going to let you break your word, less than absolute or not."

He cursed silently. He'd had his share of emotional cuts and bruises from women, but this blunt comment ran deeper than most.

"Your brother can manage," he said curtly.

"No, not yet," she refuted. "He's just . . . existing now. But even that's an improvement. You should have seen him before you gained consciousness in prison. He had completely given up. He would have—"

He didn't learn what Wes might have done. She turned her head away suddenly, but her hand remained on his arm and Rhys saw it shake slightly. God, she must be tired. Bloody hell, two invalids, a broken-down wagon, and even more decrepit nags. And she planned to travel a thousand miles or more!

Rhys, the devil help him, didn't like the sympathy he felt rising in him. Or the admiration. She was a damned stubborn fool. "Hell, he doesn't even like me," he said.

She turned back, and he thought he saw something like tears, but he wasn't sure. It might have been just the way the light from the flames caught her.

"That's exactly it. He doesn't like you, so you challenge him. You get his dander up and make him fight back. I'm just his kid sister. I don't know anything. I certainly can't tell him anything."

She wasn't bad at challenging, herself. This was the second time in the past few minutes. Rhys stifled a groan. "You're really planning to go across country in this ... this wagon."

"Until we can find something better," she said with a confidence he thought utterly ludicrous. But then didn't she have practically the whole Confederate army protecting two escaping Yankees?

"Do you have any money?" he asked, and was even a bit pleased when she looked at him suspiciously. He was glad she didn't trust *too* easily.

Instead of answering, she asked a question of her own. "Would you like some water?"

"And some food if you have it."

Susannah looked embarrassed. "I'm sorry we don't have much. I didn't have time and ... most of the stores were closed." Her voice lowered. "I do have some hard biscuits and cheese."

"Love, that sounds like a banquet." The endearment had slipped out easily. He'd said it a hundred times before, even a thousand, but never had it had the impact it did now. Susannah Fallon flushed from her head to her fingers, and probably her toes too. He noted that and smiled to himself.

Something of his inner satisfaction must have shown, for she suddenly stiffened as if struck. Or maybe she was just feeling that heated energy that so often flashed between them when they spoke like this, or when she touched him, or when ...

She moved to the wagon and returned with the food. She dropped the items unceremoniously on his lap and left him, taking a blanket to her brother. She stayed with Wes while Rhys ate slowly, letting his stomach adjust to what was becoming the rare experience of being fed.

He felt so weak. He wasn't used to being so damned helpless, to every movement being an effort, accomplished only by supreme will. The food helped, however, and so did the cup of water she'd left next to him. She was right; he was going to have to take it easier if he was eventually to be of any use. It was only then that he realized he'd made the decision to stay with them. For a little while, anyway.

His gaze settled on her again. She was kneeling next to Wes, her shoulders slightly bowed in fatigue, but still gallant. He had never used that word in relation to a woman before, or even a man for that matter. He quickly brushed it from his mind.

He lay back on the ground and closed his eyes, thinking of the way she had used the gun. But it would take more than a gun to keep him away.

He had no compunction about her recently widowed status. None at all. Most marriages in England being founded on convenience and family alliances, he had bedded many a willing wife and more than a few widows, recent and not. He certainly had damnably little conscience about doing it now.

Still, he wondered about her husband.

Rhys was still wondering when he fell asleep.

Susannah lay awake, looking up at the stars, which were barely visible through the smoky haze. She was too tired to sleep. Too tired and too tense, and her emotions too galvanized.

She was going home. Without Mark.

But going home!

Rolling hills. Wildflowers. The skies so pure and blue they made you ache inside. She hungered for it, for the way it had always soothed an indefinable yearning within her, a yearning that she was only beginning to understand. She wondered whether the Texas hills would cure her of that hunger. If indeed, she even wanted to be cured.

She looked over at Major Redding, who was asleep. At last. Just knowing he was there, seeing him, stirred a churning inside. She clenched her hands into fists, fighting it, trying to deny what was undeniable. They would be spending weeks together. Try as she might, she couldn't restrain the bubbling expectation—or the foreboding that the journey would end in disaster.

The sound of moving caissons woke her early the next morning. The sky was still dull with smoke, and the road was crowded again with Confederate troops moving slowly southwest like an endless snake. She wiped the sleep from her eyes, feeling drained and tired.

Her hair, which had been bound tightly in braids, had come loose and was falling around her face. She brushed it back impatiently, knowing she must look like the wrath of God.

She stood up and looked around. Wes was awake, sitting beside a fire being tended by her nighthawk—no, Major Redding, she scolded herself.

He stood, and she felt that raking gaze of his studying her. She felt terribly wanting at the moment, uncertain, all the confidence she'd worked so hard to gain and show him in tatters. Despite the loss of blood yesterday, and her assault on his body with a needle, each one of his movements was deliberate and exact. He looked like a brigand, his face covered with dark bristles again. She remembered how she'd felt shaving him days earlier; it had been so unnerving, her hands fairly shook. They did so now, as she remembered the intimacy of the act.

Watching him move now, she felt the warm tingling of her senses again, a painful ache that lodged itself deep within her. Self-consciously, she brushed back another lock of hair.

He smiled and lazily moved toward her.

"Mrs. Fallon," he said politely enough, yet there was a trace of amusement. "I heated some water if you would like to wash."

Susannah ignored the glint in his eyes. "Is there any news?"

He shrugged and nodded toward the Reb soldiers. "They say Lee's going to try to join up with Johnston in the Carolinas, but ... Christ, look at them. No shoes, clothes falling off their backs. No food. What can they fight with?" He hesitated a moment, then answered himself with that odd combination of admiration and contempt only he could convey. "Spirit, perhaps, enough to get a few more killed."

"The Yankees?"

"No one knows what they're up to. A man rode in an hour ago and said they've taken over the city, but apparently Grant ordered his troops not to fire on the retreating Confederates."

"Wes?"

He looked over at her brother. "He moved around a little this morning, even helped with firewood."

Susannah rubbed her eyes. "There's a handful of coffee in the bag," she said, wondering if this was the time to use it. But then why not? What would she save it for?

He looked at her with curiosity. "What else is left, Mrs. Fallon?"

Susannah wondered what she should tell him. She had so little food and so little money. Would he stay with them if he knew? She might as well find out now rather than later. From underneath the thin blanket that had covered her, she pulled out the flour sack that contained their meager supply.

He took it and glanced within, his mouth twisting into an ironic smile. "More than I thought; less than I hoped," he admitted, placing the sack on the ground.

"You don't hope for much."

"No," he agreed. "I stopped doing that long ago." There was no bitterness in his words, only a wry acceptance of the way he thought things were. That cynical acceptance was more painful to Susannah than bitterness would have been. She wondered if he realized how much it said about him. She suddenly hurt for him, but she knew she couldn't show it. He would hate it. He most certainly wouldn't accept it.

"I do have a little money. We'll manage."

He grinned wider this time. "I don't doubt it for a moment, Mrs. Fallon. I wouldn't even be surprised now if the whole Confederate Army turned over what's left of its commissary to you."

"You'll stay then?"

"I said I would," he answered lightly.

"Yep, but then you seemed to amend it. No absolutes, remember?"

"Do you always remember everything?"

She nodded. "Everything that's important."

He shrugged. "I just thought you might be thinking I'm more trouble than I'm worth."

She shook her head. "I don't think you've ever thought that, Major."

"I'm not sure how to take that, Mrs. Fallon."

"And I'm not sure I'm going to explain it," she replied. She couldn't, if she wanted to. There was such self-assurance about him, she thought it might be nice if he wondered.

He mulled over her cryptic statement for a moment, then his smile widened, touching his eyes. "Didn't anyone ever tell you to beware of strangers?"

"I don't consider you a stranger. I've seen you at your very worst, remember."

He winced, thinking of those first days in the hospital. Of the smell and the dirt and the infection.

"Major . . ."

He looked at her quizzically. "Mrs. Fallon?"

Susannah hated the way he said "Mrs. Fallon," as if he were deliberately keeping her at a distance. The magnetism between them said something quite different, that what was between them couldn't be split as a result of such tactics.

"I would be interested to know why you wanted to leave Libby."

"It's a long story."

"One you're aren't ready to tell?"

"No," he agreed with a complacency that told her she wasn't going to learn anything else, either.

He eyed her for a moment, as if daring her to ask another question and, after a brief silence, picked up the flour sack. "I'll make the coffee if you would like to do . . . whatever you need to do."

She blushed to her toes—again. Gentlemen didn't refer to necessary functions, but then she doubted if he worried much about being a gentleman. She nodded, turning away from the devilish humor she knew was dancing in those dark eyes.

She didn't even try to move, not until he was headed back to the fire. She was certain her legs would go weak under her. He had that effect on her.

Susannah looked toward her brother. He was making his way to the wagon now, and she watched his painful progress, remembering his old exuberance, his old assurance. A lump formed in her throat, so hard and big she could barely breathe. But she dared not let him realize it. Pity was the worst thing for him. That's why Major Redding was so important. He gave none. He probably had none in him. She felt her hands clench beside her as her gaze involuntarily moved in his direction. He had knelt next to the fire, his dark head leaning forward, concentrating on the coffee.

"Sue." Wes's voice was halting, unsure.

She looked at him.

"Did he ... Redding ... say anything he shouldn't?"

Susannah winced. Apparently her face had flushed even more than she'd thought. She shook her head. "No, he just said he would take care of the coffee while I washed."

Wes's eyes searched her face. "We can make it alone, Sue, if you want to go so badly. Or we can wait here for the Union troops."

And then wait weeks, possibly longer until they could get some other help? Despite Wes's assurances, he still needed physical assistance. He'd needed it last night just to get out of the wagon. He would need it if he was to ride again, or to get into a saddle, which eventually he would have to do. There were no railroads left in the South. The blockade had closed all ports. And if they waited for hostilities to cease, there might not be a home waiting for them.

No, they couldn't wait. And they couldn't make it alone.

"He's been nothing but a gentleman," she said, again bending the truth a little. She tried not to think of the teasing glitter in Major Redding's eyes just seconds ago.

Wes glanced over at the subject of their conversation. "There's something about him that's not ..." He couldn't put a word to his thought.

Susannah knew exactly what he meant, but she wasn't going to let him know it. "Maybe it's just because he's Welsh."

"So what is he doing in the Yank army?"

She shrugged. Thank heaven, Wes had been asleep during that enigmatic conversation in the hospital, when Major Redding said he was not exactly what he seemed.

"I don't like it," Wes added. "I'll be watching him."

Susannah smiled internally. That's exactly what she hoped for. Not because she was worried that the major would hurt them, but because of the spirit it brought back to Wes. The major gave him something to worry about other than himself . . . and Erin back home.

She nodded. "I knew I could depend on you."

He looked at her with sudden suspicion, but she ignored it. "Do you suppose it's safe beyond those trees?"

Wes's face cleared. "I'll go partway with you."

Keeping her face blank, hiding her satisfaction at his protectiveness, Susannah agreed.

But still she looked back. Her nighthawk had finished with the coffee and was leaning against the wagon, a self-satisfied smile shadowing his face.

Chapter 6

The rickety wagon rolled slowly on through the fifth day of their journey, three days since Susannah had stitched Rhys's wound.

She looked at him, wondering at his amazing recovery. His naturally bronze-tinged skin had further darkened with the sun, wiping away the pallor that had frightened her. And his body. The lean, muscular body that moved ... so sensually ... looked strong and fit as he again handled the reins. Susannah tried not to stare at him, but failed quite miserably. She was as attracted to him as a baby bear to a pot of honey.

She told herself it was only to ensure that he was indeed well enough to drive, but she knew in her heart that was a lie. Every time their arms brushed, or he helped her down, she felt as if someone had lit candles throughout her entire being. It was incomprehensible, frightening, but very, very real. And the more she tried to smother those feelings, the more they rebelled against any attempt to harness them.

Susannah and her two companions had left the column of Confederate troops, which had turned south to meet Lee's main army. There were still soldiers on the road they traveled: wounded going home, couriers, small units of cavalry. But the winding lines of exhausted men were gone. And the haunting glow of Richmond burning had long disappeared.

Susannah's backside was sore beyond imagination from the jolting of the wagon, her hands blistered under the gloves she wore. Hunger rumbled in her stomach, rumbled in all of their stomachs, but they had agreed to ration what food remained.

As night fell, the horses started to stumble, and Susannah realized they could probably go no farther. Nor, she thought, could she.

Major Redding apparently had the same thought. He pointed to a drive and a far light that shone beyond through the darkness. "It looks like a farmhouse. Perhaps we can get some water, even some food."

Susannah thought about the few remaining biscuits, a hunk of hard cheese and some jerky she had in her sack. She nodded.

He turned the team onto the dirt road, and Susannah saw deep ruts in the ground, which meant heavy wagons had already traveled this way. One of the wheels of the wagon hit something, and she heard the sound of splintering wood. The wagon swayed as the wheel broke, and one end of the wagon sagged low to the ground. The horses fought the traces, and the wagon wavered and then slowly collapsed. Everything, including the three passengers, slid to the left side as the frantic horses broke loose.

Susannah heard a moan from the back of the wagon, and a curse from the major as the wagon tumbled over and over.

Rhys instinctively buffered her fall with his own body, pushing her out of the path of the still-moving wagon. But the way their bodies were twisting and turning, he couldn't keep her head from hitting the edge of a wheel.

He heard a rough curse from a few feet away, and knew that Wes was, at least, still alive.

He was very aware of Susannah's body under his,

and even more aware of its stillness. He moved, taking his weight off her and sliding to her side.

The overturned wagon hid the moon from view, and he could barely see Susannah's face among the shadows of the trees. She was still. His own wound hurt anew, but he pushed that concern aside.

"Sue?" Wes's voice was nearly frantic.

"Over here," Rhys said. He found her pulse. It was even, as was her breathing. His hands moved over her; he couldn't find any open wounds. Perhaps only the wind was knocked out of her.

He felt a slight movement, and his fingers accidentally brushed her breast. Her body trembled, and then she moved again, and he felt his own breath come slowly from his mouth. He realized it had been caught somewhere in his throat. It felt bloody damn odd to care about someone else, even a little.

"Mrs. Fallon?"

Her hand came up, and he caught it in his own, holding it tight, trying to give reassurance although he knew he wasn't any damned good at it. "It's all right, Mrs. Fallon," he said in a voice much harsher than he'd intended.

He heard Wes drag himself over. "Sis?"

"What . . . happened?" Her voice was very low, the words halting.

"The wagon did what it's been wanting to do: collapse." Wry amusement was back in Rhys's voice, now that he felt nothing serious was wrong with her.

"Wes?"

"I'm all right. It's you we're worried about." Wes's voice was stronger, surer, than Rhys had ever heard it before. Maybe Susannah Fallon had been right; maybe the man had more guts than he'd believed. The self-pity was gone, at least for the moment.

Rhys felt her move again. He felt her body's strength and softness, and he knew a relief that was unique in its intensity. He didn't know when last he cared about someone, really cared in any meaningful way. He couldn't remember. Probably never. He had felt some loss when his mother had died long ago. But that hadn't been grief for a woman who had never given him a kind word, but for what little security he had had as a child.

Now he felt something else. Worry? Concern? Whatever it was, he wasn't sure he liked it. In fact, he knew damned well he didn't. It was ... disturbing.

He'd previously been in tight spots, which were too many to count. But never, not since he'd become a man, had he had this out-of-control feeling.

Christ. They were sitting on the ground between two armies, one of which would bloody well love to get its hands on him. The horses were gone, the wagon probably ruined beyond repair. No money. And in his charge, devil help him, were a woman and a cripple.

Rhys moved, testing his arms, his legs. They were all working. So was something else, he knew, as he felt Susannah Fallon move again. Hair, the texture of silk, brushed his hand. His leg was next to her hips, and the softness was like electricity in the still calm night, as if some storm lingered far away, sending arrows of static heat straight for him.

He forced himself to move. "We can't stay here," he finally said.

Wes crawled next to Susannah, who was now sitting. "I can't find the crutches," he said, sounding ashamed. If Rhys hadn't been so disconcerted over being worried about Susannah, he might have felt sorry for Wes.

"She shouldn't move," Rhys said. "I'll walk over to that light, see who and what is there. And try to find the horses."

There was a frustrated silence. "Damn," Wes swore.

Rhys heard the pain, the despair, in the one word

and again felt an unwelcome empathy. "She needs you here," Rhys said.

"I'm here," Susannah said. "Don't talk about me like I'm not."

Both men turned back to her. Her face was pale in the slice of moonlight that filtered through the trees. But her mouth had that determined set Rhys was beginning to recognize.

"I'm fine," she insisted as she tried to stand and then, with a small cry, fell back down.

Rhys's hands moved to her ankle. It was swelling rapidly. He moved it slightly. "Just sprained, I think," he said, "but she can't walk. And this wagon . . . good for firewood, nothing more. I'll see if I can find the horses.

"And what do I do if there's trouble?" Wes asked bitterly.

The gun. Rhys narrowed his eyes, trying to see through the darkness. He moved out of the shadow of the overturned wagon and searched the ground. He found one crutch and the sack with what was left of their food. He reached inside and found a dull knife. Better than nothing, but they still needed the gun.

He remembered his years in Africa, the weapons he'd carried then. He would give anything to have only a few of them now. In England, he'd carried a small derringer in the streets, and kept a brace of pistols in his London town house. But he'd never felt the need to defend his honor, since he'd never had much of it. He'd had to scrap and fight just to stay alive, and honor—whatever that meant—had been an early casualty. He'd learned never to allow the other person to attack first.

Now he felt naked and vulnerable without anything but his hands and his wits. And he didn't like leaving Susannah and her brother alone out in the night, without any protection.

Rhys continued searching for the gun among the dirt. Where in the devil was it?

A cloud flitted across the moon and limited his vision even more. But then his foot hit something, and he leaned down to find the pistol. Perhaps there was a God, though he doubted it. He automatically checked the weapon. There were bullets in the chamber, and he knew Susannah would and could use it. Rhys suddenly realized that, despite his words to Wes, his first instinct had been to give Susannah the gun, that he considered her the protector of the two. It was time the Yank became more useful. It was also necessary that the Yank learn to ride again. It was only too bloody obvious they couldn't travel all the way by wagon; it would take them forever, not to mention what it did to his backside.

He hesitated where he was standing, trying to understand all the thoughts flitting through his mind. *Them. Them* had nothing to do with him. He could summon help for them and ride on.

Rhys Redding was tempted to do just that. The bewildering emotional and sexual pull he felt toward the woman told him he ought to do just that.

Yet, he'd always kept his end of any bargain he made, despite his earlier comments to her. That had always been the beginning and end of what little conscience he had.

He chuckled mirthlessly at the irony of his situation.

"Major Redding?" Susannah's voice held the slightest bit of panic in it, and he suddenly realized he couldn't leave. Not now. Not until Wes could provide some modicum of protection, not until he felt the two might have a chance of making it on their own.

Then he could leave. Without the gut-wrenching guilt he was feeling now, guilt he'd never felt before.

But where would they get horses? For a moment he thought of his bank in London, of the very substan-

tial balance there, earned by years as a mercenary and
then by gambling and shrewd investments. But for all
the good it did him now, it might not exist at all. He
had not a farthing on him, not even a worthless Confederate dollar. Even his watch had been taken by his
captors. At the moment, he had only the pair of boots
he'd stolen from the Union officer and the borrowed
clothes on his body. Well, he'd once had even less than
that.

He walked over to where Susannah and Wes were
sitting, and he handed the pistol to Wes. "I'll be back,"
he said, then turned toward the distant light.

Rhys moved quietly among the shadows of the
trees. As he neared the light, he saw a comfortable-
looking farmhouse and barn, the house lit like a
Christmas tree flickering with candles. There were
other shapes. Ambulances in the yard. A few soldiers
around a camp fire. Obviously the place was a hospital
of some kind.

He tried to make out the uniforms. No outposts.
That was strange. Rhys crept closer. Confederate. And
just beyond them, tethered on a picket line, were
horses. Thin and tired, they weren't much better than
the ones he'd lost.

Rhys thought about approaching the men, and then
he remembered the last time he'd done that, he'd
been shot for his trouble. Yankees were not far away,
and he damn well didn't want any delays, or chance
getting caught and held by Confederates. Besides,
he'd always taken what he wanted, and he bloody
damn well didn't plan to change his habits. He certainly didn't owe the Rebs anything, not after what
he'd gone through.

A simple trade, he thought. Two of these horses, or
maybe even three, for the two that had run off. The
Rebs would find them, when they went looking for
their own horses.

Three, he thought, and then discarded the idea.

Wes and Susannah would suspect something if he showed up with three horses and said he'd made a trade for their two wretched ones. And as much as they wanted to get home, he also suspected they might object to horse theft.

With a sigh for having morality forced on him, he waited until the figures around the fire lay down, and gave them time to go to sleep. He then snaked his way to the picket line. No one was on guard. It was as if they knew the war was over, and were too tired to post even a few pickets. He suspected that these were all wounded left behind, that the horses had pulled the ambulances.

He picked two of the best-looking ones and started to cut the line, then stopped. No saddles, dammit. And there was no bloody way in hell Wes Carr could ride without one. Not yet.

The barn. He got down on his belly and crawled toward the barn. But then he heard voices, and he realized it, too, was probably sheltering the wounded.

He went back slowly toward the horses, and cut the rope from the two he'd already picked, keeping a length to guide the second horse and leading the other by the halter. Stealthily, he moved toward the woods and the road. After a short distance he mounted a horse and quickened the pace.

For the first time since she'd left Texas, Susannah felt hopeless. Despite so many disappointments and disasters, she'd always been optimistic. She would find her husband; Wes would recover and become his own self; they would make it home to Texas. But now she realized their flight from Richmond had been foolish. No, it had been even more than that. Insane, really, to leave Richmond with only a broken-down wagon and two horses she was able to obtain because no one else in the world wanted them.

She leaned against the overturned wagon. Her ankle hurt when she moved, but it was bearable, and she had no intention of letting it, or her other bruises, stop her. If Major Redding thought she and Wes might slow him down even more, it was likely he would abandon them. And Wes had enough problems of his own; he didn't need to worry about her.

Dear God, but she had been reluctant to see Rhys Redding leave. He'd faded so easily into the shadows, just like a creature of the night. It had been a reminder of who and what he was. Or wasn't! Still, she'd felt a terrible sense of abandonment, of loss. Even now she trembled, remembering the surprising gentleness of his hands as they'd examined her, the concern in his voice, even the fear that she knew was for her. She didn't like to think of how much she'd enjoyed the feeling of being protected. It had been a very long time since she'd felt that way.

But almost as soon as she'd moved, the concern was gone and the customary detached mockery was back in his voice.

"I don't trust him," Wes growled, a now-familiar complaint. "What if he doesn't come back?"

The uncertainty in his voice stabbed her to the core. "We don't have much choice but to trust him," she replied, not ready to argue with him.

She started to move toward him and couldn't withhold a gasp of pain.

She heard Wes swear again. "Are you hurt?"

"The wind was knocked out of me, that's all." She didn't mention the pounding in her head.

He moved next to her, his hand meeting hers. "Are you sure? I can try to—"

"He'll be back, Wes. I know he will."

"I don't like it," Wes said stubbornly. "Dammit, Sue, why wouldn't you wait in Richmond?"

"The whole city was on fire. What if we were caught in it?"

"The Union forces wouldn't let that happen."

She wished she could see his face, but she did feel his hand around hers. She sensed his frustration. He had always been the caretaker in the family. Strong. Responsible. In the past few weeks, he had been only a shell. "I have to get home, Wes," she said.

He sighed. "Christ, I wish I could help."

"You help just by being here."

She heard a groan of disbelief. But it was true. She'd had so many losses in the past years that Wes's survival was almost a miracle. She would take him any way she could get him, and so, she knew, would Erin.

"Have you thought about why your major was in such a hurry to leave Libby?" The question was unexpected, seemingly unrelated to the conversation.

Susannah was silent. She had the same question. Why?

"I think . . . I know . . . we can trust him," she replied.

"Yeah, but how far?"

"We don't have anything he can possibly want."

"No money?"

"Very little."

Wes sighed again. A thousand miles or more to go. "You're crazy, Sis."

"There was a time you wouldn't think anything of it."

"That's when I had two legs."

Susannah squeezed his hand. "Wes, I'm so thankful you're alive. I know Erin will feel that way."

"Maybe. At first."

"She's been waiting for you for five years."

She heard a bitter chuckle. "She'll soon know how wasted that was."

"Wes—"

"I can't even walk to get help, much less try to fix the wagon," he said. "I can't even stand, for God's sake. We have to depend on that . . ."

On my nighthawk.

The conversation died then as, lost in their own thoughts, they waited.

And waited!

Wes moved around, trying to find the second crutch. The major was obviously not coming back. Well, why should he? He knew they no longer had any money or supplies. Probably not even horses.

He hadn't trusted Redding from the beginning. There was something dark and merciless in the man, something Wes had learned to recognize over the years of soldiering. A lack of humanity perhaps. He'd watched the man turn charm off and on as easily as one opens and closes a door, and he didn't like Susannah's apparent fascination with him nor the way she'd adopted him. Even less had he liked the way they had left the Reb prison; it had been obvious to him that Redding had something to hide, and Wes didn't like the implications behind that little fact.

Yet there wasn't a damned thing he could do about it. He understood Susannah's urgency to get home. God knew she'd lost enough already without losing Mark's land too. And he couldn't protect her. Hell, he could barely stand.

If only he wasn't so damned helpless.

He cursed quietly. He cursed his injury, he cursed the war, he cursed the night and, in particular, he cursed Redding, whoever and whatever he was.

"Wes?"

He apparently hadn't cursed quietly enough. "Sue, I think your hired hand or whatever he is has taken off with the horses."

Susannah's silence told him she probably agreed with him. He saw her try to rise, gasp, and then fall back down.

"Sue?"

"I'm just a little dizzy . . . give me a minute."

Wes looked down at his stump, at the pant leg that had been folded neatly and pinned at the knee. He looked at the one crutch. He'd never tried to walk on only one before, but either he or Sue had to go for help, and he wasn't going to allow it to be Susannah, not without knowing how badly she'd been hurt.

But how?

She has the backbone of both of you. Damn, why did he remember Redding's words? Anger filled him, anger at their apparent abandonment by Redding. It was strong enough to conquer his doubts.

He grabbed the crutch and started to pull himself up. He fell and tried again. On the third attempt he came upright. He took a step and stumbled, falling down, and then he lifted himself again. This time, he knew to compensate for the loss of balance.

If only the constant pain in the missing leg would go away. If only his right foot didn't continue to tingle, to make him think it was still there, to mislead him into automatically trying to step on it. He took another awkward, uncertain step, a kind of hop, but it moved him forward.

It was going to be an infernally long walk. Wes gritted his teeth and took another hop-step.

Then another.

By God, he was going to do it!

"What in the bloody hell—?"

Wes and Rhys almost crashed into each other in the clump of trees that ran alongside the road.

"I thought I told you to stay with Mrs. Fallon." Rhys's angry voice came from atop his horse.

Wes leaned against the crutch. He hated the relief he felt at seeing the other man. "I thought—"

"Do me a favor. Don't think anymore. It might get both of us killed, dammit."

Wes felt a sudden surge of rage. "Those don't look like our—"

"They're not. A trade. Rested ones for tired ones." Rhys moved his horse over to Wes. "Hold on to my leg and give me the crutch."

Wes hesitated.

"You're going to have to ride," Rhys said curtly.

Wes didn't move.

"Listen," Rhys said. "I'll explain only once. We've been lucky because we've been on a main road, looking like innocents. I'm not about ready now to fumble my way into a Confederate camp with a Yank. I am not going to risk being held prisoner. Now get the bloody hell up here." Coldness laced his voice as he held out his hand.

Wes silently handed him the crutch and watched as Redding moved it to his right hand and then held out his left. "Take it," Redding said, and Wes did so, wondering at the strength the major had quickly regained.

With the help from Redding, Wes was able to leap up, and as he settled behind the Welshman, he felt a sense of pride.

He didn't have time to indulge it. His companion handed him the crutch and kicked the horse into a slow trot.

Chapter 7

Endless hours started to blur, one into another. Susannah had thought she was strong, even after the fall and the injury to her ankle, but she, too, was exhausted when they stopped at nightfall. If she felt that way, she wondered about her two male companions who had recently been so seriously wounded. But it was Rhys Redding who had set the pace.

"I traded horses," he'd explained earlier when he'd returned. It was his only comment about the two horses, and he'd made it plain he planned to give no more. "I think we should be on our way. There are troops down the road."

Susannah had looked up at Wes, who gave her a helpless shrug.

Rhys had quickly gathered up a few belongings, one of her dresses, what was left of their food, the sewing basket after a moment's hesitation, and stuffed them into the portmanteau. He folded three blankets over the riderless horse.

After a moment's hesitation, he gave Wes the bag and the second crutch, which he'd also found. He turned to Susannah. "You'll ride with me."

"No," Wes said.

Rhys ignored him, talking only to Susannah. "Your

brother needs the balance. If there was a saddle . . . I would feel better, but . . ."

He didn't add it was likely that both brother and sister might fall were they together, but the meaning hovered in the air.

"Both of us are very good riders," Susannah protested as Wes glared. She wasn't altogether sure what would happen if she got too close to Rhys Redding. She tried to think, but there was no time.

Rhys was brutal. "Your brother has one leg, you a sprained ankle, and none of us have saddles or reins. We don't need any more accidents. If you go with me, you ride with me.

He turned around and it was obvious there was to be no appeal. He moved to a tree stump and mounted the riderless horse, then held down his hand for her, giving her no choice. She took it and swung up behind him, her dress bunching up in front of her, leaving bare most of her legs. She wished for the britches she sometimes wore on the ranch.

His legs tightened against the horse's belly, and they moved into a fast walk. She knew almost instantly that he was an excellent rider, as good as Mark.

Just the touch of her hand on the lean body had sent fire through her, and she jerked her hand away with the silent excuse that she did not wish to do further injury to his wound. But that wasn't it at all. Her bare legs touched his trousered ones, and she could feel the muscles, the strength of them, spreading that fire up into the core of her. She simply didn't understand the electricity that ran between them, that vibrated and tingled like streaks of lightning.

She tried to ignore it, tried to keep her hands on her own thighs and tried to think of other things: of home, of the river that fed the rich pasture, of the hills sprinkled with blue flowers in the spring. She closed her eyes, trying to concentrate on them, but instead she felt the warmth that came from his touch after the wagon had overturned, saw images of being held tight, of protecting arms. Tenderness. Gentleness. A dream. Moments so incredibly pleasant, like nothing else she'd ever felt. She'd never felt that kind of ... belonging with Mark. She should have. She certainly should have with Mark rather than this dark enigmatic stranger with so many secrets.

Home. Think of home. And Mark. Memories of Mark. Don't think of the man whose back touches your chest. Don't think of the way his hair curls slightly in back or the masculine odor of leather. Don't think of the way he makes you feel so alive, as if you'd been awakened from a long sleep.

Hours of this nearness. Days. Weeks. She had been an idiot to consider it.

Yet shivers of excitement crawled enticingly through her in anticipation of exactly those days and weeks.

She was going home. With the nighthawk.

Susannah bit happily into the roasted leg of a chicken, allowing the tantalizing smells and taste to drown what little crumb of conscience she had left.

The only comfort she gave herself was that she, at least, worried about her conscience. She didn't think Major Rhys Redding fretted himself at all about his lack of one.

In fact, when he had appeared out of the night with two chickens, he seemed very pleased with himself. They were very likely stolen since he had no money, and nothing to trade. He had regarded his two charges with amusement as he presented his bounty, obviously expecting questions and just waiting to give them answers he must have known she and Wes didn't want to hear. But they had had no more than the hard biscuits they had salvaged from the ground two days earlier and neither she nor, apparently, Wes was going to suggest their provider return the scrawny chickens.

So she and Wes, both tired and sore to the point of collapse, watched without comment as Major Redding built a fire in the small clearing far away from any road, and cleaned and spitted the chickens with an expertise that she had come to expect of him in every enterprise known to man and some probably only to the devil.

She enjoyed the greasy feast, licking her fingers to capture the very last, tiny drip of nourishment and taste. So did Wes, though his demeanor was grudging and reluctant and suspicious of their benefactor.

She looked over at Major Redding, and knew he had been watching her. A gleam lightened his eyes as he imitating what she had done, very slowly licked his own fingers. She suddenly wondered if she had looked as sensuous, doing something that normally would be considered bad manners. The obvious physical pleasure of taste, the deliberate movement of his tongue, the lazily suggestive movements seemed to say he would like to be tasting something else altogether.

Susannah was sitting next to him, and her glance locked with his, and she felt the heat radiating from him, inhaled the lingering aroma of chicken mixed with his own male warmth.

She felt her blood become heated, pulsing. She swallowed deeply, trying to slow the race of her pulse, even as everything else in her had slowed to a tantalizing rhythm.

She knew she had to shake the spell, or she would move directly toward him, despite the fact that her brother sat only feet away.

"Major Redding . . ." she started, astonished as she heard the unfamiliar huskiness in her own voice.

He gave her an innocent grin that she knew had no innocence in it. "I think the time for formality is near its end," he said lightly, "and major isn't quite . . . accurate. Call me Rhys." The deep, strangely attractive, almost musical accent made the name hum in the air.

The comment stirred Wes, who had been staring out into the dark, thinking glum thoughts or else just numb from the day's ride.

"What *is* accurate?" he asked.

"I suppose you could justify captain," Rhys said with a smile deepening on his lips. He was only causing more mystery, not explaining, and he obviously relished it.

Wes flushed, also realizing Redding was playing a game. But still, he bore in. "Who are you, anyway? It's damn well time we knew."

Rhys shrugged. "Why? What would you do?"

One of Wes's fists tightened where it lay on the ground. "We don't need you."

"Yes, you do," Rhys said brutally. "Or would you prefer to have eaten the last biscuits tonight?"

Susannah felt the hostility radiate between the two men, relieving that heated moment of intimacy between herself and . . . Rhys. She felt both relief and an aching regret. Why did he always do that to her? Ignite such conflicting emotions?

She looked at the man, and his eyes moved back to her, and she knew that heat hadn't completely dissipated. "Captain of what?" Her own question came softly, the huskiness still in her voice.

With a mocking glance at Wes, he turned back to her with a small grin. "I was a sea captain of sorts. A blockade runner."

Susannah knew her mouth must have dropped open. In all her wild speculation, never, ever did she imagine that. "Blockade runner?"

One side of his mouth twisted upward in a half-smile. "A would-be blockade runner, I should say. I was blown out of the water on the first run into Charleston. An adventure, you could say, gone awry."

Susannah was fascinated by the expression on his

face. Part wry, part amused, as if it had been someone else's tale. And tale it could be, she thought.

It was Wes who voiced the obvious question. "Then why didn't you tell the Rebs?"

Rhys shrugged. "I didn't think they would believe me. No identification. A Union major's uniform—"

Wes's eyes could have been daggers. "That brings up another question."

"I was captured by the Yanks and was being taken to Washington when I escaped to Confederate lines in the uniform I—" Rhys hesitated as he cast a look at Susannah, then added, "That I appropriated. Unfortunately, the Rebs didn't wait for me to explain. I didn't expect much better in Libby Prison."

At the word "appropriated," his eyes grew darker, and Susannah heard death in the word, if that was possible. His eyes had suddenly turned cold and hard, and she felt a shiver run up and down her back.

She knew Wes had heard it, or sensed it, too. He'd stiffened. "Murdered, you mean."

"Is that what *you've* done?" Rhys stared at him, his gaze unblinking and dark. "Murder these years, or kill the enemy?"

"It was war for me," Wes said. "What did you call it, an adventure?"

"So it was," Rhys said. "I don't believe in causes."

"Do you believe in anything?"

Rhys laughed. "Myself, Colonel Carr. Myself." And then he rose lazily. "And I'm very bored with this conversation. I'll take another look around. Make sure no one saw that fire."

"Redding?" Rhys had taken several strides and now he hesitated, finally turning around at Wes's command. He raised an eyebrow.

"That's the most preposterous story I've ever heard."

"It is, isn't it," Rhys agreed with a deepening grin

that allowed room for either Susannah or her brother to wonder whether indeed there was any truth in it.

Except for that one comment about causes.

Rhys Redding was uncommonly laconic and distant for the next few days, as if regretting he had revealed what little he had that night. And he drove a relentless pace.

She and Wes managed to do little more than collapse on the ground when they finally stopped for the night, while Rhys Redding went foraging. She had always been a good rider, but now her legs were chafed and terribly sore from rubbing against the sweaty sides of a horse. Neither did the horse's bony backside do anything for the rest of her body.

A week. No, more than a week since they'd obtained the new horses. Rhys—she had started to think of him that way now—was indefatigable and gave no quarter. Wes's face was lined with pain, his lips set in a grim line, yet he stubbornly refused to ask for any additional rest.

Neither would Susannah. Something was driving Rhys Redding, something she didn't understand, but it was working in her favor, in her effort to get home as quickly as possible, and she was loath to question it.

And the weariness that now never left her partially numbed the effect of her body next to his. The electricity was still there—she suspected it would always be there—but now when they stopped, all she wanted was to sink into sleep's oblivion. Even a bed of hard ground was preferable to the bare back of their horse.

Now that they were on horseback, they skirted the roads to avoid any troops, or for that matter anyone at all. After stopping each night, Captain Redding continued to disappear without explanation, bringing back berries one time, a rabbit another. He was a forager of no small consequence, Susannah and Wes soon discovered.

The next major bounty was a saddle and clothes.

It had been more than a week since they had left the wagon behind when they stopped for the night at an abandoned farm. It was past dusk, as it usually was before they stopped. Rhys—the name was coming easily to her now, too easily—had disappeared again, and Susannah sank down next to Wes who was resting against a tree. It was later than usual, but their ... guide always waited to stop until he could find an isolated spot, preferably near water. They were still trapped somewhere between two armies, and their horses could easily be confiscated, since they had only one gun between them.

So this place had been a stroke of luck. It had apparently once been a small farm, but now all that remained was a skeleton of a house, and ashes where a barn had once been. It was deserted now, but Rhys had found a well in back, and a large oak tree for shelter. He'd then disappeared on his nightly foraging.

Susannah and Wes drank their fill from the well and Wes watered and rubbed down his horse, something he did religiously no matter how tired he was, or how difficult when he had to balance on two crutches. When he'd finished he hobbled over to where Susannah had gathered wood in preparation for a fire.

He collapsed to the ground without saying anything. Like the other nights, they would have to wait. And she knew how much Wes hated that, how much he hated their dependence, but he was still weak, still learning how to move on only one leg. And Susannah saw the pain that persisted, the sudden flashes of agony that occasionally swept over his face. He'd told her that he still felt the missing foot, that sometimes it itched so badly he could barely stand it, and yet how could you scratch something that wasn't there? And the stump itself had not yet entirely healed. The jolting it received on the bare back of the horse had not helped and she had watched in helpless empathy as he had rebandaged it several times, no longer allowing her to do it.

Susannah eyed the gathered firewood with wry wistfulness. Unless their provider brought food, there was no need for a fire. They didn't want to attract any unwanted attention, not without their strongest member there. Rhys Redding had assumed control of their one pistol since the wagon turned over. He had simply taken it upon his return with the horses, and Susannah, who still feared he might leave, had said nothing.

He should be back by now. He had never been gone quite this long before. Anxiety pricked at her, and she went over to Wes. His eyes were closed, his one good leg bent at the knee. She couldn't see his face in the moonlight, so she kneeled down. He looked so tired, so drawn.

His eyes opened slowly, and one of his hands went out to her. "You must be tired too, Button. I should have helped."

She shook her head, denying his words although her spirits rose at his endearment. It had been years since he had called her "Button." She bit back the emotion. "You have to get your strength back."

He didn't answer that question, only looked doubtful, then asked one of his own. "Where's your friend?" It was always like that now. Wes removed himself as much as possible from Rhys Redding. The animosity between them was like a live thing.

Friend. Rhys Redding was many things, but Susannah did not fool herself as to that relationship. She had tried to develop something like a friendship, but unlike his easy wit when they'd first met, he'd turned silent, or perhaps he was just as tired as they were. He certainly should have been. But then several times, she had heard him getting up in the night and moving around, returning only after what seemed like hours. Yet the next morning, he'd seemed far more refreshed than either she or Wes.

He was still a complete puzzle. And she was no closer now to solving it than the first day she'd met him. She still wasn't sure why he remained with them; it certainly wasn't fear for himself because he appeared fearless, even nerveless. He was always ready with a new solution, or lie, to combat any crisis. Neither had she seen any warmth in his eyes, although there was constant speculation.

Instinctively, though, she knew he was no more immune to the attraction between them than she; she had seen his body tense when she touched him. She had seen his jaw set with control. She was beginning to really dislike that terribly rigid control, to wonder what it would be like if he lost it.

Dangerous thought. But then she was getting used to danger, even to like it. That was even a more dangerous thought.

She sensed Wes's sudden tension, and she looked up. Captain Redding was riding toward them. The horse and rider were only a dark silhouette, and yet she knew it was him. There was a certain elegance about the way he rode, the way he held himself, a kind of fierce pride that dared, that challenged, in a way she'd never seen before. Her heart suddenly raced into a gallop, and her hand went involuntarily to the back of her hair, trying to smooth wayward strands into the long braid.

It was then she noticed something different. She rose to go meet him, the fatigue leaving her as he approached, his body resting easily in a well-worn saddle. His hand held a bundle, a pair of boy's trousers, which he dropped in front of her.

He gave her a wicked grin and spoke softly in an intimately warm voice that she knew couldn't reach her brother. "As much as I like to see your legs," he said with a provocative gleam in his eyes, "I've noticed they're getting in a wretched state."

Susannah turned several shades of red, despite her attempt not to do so. How could he hide his emotions so well, when she couldn't do it at all? She had tried to hide herself when she had studied her chapped, sore legs. Obviously, he had seen more than she thought. And how had he known how much she coveted exactly what he'd brought.

And the saddle. Dear Lord, how much they needed that, how much Wes needed that. Wes, though an excellent horseman, had struggled each time to get astride the bare back of the horse. It galled him, Susannah knew, to accept Rhys's help, but it had been necessary. Now, with the saddle, he should be able to mount by himself. She didn't even question that the saddle was meant for her brother.

Rhys had something else to offer, however. He swung down, walked the horse the last several feet, and glanced down at Wes. "General Lee has surrendered," he said.

Wes sat up, all attention now, his eyes flashing with a brightness Susannah hadn't seen in four years. "It's over? You're sure?"

"As far as Lee is concerned. The word is being spread now by couriers. I ran into one on the road. The Confederates are being allowed to keep their sidearms and horses. It's generous terms, I was told, but there certainly wasn't any bloody celebrating."

"As far as Lee is concerned?" Wes repeated the words softly. "What about the other armies? General Johnston in the Carolinas? Kirby Smith in Texas? The others?"

Redding shrugged. "Lee surrendered his army. That's all anyone knows."

Susannah closed her eyes and whispered. "Over."

Then she opened them wide again. "Dear God, so many dead."

"And you, Redding?" Wes asked, his glance penetrating as it once had been. "Is it over for you, now?" He was asking for answers, more than the one just voiced.

"I don't know," Rhys said honestly. And he didn't. He'd still killed a Union officer when he himself was not really a combatant. He shrugged without conveying any of the thought to Wes or his sister. "But it should make things easier for us. There's going to be a lot of people moving. Soldiers going home, both ways. We won't look any different."

Wes looked toward Susannah. "There's going to be a lot of bitterness back home, Button."

Rhys looked from one to the other, a question in his usually oblique eyes.

"Most of the people in our county were southern sympathizers. Nearly every family has lost someone to the North," Susannah explained.

"Except the Martins," Wes added bitterly.

Again, Rhys questioned with his eyes.

"A very greedy family who sat out the war and is now trying to take advantage of it," Susannah answered with every bit as much bitterness as her brother. "They've been trouble for years, and recently there's been no one to stop them." She turned back to Wes. "And it doesn't make any difference what anyone thinks. I need you, Wes. I can't do it alone now that Mark . . ." Her voice trailed off.

She turned away suddenly, aware that she had not thought of him in the past few days, and sudden shame engulfed her. Shame and an emptiness that made her heart ache. So much had changed since she and Wes and Mark rode the plains and swam the river and dreamed alongside its banks. Had there ever been that kind of peace? They were all gone now: her mother and father, Mark, and even Wes. Not the physical part of Wes, but that brash, confident brother with his strong sense of duty and the courage to follow it. He looked so uncertain now, afraid he was more a burden than a savior, and she wanted to go to him and bury his head in her arms.

But that would be the worst thing she could do. He didn't need pity. He needed to feel like a man again.

Her eyes went back to Rhys Redding, a stranger despite the number of days they'd been together. He was leaning against a tree, watching them both carefully as if they were actors in a play. There was no more emotion in his face than that of a spectator, curious, perhaps a little bemused as he waited for Wes to respond.

"I'll go on," Wes said finally, "until Texas." And his eyes went toward Rhys, the message very clear: *I don't trust you with her.*

Rhys merely shrugged, as if he cared little about Wes's opinion, which, Susannah knew, was quite true. He squatted down, balancing himself on the balls of his feet and regarding the pile of unlit kindling with interest.

"Great expectations?" he observed dryly. Rhys had been out to scavenge, but he'd run into a Reb courier, a single horseman, whom he had stopped and relieved of his saddle. He figured Wes's need was greater. The fact that the slender young man had a second set of clothes in his saddle bags had been an unexpected bonus. He'd decided against taking the lad's last food and had left him loosely tied, his horse hobbled nearby. The Rebs, after all, had wounded and imprisoned him, and he felt entirely justified in this rather mild retribution.

But he had no food to offer this time. The courier, no more than a boy, had had only some hardtack and looked famished himself. And Rhys thought his news would be more important to his two charges than food.

He had expected more of a happy reaction, but Wes's expression appeared only more troubled, and Susannah's was bleak, her gaze fixed on something far away. *Her husband.* The lost husband. Rhys felt unexpectedly lonely then, a feeling he thought he'd banished long ago, but now feared he'd just covered under a veneer of indifference.

The bloody devil knew he had certainly not been indifferent during the past days to the feel of Susannah's body next to him, to all the gently rounded places that fitted so neatly into him, particularly when she was tired, and the tenseness left her and she rested her head against his back. It had been all he could do to appear unaffected, and so he had pushed and pushed and pushed them until at night they were all too tired to think of anything but rest. Even then, his natural restlessness, exacerbated by his growing physical need for her, sent him out alone: scouting, hunting and even indulging in a bit of thievery.

He had learned the latter as a boy. Unable to stay in a place which constantly reminded him of his humiliation and pain, he'd left that inn not long after his beating, and he had survived by stealing. His future might well have been the noose, or transportation, had he not met Nathan Carruthers and, under his tutelage, learned to read and write. And a great deal more he'd rather not think about now. There had been instant recognition between them, two of a kind, and they'd joined forces for more than ten years. Nathan had been his teacher in speech, manners, reading, and writing. Rhys had been the teacher in sleight-of-hand and other dubious skills. It had been an enriching, if not ennobling, experience for both.

Rhys was suddenly aware of two pairs of eyes directed at him and of the silence hanging heavily in the air.

"I'll put the horse up," he said abruptly, and rose

gracefully. "I didn't find any food, so there's no use for a fire. No advantage in directing attention this way."

He reached the horse and his hand soothed its shoulder in a gesture of affection, earning him a grateful nicker. Poor beast. He, too, had whip marks on his back and, if Rhys was any judge, had been thoroughly mistreated in his life. Yet both horses had held out far better than they had any right to expect.

"You deserve a good rest," he said in a low voice to the horse, "and some oats. Be ever sure I'll find you some before long." Another nicker answered as the horse tossed his head in one of the first spontaneous movements Rhys had seen it make. "Coming back to life? Maybe both of us are."

He led the horse to an area with tall grass and hobbled him. He wished like hell he could find another horse to keep this one from carrying such a heavy burden. He had been on the outlook for a single rider, either Yank or Reb, but he'd spied nothing but the courier, and something had prevented him from taking the animal as well as the saddle. The courier, not much more than a boy, had looked so tired, so defeated. A military saddle could easily be replaced, a horse perhaps not so easily.

Bloody Christ, he hoped he wasn't going soft.

With one last soothing stroke, he left and started toward a clump of trees to the left. He needed the exercise, he told himself, to stretch his legs after all day in the saddle. It was certainly not to get away from a certain young lady whose violet eyes had a way of reaching into him and awakening memories and feelings he didn't want.

When he reached the trees, he discovered it was a small family cemetery surrounded by a small iron fence. A huge oak sheltered the small plot dotted by headstones with carved remembrances. He read several of them. Generations of a family. *"Sylvia, Born 1808, Died 1815. Joined the Angels in Heaven." "David*

Metcalf, Born 1840. Died 1861 With Honor at Manassas. He was our Hope."

There were others, a history of a family. He thought of the epitaph, "Died With Honor . . . He was our Hope." Rhys had never really believed in honor. Still, he thought as he glanced over the graves, it might have been interesting to have a family. The messages seemed to say they cared about each other. What would it be like? He couldn't even imagine.

"It's so peaceful." The voice was soft and sad, and Rhys stiffened. He had not heard Susannah approach, which meant his concentration had slipped. Not good. Not good at all. Was it weariness? Or her?

He didn't turn to look. "Peaceful?" The word was wry, almost mocking, a part of the facade that was becoming harder and harder to hold in place when she was around.

Her voice trembled slightly when she answered. "I have to think that."

He turned then and looked at her. Her lips were quivering slightly. "Your husband?"

"And so many others." She looked up at him, a tear hovering in the corner of one of her eyes. Rhys foolishly, recklessly, held out his arms and she moved into them, as if they were both metal objects, magnetically attracted to each other, and not human with human choices at all.

Rhys felt a new ache, a need to comfort, and he didn't know how. His arms, seemingly of their own volition, closed tightly around her, around this strong, independent woman with tears in her eyes and sadness in her voice and agony in her bearing. He suddenly wanted to take them all on himself. It was such a unique thought, one so foreign to him, that it shook him as little else in his life had.

He told himself to step back, to take a long breath and think things through. The cold analytical part of him demanded that he do just that. But there was something even stronger now, a curious longing that spurred him ahead.

His head bent and his lips touched the dark hair with a gentleness that surprised even him. It felt good, that hair, soft and silky. Soft and inviting. His lips moved down to her forehead, and her head bent back until her eyes looked directly up at him.

There were so many questions in them. Yet there was also an invitation, a need she couldn't hide. And fear. A fear of the unknown, of entering uncharted waters.

A gentleman would respect that fear. But he was no gentleman. He had never been a gentleman. His lips moved down to hers, expecting experience. Expecting response.

There was the latter but not the former. He saw the surprise in her eyes as his lips captured hers, the wonder as they pressed together, first gently and then with a kind of desperate need. Yet there was an innocence about it he hadn't suspected in a woman who had been married. As if she didn't quite know what to do.

He did.

Rhys felt her body quiver ever so slightly as his lips invited her mouth to open. His kiss deepened and his mouth moved against hers with a fierce urgency. He had to hold back to keep from devouring her, from bruising her with the violence of a kiss that grew in intensity. His tongue slowly invaded her mouth, caressing, searching, demanding. It was her uncertainty in meeting his movements that fueled his need. Married or not, he sensed she'd never been kissed like this before, that she had never responded to anyone like this before. He sensed it, and knew it, although such innocence was new to him . . . new and touching and bewildering.

He felt the tension coil in his body and knew she shared it because her body trembled so against his, because her lips pressed tightly against his, and her hands climbed to the back of his neck and curled possessively around it. He knew because cautiously, so cautiously, her tongue met his in a low sensual exploratory dance and her eyes widened as the attraction between them flamed into desire so powerful they were both engulfed in something they could no longer control.

The slow sensual meeting of tongues became a wild dance of desire until the embers smoldering inside him flamed into a need so strong he wanted to take her there and then. But still there was a hesitant quality in her, in the shy wantonness of her touch that warned him to go slowly.

He moved his mouth from hers and looked down. "Susannah," he whispered, the British accent giving the name a slight singsong sound. He heard himself draw it out, as if it were a love word. He hadn't meant to do that.

But then he hadn't meant to feel this way either.

As if to verify those feelings, his gaze settled on her and his finger went up and traced the hollow of her cheek up to the corner of her eye. He carefully wiped away the small smudge, the result of that teardrop he'd seen hovering there. The violet of her eyes was slightly misted, like dew-touched flowers, the gaze wondering as they seemed to search his own face.

He didn't know what she would find there, so he fit his lips to hers, this time harshly as if trying to expel the gentleness, to make the kiss into something common, something easy to understand. A man's simple attraction to a pretty woman. A lonely woman. Nothing more than that.

But it didn't quite work that way.

As his lips met hers, they instinctively softened as he again savored the sweet taste of her and knew a craving he'd never felt before. It was not lust alone; that he could handle. But his need went far beyond that. He had never felt so alive as he did this minute, had never experienced so many new sensations. The adventurer in him was snared, completely and totally. Dangerous sensations, he told himself. But he was beyond caring. His body coiled like a tight spring as he struggled for control, but it was not listening to him. The kiss deepened, taking on a wild, fierce quality, given and reciprocated, until both of them were oblivious to the world around them.

And then the blaze started. He felt it deep within, and he felt it spread, and he knew she felt it too as her body pressed even closer to him, clinging to him with a need that equaled his own.

His hand automatically reached for the button of her dress, as his mouth moved from her lips up the side of her face, and then he felt a wetness on his cheek. Softer than rain. More painful than slices of a knife.

With an effort, he lifted his head. The one tear had turned into so many more. Quiet tears, which made them all the more potent. The kind of tears that could rip a man's soul out—if he had one. Rhys was afraid now he just might have one.

In an effort to wipe the tears away, his tongue traced their path, sweeping up the salty residue in an infinitely tender way until his mouth reached hers again. He hesitated for the slightest fraction of a second, then kissed her lightly and, in an incomprehensibly quixotic gesture, considering the urgent condition of his body, he stepped away, calling himself every sort of a fool for doing so. She was vulnerable, a mere step away from seduction.

But he found he couldn't take that step. Not now. Not with those tears hovering in eyes that looked at him as if he was something more than he was.

Rhys grew rigid as her hand did what his hand had done moments before, ran an invisible line along his face as if to imprint it on her own mind. The touch was so light, so tender that he was transfixed, unable to move. He had never been touched like that before.

He felt a pain so different from all the other physical wounds he'd suffered. He hurt in places he hadn't known existed, and one he had. And that hurt was particularly agonizing. Bloody hell, but he throbbed for her. He reached for her again, but she backed away.

"Mark—"

"Your husband is dead." The words were almost cruelly said, and Rhys watched her eyes flare with hurt.

"I know, but . . ."

But her love, or something, was still there, Rhys surmised. Why else would she hesitate when her body was so obviously willing? He tried to will his body to relax. Bloody hell, he didn't like the idea of competing with a dead man, not now, not ever. It was an uneven contest, and he didn't like uneven contests unless the odds were on his side.

Still, his voice gentled persuasively. "But what?" It was almost a croon, a very seductive croon as his deep voice drew out the two words and allowed them to hover in the air.

"I don't know . . ." she cried, her words trailing off as she stared up at him through shimmering eyes. His voice had a hypnotic pull to it, like that of a tiger's rumbling purr before his next meal. There was even a predatory gleam in his eyes, yet there was something else there too, that ironic twist of his mouth that struck her with a particular poignancy. No one should be so cynical, and she knew there had to be reasons. At least, she thought so, and the thought hurt. She suddenly couldn't bear the thought of anyone hurting him, even while she knew such feelings were ridiculous. Rhys Redding could obviously take care of himself. Yet . . .

Yet, she couldn't stop thinking of that hawk she'd found, the wild thing she'd tried to help. It had turned on her in its pain, and bitten her, and yet something about it had touched her beyond most things. Its frantic battle for freedom, its defiance.

You can't compare the two. Rhys Redding is a reasoning person; the hawk, an instinctive creature. But she wondered whether she would ever separate one from the other in her mind.

Run. Run like the devil was after you. She knew she should, but her legs wouldn't move. Not even the thought of Mark could make them move. Mark, her friend, but never really her husband. She had never wanted to reach out and touch him like she had Rhys Redding. She had never felt the volcanic bubbling in the pit of her being before, nor the unaccountable tenderness she had when she looked up at her nighthawk. She had never known there could be such emotions as she felt with him, so many contradictory feelings that somehow came together in a nonjarring way: trust and fear, safety and danger, tenderness and yet a violent desire that ran to the core of her.

Run. She looked up at him. His eyes were enigmatic again, watching. Waiting. The side of his mouth was curled in a challenging, inquisitive manner.

Susannah did the only thing she could. Susannah—who had run two ranches on her own, who had traveled alone through blockades and a war-torn country, who had battled the Martin family—did what she'd sworn she would never do. Susannah, who prided herself on never running, ran.

At least in her mind, she did. Physically, she merely turned around and walked away.

It was the hardest thing she'd ever done in her life.

Chapter 8

The next morning was among the most difficult Susannah had ever spent, and that was saying a great deal indeed.

But how do you resist the irresistible? Even when you know you must?

Susannah had spent a sleepless night after the kiss. She thought about riding with Wes; she knew that would be the wise thing to do. But she dismissed the idea. There simply was no room on the saddle after Rhys fixed straps to accommodate the crutches and the portmanteau, which she and Rhys had formerly taken turns holding.

At least, that's what she told herself. She also didn't want Wes to think there might be a reason behind a switch in riding arrangements. He had enough to worry about.

But truth be told, she couldn't force herself to be wise, to surrender all the wonderful, bubbling, exciting feelings Rhys Redding ignited in her. She *could* control them, she told herself over and over again.

She found that he apparently had not been affected as she had. He was whistling this morning, a bittersweet melody, and the look he gave her had nothing of last night's passion—or gentleness. His eyes danced with sardonic amusement when he eyed her in the trousers he'd appropriated. They were a bit tight in the hip, and she knew they must reveal every female curve she had.

"Fetching," he said, and she didn't know whether it was sarcasm or admiration that made the soft rhythm in his voice even more melodious, but whatever it was, it ran up and down her spine like a lava flow of warm honey. But his hand held hers just a second more than necessary after he had helped her up on the horse, as her legs fitted so much more easily within the muscled curves of his own.

And after last night, the electricity between them seemed more potent than ever, at least to her. Every time her body, her hands, her legs touched any part of him, the affected part tingled. No, not tingled. Sizzled. Sizzled and burned because there was always heat between them now, a warm current that surged and ebbed but was always there, ready to flame into something greater at the slightest provocation.

She watched as his back braced, as if receiving a blow, when her arms went around his waist. She sensed he was waiting. She wasn't sure what he was waiting for, but she knew, right down to her toe tips, that he lay in wait for something.

Her brother seemed to know, too. As Wes mounted, by himself, in the appropriated saddle, his eyes seldom left Rhys Redding, even as he avoided much conversation with the man. It was as if he, too, were waiting, building his strength for some confrontation, holding back.

As they rode throughout the morning, tension was constant, so many different kinds of tension, alive and vivid between them. Making them all strangers, even Susannah and Wes, who once had been so close. Yet she couldn't penetrate Wes's bitterness, the way he'd closed himself off with a self-pity that warned everyone away.

Susannah wondered how long this tension could

last without an explosion. And yet she couldn't even imagine asking Rhys Redding to leave them. It was he who had gotten them this far. His charm, his initiative, and his lies.

She had to remember that. He was a consummate liar. She'd seen him do it over and over. But then she'd lied, too. To survive. To help Wes. To help Rhys Redding. To help ... herself. To get home to Texas.

Only the pace Rhys continued to set saved her from doing something impossibly foolish: giving into feelings growing stronger by the day. She sometimes wondered why he was pushing so hard, why he seemed chased by demons of his own.

Perhaps, she thought unhappily, he merely wanted to rid himself of the burden he'd so reluctantly committed himself to. Susannah tried to keep the latter thought in mind. Even if it hurt. And it did, God help her. It did.

Two days later, the three heard that Abraham Lincoln had been killed ... shot while attending a Washington theater.

They heard the news in a small Virginia hamlet not far from the North Carolina border. Rhys decided to take a chance and stop at the small town they saw from the top of a hill. There was a scattering of buildings: a school, church, blacksmith shop, mill, and store. This was hill country, dotted with small farms, and there were no troops, no uniforms in sight.

There had been no game in this area, the army apparently having hunted it bare, and Susannah had reluctantly suggested they use some of their limited money to buy grain for the horses, and eggs and flour for themselves. Perhaps even some bacon and coffee, if possible. She had admitted to Rhys, finally, the extent of her money: thirty dollars in gold and two thousand in Confederate scrip which was now all but worthless. But they'd had precious little to eat, and the horses desperately needed more nourishment than the grass they found hobbled at night.

Susannah had changed into a dress that morning, which forced her to ride in front of Rhys, both of her legs on one side. It meant even closer contact with him, but she knew that, despite the devastation of the war, certain customs didn't change, and she didn't want to risk alienating help they needed.

There were several wagons in front of the store as well as saddled horses, and a small clump of men talked grimly on the porch outside as Rhys, Susannah, and Wes rode up.

As if by unspoken common consent, the men in the clump all turned and stared at the three riders. There were six of them, four older men and two younger men; one of the younger men wore an eye patch, the other an empty sleeve. Their expressions were wary, yet one man took off his hat as he saw Susannah, and the others followed suit. A seventh man stood apart from them, as if he didn't belong, and he kept his hat intact on his head, although he moved closer to listen.

Rhys helped Susannah down, and then followed her up on the porch. Wes, whose missing leg made it so difficult to dismount and mount, stayed on his horse.

"Ma'am," one man acknowledged, a question in his eyes.

Susannah looked from one face to another and saw something more than obvious interest in a stranger. There was a gravity that hung in the air, like the sultry, tense expectancy before a storm.

"Has there been any news? Other than Lee's surrender?" she asked.

One of the men chomped down on what must have been tobacco. "Yes, ma'am, you could say so. Lincoln's been shot. Killed, according to the telegraph."

Susannah closed her eyes in something like pain.

Neither her brother nor her father had voted for Lincoln four and a half years ago. But from everything she'd heard he'd been a good man, a decent man. She looked up at her brother, and saw pain dart across his face, his hands tighten around the edge of the saddle. But he said nothing.

"There'll be hell to pay now," one of the men said, adding quickly, "begging your pardon, ma'am. They're saying it's a southern conspiracy."

"And Jefferson Davis's skedaddled to Charlotte, North Carolina," added one of the other men. "Whole damn Yankee army after him."

"Is it over then?"

"No, ma'am. There's still those holding out in North Carolina, Georgia, Alabama, even Texas, I hear."

The man with the eye patch added, "Old Kirby Smith, he won't ever give up down there in Texas."

Rhys broke in then. "Any Yank troops nearby?"

"Sherman's all over North Carolina, looking for Jefferson Davis," one man said. "Hey, what kind of talk is that?" They all looked at him suspiciously.

Rhys gave them a disarming smile. "English. And I bloody well don't want to run into any Yanks." It was enough to diffuse the hostility.

One man stepped out. "Can I get something for you folks?"

"You the storekeeper?"

The man nodded.

"We were hoping to buy some supplies . . . flour, bacon, perhaps some grain."

"Confederate money?" The man's eyes had narrowed. Obviously business had nothing to do with patriotism.

Rhys shook his head and took out the coin Susannah had given him earlier. "Gold."

The storekeeper nodded, his dark expression lifting slightly. "Don't have much left. Army took most of it, left worthless scrip. But I do have some flour and bacon. No grain, though. Soldiers took all that." His face brightened. "Have some fresh eggs." His eyes took in the somewhat worn clothes of his visitors. "You got any more of that gold, I got some ready-made clothes."

Rhys shook his head. "Just the food, if you will, sir," he said with the polite formality that usually brought quick results. He gave the man a pleasant smile which Susannah saw didn't reach his eyes.

It took them only a moment to select what they wanted. Even the five-dollar gold piece didn't go far in a store where goods were scarce. They emerged with a small sack of flour, a hunk of bacon, some hard biscuits, and six dearly purchased eggs. There was no salt, no grain for the horses, no coffee.

Rhys gave the sack to Wes and then swung up on his horse, helping Susannah up in front of him, the only place she could ride with the dress.

The storekeep had come out with them. "There's deserters all over these hills," he said. "A band of them been hitting travelers and small farms. You be watchful, now."

Susannah gave him a blinding smile, and six hats came off again.

Halfway down the dusty road, Rhys looked back. The six men were still standing there, but they had resumed their conversation.

The seventh man's stare, however, lingered as the others turned around. Rhys had noticed the man earlier, and the intense interest he'd shown in the gold piece, and in Susannah.

A chill suddenly darted down his back. And he knew his old instincts had returned.

Rhys drove them longer and harder than before, and that was very long and hard indeed. Even Susannah, who was used to long hours in the saddle at the ranch, nearly fell when they finally came to a halt.

They had left the farming community and climbed up into the forested hills.

Susannah was very aware that something was bothering Rhys, but he said nothing. He backtracked several times and once followed the streambed, obviously trying to obscure their tracks.

She didn't know why. The men at the store had seemed harmless enough, and Susannah hadn't seen any troops in the past few days, neither blue nor gray. But there was no question that her nighthawk was tense. She wondered if it had to do with a predator's natural wariness. And then she wondered why she always thought of him as a predator, even as she trusted him. As she had entrusted her brother and herself to him.

When they finally stopped for the night, Rhys helped her to the ground and waited until Wes safely dismounted and reached his crutches. Rhys, who had not dismounted, then gave her a brief salute and trotted off, just as he usually did.

Unaccountably disappointed, Susannah wondered whether he was purposefully keeping away from her, whether their brief encounter days earlier had made him think of her as nothing but a silly woman who didn't know her own mind.

She didn't. No, that wasn't correct. She did. She was just so very confused about it. Even befuddled. She had always been intensely loyal to her friends and family. Her family had always been the most important thing in the world to her. And because of that, she had married Mark; she owed him every bit of that loyalty for what he had done for her and Wesley. Even Mark's death shouldn't change that, and she felt guilty and sad and unworthy for harboring these kinds of feelings so soon. But, dear God, she had never known she could quake at the sight of a smile, wry as it was, or melt when he touched her, even when it was merely to help her mount or dismount. She had never been touched as he had touched her the other night, not with that mixture of fierceness and uncharacteristic wonder. Nor had she ever missed anyone so when he disappeared on his mysterious errands. It was like the moon being suddenly plucked from the sky.

Foolish dreamer! Susannah scolded herself. She didn't have time for this. The moon was there, full and beautiful, and bright enough to search for the makings of a fire. Eggs. They had eggs. And bacon. And flour. A little water and she could make biscuits.

Wes was unsaddling his horse. It wasn't easy, but he had been doing it for the past several days, and Susannah was noticing a new spirit, even confidence, creeping into him day by day as he discovered he could do things he once thought impossible. He still fell occasionally, but his movements were surer, and some of the taut lines of pain around his eyes were fading. Rhys—Susannah thought of him that way now since neither captain nor major seemed to fit anymore—never assisted him with anything but seemed to expect of Wes what he would of any man. Susannah had worried that he expected too much, before realizing how well it worked. Wes obviously detested and distrusted their companion and was unwilling to ask a favor of him. So Wes found his own way of doing things, whether it was taking a bath at a stream or saddling a horse.

Her brother hobbled his animal and rose with the help of a crutch, hobbling over to a tree and leaning against it, breathing heavily from the exertion. "Where in the hell did Redding go now?"

"Maybe he just wanted to be alone for a while."

"He's always alone," Wes shot back, and Susannah thought how accurate that observation was. Even when he was with them, he was alone. Even when he smiled, he was alone.

Except for the other night, when for the briefest of

moments he had been truly with her. And then the moon had been brighter than ever before.

She leaned over so her brother couldn't see her face darken in the moonlight, and she gathered some fallen twigs. It felt good to stretch and walk after the long ride, and she soon had a very nice pile of kindling. But she remembered what Rhys had said before about a fire, and she decided to wait to ignite one until he returned.

Wes had allowed himself to slide to the foot of the tree, and was sitting against it, obviously very tired. He was still weak, and their diet unfortunately had not done much to improve his half-starved condition.

There was a noise, a rustling, and she looked toward the direction of the sound. For some reason, she felt her nerve ends crawl, and it wasn't because she thought Rhys Redding was approaching. He would have come on in, not hovered somewhere outside the clearing.

Dear God, Rhys had their pistol, their one and only weapon except for a knife still in the saddlebags Wes had just thrown on the ground. She saw that her brother, too, was sitting up, as if he sensed danger, and she nodded toward the saddlebags before carefully walking over to them.

She stooped over them and tried to place herself between the direction of the sound she'd heard and the saddlebags as she slipped out the knife. Where to put it? She had changed back into the trousers and shirt shortly after leaving the farming community, and she slipped up her trouser leg and stuck the knife in the side of her boot, feeling the dull edge of the point against her skin.

Just as she rose, three men walked into the small clearing, one of whom she recognized from the porch of the store. He was an older man, but the two with him were much younger.

"Where's the other gent?" he asked sharply, not even trying to hide his intent.

It was Wes who answered. "We had an argument, and he left us."

The two younger men looked at the man who had been at the store; he was obviously their leader. "Ain't no never mind, anyway," the man said. "He was a foreigner . . . couldn't even talk right."

"Jest you and the little lady, then," one of the younger men drawled.

"What do you want?" Wes demanded, his voice reminiscent of years back, full of authority and command.

"Why, yer money. We figger you must be Yanks, what with gold and all. Only fitten to pay us back for what you took."

"That coin was the last of it," Susannah said, hoping her voice was steady. Steady and loud in case Rhys was on his way back. "That's why the other man left."

"Don't believe you, missy. Might be 'siderable fun to find out where you hid it."

One of the men started to approach, and Wes reached for his crutch and started to rise. One of the men stuck his foot out and kicked it out from under him, laughing as Wes fell. He then picked the crutch up and threw it and the other, which lay nearby, into the woods.

Then he moved again toward Susannah. She started to reach down to her boot, but she didn't have time. He caught her arm in one of his hands and twisted it behind her. "Right pretty lady, ain't she?"

"She's no lady. Ladies don't wear pants." The older one approached her. "Where's the rest of the gold, girlie?"

Susannah thought about telling them. The gold wasn't worth their lives, but she knew if she did their lives would probably be forfeit anyway. Rhys. Where was he? How far away? She had to warn him.

She screamed, a bloodcurdling sound that echoed through the woods, and immediately a hand went over her mouth. She bit it, and the man cursed, dropping his hand for the barest second, and she screamed again. The older man pushed a piece of cloth into her mouth and bound it there.

"Christ, the whole world could hear her," he said.

"Ain't no one around to hear."

"'Cepting maybe that foreigner," the older man said. "Mebbe she lied to us." He looked at one of the younger men. "Ollie, you go keep watch, jest in case they lied."

"But Pa—"

"Do as I say. You can have your turn when Amos relieves you."

Sullenly, the man with the bitten hand still dripping blood turned and walked into the woods, a shotgun in his hands, and Susannah shivered. What had happened to Rhys? She realized again she didn't know anything about him, or how good he was with the gun he had. Perhaps he would even run out on them, now that real trouble was here.

But she didn't have long to consider that possibility. The older man approached and tore a strip of material from her shirt to tie her hands behind her. She glanced at Wes. He had moved slightly forward while the attention was on her, but he had to drag himself, and his face was white with frustration and rage.

The man moved his hand inside what was left of her shirt and fondled her breast. "That cripple your man?"

Susannah stared at him with defiant hate in her eyes.

"I like fire in my women," he said. "But first I want that gold, or I'll cut that man of yours. Think 'bout how he'll do with no legs. Now you just nod, missy, when you're ready to tell me what I want to know."

He handed Susannah over to the other man and

walked menacingly over to Wes, taking a knife from his belt. His rifle, the weapon the stranger had approached them with, had been set against a tree.

Susannah watched Wes tense, and saw the sudden fire in his eyes. She had seen it there before, and God help the person who put it there. But he was so weak.

Yet she wasn't surprised when his hand whipped out and grabbed the wrist of the hand holding the knife, forcing the larger man down on the ground. He moved his body with a speed she scarcely could believe, and the two were rolling on the ground, struggling for the knife as the other man held her.

The older man hollered as the knife struck him, and he kicked out, hitting the still-tender nub of Wes's amputated leg. Her brother doubled over in agony as the man rose to his feet, sweeping up the knife as he did so.

"Now I'm going to take off that other leg," he growled as he stumbled back toward Wes.

Susannah fought against the man that held her, but with her hands tied behind her she could do nothing. Desperately she threw her body into that of her captor, sending both of them to the ground and distracting the man leaning over Wes.

A shot rang out, and Susannah was thrust aside as the man who had gone down with her cursed and tried to stand. She heard a grunt and struggled to her feet, her eyes frantically searching the place where Wes had been.

His attacker was doubled up on the ground, cursing as blood puddled on the ground from a wound in his leg. Wes was struggling up against the side of the tree, trying to stand. Across the clearing, Rhys Redding stood in the moonlight, his stance seemingly relaxed, but his intent obviously deadly. His expression, barely visible in the moonlight, was grim, and she saw that his hand was very, very steady on the pistol. In the other hand, he loosely held the shotgun the third man, the man who had been dispatched to the woods, had carried.

"Come over here," he said to Susannah, his British accent clipped and abrupt. She looked at the man who had held her, who now stood just feet away. Fear seemed to paralyze him. Fear would probably paralyze her, too, if she were facing the man holding the gun.

Perhaps it was the cold fury that radiated from Rhys in nearly visible waves. His eyes, in particular, were frightening. There was something in their complete lack of emotion that chilled the air around him.

"Over here, Susannah," Rhys said again, and it was the first time he had used her given name. Yet it had a very cold sound to it, as if said by a stranger. Slowly, she moved to his side. He glanced at her hands drawn behind her back and motioned to Wes. "Toss the knife over here."

As Wes obeyed silently, Rhys dropped the shotgun and easily scooped up the knife, swiftly cutting her hands loose.

"Now get that rifle." He watched carefully as she did so.

Redding then turned his attention to the man on the ground. "So you thought to eliminate his other leg," he said in a conversational, almost supercilious tone that belied the deadly intent underlying it. "I wonder how you might face the same fate. How do you think *you'd* do without any legs?" No one at this moment—not Susannah nor, from the fear on his face, the man on the ground—doubted he meant every word.

Before Susannah or the man could say anything, Rhys very carefully aimed for the attacker's leg, the one without the wounds already inflicted by Wes's knife and Rhys's bullet.

"No," the man screamed.

Rhys looked up at Wes. "What do you think?"

Wes had managed to find one of his crutches and

stand. He looked at Susannah, and she knew that he didn't want her to see what Rhys was obviously planning. "Let them go."

"You have a noble heart, Colonel Carr, much nobler than mine," Rhys said with a slight smile that did nothing to alleviate the threat still in his words.

"Where's Ollie?" said the man who was still standing. "Where's my brother?"

"That miscreant," Rhys said in the haughtiest of the haughty upper-class accents he'd picked up over the years. "I'm quite afraid he's dead. A bit of misjudgment on his part, you see. Nothing personal." His eyes went to the man who had held Susannah. "Now you there . . . mistreating a lady. That *is* personal!"

"Redding." Wes's voice was cool. Calm. "Let them go. They can't do any more harm."

"Susannah?"

Susannah slowly nodded. Her anger and fear were fading now. And Rhys Redding's coldly menacing face frightened her even more than the three men had.

Rhys hesitated, and the other four—Wes, Susannah, and the two robbers—watched as his hand tightened on the pistol, as if he were itching to pull the trigger. He seemed almost soulless then, weighing his own inclination against that of the brother and sister. He finally shrugged.

"You're not worth a bullet," he said finally, almost regretfully. "But there's a certain penalty involved in attacking a woman. You can walk back. We'll take the horses in tribute."

"Tribute?" growled the younger bandit.

"An old English custom, my friend. Something along the lines of the victor takes the spoils. Now you and your friend have about three minutes to disappear. In the opposite direction of the horses you so kindly left for us. I'll follow for a while, just so you don't lose the way."

The man on the ground tried to stand. "I can't walk. . . . You wouldn't leave us . . ."

"I could always kill you instead," Rhys said in a conversational tone of voice.

"Damn you to hell."

Rhys smiled. "You're wasting time. Three minutes, remember. Something like two and a half now."

The wounded man turned toward Susannah. "Lady . . ." His voice begged.

Susannah turned her back on him and went over to Wes.

"Two minutes." Rhys's icy voice left no doubt as to the outcome if the intruders didn't leave within the allotted time.

"My brother's body?" The younger man said, looking toward the woods.

"He won't miss you," Rhys said. "You can come back later and bury him with proper honor. If you see a need for such formalities." He might have been addressing a room full of lords, Susannah thought, for all his coolness, his tone almost polite if you didn't hear the total lack of feeling behind it. "I think you might have a minute left."

There was no more talking. The man called Amos went over to his fallen comrade and helped him up, stumbling as he did so. He made one last plea. "You can't leave us like this, not on foot, not without weapons."

"Oh, I can. And I will. I doubt if you had anything better in mind for my friends here."

"This ain't over."

"No,'" Rhys replied pleasantly enough. "I'll always remember your faces, and next time there may not be a lady with me." Only the almost invisible throbbing of a muscle in his cheek betrayed his mild tone.

When the two men had stumbled out of the clearing, Rhys looked at Susannah. "Are you all right?"

She nodded, too numb at the events to speak, too

completely astonished at the cold distant stranger who had been so ready to kill without any compunction at all.

"Carr?"

Wes looked directly at him, but the dim light disguised whatever was in his eyes. There was, though, a certain defeat and bleakness in the way his shoulders bowed. His mouth worked for a moment as if he could barely spit out the words, "We owe you, Redding."

Rhys returned his steady stare. "You did everything you could."

Wes laughed without mirth. "Yeah," he said bitterly. "Everything I could."

Rhys turned back to Susannah. "Can you get their horses? They're just north of here. I moved them before coming in. I'm going to follow our visitors for a while, make sure they're going in the right direction." He took the rifle Susannah was still carrying and walked over to Wes, thrusting the weapon into his hands, turning away before the man could protest.

And then he disappeared once more into the woods.

Susannah didn't look at Wes but went to where his other crutch had been thrown and brought it to him. He tucked it under his arm without comment, his brows knitting together over eyes that were desolate.

Susannah felt every bit as uncomfortable as he did. She had fooled herself into believing she knew something about their companion, but the last few minutes proved she knew nothing at all. She had never seen anyone before who displayed so little emotion and yet had been so willing to maim or even kill a man no longer a threat. Rhys Redding had protected them, but there had been a detached air about him, as if nothing really meant anything to him, except, perhaps, winning.

Or maybe he just wanted Wes and her to believe that. She suddenly recalled that throbbing of a muscle in his cheek, the constrained fury that he hid almost immediately. Or had she seen that only because she wanted to?

"I'll go find the horses," she said to Wes.

Wes moved slowly on his crutches, having obvious difficulty in keeping the rifle with him. He tucked it in the handle of the crutch, but it was awkward, and he moved slower than usual. "Button," he said slowly.

Susannah looked toward him.

"Don't you think it's a bit odd that he appeared when he did . . . almost as if he expected them?"

"How could he?" she said. "You saw how careful he was coming here, how he backtracked."

"Another skill I doubt many blockade runners or English gentlemen would have."

Susannah stared at him. "What are you implying?"

"I don't know," Wes said slowly. "I wish I did. I just know there's something not quite right about him. I wish you wouldn't trust him as you do."

"But tonight—"

"Tonight, he got exactly what he wanted. More horses. Think about that. Think about when he arrived. Think about how completely at home he is with a gun."

But Susannah didn't need the words to warn her. She was already thinking about everything Wes had mentioned. And more.

A great deal more.

Chapter 9

Rhys followed the two men long enough to know they were heading away from the clearing. He also used the time to suppress the deep simmering anger inside him.

He hadn't felt anything like it since he'd been a boy. He'd learned to control his emotions as a child locked toys away in a box. He couldn't afford anger or mercy or grief, and so he'd simply willed them away. They were luxuries for someone like him.

Someone like him. He was really no better than the three men who had just attacked Susannah and her brother. Except he wouldn't have been so crude about it. Nathan had taught him more sophisticated methods of obtaining what he wanted.

Bloody Christ, he didn't need this! He didn't need to nursemaid two innocents, and Wes Carr was apparently just as soft in the head as his sister about bloodshed. Strange in a soldier. Rhys felt deep in his bones he should have gone ahead and killed those two men, just as they would have killed Carr and Susannah. And worse. And now he anticipated more trouble in his gut, a most reliable omen in the past. The man at the store had said there was a band of deserters prowling these hills; these three had probably decided they were easy pickings and decided to come on their own. But they might have friends nearby.

Because of Susannah, Rhys had tried to avoid an attack, which was why he had snaked all over the country today. If he had been on his own, he would have openly invited a visit, just to obtain the horses. Still, that strange sixth sense he had about trouble, which had stood him—and Nathan—in good stead in Africa, had warned him what would happen. In the back of his mind he knew he had not been entirely distressed about it. It was his chance to get the horses they needed, and a few more weapons.

The Rhys Redding who was an opportunist and scavenger had gloated; the slowly emerging protector in him had winced but had easily been overargued. He had decided not to warn his two charges, afraid that it might ruin his surprise. Just in case they did have a visit.

So he had waited in the woods, watching the three men approach carefully, and had waited until the one man had been dispatched as lookout. It was easy enough to take him silently with an arm around the throat, giving it a certain deadly twist. He'd then moved the horses so the other two men, if they somehow managed to escape, wouldn't find them.

Everything had gone according to plan, except his reactions when he saw Susannah mishandled. Rhys had not been prepared for the fiery knot of rage that formed in the pit of his stomach, the raw fury that he just barely held in check.

He didn't like that feeling, that invasion into places he'd locked off. He didn't like the lack of control it implied. He didn't like the implications at all. Susannah Fallon had been only a means to an end, nothing more, and she was just a woman, like all the women he'd known.

He wasn't going to let it become anything else. He'd already done something tonight he wouldn't usually do: let the scum live, perhaps to return another day. Yet he had stayed his hand. It was an incongruity of his usually more expedient nature.

He bloody damn didn't want to change. He had never needed anyone in his life, not even Nathan. Nathan had been a useful companion, never a friend. Rhys had recognized from the beginning that their relationship was founded on mutual advantage, that Nathan was incapable of caring for anyone, and that to think otherwise could be a fatal mistake. Rhys Redding did not make fatal mistakes.

Up until now, he warned himself. He would come dangerously close to doing so if he allowed himself to care for two people who would detest what he had been, what he still was. And his emotions *were* something he could control. He had watched them make fools of others.

Still, he couldn't forget the momentary horror in Susannah's eyes as he had so casually proposed maiming, even killing, two people, nor the apprehension, even dawning understanding, in Wes Carr's face. Rhys shook his head. There was no time to ponder the imponderable, to indulge a sudden vagary. With a snort akin to disgust, he turned back toward camp.

They needed to leave tonight. Now. No matter how tired they all were. He didn't know how far the rest of the deserters were, and he couldn't take a chance on the two getting reinforcements. Now he had three good horses. They could make good time now, bloody damn good time, and he could rid himself of the brother and sister. He would find a bank, arrange for a transfer of funds, and then locate a good hotel, excellent wine—God, how he missed that—and a woman. A woman with experience.

But for some reason, the combination did not hold the allure it usually did. Swearing particularly crude oaths he remembered from the streets of London, oaths that would probably embarrass even the upstanding Wes Carr, he made good time back to the clearing. The three horses were there, and now Rhys had a chance to take a good look at them in the moonlight. He didn't miss the U.S. Army brand on them, nor their obvious quality. They all had good saddles and stuffed saddlebags.

Rhys paid no attention to Wes or Susannah but, in his best brigand manner, went through the saddlebags. There was jewelry, a man's watch, worthless Confederate scrip, and a limited number of U.S. dollars. He silently counted them. Eighty dollars. The jewelry would bring more.

He repacked the bags and turned to his two silent watchers. "We'd better get going. They might send some of their friends after us."

Susannah hesitated. "The jewelry . . . it would mean something to someone."

Rhys glanced at her with ill-concealed impatience. "You still don't understand, Mrs. Fallon." His renewed emphasis on the "Mrs." placed them a hundred miles apart again after their enforced intimacy on the horse and those few moments in the graveyard. It was as if he were willing them away. "They would have killed you and your brother, and not quickly. Just as they probably killed the owners of that jewelry. But if you feel that strongly about it, you can always take it back to the store and tell them what happened."

"And you?" she whispered.

"I'm heading west. With or without you." Rhys's voice was flat.

Susannah, obviously in an agony of conscience, looked toward her brother.

Wes had set the rifle against a tree, and now leaned wearily on the crutches. "He's right," he said reluctantly. "The owners are probably dead and, if not, impossible to find. We can always send the jewelry back here."

"You're so tired," Susannah protested again. She

wasn't sure which man she meant, although she looked at Wes.

"Better tired than dead," Rhys observed with that smile that mocked.

Wes's shoulders slumping, he leaned over and picked up the rifle and awkwardly walked to one of the three fresh horses, resting on one crutch as he fitted the rifle into the scabbard. He hesitated. "What about our horses?"

"We'll take them up into the hills near some water and let them go. There's good grass there. They deserve a good rest."

Wes nodded and grasped the horn of the saddle. This horse was more spirited than the one he had been riding and suddenly it moved, spilling Wes to the ground. For a moment he didn't move, and then he buried his head in his hands, defeat written all over him. Heartsick, Susannah looked toward Rhys, who shook his head, warning her to keep her distance.

Neither moved for the next few moments, and then, slowly, with the help of the crutch, Wes finally rose. This time he spoke to the horse first in low soothing tones, or perhaps he was talking to himself, giving himself courage. Once more he took the saddle horn and this time he struggled up into the saddle.

Without a word, Susannah went to another one, and Rhys was suddenly there, his hands folded to give her a step up. She'd always been surprised by his strength when he had lifted her up next to him, and now was no different. There was a wiry power in those hands, those arms, that belied the gentlemanly English accent. Everything about him belied that attractive sound, and now she knew how much.

She shivered suddenly, shying away, not so much from him but from from her reactions to him. He hesitated no longer, but sent her into the saddle and moved quickly away, as if burned. *I didn't mean it*, she wanted to say, but his back was stiff, just as Wes's had been during so much of this trip. Unapproachable. With Wes, it represented a hurt too deep to express.

But what was it with her nighthawk? Impatience, probably. Certainly not hurt.

She watched as he gave Wes the reins of one of their original horses and he took the other, and then he swung into his own saddle with tireless grace. As he led the way out of the clearing toward a barely visible path, she knew he hadn't felt hurt at the way she had shied away. Once more he seemed alone and invulnerable—and obviously preferred it that way.

They didn't stop until noon the next day. They had made perhaps thirty miles, and all of them, including the horses, were exhausted.

Wes was barely hanging on. He knew it. He prayed to stop, and yet he couldn't force himself to ask it of Redding.

The humiliation of last night was still too alive, too bitter. He had been unable to do anything to help his sister. The episode had shown him exactly how much he had lost of himself, how little he had left.

The hopelessness that had haunted him since the surgery in the reb field hospital hit him anew. For a while, during the past few days, he had regained some confidence. He had learned to walk, had ridden again. But all of that was gone now, kicked away just as the crutch had been kicked away.

He tried not to think of Erin. He had allowed himself brief glimpses of her in his thoughts in the past few days, when he'd thought there might be some hope for a normal life, but now . . .

How could he ever protect her?

It was a miracle she was still waiting. Sue said she was. It had been four years since he'd seen her, since he had gently tried to break their engagement. But she had refused and had sent wonderful letters that had kept him going those bitter years. She was one of the few people in the area who had understood his decision to go with the north. She and Mark. His friend, Mark. His sister's husband.

But Mark was dead. Mark had been one of the most thoroughly decent men he'd ever known, although Wes had questioned the marriage. He feared that Sue had married out of gratitude and friendship rather than the kind of love a woman should have for a man. The kind he'd had with Erin, when the air virtually sang during the moments they were together.

He'd wanted Sue to have that kind of joy, to watch her eyes dance and her smile come easily again. She'd had too much of a burden these last years.

But it scared him now the way her eyes flashed when she watched Redding. It scared him to the core—and never so much as in the past few hours. He had seen a lot of killing in the past few years, but there was a cold-blooded ruthlessness in Rhys Redding that chilled him. And the upper-class English accent apparently hid a past that was very familiar with violence. Redding had held the gun as if it was a friend; every move he'd made, including the silence with which he had approached the clearing last night, spoke of more than a passing acquaintance with duplicity.

And he hadn't missed the hunger that occasionally flared in Redding's eyes when the Brit thought he was unobserved, when he looked at Susannah.

Yet now, more than ever, Wes couldn't say anything. Not after last night. Not when he knew how little protection he himself could provide. Not as long as Susannah persisted in this trek to Texas, and he knew her well enough to know she couldn't be deterred. She was as stubborn as a Texas mule, and God knew there were few creatures more set-minded as that. Her marriage was a perfect example. No one could persuade her against it, not when she thought she was right. And now she believed she was right again.

Just as she apparently believed in the man riding with them, a man Wes distrusted with every instinct in him. Especially when he flashed that easy smile, the smile that never quite reached the eyes. Or, Wes suspected, the soul.

The one thing Wes didn't understand was why he stayed with them. In the beginning, Rhys Redding had needed them, needed Susannah, but now the coin had flipped. As much as Wes hated to admit it, they needed Rhys Redding, and he no longer needed them at all. He could do much better on his own. It didn't make sense. Wes would have sworn from his own knowledge of men that Redding had little or no sense of obligation. He had expected Redding to quit them long before this, perhaps taking everything with him.

The fact that he had remained jarred Wes. There had to be some kind of motive, and not a noble one, behind it. A job as a Texas hand didn't meet that criterion. Rhys Redding was one of those men who would survive under any circumstances, and he couldn't picture the graceful Englishman with the upper-class accent and mocking smile herding cows.

The only thing that made any sense was Susannah. And yet, except for a rare hungry glance, the Englishman had shown little real interest in his sister, treating her little better than himself.

Still, that was the only explanation. And all Wes could do was make sure they were never alone. One way or another, he would make sure of that.

Day blended into day. They traveled thirty to forty miles a day by Wes's reckoning, and he had become an expert on judging distances after four years of forced marches. It was a killing speed for both humans and horses, but none of the former objected. Wes suspected they all had their own devils driving them, even Redding, if the pace he was setting was any indication. Or perhaps he just wanted shed of them.

The evening ritual never changed. Once they stopped for the evening, Rhys would disappear, often returning with a rabbit, once with the haunch of a deer. When he returned, a fire would be ready. Usually they camped near a stream, and Susannah would wash or bathe while Rhys was gone, and Wes would tend the fire.

Susannah tried to draw out their reclusive companion, the few times he shared their meal with them. She would ask about London, and London fashions; he would answer readily enough and with an amused charm that obviously entranced Susannah and annoyed the hell out of Wes. But any attempt to probe any deeper into his background always met with an indifferent shrug of his shoulders.

On one evening, however, Wes bored in. "Were you with the British Army?"

Rhys looked amused. "I'm afraid I'm not well suited to army discipline."

Wes would have wagered on it, but that didn't answer his question. "Where did you learn so much about . . ." He hesitated.

Rhys raised one of his dark eyebrows in question, almost daring him to continue.

"Guns."

"All of us British hunt," Rhys answered with a grin. "Haven't you heard? Favorite English pastime."

"But not usually humans."

"You must be referring to our friends back there. You do them a service by calling them human."

"You're changing the subject, Redding."

"Am I?" he asked. "What *is* the subject?"

"Your past. I think we have a right to know it."

"My past, Carr, is none of your bloody business."

The humor was gone now; only a hard glint shone in Rhys's eyes.

"Dammit, Redding, it is, as long as you travel with my sister and myself."

"As long as you and your sister travel with me," Rhys corrected him. "That can change anytime you want."

Susannah broke the sudden tense silence. "You said you were a blockade runner. Are you a sailor?"

Rhys's expression softened slightly as he turned to her. "Only as a passenger."

"Then how?"

Rhys shrugged. "A matter of bad judgment. It happens when you start feeling invincible. Or bored."

"And you were feeling both?" she queried softly.

"An occasional failing," he said with the briefest of wry smiles.

"And that's how you ended up in Libby Prison? You were feeling bored?"

Rhys looked up at her with shuttered dark eyes. He wondered how anyone could look so pretty after riding all day, especially in the boy's clothes she continued to wear. But her dark hair had a reddish glow in the firelight, and the violet eyes were softly persuasive in the dim light. She had consistently surprised him with her strength. She never complained, not even when he knew she was ready to drop from exhaustion. He had driven her to that more than once to discover her limits. But neither the brother nor the sister had given in. He even grudgingly respected Wes Carr for that tenacity. But he didn't like him.

She was waiting for an answer. Rhys had to search back to the last utterance, her question. *You were feeling bored?*

"A little," he replied.

"Why?"

"I tried to be a country gentleman. It obviously didn't suit," he replied with the wry self-mockery that was so irresistible to Susannah. She could withstand anything but that, but there was a vulnerability in that mockery that touched her, and made her ache inside.

"You were a country gentleman?" There was a world of doubt in Wes's voice.

"And a son of a lord," Rhys said, the mockery even stronger. "And now you know my past. Satisfied? Does that make you feel safer?" He stood up. "I'm going to wash up. You both better get some sleep. We leave early in the morning."

The words were unnecessary. They left early every morning, right at sunrise. Susannah wanted to stop him, but there was something new hovering around him, an explosive quality she hadn't seen before.

Wes was silent, as if he felt something odd, too, that they had stirred something better left alone. After several moments, he said, "He's right, Sue. Go to bed." As if to convince her, he lay down, and soon she knew from the sound of his steady breathing he was asleep.

But she couldn't do the same. She kept hearing Rhys's last words, "a son of a lord," and they were more puzzling than anything he'd said before, particularly in the tone he had used. He could certainly pass for a lord with his accent, speech, and bearing. But nothing else fit. But then ordinary descriptions had never applied to him.

She knew where he would be, as well as she knew anything. Something undeniable directed her, although she had tried to avoid seeing him alone since the confrontation in the woods. She had seen a side of him then that had frightened her in a way she wasn't usually frightened. Not exactly of him, but of the different elements of him. It was like looking through a prism and finding the object distorted or slanted or colored. She never knew what she would find. It frightened while it fascinated. Or was it the fascination that frightened?

Susannah didn't know. She only knew how much she missed riding behind him, feeling his body next to hers. She only knew how she'd remained sleepless at night thinking of that kiss, of the violence behind that barely controlled tenderness. She trembled when she realized how much she wanted that violence, that passion that he kept so tightly locked within him. She wanted him to feel, so she could feel again. It had been so long since she'd done that; she knew that now after the other night. She had turned herself off these past years, surviving in the best way she could as she lost everyone dear to her, one by one. She had turned all her passion to the land, and now she knew that was not enough, would never be enough.

And Mark. A terrible sadness filled her at the thought, at the memories. She had tried to keep him alive, partly because of the guilt that had grown even stronger in the past weeks because she realized now what she had not given him. She had never shared with him this wild wanton need that made her so electrically alive. She felt real for the first time in her life. Up to now she had been playing only a role, doing what was expected, what was needed, what she thought she should do.

In those few moments the other night, he had split her open as one might open a pea pod to expose the core inside. He had done that, and now she wanted to do the same, to expose all the layers that protected who and what he really was.

She found him where she expected, as if she had been drawn like a planet to its sun. He was leaning against a tree that overlooked a stream. But despite the casual-looking pose, his body radiated an untamed energy, a tension that bespoke internal turmoil. She recognized it now, because she shared exactly that feeling.

He turned as if sensing her silent perusal. "You should be getting some rest," he said.

"So should you," she countered.

"I don't need much," he said shortly. "I never have."

"Unlike ordinary people," she finished softly.

"Go back to camp, Mrs. Fallon."

"I can't sleep.'"

"That's your problem."

Susannah ignored the almost hostile tone. "I haven't thanked you for the other night."

He turned and strode over to her, his hand touching her chin and bringing it up so she had to look straight into his eyes. "I scared the bloody hell out of you."

"Yes," she said, meeting his eyes, knowing she had to be honest with him. "You seemed to change into a different person."

"Not a different person, Mrs. Fallon," he said, again emphasizing the "Mrs." His eyes were like the hawk's again, glittering with defiance. "You just saw what you want to see, believed what you want to believe. And then you saw the real thing, and you ran like hell. Run again, Mrs. Fallon, before you see more than your stomach will take."

There was a deliberate crudeness to his tone that she'd never heard before, but she couldn't stop, she couldn't retreat, no matter how much her normal good sense urged it.

"Is there more to see?" Susannah felt like a child taunting a tiger, not knowing the strength of the beast but foolishly, suicidally continuing as long as the tiger didn't do more than roar.

He chuckled mirthlessly. "You and your brother are so curious. Would you like to hear how I obtained the uniform I was wearing in Libby?" It was a challenge, said in such a way that Susannah knew she didn't want to hear.

"Or how I happened to be on a blockade runner?

I said it was a matter of bad judgment and boredom. Do you want to know exactly how I indulge fits of boredom? They come very frequently, you know. In this case, it was a game of chance with an American lady. Her virtue against something she wanted very badly for the man she . . . thought she loved. So I took her to a place of assignment, a rather well-known trysting place, and we played a game." He stopped, as if for emphasis, then continued. "I played a game, Mrs. Fallon, with her honor and reputation. That's what I do. Play games. And I really don't think you want to play one with me."

The tiger had shown his teeth. But the child couldn't leave. She was mesmerized by both the beauty and the danger of the beast.

"Why haven't you left us, then?"

He gave her that slightly twisted, mocking smile. "It's been interesting."

"Another game?"

"Wise lady," he said in apparent agreement.

"When are you going to get bored with this one?"

"I already am, Mrs. Fallon."

Susannah knew she should leave. She had known it almost instantly. He was obviously in a dangerous mood, and she knew she was, too. She felt an incredible longing inside, an agonizing ache to touch him, to feel that tenderness she now wondered whether she had imagined.

But she could only stare up at him, at the hawklike features that had such cold strength. There was no tenderness in them now, no gentleness, only a harsh reality.

She wanted that reality. Almost without realizing it, she rose up on her tiptoes, her face nearing his, her hand reaching upward to soothe the frown that burrowed between his eyes.

"Don't," he said, but it wasn't denial so much as

surrender. His lips went down and took hers, just the way she had dreamed they would. There was anger in the kiss—cold, hard anger—and she wished she knew where it came from. But there was also life, a sudden surge of passion that ripped through both of them as a tornado rips through air, taking everything in its path: every caution, every fear, every inhibition. His arms went around her, and hers around him, until they were one. Their lips joined with a fierceness that nothing could break, a natural joining of something right and meant and destined. Susannah knew it to the marrow of her bones. She was made to be here, now, at this odd moment in time and place. His mouth opened and her tongue met his naturally, and she knew immediately how to seduce, just as he was seducing her, and she wondered at the magic of knowing, coming to the conclusion that every woman must know when the time was right.

She felt his lips move downward to the softness of her throat and hesitate as his breath sent tremors down her body. He nuzzled her there for a moment, and one of his hands moved to her breast, shaping his long competent fingers around it and cradling the mound as it grew hard. His lips moved up to her ear, licking around the lobe until she thought she would go mad with sensation, with the hot longing that screamed for something more. Her hands moved up to his neck, and her fingers twisted in his thick black hair.

"Bloody hell," she heard him moan, and she knew that damned cool mask had slipped at least a little. There was nothing cool about either of them as heat rampaged through her body, seeking companion heat.

She found herself down on her knees, Rhys beside her, his hands exploring her body, making their way into her blouse and the camisole that was her last wall of modesty. She, on the other hand, was exploring the hard body underneath the rough cotton shirt. It was so hard, so enticing, as her finger found the skin just inside the collar. He trembled slightly as her hands kneaded that skin, kneaded and then touched lightly, drawing imaginary circles with fingers so gentle one second and so very demanding the next.

He pressed his body against hers, and she felt his hardness against the crease between her legs. She felt the throbbing, the heat, and it reverberated inside her, causing quakelike tremors throughout her body. His mouth was covering hers again, hungry yet somewhat hesitant all of a sudden. He drew back.

"Are you sure, Mrs. Fallon?" Once more he'd used her marital address, as if to remind himself. Or her.

Her lips moved along the bronze skin of his face, darker now after days in the sun than even his natural complexion. He tasted so good. She nibbled slightly.

"Mrs. Fallon?"

"I thought you liked playing games," she said softly, wondering at her own sudden brazenness.

His finger ran down her cheek, stopping at the edge of her mouth. "Only with those who know the rules."

"Did that other woman know the rules?"

"Better than I did," he said wryly.

She suddenly grinned. "Outfoxed?"

"Perhaps."

"You always speak in riddles," she complained softly, her hand still playing with the back of his neck. "If you speak at all."

Instead of answering, his lips touched hers and caught on fire again, their bodies locking together in sudden desperation, she because she was losing him in some way again, he to stop the questions that had no answers he could give. He had hidden them too long, too deeply. Sometimes even he didn't know who he was any longer.

Chapter 10

Rhys Redding had never had a noble, honorable, or unselfish thought in his life.

Except perhaps once, and that had ended in something less than desirable results. Even then, however, he had done it as much for his own amusement as for anyone else's benefit. A study in human behavior, he'd comforted himself at that time. A game, as he'd told Susannah. And so he had disqualified that experience as anything more, and continued to take pride in his invulnerability to common human emotions.

He was, therefore, quite annoyed with himself that now, after all these years, there might be the barest glimmer of an emotion fighting to emerge.

Otherwise why didn't he take advantage of what was being offered?

Rhys knew now he could have Susannah Fallon almost anytime he wanted. He knew it as men always knew. He'd known it that night when Wes had interrupted what might have proved to be a most enjoyable interlude.

He told himself it was lack of opportunity. But he had always been more than capable in the past of making opportunities.

The unfortunate fact was he liked her.

He'd never liked anyone before, and he wasn't sure

how to handle it. But something deep inside rebelled at the idea of hurting her, no matter how hard he tried to squash the notion.

He liked everything about her, although he had tried hard to find a reason not to. He liked the way she lied when she had to. He liked her unflagging determination. He liked the way she never complained, no matter how hard he drove her. He liked her lack of hypocrisy. No hand-wringing over morality when he produced something they needed.

Her determination to get home, to take care of Wes, was altogether as strong as his had been years ago to make a fortune. The goals were different, his less altruistic than hers, but the core strength was there.

He also liked the way she blushed, the way her violet gaze lingered on his face as if there was something to admire there. He liked the way she looked in trousers, the way the material hugged the soft hips. He especially liked the way her body had fitted into his when they rode together, her arms around him so trustingly and her head resting against his back.

He missed her there.

Rhys knew he had often left destruction in his wake. He had never really cared before. It had mostly been deserved. His victims had been victims because of their own greed. But he sensed now if he left Susannah Fallon a victim, he also would become one. And that he would not do.

And so Rhys avoided Susannah completely as day by day went by, and he never indicated that anything, anything at all, happened that night.

Susannah wished it had, that he had not disappeared as he had, but she sensed he had done it for her, to keep Wes from knowing what had almost happened. She also thought this was most unusual behavior, indeed, for a man who declared he enjoyed playing games.

Why was he staying away from her? She had absolutely no idea, particularly since occasionally she saw the hunger in his eyes and knew his retreat was not due to lack of attraction. She herself wouldn't feel it so strongly if that was so. And since he so often derided honor, she had to dismiss that idea, also.

When, a month later, they approached the Texas border, she knew little more about him than she had at their first meeting, except for his extraordinary survival skills.

They were strangers still, the three of them: she, Wes, and the nighthawk.

It was odd, Susannah thought with the wistful ache that was always with her now, how someone could simultaneously be a part of a group and yet not a part. It didn't make sense, but then nothing about Rhys Redding made sense.

Rhys had faded into the darkness that night, after another exclamation. "Bloody hell. Your brother has the worst timing . . . or maybe the best." She'd just barely had time to button her blouse and smooth her hair when Wes appeared, his face knotted with worry.

He had looked around, but there was nothing to see but Susannah and she had brushed aside his questions, saying she had only been seeing to personal needs. He had accepted the explanation.

She had not seen Rhys again that night. He must have returned after she had finally fallen asleep. In the morning, he was up, saddling the horses, whistling cheerfully as if nothing at all had happened.

During the following days, Rhys became even more of a phantom. He always disappeared at night, like some wild thing, and she worried that he wouldn't return. But in the morning, he would be in camp, that damned charming smile in place while his eyes remained as inscrutable as always. He would sometimes take meals with them, sometimes not. And he and her brother continued a guarded, wary civility that had nothing to do with liking. Since that night Wes had come after her, he had rarely left her alone, not, she knew, that it mattered. Rhys Redding had, apparently, found her lacking.

It hurt. It hurt almost beyond bearing. How could he not feel the heat that always flooded her when he helped her on the horse, or accidentally touched her in passing? How could he forget that kiss, the passion that had almost overtaken both of them?

But even if her pride would allow her to question him, which it didn't, she knew she wouldn't receive an answer. At least not one that would mean anything.

And so they ate up miles, each day traveling until the horses could go no farther. And then Rhys, together with Wes, would carefully rub them down, water them with care, and whenever possible find them grain. The two men would go hungry before they allowed the horses to do so. It was the only thing they had in common.

As they drew closer to Texas, Susannah also noticed changes in Wes. He had grown more proficient on the crutches and in the saddle, but he had also grown more morose. One day after stopping in a small Mississippi town for supplies, he had disappeared for a while, then returned smelling of whiskey.

At Susannah's questioning look, Wes glared at her defensively. "My leg is hurting."

But Susannah knew it wasn't his leg. She knew he had endured much greater pain. It was the bleakness in her brother's eyes that worried her. It seemed to grow greater the closer they traveled toward home. And the bleakness had nothing to do with physical pain.

"Whiskey won't help," she said, all the time knowing her words would do little good.

"No? What will help, little sister?"

Susannah wished she knew. She knew he dreaded seeing Erin, and confronting his past life when he could ride better, rope better, fight better than anyone in the county. He had gotten some confidence back until those . . . deserters.

"Not whiskey," she said more sharply than she'd intended and saw the sudden surprise in his eyes. It was the first time she'd been critical or impatient. "And we need that money," she added. "We have so little left."

Susannah had given Wes what money she still had, believing he needed the responsibility. Rhys had kept the money they had found on the thieves. Both men had used it carefully until now; the only purchase other than small amounts of flour, bacon, and coffee had been a small derringer Rhys had found in a store and bought for Susannah as an extra precaution. He had shown her how to conceal and use it.

Now Wes's face flushed, and his eyes didn't quite meet Susannah's, which was completely unlike the brother she had known. She wanted to cry, but she knew that would only make things worse. Anger was fitting. Pity was not.

They stopped occasionally at farmhouses or plantations along the way. During one of those visits, she discovered something else about Rhys Redding. He was a chameleon and an actor. She was astonished to hear him fall into the Texas accent of her brother at one of the brief stops they made: a plantation in northwest Mississippi. The heat had been terrible, and they stopped to water the horses. Wes had fallen behind, and Rhys was leading the small party when a woman looked up from the field she and five children were working. The fear in her face was obvious, and Rhys had immediately put her at ease, his voice falling into a slow Texas drawl.

"Ma'am," he said easily. "We'd be most beholden for some water."

The woman immediately melted under his smile

and soft drawl. She even offered them all some stew simmering for supper.

Rhys appeared pleased with himself when they left, and Susannah looked askance as Wes bluntly demanded an explanation.

"A small talent of mine," Rhys said easily with that challenging smile that could be either engaging or annoying, depending on the subject. "I have an ear for languages and dialects. I've been listening to you for the last month and decided to try it out."

"What other *small* talents do you have?" Wes asked, his lips in a tight grim line.

"I'm a bloody damned good gambler," Rhys replied modestly.

"Christ," Wes mumbled, but he didn't ask any more questions.

Nor did Susannah. Every question invited more questions that both of them knew Rhys Redding wasn't going to answer. The longevity of their association with Rhys seemed always to create more questions than answers.

She knew he enjoyed goading Wes, though she didn't know exactly why. In the beginning, she had naively thought his motives altruistic: an attempt to challenge Wes to do more. Now she wondered. Rhys whistled often, always one of two melodies, both as contradictory as he was. The first, he said, was a Welsh lullaby, and the second an English sea chanty called "The Drunken Sailor" that drove Wes nearly crazy. Which was exactly, she suspected, why Rhys Redding did it.

There would never be love lost between the two men.

More and more now, she wondered what would happen when they reached home. Part of her ached for the log house she'd grown up in, even more so than the larger, more luxurious Fallon home where she had lived since her marriage. Another part cringed at the thought of losing Rhys Redding. It created a dilemma that was tearing her apart: Despite her eagerness to get home, every hour was tinged with a sadness that she might lose the one thing that had brought her back to life.

Resting in the saddle of his horse, Rhys Redding gazed at the Sabine River. Texas.

He had read of Texas in England. The English had a fascination with the American West: a wild, uncivilized land said to be full of Indians and adventurers. And then he had heard Susannah and Carr speak of it with something akin to reverence. He didn't really understand their commitment to the land. He had tried farming, after a fashion, when he had won an English estate, and he had hated it. He had thought it might bring him some measure of acceptance and peace, but he had soon grown restless and found he had little interest in planting and harvesting crops. He had hired a manager who had turned out to be dishonest, and the acceptance he had expected never came. He'd found himself more alone than ever, even the object of scorn for trying to be something he could never be.

It was a mistake he would not repeat.

Texas! It seemed to have some kind of magical impact on his two charges. But to him, it represented only his obligation for their help in escaping Libby. He continued to think of them that way: his charges, his dependents. He had to think of them that way. Nothing more. He had done everything he could to keep any deeper relationship from developing.

He sighed. Susannah and Wes were behind him now, perhaps a mile or two. He had ridden ahead as he often did. Anything to keep from seeing those expressive violet eyes that seemed to bore their way through all his defenses. She had learned, however, to stop looking at him as if he were hero material. She had a guarded look now and, though it hurt, he knew it was far better for both of them.

Another week! Another week and they would be delivered safely. He had already made his own plans. Susannah's and Wes's land was some forty miles from Austin, and he knew Austin, as the state capitol, was large enough to have banks. He could send for funds and find passage from Galveston back to England. The thought, however, held frighteningly little appeal.

He knew, though, that he could not stay. Bloody hell, but his defenses had been pulverized in the past weeks. It had taken all his formidable willpower to keep away from Susannah since that night he had almost taken her. If he had thought he could merely bed her and forget it, he would have done it in a fraction of a second. But as much as he hated to admit it, he knew that was no longer possible.

She had struck a chord of tenderness he'd never known he possessed, and nothing good could come of it. Certainly not for him. He had learned that weakness invoked carelessness; trust, disaster. If you didn't trust, you couldn't be hurt; if you depended only on yourself, you were never disappointed.

So he had kept his distance, pushing his companions until they could do little but fall asleep when they stopped for the evening, and himself even harder so he couldn't feel anything but the numbness he welcomed. He always slept apart from them and when he wandered at evenings, he made sure he wandered far enough that Susannah wouldn't find him. He often rode ahead, looking, he told them, for trouble. He'd always been able to sniff trouble, and it had served them well.

If it had not been for Susannah, and the unsettling effect she had on him, he might even have enjoyed the experience. They had ridden through the forested foothills of Tennessee, the rich Mississippi Valley, the hills of Arkansas, and the sultry tip of Louisiana. Mile by mile, he had felt his strength increase, his instincts become razor sharp again. He had forgotten, during the past few years in London, the simple pleasure he derived from stretching every physical and mental skill. He realized now that London had wounded him, had dulled what he was when he tried to be something he wasn't. So why was he even thinking of returning?

Because he couldn't stay here. Not with a woman he wanted in ways that would eventually destroy him. She was attracted to what she thought she saw, to a man who had helped her, albeit for selfish reasons of his own. She did not see what he really was: a bastard and a thief and a pretender. A fraud. It was enough for him, but it would never be enough for someone like Susannah Fallon.

He wasn't going to wait for her to find that out.

They made camp that night on the Louisiana side of the Sabine River. They would cross in the morning.

This night, Rhys joined Wes and Susannah after they had stopped for the day. They had a special treat for supper, a wild turkey Wes had shot earlier in the day. There was a special pride in that accomplishment, and Susannah had been delighted to see the brightness in his eyes as he retrieved it.

Even Rhys had acknowledged the accomplishment with a nod of his head, the usual mocking challenge gone for once.

It was earlier than they usually stopped, still daylight although the sun was now falling rapidly. They had ridden downstream to where the river narrowed, and found a quiet, private place. Rhys's first instincts were to cross the river, but he saw the tired lines in Susannah's face, the grimly pressed lips of Wes Carr. The man had done far better than he'd suspected, except for the drinking during the past ten days or so.

He even felt a grudging admiration. Rhys hated to admit it but he doubted he would do much better, considering the circumstances: a crippling wound and a home where, apparently, he was hated. It took a hell of a lot of guts for him to return.

But that was Carr's problem. Not his. He would be gone. Free again.

Rhys watched with bemusement while Susannah cleaned the turkey, her hands efficiently pulling feathers from the bird after it had been dipped in boiling water, and she looked up, obviously catching his measuring look.

Susannah flushed, forcing her eyes away from his. She wondered how she must appear: travel-stained clothes, her hair unwashed and tacked into a careless braid, her hands now covered with blood.

She bit her lip. "I used to do this at home."

"I thought most southerners had slaves," Rhys said.

"Father didn't believe in slavery. That's why he and Wes supported the North." She glanced at Wes, who was busy tending the fire and preparing a spit for the meat.

"He fought with Sam Houston for freedom. He didn't understand why he should have it when others didn't," she added.

"And you?"

"I agreed with them."

"But your husband didn't?" It was the first time he had asked about Mark.

"He did about slavery, but then he thought Texas had a right to secede."

Rhys was quiet for a moment. "Contradictory ideas."

She nodded. "It wasn't easy for any of us."

"But honor won?" The mockery had crawled back into his voice.

"I don't know," she said wistfully. "I don't know anything anymore."

"You know how to pluck that turkey."

She grinned suddenly, relieved to change the topic. "I guess I can do a lot of things. Our father raised cattle, or tried to. He wanted to improve the breed and spent everything he had trying to find the perfect bull. His law practice suffered, and Wes and I did everything around the ranch."

"Is that how you learned to shoot?"

She nodded. "That's a necessity on a Texas ranch. You'll discover that."

There was a silence, and Susannah realized she had slipped, assuming out loud he would stay with them.

He let the words go without comment, but he stood. "I'll wash up before supper."

It was dusk when she finished and Wes put the turkey on the spit he'd made. Rhys had not returned yet, and Susannah wondered whether he would eat with them after all. She knew he was meticulous about washing, had been from the beginning. He had purchased a change of clothes, as had Wes, and washed them frequently, never assuming she might do it as she did her own and Wes's. He also shaved each evening, smoothing away the daily heavy beard that darkened his face and made him look even more like a bandito.

She looked at her own hands. She wondered which direction he had taken, because she thought to take the opposite one. He had made it only too clear that he wanted to avoid her as much as possible. She decided to turn left where the trees were thicker alongside the bank.

The river was shallow and muddy, the water moving sluggishly, and she longed for a clear spring where she could wash her hair and her body, and truly feel clean. As it was, she feared she would only exchange the blood on her hands for dirt. Still, the air was terribly hot, and the water for all its dark texture would be cool.

She ducked her hands in the water, finding it more pleasant than she had anticipated. Susannah scrambled back up the bank and took off her riding boots and the cotton stockings she wore under them. She then rolled up the pants legs as far as she could and stepped into the water, feeling a little reckless as she had as a child, holding up her skirts in a deliciously naughty way.

Her toes went into the mud and wriggled there. Even the cool ooze felt good after the hot boots, and the water was refreshing around her ankles. She heard splashing then, and cautiously she waded through the water around a bend, and saw a man swimming in what must have been a deep pool in the middle of the river.

The dark hair told her immediately who it was. As she watched, his shoulder broke the surface and she saw his broad naked back. With sure strokes, he moved lazily in the water as if he belonged there. She wondered if the rest of him was as bare as his shoulders.

Turn back, she told herself. But she couldn't. She was as caught in a spell now as she had been that night he had kissed her. Just then his head turned toward her, and she saw from his startled expression that he had seen her. She stepped back suddenly, completely mortified that she had been caught staring at him like a Peeping Tom, or worse. Her foot caught a root and she went tumbling down into the water, her hand stretching out to break the fall. She tried to get up, but her foot slipped again, and she landed smack on the bottom of her britches. She was only glad that the trees of the bend now shaded her from where he had been.

For a moment, she buried her head in her hands. Where had the sensible, controlled Susannah Fallon gone? She was so rocked by different needs, so completely bewildered by what was happening to her.

She wouldn't cry. She wouldn't. The last time she'd cried was at the cemetery when she heard about Lee's surrender. She'd cried for all of them then, for all the loss and suffering and loneliness. Now, she wanted to cry for herself, for everything she didn't understand, for wanting without being able to have, for feeling this terrible desperate craving.

Unexpectedly, like a flash of lightning on a clear summer day, she felt his hand on her shoulder and she looked up through eyes shaded by her lashes. She very briefly wondered what she looked like, sitting in muddy water like a desolate waif. She didn't want to look at him, but she couldn't help doing so.

And then she couldn't look away. He had, apparently, hurriedly pulled on his britches. They stuck to his wet legs like a second skin, and the rest of the naked beauty of him glimmered with drops of water reflected by a setting sun.

He had been so thin in the prison, but now, despite a limited diet, his upper body was magnificent, the shoulders broad, the chest muscular without an ounce of fat. His lower body was almost as revealed with the now wet trousers clinging to him, and her glance lingered at the lean hips and muscled legs. She tried to avoid the obvious but she couldn't. The pants outlined a manhood that was more than a little aroused. She couldn't imagine why as she pictured herself in her mind.

Until she looked down. Her own shirt was as plastered to her form as his britches were to his legs. The last months, she realized, had probably done as much for her as for him, trimming whatever excess there had been, the endless riding firming every muscle.

She looked back up to his face, and for the first time his eyes had lightened, dancing with some kind of merriment that went beyond the usual mockery.

"You can take a better bath where I was," he said mischievously, with such rare lightness that all the gloom instantly lifted from her. "There's a bit of a current, and the water's cleaner."

He took her hand and pulled her up, giving her a quizzical once-over, and again she felt every bit of her dinginess. She wistfully touched her hair, and he grinned in understanding. His hands took her braid and undid it, his eyes warming as her hair fell around her shoulders in waves. "I'll go with you if you can't swim," he suggested.

The offer was so totally astounding that all she could do was simply stare at him. He gave her the crooked grin that usually held some hidden meaning of his own. "I'll even keep my britches on, and yours . . . well, they're already as wet as they can get."

"I can swim," she said.

"I somehow guessed that," he said, and she knew from the approval in his eyes that it was a compliment. She felt a warm fuzzy feeling crawling up her back. Her legs didn't want to move. She wanted only to bask in that approval, in those dark eyes with the curious light in them.

"Come," he said and held out his hand. She stepped out of the water, her clothes dripping as she did so, and she hesitated and looked at her boots lying on the bank. He saw them at the same time and leaned down, picking them up with his free hand. "We'd better hurry," he said wryly, "or your brother will come after us with the shotgun."

"He's busy with the turkey."

"For the moment," Rhys said, amusement back in his voice, and she knew he was remembering that evening nearly a month ago.

She didn't know what to say. Rhys had been so distant since that evening. She darn well knew he wasn't afraid of Wes, but she couldn't question him, couldn't break that magic that now seemed to envelop them, just as it had in the cemetery. The magic that was there when he allowed it to be. The thought was suddenly disturbing.

But then they were around the bend, and he'd dropped her boots and picked up a bar of rough soap he'd apparently been hoarding in his saddlebags. She realized again how apart they were despite the fact they had been traveling together. Just as he'd never asked her to wash anything of his, as if that would create a dependency or obligation he didn't want. Yet, she and Wes owed him so much. He shrugged when he saw her momentary realization, and she knew he'd read her mind.

"I like doing things for myself," he said with that crooked smile again. This time, his eyes didn't smile.

She felt an altogether too familiar ache. He was closing the door again, the door that had opened for such a tiny piece of time.

She waded into the water, going directly to the place she had seen him. The bottom fell out from under her feet and she felt the cool current. The water *was* cleaner here. She swam back to where she could touch and ducked her head, soaking the thick hair. She soaped it and then ducked her head again, rinsing it before running the soap over the rest of her body and her clothes. When she was through she stepped back into the current, into the pool where the water was cool, and swam a few strokes, remembering how she and Mark and her brother used to go swimming secretly. Her father would have been appalled. Mark would bring an old pair of his britches and shirt for her to use, so her dress wouldn't get wet.

She swallowed suddenly, her throat thick. Those days were gone forever.

She swam back to the shallow part of the river. Rhys was sitting on the bank, watching. He had pulled on his shirt and boots and run a comb through the thick tangled hair. Dusk was giving way to night, and stars blinked overhead while a quarter moon hung precariously in the sky. She wished she could see his expression as she climbed the bank, but she only detected a sudden watchfulness.

"You look like a river sprite," he said.

"I'm afraid to ask what a river sprite looks like."

"Much too appealing," he said quietly. "We'd better get back."

She hesitated. She didn't want to leave this spot where, if only for a few moments, he'd lowered his guard. "May I use your comb?"

He said nothing but reached inside the saddlebags he was carrying and pulled out the comb, watching as she ran it through her tangled hair, yanking impatiently on snarls.

Without a word, he took it from her and gently guided the comb through the snarls with a patience she would never have expected. There was an intimacy about the act, about the evocative way he touched her, that made her senses erupt, just as they had before.

She felt as if she were falling into a jar of warm honey. It felt so good, yet she could easily drown in it. Quicksand. She had been here before, in this warm, intimate world he and she created together, and she was suddenly afraid that he might leave her again, allow her to sink to oblivion in her own emotions.

He finished, but his fingers hesitated just a second against her face. She turned around to look up at him. "Rhys?"

"Hummmmmm?"

The sound was something between a groan and a sigh, and she knew he was feeling the same onslaught of feelings, or at least some kind of feeling.

Susannah found herself leaning against him, sharing a momentary warmth that had as much to do with belonging as passion, though that too was present. She felt it in herself, in him. In the reactions of both their bodies. In the sudden sensitivity of her breasts against him, in the growing hardness of his manhood. She swallowed hard against her reaction, against the compulsion to say things that might push him away again, or create a barrier she feared she could never breach.

"Susannah, you don't know what you're doing."

She looked up at him. "Yes," she said, disagreeing.

He chuckled then, the first time she heard real amusement in his voice. She felt the rumble in his chest and turned her head against it, where the laughter mixed with his heartbeat. They were both such fine sounds in tandem.

"You were once afraid of me," he reminded her.

"I think I'll always be a little afraid of you," she said honestly.

"Wise lady."

"But it doesn't seem to matter," she added.

"Foolish lady."

"I know."

"Oh, bloody hell," he said ruefully. "Save me from American women."

"Tell me about the other one," Susannah said.

"Someday," he said, and Susannah knew that he was backing away again.

"Will there be a someday?" Her question was wistful.

He didn't answer, but turned instead toward her boots. "You'd better put them on. I'll go on ahead."

"Rhys, will you stay with us? When we get home in Texas? We ... I ... need you."

"You need me like you need the pox." His voice was light but there was an underlying current. One she couldn't identify. Irony, perhaps.

"Is that why you keep running away?"

He stopped then. "I don't run away."

"Then stay." It was a challenge, just as he had challenged Wes so many times.

"I only said I would get you to Texas."

"Are you so eager to return to England?"

There was a silence. It was an answer of sorts, and again she wondered about his past, his life.

He turned back to her. In two long strides, he was in front of her, the dark eyes stormy. He leaned down and kissed her, a hard, punishing kiss with no gentleness this time, only a violence that had no restraint. Susannah felt a new kind of fear then, that she had tweaked the tiger too long.

He wasn't giving her an opportunity to respond; he was merely taking in the roughest possible way. She remembered the coldness in him when he had almost killed the thief, and the cool analytical way he had gathered the thieves' belongings, without compassion for the previous owners.

Susannah realized he had been right weeks ago, when he told her she saw only what she wanted to see. And she was suddenly frightened, more frightened than she'd ever been in her life. Frightened of her own volatile feelings, frightened of the ruthlessness he was displaying.

It was as if he took a certain satisfaction in the fear she knew was reflected in her eyes, and the way she started fighting him.

He suddenly stepped back. "Never tempt a wolf," he warned, and she wondered again how he knew exactly what she was thinking. Tiger, wolf, hawk. They were all predators. She felt herself tremble from reaction, from that moment of violence. Her lips were painful and swollen and she felt a tight tension behind her eyes. She closed them for a moment and when she opened them again, he was gone.

Chapter 11

Rhys felt uncomfortably like a bully who had kicked a kitten as he made his way back to the camp fire. And of all the things he'd been in his life, he hadn't been that. He took from those who deserved it.

Bloody hell, he should have gone straight back to the camp, but Susannah had looked so incredibly desolate, and appealing, sitting on her backside in the water. He had not been able to pass her by—as he should have.

He had made things so much worse. And yet, when she had looked at him with something close to real liking in her eyes, he knew he had to do something or they both would be lost.

It had been one of the hardest things he had ever done, not to let his lips be gentle as they were wont to do when touching her. But he had to make her understand what and who he was, to rid her of that damn hero worship. It was even beginning to get to *him*.

Wes was still tending the fire, although in the dusk Rhys didn't miss the quick search the man's eyes made.

"Susannah?"

Rhys shrugged. "I went downstream to wash and shave." He changed the subject. "Smells good."

Wes looked at him suspiciously, then, apparently

seeing nothing to criticize, seemed to relax. A muscle jerked in his cheek for a second as if there was something he wanted to say. Whatever it was, Rhys was sure he didn't want to hear it.

He stooped down, tearing a piece off the turkey. "You're almost home," he observed unnecessarily.

Wes stirred some embers in the fire. "I wonder if there is such a thing for me," he said almost absently. "If it hadn't been for Mark, we probably would have been burned out long ago. I sure don't know how Sue expects to fight them. God knows I can't help her." He reached down and picked up a canteen, took a long swallow. Rhys realized almost immediately it wasn't water, partially by the faint slur in Wes's voice, partially by the lack of his usual caution, partially by the way the man's lips savored the mouth of the canteen. You did that when you'd gone a long time without water, or when you were drinking something else.

"Them?"

"The whole damn country. Particularly a family named Martin. They wanted our land before the war, tried to buy it, and when everyone knew I was staying with the Union, they tried to run us out. But my father and Susannah were tougher than they thought, particularly Sue after he died. God knows what's happened since she's been gone."

Rhys didn't want to hear any more. He didn't want to know about their problems. They weren't his. He'd promised to stay this long and no longer. And now *she* wouldn't want him to stay. He'd made bloody damned sure of that.

"Redding . . ."

Rhys didn't want to hear it. He got to his feet.

"That job Susannah offered. Will you take it?"

"No," Rhys said flatly.

"If . . . I were to ask?"

Rhys stared at him in surprise, his usual nonchalance shaken by the hesitant request. "You never wanted me along."

Wes hesitated, a throbbing muscle in his cheek showing how difficult this was for him. "I might have been ... wrong about you."

"No, you weren't. You and your sister were convenient for me. Nothing more."

"Why? I've been wondering about that."

There was no reason to be silent any longer, and every reason to be frank. If Susannah wouldn't understand what he was, well, perhaps Wes would. "Because I killed a Union major, Colonel," he said coldly. "One of yours. I couldn't risk staying in Libby and being ... liberated. And exposed."

"So you really were a blockade runner?"

"Briefly."

"Why didn't you tell the Rebs?"

Rhys shrugged. "I had no identification. It was my first run, and no one knew me. I didn't really think anyone would believe me."

"How did you learn to handle a gun like you do?"

Rhys's eyes glittered. "You're full of questions."

Wes smiled grimly. "You've just handed me a weapon, Redding."

Rhys stared at him, realizing he'd done just that. He had intended to do what he had done with Susannah, to disgust Wes, to turn around the implied gratitude he didn't want. Instead, he had handed Wes his life, or at least a complication. "I doubt if anyone cares now."

"If you were a blockade runner, you were a civilian," Wes said. "You could be accused of murder."

"I could, of course, kill you," Rhys said conversationally. "Or just disappear."

Wes's eyes didn't waver, although he took another pull on the canteen. "You could," he said agreeably, "but I don't think you will do the first. As to the second, the Union will soon control every port. If it doesn't now."

Rhys clenched his teeth. He didn't like being out-maneuvered. Nor did he enjoy underestimating someone. "What do you want?"

"A few more weeks of your time. Until we know what we face back home."

"You surprise me, Carr. I didn't think you wanted me around your sister."

"I don't. But neither do I want her to die, and she's reckless enough to do just that." He looked down at where his missing leg should be. The muscle throbbed in his cheek again. "We need you. God knows I hate that fact, but I haven't many options now."

"Except for blackmail?"

Wes stared directly at him. "Yes."

Rhys smiled bitterly. "I was wrong about you, too."

Wes didn't flinch. "And Redding, stay away from Susannah."

Rhys smiled, without humor. "Go to bloody hell."

Six days later they approached the Carr homestead. Rhys knew by now that the land belonged to Wes, while Susannah, as Mark's sole heir, owned Land's End, the property next to the Carr place.

He also knew that both pieces bordered the Colorado River, although Land's End was three times the acreage of Wes's land. The original acreage had come to the Carr and Fallon families as members of the Old Three Hundred, original colonists brought to Texas by Stephen Austin. The Fallon family had bought out several of the original families . . . and expanded its holdings; the Carr family remained on its grant, its male members engaging in law rather than in farming or ranching.

Part of this he had learned during the month and a

half of travel. The remainder he had learned three nights earlier.

It was then Wes announced that Rhys would be staying a while, and Rhys had seen the flare of surprise and then wary pleasure in Susannah's eyes, a pleasure that clouded when she gazed at him and saw the set grimness of his face.

He also was told everything about the Martins—Hardy, Lowell, and Cate. The Martins, Susannah explained, had cast greedy eyes on both pieces of property, which were among the most fertile and desirable along the river, for years. They had used the war to obtain other tracts, and now the Fallon and Carr properties stood in the way of their dominating the east side of the river.

He'd also heard more than he wanted to about Mark Fallon, Susannah's husband. Mark the noble, Mark the loyal. Mark, the one man who had stood up for the Carr family when Wes and his lawyer father sided with the North. A heated jealousy had nearly consumed him, surprising him with its intensity. Why did he give a bloody damn about a dead man?

Because he'd had Susannah. The thought was absurd in the extreme. He could have had Susannah easily enough, and for some damn fool reason had not taken her. He had given himself a dozen reasons. He didn't take vulnerable innocents; they were simply too much trouble. Give him an experienced whore any day. And God knew he didn't need complications in his life, or anyone who would impose on his freedom.

Only once, in a split second of self-honesty, did he admit another reason: a deep unreasoning fear of exposing himself to someone he suspected could wound him in a way he'd never allowed anyone. Once Susannah knew who and what he really was, she would turn on him with horror and outrage, and he didn't think he could bear that particular burden.

And so he wondered why in the bloody hell he was

staying. He'd half convinced himself in the past few days to disregard Wes Carr's threat. He'd been able to get out of London when he had to. He could do the same here. There was no way Carr could really stop him, not with his talent for accents and languages. Rhys knew he could well act the part of a French sailor if necessary. But he had to get money, and Carr *could* make that difficult.

The fact, however, that Wes Carr had used the threat was intriguing. Rhys didn't believe for a moment that Carr had changed his mind about him, only that Rhys had shown himself to be useful, and Carr was a pragmatist after all. The thought made him smile bemusedly. How far would Wes Carr go?

They had stopped at a trading post and received the latest war news. Jefferson Davis and what remained of his cabinet had been captured in Georgia on May 10; William Quantrill, one of the last guerrillas, was rumored killed; and Kirby Smith, who commanded the last remaining Confederate force, was apparently discussing surrender terms. Part of Texas still remained in Confederate hands, but its soldiers, realizing the war was over, were deserting by the thousands, often pillaging and robbing as they traveled.

There was little law in Texas, they heard. The ranks of the Texas Rangers, once the chief law enforcement, had been decimated by the war, many of its companies being drawn off into the regular armies. What was left of them had been disbanded in federally controlled areas of Texas. No one knew what would happen now.

As they left the main road for the Carr homestead, Rhys couldn't keep his eyes from Susannah's face, from the eager expectation, the way her back straightened. They would stop there first, for news, and then continue on to Land's End.

He slowed his horse, allowing the brother and sister to go on ahead as they moved onto a dirt road. A wooden arch framed the road, the words "Carr" carved into the wood overhead.

The brother and sister urged their mounts into a trot, and Rhys followed at a distance, content with being a spectator to the homecoming. And then he saw it, at the same time Wes and Susannah did: the burned rubble of a house. Only a stone fireplace remained, a silhouette against the cloudless blue sky. To the left, there were more remnants, apparently a barn. Fences were torn, the posts scattered; and the entire scene, atop a hill overlooking the river, looked lonely and desolate. There was the carcass of a cow, half eaten by scavenger birds.

There was not a living creature in sight.

Rhys moved up until he was beside Susannah. Her face was white, stricken. Wes looked frozen, his hands still on the reins of his horse.

Rhys dismounted, walked over to the carcass. Whatever had happened here occurred not too long ago. Otherwise there would be only bones. He strode over to the ruins of what must have been a fair-sized cabin and leaned down, his hands running through the ashes.

He turned back to where Wes and Susannah still sat astride the horses. "Should anyone be here?"

"Miguel," Susannah whispered. "Miguel and his sons. They were looking after the place for Wes. And me."

Rhys walked around. There was a cornfield planted just below the hill, but it too was burned; only a few charred stalks gave indication of what was once there. This was no accident, but a very thorough act of destruction.

He went back to the horse. Susannah looked at him. "The animal . . . it wasn't a bull . . .?"

Rhys shook his head and mounted his horse. "No."

"My father was trying to crossbreed, raise a better

breed of cattle. We had a bull he imported from up north. King Arthur."

Rhys's lips twisted into a slight smile. "That was not King Arthur." His gaze moved over to Wes, to the grim mouth, a burning, hopeless anger in the Texan's eyes. "What now?"

Wes didn't answer. Instead he guided his horse over to a small fenced area behind where the house had once stood and dismounted, taking his crutches from the saddle. Rhys silently watched him approach what must be the family cemetery and stand in front of a headstone, his head bowed slightly.

Susannah turned to Rhys. "Our father died two years ago. Wes ... couldn't come home."

"Your mother?"

"Fifteen years ago. In childbirth."

"There's no one else?"

Susannah shook her head. "There were two other brothers. One died of snakebite when he was five; another was killed by Indians years ago."

Rhys's mount moved restlessly under him, and Rhys knew that the horse was only reflecting his own sudden tension. "Why don't you join your brother?"

"I think he needs time alone." There was a soft understanding in her voice that rippled through Rhys like distant thunder. She turned to him. "Do you have family?"

"No," he said abruptly.

"Your mother and father?" The violet of her eyes was muted, as if she was holding back a storm of emotion by sheer will. She was obviously asking questions in an effort to take her mind from the destruction. Bloody Christ, but she was gallant.

He looked around again at the desolation around him, at the ruins of the home where she must have grown to womanhood. Perhaps he had been lucky after all. If you hadn't had anything, you couldn't miss it. Or could you?

He could imagine a certain peace here once. There were giant cottonwoods and wildflowers, rolling hills and rich bottom land, and a sky so blue it hurt the senses. He could almost imagine Wes and Susannah playing as children, a father watching benignly, and a woman sweeping a porch that looked out over a river.

Gone now. The house. The peace. Dreams. He looked over at Wes, whose head was still bowed as he leaned on crutches. Better to have no dreams at all. And yet he felt drained by an emptiness that was so much more painful than the wounds he'd received so recently. He'd always been alone, and he had told himself that didn't mean he was lonely. He had never allowed that thought for fear it might corrupt what he had fashioned in the stead of companionship. Complete and total self-reliance.

"Rhys!" Her voice broke his thoughts.

He reluctantly looked back toward her in acknowledgment.

"I was asking about your family?"

His eyes met hers, and he saw her body suddenly flinch. He didn't know what she had seen in his gaze. He didn't want to know, but apparently it was enough to stop her from asking questions.

He wanted to comfort but at the moment he didn't know how. The bleakness in him was too deep, the habit of withholding feelings too ingrained. He turned his horse away and moved up the hill where he could look around. There was an unusual stillness, as if all the usual creatures had been frightened away. Violence lingered here, and, if he didn't know better, a sense of evil. But he did know better. This was simple greed, human behavior he'd seen over and over again. It shouldn't affect him as it did. He had seen so much destruction during their journey across a war-torn country. Burned and abandoned houses. Destroyed fields. Hate. Grief. Desolation.

Yet it had never really affected him until now. And

he didn't understand why it did at this time. He was an onlooker, nothing more. An observer, as he'd always been. A man who took opportunities where he saw them.

But it did. He felt his own dormant sense of anger fill him at the wanton destruction and he could attribute it only to, God help him, his interest in Susannah and even, confound the devil, Wes Carr. He was beginning to feel like a damn nursemaid. He sat astride his horse, and waited. And wondered what in the bloody hell was happening to his judgment.

Wes felt the sting of tears behind his eyes. He hadn't cried since he'd been a kid, since his first dog had died. Now there was too damned much to grieve for. There weren't enough tears in the world. Even if he could let them out, and he couldn't. Not in front of Sue. Not in front of the Brit, who, for all Wes had observed, had never had a legitimate feeling in his life.

He looked at his father's gravestone. His father's heart, Susannah had written in a letter. Wes suspected it had been broken more than worn out. His father had fought at fifteen with Sam Houston for an independent Texas and then later took a major part in pursuing statehood. He had stood with Sam Houston in fighting secession in 1861, earning the enmity of all his one-time friends.

And Wes had followed suit, his loyalties shaped by his father's unwavering allegiance to the Union. He had traveled east and joined a regiment there, so he wouldn't have to fight his friends. Honor had dictated some decisive action; he couldn't stay at home and do nothing while so many others fought for their beliefs, whichever way they chose.

Now everything he loved was gone, except Sue. His father, whom he'd so admired. The home he had expected to be his. And Erin, whom he had once hoped to marry, was beyond him now. And he had damned little to fight back with. He'd come home a cripple who couldn't even protect his own sister, much less his home and heritage.

There was nothing left with which to rebuild, either physically or financially. They'd never had much money. His father had been a lawyer in a state that probably had more lawyers than any other in the country, but both he and Wes had had the same dream.

Cattle ranged wild in much of Texas, but they were tough and ornery, not much to look at and even less edible. Wes's father had proposed crossbreeding eastern beef with the hardy prairie stock. They could produce a small select herd which they could then sell to improve other herds, making a real contribution to this part of Texas. There had been little demand for cattle prior to the war, but Wes and his father had looked ahead, to the growth of the West and the development of railroads.

But the dreams were gone now, crushed by four years of death and killing, and Wes had no heart for rebuilding. He could only try to see that Susannah was safe. Even in that, he thought bitterly, he had to resort to blackmail. He still wasn't sure whether the Brit was staying because of his threat, or for his own oblique reasons. Wes didn't trust the Englishman, had never trusted him, although their enigmatic companion had, apparently, maintained a certain distance from his sister.

In his desperation, he had hoped that Rhys Redding was less dangerous to Susannah than the Martins. At least, Wes knew he would be around to make sure of that.

He reached out and touched the stone that marked his father's grave, that marked the passing of an era, that marked the death of dreams as well as the human body. "I love you," he whispered. "And I'll take care of Sue. Some way, I'll take care of Sue."

Swallowing a lump that almost choked him, he slowly turned around on his crutches and walked back to where Sue waited. "Let's ride to Land's End."

Even from a distance, Rhys was impressed with Land's End. He had not expected much, not after seeing the Carr home. He had realized from the ruins that it had not been a large structure.

Like Wes's home, however, the house at Land's End stood abreast a knoll. The long ranch house spread out along the width of the hill in casual elegance. Below it stood an equally impressive barn, a long building that he guessed housed the workers, and a series of fences. He wondered, for a second, how Wes felt, now that his sister so obviously owned more. It was a situation which in England often produced ugly relationships.

But Wes's face showed only relief as they rode up. Horses milled about in several corrals, and a number of bronzed-skinned men were working around the barn.

One separated from the others and sprinted toward the horses. "Señor Wes, Señora Fallon. You have come home." He genuflected. "Gracias, Mother of God."

Susannah flung herself down from the horse. "Miguel. Thank heaven. We went by home and ..."

The Mexican's face seemed to shatter. "They killed Ramon. Jesus heard there could be trouble, and we were taking King Arthur to Land's End. Ramon stayed behind to watch—"

"When?"

"Four days ago, señora."

Susannah closed her eyes. If only they had traveled faster. She took Miguel's hands in hers. "I'm so sorry. Do you know who?"

"Sí, we know. But prove? The sheriff says we must have proof."

"Sheriff Paley?"

The Mexican shook his head. "He, too, was killed ... not long after you left. About the same time as Señor Green."

"Jaime?" Jaime Powers had been assistant foreman to Stan Green, Mark's foreman for many years.

"He's here, but each week we lose more cattle and horses. That's why so many here. Now that you and Señor Wes ..." He looked up, and the sad smile deepened as he noticed, for the first time, that Wes's right stirrup was tied, that his leg ended at his knee. *"Por el amor de Dios."*

For the love of God, she silently translated. She watched Wes flinch, and she immediately turned Miguel's attention to the other rider. "This is Señor Redding, Miguel. A friend."

The Mexican nodded warily to Rhys, then turned back to Susannah hopefully. "Any news of Señor Fallon?" He knew that had been the purpose of Susannah's trip east.

Susannah stilled. The ache, the terrible guilt she'd tried to bury under the weight of the journey, under her worry over Wes and the ranches, struck her with renewed force. Mark seemed so real again, here on the land he'd loved, where he'd grown to adulthood. She could almost see him standing on the porch, his lips creasing into a slow, welcoming smile. "He's dead, too, Miguel. In Virginia."

Miguel bowed his head. "I am so sorry, señora. So many fine men."

She nodded. "I know," she whispered.

"I will go find Señor Jaime. He will be glad to have you back. You and Señor Wes."

A younger Mexican, a boy of no more than twelve, approached and took the reins of the horses as Wes and Rhys dismounted and followed Susannah as she went up the four steps to the porch of the ranch house, hesitating before going in. Mark's home.

I want someone to have Land's End who will love it as I do. She remembered Mark saying it as clearly as if he were saying it now.

"I will," she promised him silently. "I'll take care of it for you."

She heard the clump of Wes's crutches behind her, and she opened the door to the large room that dominated the ranch house.

It was just as she had left it. A huge stone fireplace centered the back wall. A rack of rifles, which had been there as long as she remembered, decorated another side. A colorful rug covered the pine floors and large stuffed furniture welcomed weary travelers. She had always liked this room: the masculine nature of it also stressed comfort. She remembered Mark and his brother and father sprawling over the chairs, dogs at their feet. All three were dead, and although she had lived here the last four years, she suddenly felt like an intruder in a room full of ghosts.

"Susannah?"

She turned at the sound of her brother's voice. He stood just inside, resting on the crutches as his face searched hers.

"There are so many memories, Wes."

"I know," he said, his hand going out to hers and clasping it. Susannah held tight to it, allowing the emotions to wash over her. Somehow part of her hadn't accepted the fact that Mark was really gone. Why hadn't she loved him more? But she had. She had loved him dearly, just not in the way he'd so wanted.

She bit her lip, forcing the tears back from her eyes. She couldn't give in now. There was too much to do. Susannah had the terrible feeling that if she ever broke, then she could never repair herself again.

Susannah turned back toward the door. Rhys was

standing there. No, not standing, but leaning against the doorjamb carefully surveying the room inch by inch, his posture lazy but his eyes dark and piercing, obviously absorbing every detail and making judgments.

She felt the familiar thrill, the bright flashing pleasure that always assaulted her when their eyes caught, and waves of guilt immediately followed. Guilt and a kind of sad disloyalty. This was Mark's house. Surely, she should be able to mourn him here without ...

She turned away suddenly, not wishing Rhys to see a sudden film clouding her eyes.

Hannah came in then, rubbing her hands on the apron she always wore. Hannah, the daughter of one of Texas's original German settlers, had been housekeeper and cook for the Fallon family for as long as Susannah could remember. And mother to the boys. And often to Susannah herself.

Her eyes were red-rimmed now as she hurried toward Susannah, her hands outstretched. "Miguel told me about Mark," she said in a voice that broke.

Susannah allowed Hannah to enfold her in the large creases of her body, feeling the comfort flowing from her as she had when she was a little girl. Hannah was a constant in her life. The only constant now, for even Wes had changed into a different, distant person.

She finally backed away. "Hannah, Wes will be staying here, and so will ... Mr. Redding. He helped bring us home."

Like Miguel, Hannah's look was measuring when her gaze turned toward Rhys.

"He'll be staying in the bunkhouse," Wes interrupted, although he managed a small smile for Hannah.

Susannah turned and looked at her brother, and then Rhys, who was still lounging against a doorjamb. Although his pose was relaxed, Susannah noticed a certain stiffness. She doubted whether anyone else would have noticed, but she had seen that gesture several other times, when he seemed to mentally retreat even more than usual. She half expected him to disappear out the door.

But then he caught her gaze on him and shrugged. "The bunkhouse is fine," he said. "I won't be staying long."

His voice again carried the English accent, rather than the Texas drawl he'd been practicing, and Susannah saw the surprise on Hannah's face at the foreign sound. There was something odd about Rhys now. The control, that assurance that had always drawn her so, was gone. So was the odd wariness with which he had viewed this room. He looked different, even in the same clothes he'd been wearing. He looked ... somehow ineffectual. She wondered how that was possible after all that had happened, how that strong harsh face could somehow become almost slack. She had seen actors do that, become other personalities, and now she was seeing a man transform himself in front of her own eyes. She looked at Wes, and noticed the astonishment in his eyes.

She had seen so many sides of him during their weeks of travel. This was yet a new face. But why? Knowing Rhys, there had to be a reason.

But what was it?

Chapter 12

Rhys settled back on the lower bunk, trying to get comfortable. Even the thin lumpy mattress was too soft after the last month and a half on the ground.

And he had grown accustomed to the sound of evening creatures lulling him asleep, not the snoring and heavy breathing of fellow humans.

The bunkhouse was only about a quarter full, about ten men, six of whom were Mexicans, who eyed him with something akin to distrust, an attitude he did nothing to dispel. The other four men were young, not much more than eighteen, and Rhys figured the curious mix resulted from the war and the draft he'd heard about.

Jaime, the foreman, was also young, too young for that kind of job, Rhys thought, but apparently he was the most capable man remaining when the older foreman was killed. Overall, Rhys judged the group to be woefully deficient, if not downright ludicrous, compared to what he was hearing about the Martin brothers.

It was none of his business, he assured himself. He'd fulfilled his part of the bargain and, blackmail or not, he would stay just long enough to get some money from an Austin bank.

He'd made that decision when he'd seen Susannah's eyes fill as she entered the ranch house, when he glimpsed the grief in so many faces at being told of Mark Fallon's death. Mark Fallon was evidently a well-liked man. A good man. An anathema to Rhys, who had always steered clear of such paragons. Well, let Susannah keep those bloody damned memories and live with them. He had no intention of changing who and what he was. He was quite content with his character, such as it was.

Still, for some reason, he had decided to show a weak face to those around him. He wouldn't fool Wes or Susannah, of course, but there was no reason to reveal certain talents to the world at large. Not yet. Ignorance in others, he had discovered in the past, yielded a certain advantage.

A particularly loud snore emitted from a man two bunks away, and Rhys felt the urge to demonstrate one of his more deadly skills right then and there. He sat up. It was hopeless. Bloody hell, he hadn't slept in a room with so many men in years. Wealth, he knew, had certain advantages one tended to forget.

Wes, he thought balefully. Wes knew exactly what he was doing. He thought he had Rhys tied in a knot. He thought he could keep him away from Susannah. He had another think coming.

The only reason he'd kept away from Susannah was for his own sake, not hers, not Wes's. And he was staying only because Land's End was as good a place to wait as any while he tried to retrieve some funds.

He stood and walked to the door, opening it quietly. There was a slight breeze fanning out from the river, but the sky was clear. He walked out to the corral, where a man leaned against a post, a rifle in his hand. Miguel. He nodded to him and walked on.

"Do not go far, señor. One of my sons watches below, and he is ... how do you say—nervous?"

"Do you expect trouble tonight?"

"I do not know whether the cursed dogs realize

the señora is back. I fear for her." He looked at Rhys, his gaze moving down to Rhys's hips, and disapproval, or disappointment, glittered in his eyes. "It is not good to wander around here without a gun."

Rhys shrugged. "It could be more dangerous with one."

"You are not familiar with guns, señor?"

Rhys didn't answer the question directly. "We do not need guns in England."

"You must be very careful then. You are the señora's friend, and you will be a target, as we all are."

"Why do you stay, then?"

"My father fought with Señor Mark's grandfather at San Jacinto. He saved my father's life. We have been with the family ever since." He shrugged. "Their destiny is our destiny."

"Even to die?"

"Even to die, señor. Do you not have loyalty in your country?"

Loyalty is for fools, Rhys wanted to say, but the words obviously would have little impact. What in the bloody hell had he walked into, anyway?

"Will you be staying long, señor?"

"No," he said shortly.

"But you came all this way ..." The question was in his voice, an insistent question.

"I made a bargain." Rhys said. "Mrs. Fallon needed help with her brother. I have a strong arm."

Miguel's eyes were steady. "You came a long way, señor, during very troubled times. There was no ... danger?"

"I've learned how to avoid trouble."

"And you will avoid it now?"

"Yes."

The Mexican's eyes again reflected a measure of disappointment as he turned around, dismissing Rhys. "Remember, señor, my son might shoot at shadows. I would dislike him being responsible for your death."

"A sentiment I share," Rhys said courteously, almost priggishly. He inwardly grinned at the Mexican's look of distaste. He congratulated himself. At least, he still had that particular ability, to become whatever he wished to become.

He nodded pleasantly, something he had not done since he started on this insane journey. "I will go back to the bunkhouse then." He was rather pleased at the look of disgust on Miguel's face, even as he wondered why he was performing this charade.

Yet his instinct had prompted it from the moment they'd approached this place, and he always, always trusted his instinct.

And God knew he had played the fool before. In more ways than one.

He wondered whether that particular tendency applied now.

Wes waited up with Susannah until Jaime returned that night to the ranch house. The young foreman's youthful face was tight with weariness and responsibility. He gave Susannah and Wes a brief smile, then blinked when told of Mark's death. He was still not too old to spare a tear. But after a brief moment, he was all business as he told of "the troubles."

He had just returned from bringing in a small herd of horses. Instead of letting them roam as they once had, riders took them out each day, watched them as they grazed, and then returned them to the corral at night.

It was a wearing exercise, keeping them from other duties. The small herd of cattle was being depleted daily by rustling, but the horses represented Land's End's survival. They were among the best raised in the territory, a mixture of the rugged range horses, wild descendants from those animals brought to the new world by the Spanish, and thoroughbreds im-

ported from the East. While Wes's father had concentrated on cattle, Mark's family had emphasized horses,
which proved to be the far better investment. Texans
loved good horseflesh; races had been the prime en-
tertainment before the war, and, during the war,
horses had been in demand for another more ominous
reason. Land's End offered the best horses available,
then and now.

The demand for cattle, however, had not been so
strong. The push west, envisioned by Wes's and
Susannah's father, had not yet fully materialized and
there were plenty of wild cattle to satisfy present demand. Wes knew the time was coming, now that the
war had ended, for the expansion of the cattle market.
The railroads would move west rapidly, and there was
bound to be a strong migration. The South was worn
out; the soldiers from the North would hunger for
something more than factory jobs; he had seen that
hunger in the men of his company as they'd expanded
their knowledge and skills. The West would be a
promised land for families from both the North and
the South who needed new beginnings.

His father had been a visionary, years ahead of his
time. Now the vision would be realized. But not by
Wes. By others.

Jaime and Miguel had made that clear. The carefully bred cattle which had consumed Frank Carr's life
and what little money he earned or could borrow were
gone, leaving debts Wes doubted he could meet. Only
King Arthur remained. And Wes knew he wasn't up to
starting over again. He looked down where his leg
should have been and knew he didn't have the
strength—or even the will—to rebuild. For what? He
wouldn't have a family now. He couldn't marry Erin,
not like he was. He couldn't even hate anymore. Not
the Martins, not anyone. Four years of war had
drained him of hate, of most emotions.

The fact that he had tried to blackmail the Englishman, or Welshman, or whatever he was, showed how entirely impotent he was.

Susannah went up to bed when Jaime left for the foreman's cabin. She had refrained from saying anything about Wes's banishing Redding to the bunkhouse, though her eyes had questioned him. He knew he really had no right to do what he had done. This was Susannah's home now, and he'd half expected, no, fully expected, an argument, but it had not come.

After she disappeared down the hall, he sat silently for a while in the lonely room, brooding, pondering a future that looked empty. He finally rose and found Mark's supply of liquor. He selected a bottle and sprawled back in a large chair, letting the crutches fall where they may. He took a long swallow, and then another. He felt the tingling of nerves in the leg that no longer existed, and he cursed. Why didn't it stop, dammit? Maybe ... but then he looked down again, and it hadn't been a dream. The leg was gone, the pant leg neatly folded and pinned up. Why did he keep doing that? He took another long pull from the bottle.

Susannah found Wes in the chair in the morning. Hannah had probably seen him too, since Susannah appreciatively sniffed the smell of coffee wafting through the house. The joy of such a simple pleasure was dulled by the sight of Wes. She knew he had been drinking on the trail, but she had never before seen him passed out like this, his jaw slack and his breath smelling of whiskey. An empty bottle was turned over next to him.

She went over and shook him gently. "Wes."

He woke slowly, opening one bloodshot eye and peering at her before opening the other. He groaned as daylight, and reality, penetrated. "What time is it?" he mumbled.

"Breakfast. You know. Coffee. Real coffee. Bacon."

He closed his eyes and groaned again.

"Wes," she said softly. "Don't do this. I need you too much."

"Forget it, Sue. I don't need your lies, dammit. I don't want them. You and I both know how much good I am. You saw it when those damned bushwhackers hit us."

"I know you can do anything you *try* to do," she said with a trace of impatience. "You made it halfway across the country."

"Because of that goddamned Brit," Wes said bitterly.

"Is that why you wanted him to sleep in the bunkhouse?"

"Did you want him to sleep somewhere else?" Wes's question was unusually sharp.

Susannah disregarded the implication as unworthy of her brother and indicative only of his morose state.

"You just said we owed him."

"That's not what I said at all," he retorted. "You can bet he had his own reasons for coming."

"But not for staying."

Wes didn't reply, not immediately. When he did, he sounded defeated. "Don't be so sure of that, Sue. Stay away from him. I've seen men like him before. No conscience. No soul. Perhaps we need that part of him now. But don't kid yourself that there's any more." His hand went up, and he felt the stubble on his cheek and smelled his own whiskey breath. He wondered whether he was any better than Redding. "I'll get cleaned up." He tried to smile. "The coffee does smell good."

Leaning down, he found his crutches and slowly got to his feet. Christ, but he hurt. His head felt as if it were exploding, his mouth as if he were gagged with a handful of cotton.

"Wes?"

He heard her soft voice, and he turned around.

"I'm so glad you're here."

Wes felt even sicker. He could only nod, and hobble out of the room.

She had some time before breakfast. She knew she had time to go out and see him. Rhys Redding. It seemed so strange this morning to wake in her own bed, and alone. She had grown so accustomed to seeing him moving around, his hard lean body so effortlessly saddling the horses, packing what little supplies they had. She was used to studying his face, the angles and planes that comprised such an intriguing whole. She'd never tired of looking at it, wondering what lay behind those dark eyes.

Even now, in Mark's house, that face blinded her to everything else except the guilt that filled her for feeling so.

She went out on the porch and looked toward the bunkhouse. Men were in their saddles, cutting out a string of horses to take to pasture. She looked for Rhys's tall figure, but she didn't see him. She saw Jaime, who was competently giving orders, and again she marveled at how much he'd matured in the past few months.

Where was Rhys Redding?

She looked for his horse in the corral, the one he had been riding, but she didn't see it. Had he finally left? Had he taken Wes's order last night as an insult? Somehow, she doubted it. She had seen his amused reaction to Wes's truculence too many times. Rhys would take it more as a challenge than an insult, a challenge to throw it right back in Wes's face.

How did she know that?

But she did. She ached now to go saddle her own horse and ride out and find him. But she couldn't. Not as long as Wes was in his current mood. As much as she yearned to do otherwise, she had to support him, to give him back the confidence he'd once had. She couldn't do that by defying him openly or opposing him in front of others. So she went inside and asked Hannah if there was anything she could do to help.

At her request, Miguel joined them for breakfast. They still had a lot to catch up on. Miguel was tending to what stock he managed to salvage from Wes's place. When Frank Carr had died during the war, Susannah had sent Miguel and his sons over to take care of her old ranch, and they had been there, managing the herd and the property, until the raid. Now his remaining sons worked for Jaime, and Miguel was on a par with the foreman.

She couldn't resist the question most on her mind. "Have you seen Señor Redding?"

"Sí, señora. He left this morning for a ride. I was able to stop him last night from wandering around, but this morning . . ." He lifted his hands in a gesture of hopelessness, a gesture Susannah understood only too well. She knew how difficult it was to stop Rhys from doing anything.

Miguel continued, his face earnestly persuasive. "I think we must teach Señor Redding how to shoot."

Susannah and Wes looked at each other, both trying to keep any knowledge from their faces.

If Rhys Redding was playing a role, he must have a reason for doing so, no matter how opaque it might be to her.

Wes seemed ready to say something, and Susannah threw him a warning glance. "I suspect he can take care of himself," Wes finally mumbled.

"He rides well," Miguel said, "but he does not carry a gun. He does not realize the danger. He is a—" Miguel hesitated, not sure whether he was insulting a guest—"a tenderfoot?"

The description almost made Susannah choke. Her nighthawk was even better at pretending than she'd thought. But why was he playing games? She remembered what he had said that night weeks ago. *That's what I do. Play games. And I really don't think you want to play one with me.*

She wished she could be as sure. But what game was he playing now?

"I wouldn't worry overmuch," Wes said dryly.

"If you say so," Miguel said reluctantly. "He is your friend."

"Hardly that," Wes mumbled again, and Susannah hoped she was the only one who heard—and understood.

"Do you know where he was going?" she finally asked, braving Wes's baleful look.

"Along the river," Miguel replied. "He went toward your ranch."

"I will advise him," Susannah said solemnly, "to learn how to shoot."

"*Gracias.* I do not want another killing."

"Can we stop it?" It was another question on Susannah's mind.

"I do not know." He looked doubtful. "Perhaps now that you are back . . ." His voice trailed off. "If only Señor Mark . . ."

"I know, Miguel," Susannah said softly. "He could bring everyone together. I don't know if anyone will listen to Wes and me. Not if feelings still run so strong."

"So many are dead, señora. Many families have lost their men and given up, selling out to the Martins. The ones that are left are like us . . . they lose cattle and horses and other livestock. Many have borrowed money to survive the war since they could not bring in crops alone without their men, and now they cannot pay. The Martins are buying up the notes." He shook his head.

Loans. Susannah knew Mark had taken out loans to buy the thoroughbreds he'd needed. She'd been able to make payments by selling a few of the horses over the years, but now, she knew, they needed what stock they had left for breeding. If some had been stolen . . .

"Are we missing any horses, Miguel?"

· He nodded. "Ten so far. That is why Jaime now brings them in each night."

Susannah closed her eyes and figured. They needed that money, every dollar of it. And Wes would need additional funds to get started again.

They couldn't lose any more.

She finished eating. "I'll go find Señor Redding."

"Not alone," Wes said.

Susannah looked at him with patience. "I've been riding alone the last four years, Wes. And I'll take the rifle. I promise to be careful. Will you look at the books?"

He hesitated. He felt like hell warmed over. "I don't . . . know . . ."

Miguel broke in. "The trouble always comes at night, señor."

Wes looked over at Susannah. "You'll be careful?"

"I'll stay on our land," she promised.

"If you're not back within a few hours—"

"You can come find me," Susannah finished. Before he could say anything else, she went to her room to change clothes, her mind in a muddle. She was suddenly seized by anticipation, the excitement that was always with her when she was with Rhys Redding, or even thought of him.

She put on her old riding habit, a violet color that matched her eyes. He had seen her in little but faded dresses and masculine clothing for the past months. She brushed her hair, which she had washed last night, and tied it back with a ribbon. She took a quick glance in the mirror and, though her face was thinner than usual, she no longer felt like a ragamuffin.

Susannah took one last look around the room. She had shared it for one night with Mark four years ago. There was a ghost here, but it was not nearly as strong as it was downstairs where she had spent so much time with the Fallon family. "I *do* miss you, Mark," she whispered. But it was the friend she sensed in the room, not a husband. She wanted to think he was smiling at her.

She passed up the horse she had been riding and saddled her mare, Fancy. It nickered with a soft pleased sound as Susannah ran her hand along her neck. The mare was small but fast, its color that of midnight and its manner most ladylike. A present from Mark, the pretty little mare had a fancy step that made riding a pleasure. Susannah saddled the mare herself and used a block of wood to help her into the sidesaddle. She did not want to bother the few hands working the horses. The ranch was short of men already, and she was used to doing for herself. And she didn't want questions. Or warnings. She just wanted . . . to see Rhys Redding, to know he was still here, to know that . . .

She didn't know what. She only knew she wanted to be with him, to feel that safety she felt only with him.

Susannah followed the well-worn path that skirted the river between the Carr and Fallon ranches. The two families had practically lived together, a closeness that started with their fathers.

She didn't know where Rhys would go, or when he would return, or whether he would return at all. It was absurd how little she knew about him. She had known everything about Mark. She could predict his every move, his every action. He would, she knew, always do the right thing.

Was that why she was so intrigued by Rhys? He was the opposite side of the coin, as unpredictable as a summer storm. She reached the hill where the Carr ranch had once stood, and she saw a horse grazing there. *His* horse.

It neighed a welcome to her mare, who pranced an eager little step and turned her head as if to ask Susannah her permission to greet the stranger. Her horse was not one whit better than she, Susannah thought disgustedly. Lured by an attractive face.

But still she gave the horse its head, her heart thumping just as she felt the little mare's heart accelerate.

She saw Rhys kneeling in the grass, and she dismounted, which was much easier than mounting on a sidesaddle, and walked toward him, holding the reins as the mare nickered softly.

Rhys seemed to be shifting through tall grass with a long stick, looking for something. His movements stilled, and he glanced toward her, as if surprised. She knew, however, that he must have been aware of her approach. He was much too intuitive and careful not to have been. He stood as she approached, and she thought how tall and handsome he was. The gun that he had kept tucked in his belt those long weeks was gone, and he looked strangely naked without it.

"Mrs. Fallon," he acknowledged with the heavy mockery he used so often.

"*Major* Redding," she retorted.

He grinned. "All right. Susannah, then."

"I like Rhys better, too."

"What are you doing here alone?" he asked, ignoring the comment.

"I'm not here alone," she said with no little satisfaction.

"Ah, you have me there, Susannah. What are you doing here *with* me?"

"Trying to convince you to learn to shoot," she said with fiendish delight in her eyes. "Miguel is worried about you."

"Good."

"Why the charade?"

"Never let anyone know your strengths."

"Or weaknesses?"

"Especially those."

"Do you have any?"

He smiled and it very briefly touched his eyes, and then left them as cold as ever. "Of course not, Mrs. Fallon."

She chided him with her eyes. "You can trust everyone at our ranch. They've been with us for years."

"I don't trust anyone," he said, all traces of the smile gone.

"No one?"

"No one."

"That must get lonely."

He shook his head. "It keeps me alive," he said.

She tried again. "Not even me or Wes?"

"Especially you and Wes."

"Why?"

He leaned his head to one side and gave her a quizzical half-smile. It could, she thought, even have been termed a sneer, obviously meant to intimidate. "I never trust pretty women, Miss Susannah, or honorable men. I would have detested your husband, from all I have heard."

"He would have liked you."

Her statement made one of his eyebrows raise in doubtful question.

"He liked competence," Susannah said.

"He sounds like a paragon." It was not a compliment.

"No," Susannah said slowly. "He wasn't that. He was dear and he was loyal, but he was also reckless and he had a fierce temper. He liked a fight."

"And you loved him?" He tried for derision, but it didn't quite work. He hated the almost wistful request for denial in the question. He hoped like bloody hell she didn't hear it.

Susannah looked up at him, misery and guilt in her eyes, emotions that caused havoc inside Rhys. The part of him that was discovering he might have just a little heart after all hurt for her. The disciplined, analytical, don't-feel-anything-for-anybody part took a perverse pleasure in the instinctive knowledge that all had not been perfect. He smothered down the first vulnerable emotion. Or hoped he had. He waited for her to answer.

"He was my best friend," she said simply.

Rhys didn't like the sudden ache that ran through him. Such simple words she'd said. Yet such alien ones for him. He'd never had a friend. Never trusted anyone that much. The only time he'd ever held out a hand to someone was to Lauren Bradley months ago, and God knew what that had cost him, physically and financially. Bloody hell, even emotionally, as much as he hated to admit he had emotions.

"I don't think that answered my question," he said, despising himself for pursuing something he wasn't sure he wanted to know. Yet, he couldn't help himself.

The look in her eyes was almost tragic as she studied his face, searching for something. And he knew why. Instinctively, he knew why. She was hunting a reason to reveal something so very personal.

Suddenly, he didn't want to know. He didn't want her to find the reason she was seeking. He stepped back, a movement that was more than a physical motion, and he saw she understood.

"Why did you come back here?" she said, trying to pretend that nothing had happened, that the strong tide of attraction wasn't there at all, that she hadn't felt that momentary reaching out from him to her, or her to him.

He shrugged. "I don't really know. Just looking. It seemed as good a place as any to come." He didn't mention the portion of a spur he'd just pocketed.

"You could have gone with Jaime."

"I'm not a cowhand," he said abruptly. "I don't intend to become one."

"What do you intend to do?"

"Ask your brother," he said.

"Why?"

"A bit of blackmail, I'd say."

"I wouldn't think that would stop you ... if you wanted to go."

Bloody hell, she saw too much. "It wouldn't," he agreed, to his own surprise. "But I have a few things to do first. I plan to go to Austin tomorrow."

"It's a hard ride."

The eyebrow raised again, and she looked sheepish. A difficult ride would be the last thing to bother him.

"Come with me," she said suddenly.

"Where?"

"One of my favorite places." The hope in her voice was irresistible. She held out a hand to him and Rhys found himself taking it. He also found his spirits lightening in a most peculiar way.

She took him up to the top of the hill and partly down to where an old weathered oak tree, its leaves still the color of the young hopeful green of spring, sat in solitary splendor. She drew him to its trunk and directed his eyes downward, where a patchwork of wildflowers carpeted the side of the hills in intricate patterns. The sun shone bright on them, bringing out the various hues of gold and yellow. Below them stretched a plain that seemed endless.

"Our cattle used to graze there," she said. "It always seemed so peaceful and safe to me, though Indians used to raid this area."

He felt it too, a peace, an inexplicable sense of belonging that rocked him. He had never felt as if he belonged anywhere, that he was a little like a leaf blowing in the wind with no anchor. He'd tried to anchor himself once and it hadn't worked. He'd been a misfit, just as he'd always been.

Unlike Susannah. She appeared to fit everywhere. Bad luck seemed to have dogged her steps, but she still had a kind of radiance about her, an endurance and hope that never really flagged. He had seen her work magic with Wes, had watched her travel, without complaint, distances that would have daunted most men. She mystified him. Bewildered him.

And more.

Her hand was still in his, and now it seemed to curl around his fingers in an intimate way that sent fire racing through his veins.

She looked beautiful this morning in the riding dress, her hair tied back by a violet ribbon. She looked fresh and untouched and wistful. And so sad as she looked down. Memories, he supposed. Memories of her family. Of her husband.

He swallowed hard. He had been able to keep away from her only through the strong personal discipline he had mastered during the past two decades. He told himself it had been for his sake, not hers, that he exercised it.

And now for some reason neither seemed to matter. He wanted her! He didn't want her thinking of another man. Not even a dead man.

Rhys felt the pressure build inside him, the raw, hungry desire that defied his control, defied every rational thought, every warning signal. The pressure made his breathing difficult; he had to work for every swallow of air as his arousal strained against the trousers he wore. He had lusted before, but never had he felt this kind of uncontrollable craving, an obsession to bury himself in her, not just to experience erotic pleasure but for some more powerful inexplicable need.

His hand tightened on hers as the other went up and caught her chin between his fingers, roughly holding it there, and he felt a shudder run through her body as his flesh pressed against hers. Her eyes met his, the violet deepening with passion that also flushed her face a soft pink. Her lips trembled slightly as she watched him, an expectancy in her face flaming the already glowing coals in his loins.

She stood on tiptoes, her head barely coming to his chin.

His lips met hers, and there was such wistful innocence in her response that all his defenses exploded. This time, he knew he wouldn't, couldn't, stop.

He was going to take what as offered. And damn the bloody consequences.

Chapter 13

Rhys had never dreamed heaven existed. Even when he first saw Susannah in the prison hospital and wondered so fleetingly if she was an angel, he still hadn't believed heaven existed. For him, anyway.

But he knew he was coming as close to it now as he ever would.

How else to explain the feelings running through him like wildfire? Even, devil help him, through what must be the heart he thought he'd thoroughly tromped years ago. He had thought to kiss her hard, expending some of the physical need he'd been storing these past weeks, but the moment his lips touched hers they unaccountably gentled. He felt tension thrumming through his body, causing a terrible ache in a very reactionary part of himself. She was so soft and sweet-smelling. Not like the expensively perfumed ladies in London, but like the clean fresh scent of soap and the slightest hint of flowers.

She didn't use the usual tricks of women he'd known: the overdramatic fluttering of eyebrows, the conscious teasing and touching that had nothing of caring behind it. There was only an honest wonderment of feelings reflected in her eyes, an absence of pretense or false indignation. Again, he thought of innocence; yet how could she be innocent? She had been married. And to a man she'd obviously cared about. Whom everyone seemed to care about. The thought made him suddenly, unaccountably, angry, as did his former gentle impulses. His mouth covered hers with a savagery he'd controlled until now.

His arms pulled her to him with fierce, uncontrolled want. He wanted to frighten her, to scare her off, to wipe away that look that made his heart beat faster, and that told him his soul just might be intact, after all.

He didn't want anyone to look at him that way.

So why did it affect him this way? Why did it make him want to soften his kiss, to tempt rather than demand? One of his hands went to her left breast, his fingers playing with it, erotically, intimately, feeling its every response: the swelling, the hardening of the nipple. Her body was reaching for his, her hand touching his back, the fingers moving inside the shirt where his skin was burning now.

"Susannah," he groaned as his lips moved down to the throbbing pulse of her throat and nuzzled it, feeling her quiver, almost vibrating under his touch. He felt sensations ripple through her as they rippled through him too. His body was no longer his own to rule.

"I told you not to tempt a wolf," he whispered in a rich sensual voice as his mouth moved to her ear, his tongue playing with the sensitive lobe, creating even more spasms that crossed over to him and back again as her body melded against his, his almost bursting manhood pushing against the cloth of his trousers and against the cloth of her skirt. He swallowed hard, trapped by his own need.

He knew how vulnerable she was at that moment, vulnerable in so many ways. How ready was she for him? Or was she ready for anyone? She'd had more grief than most, more to bear than most. And as determinedly independent and competent as she seemed most of the time, Rhys had seen that occasional lost look, the relief in her face when he had returned after one of his disappearances. He had come along when she needed someone. It was no more than that. Need.

And he needed a woman. Bloody hell, how he needed a woman. No more than that.

He took his eyes away from her long enough to scan the countryside. A rabbit moved down below, and a bird flitted above. The horses were making get-acquainted nickering noises from where he had tied them. A bee buzzed among the wildflowers just a few feet away from them. Other than those natural stirrings, there was quiet, an undisturbed stillness that proclaimed a certain peace. For the moment, anyway.

Rhys leaned over and picked her up, carrying her to a place where the grass looked soft and green. He kissed her long and deep and hard as he laid her down and dropped next to her, one leg stretching out while the other bent at the knee. He rested his chin on his knee for a moment, searching her face as one hand ran trails along her wrist and up her arm.

"Pretty Susannah," he said. "Come share an adventure with me." It wasn't a question at all, but a velvet invitation.

He saw some of the glow in her eyes dim. "Is that what it is, Rhys? An adventure? A . . . game?"

"It's all I have to offer, pretty lady. Nothing more. Not even tomorrow."

She bit her lip, and he knew she was trying to keep it from quivering. He knew she didn't want to show she'd been wounded by his words. Her lips were already slightly swollen from his kiss, and now, with the slightest tremor, they were beguiling, enchanting. They were also incredibly dangerous. He wanted to take back his words, to offer her something else, something that would make the eyes shine again as they had occasionally during the long trip together.

But, capable liar that he was, he couldn't lie about this. Not to her.

He knew he didn't have to. He knew, as he had that night at the river, that she felt the same aching attraction, the same electricity that made his body react in ways not altogether familiar. His teeth nibbled at her earlobe, sending shivers of anticipation through her. And through him.

He had bedded some of the most gifted courtesans in England, but he'd never before felt this level of anticipation, of need, of raw, naked, physical appetite. He'd never felt this drumming in his heart, nor the intensity of the white-hot heat that ran through his body when he touched her, even looked at her and saw his craving reflected in her eyes. There was something so honest and right about her, about everything she was. He wondered for the briefest second whether it was that quality he was seeking to conquer. And quench. An attempt to make her like him, to corrupt her?

What kind of bastard was he, anyway? Besides the legal one?

But he was beyond redemption. He knew he couldn't stop now even if he wanted to, not with her slightly misted violet eyes gazing up at him with such desperate, expectant wanting of her own. And trust. God help him, the trust. But together—desire and trust—they were irresistible.

His hands undid her buttons, slowly and sensuously, his fingers lingering possessively on her skin. Heat rippled through him in hot waves, and he had to force himself to go slowly, to not suddenly take her roughly as his physical need urged him to do. A camisole lay under the dress he managed to tug off her, and her breasts stretched taut against the cloth. His hands went inside and stroked, then tugged the camisole up until his mouth could reach the left nipple. He nibbled and tasted, again feeling shivers rack her body as her hands stole up and tangled themselves in his hair.

They were stretched out along the ground, his body rigid and tense with need as he made hers sing. He saw the surprise in her eyes, the astonished pleasure that shone there, and he wondered that she seemed to experience these things for the first time.

He took his hands from her and unbuttoned his own shirt, throwing it several feet away. He then unbuttoned his trousers, but hesitated at pulling them off. She was watching him solemnly, her face still flushed with warmth, her skin hot, even a little damp now. Her hand inched up and caught the dark hair on his chest, ran her fingertips over his chest and downward, along the skin that stretched taut over the ridged muscles of his body.

Now it was his turn to shudder, to try to control the spasms her touch created. But he couldn't. All his fabled control was crumbling, pulled down by a wisp of a woman with gentle hands and eyes which were at once determined and expectant and even a little frightened. The combination was potent. He wanted to reassure her, which was the last thing in the world he could do. He wasn't going to stay. He'd never intended to stay. There was nothing here for him. If he stayed, she would, one day, discover all that he was, and he didn't intend for that to happen. And he had no wish to compete with a memory.

But his body was paying no heed to his mind. It had no scruples, or fears, or reservations. It had only want. And it was exercising that want in the most blatant way, responding to her every touch, and making its own damnable decisions.

He felt her mouth on his chest, nibbling fiery paths along a ridge of muscles, and he couldn't hold back any longer. He pulled down the pantalets she was wearing, and his hand went between her legs. He heard the tiny gasp of surprise, and then a sigh of pleasure as her body seemed to arch toward him.

She cried out his name, and the sound of it on her lips sent a rush of pleasure through him. Not just physical but something even more satisfying. She wasn't thinking of her husband now. He twisted his body to meet hers, his mouth touching hers, and it opened to him.

It was that bloody trust that did it, that made his heart stumble and his will weaken, and his judgment move somewhere to the left of lunacy. He slipped his tongue inside her mouth and explored and plundered and then gentled, finding, oddly enough, that he wanted to give as well as take.

He drew off his boots, sliding a knife from a strap around his ankle into one of the boots, and then slipped off his trousers. His body moved next to hers, kindling a flame within him that he knew would have to burn itself out. Lightning leaped between them, jagged and violent yet binding them with its intensity. Need took over, a need so great it threatened to consume him. He crushed her to him, his mouth insatiable as it tasted and wanted more. His hands ran up and down her body, feeling the heat run between them, scorching and branding.

He felt her breath, warm and quick, as she drew him to her, and he felt the last vestige of control go as he entered her with an impatience he tried to curb. Slowly, something told him. It must have been years since she . . .

And he didn't want to hurt her. Everything within him rebelled at bringing any more hurt to her, although he knew that just being here, just by submitting to his own desires, he was hurting her. Yet, he couldn't stop. He had never known this storm of feeling, the sweetness of trust, and that, he knew, was what she was giving him, no matter what he had said to her.

For this moment he would take it. He probed deeper into her, feeling the honeyed warmth of a shy yet willing eagerness. Her arms went around him, holding him tight, and she whimpered as he went deeper and deeper, feeling her body tremble as it welcomed him and instinctively moved first with him, then against him, as sensations kindled and flamed, sending shimmering waves of heat through every part of him. He moved in a rhythm that grew more and more frantic, a whirlwind of power and response as he heard her cry out in something like agony.

But he couldn't stop. Not now.

He heard her moan with pleasure, felt her lips brush kisses against his skin as her body hugged his, claiming it in every possible way. He sought to prolong her pleasure, his pleasure, the infinitely precious moments of intimate belonging. He felt her teeth on his neck, nibbling with an erotic hunger that made his body convulse.

Susannah thought ... dear Lord, she didn't know what she was thinking. Glory, sheer wonderful glory and splendor as waves and waves of sensation rolled through her body. He fitted as if he was personally made for her, throbbing against the ever so sensitive interior, each movement taking him deeper and deeper into the core of her until she felt she would explode with pleasure so great it was unbearable. She cried out with the sheer joy of him, yet ... she knew there was more though she didn't know how she could bear more. Her body reacted with centuries-old instinct, arching toward him, taking him deeper and deeper until ... she felt the magnificent explosion inside. Bursts of wonder and thunderous waves of pleasure swept through her like a great tidal wave, paling in comparison to anything she'd ever felt before in her life.

Rhys thought he must have shattered into millions of brilliant pieces as he drove into her one last time and found his own release. He closed his eyes, allowing himself to relish every exquisite quiver as her muscles contracted against him, reluctant to let him go. He looked down at her face, afraid of what he might see—fear, loathing—but there was neither, only a soft wondering glow that was suddenly the greatest gift he'd ever known.

The only gift he'd ever known.

He held her, resting his face against hers with a tenderness that made him ache. How could she accept him so readily? Knowing so little about him?

She looked at him with the large violet eyes. "I didn't know it could be like this."

The words came as a shock, even though some part of him was aware that she'd had very little experience. She'd been tight, so very tight, and she had moved as if exploring for the first time. The exclamations of surprised pleasure had been both astounding and immensely gratifying. He had never been a considerate lover, had never really known what it meant to try to give pleasure rather than take. He'd never had complaints, but now he knew there was a difference as his arms sheltered her in ways that were new and tender and protective.

I didn't know it could be like this.

"Your husband?"

"He left . . . for Mississippi with his unit the day after we married." The glow in her eyes faded a little, and Rhys wanted to comfort. But he also wanted to know more. His eyes questioned.

The rosy blush on her face from lovemaking grew deeper, but she didn't say anything. She turned her gaze from him to overhead, where a hawk wheeled about in the sky, apparently spying some prey on the ground. It dived suddenly, out of sight, and she felt herself tremble. Rhys's eyes, which had softened during their lovemaking, were hard and curious again.

Dark. Secretive. Probing. Like the hawk seeking a victim to consume.

And yet his hands were still so incredibly gentle that he seemed to be two separate people. She didn't know which one to trust. But she already had, hadn't she? She had just given him a part of her, a part she had been unable to give to Mark, who had wanted it so badly. She didn't want to think about their wedding night four years ago. Mark's expression when she was unable to respond, when he realized she was trying, pretending. "It will come," he tried to assure her, but she had seen the desperate hurt on his face, and she knew the marriage had been a terrible mistake. She knew she had cheated him when she had only wanted to give to him a portion of the loyalty he had given to her and her family.

She hadn't had to try with Rhys Redding. She had never really believed the adage that for every woman there was one man. Not until she had seen Rhys in that hospital and something in her had so completely and fully experienced a stunning recognition, a . . . rightness, a belonging, even fate, if she wanted to be whimsical. She had tried to fight it, particularly after the confrontation with the deserters, because she recognized a ruthlessness in him she wasn't sure she could accept, but it was like trying to stay away from the sun, which gave and nurtured life.

But she couldn't talk about Mark. It still hurt, that loss, that guilt that she couldn't be as he had wanted.

She had wondered if there was something wrong with her as a woman, but now she knew there wasn't. Her body still quaked with the aftermath of sensations so splendid they could never be described, with the warmth he had brought to her soul. Still, despite those wonderful intimate moments of warmth and closeness and incredible feelings, she still felt the aloneness in him, the silent struggle to distance himself. She saw it in those hawk eyes of his.

But even hawks mated.

The hawk was back in the sky, a lifeless rabbit in its beak, and she suddenly realized that the noises around her had quieted. There was an ominous stillness in the wake of the bird's catch.

Susannah looked back at Rhys. His eyes, too, had been following the hawk. Her hand went up to his face, the stark harsh features that comprised such a compelling whole. The dark unfathomable eyes softened for a moment, and a muscle pulsed in his throat in an uncharacteristic show of emotion. "You remind me of a hawk," she said with a smile.

Those wonderful dark brows of his lifted.

"A nighthawk," she added.

"Do I dare ask why?" There was real amusement in his voice, not the mockery he usually hid behind.

She cocked her head to one side as she considered her next words.

"The hawk is a rather striking creature."

He laughed. For the first time since she'd met him, he actually laughed. A smile even reached his eyes, and she thought how extraordinarily it changed him, softened him, made him even . . . approachable. "I wonder how you mean that," he said after a moment, grinning.

Susannah thought about her words. She had meant in appearance, but the words could mean something else altogether. She smiled back at him. "Every way, I think."

"A good thing to remember, love," he said as his fingers wandered down the small of her back, making her tingle all over again.

Love. The word was lazily, sensually, said, and the tingle along her back moved inward, even though she knew he meant the word lightly. Still . . . it had a very nice sound, particularly in that deep-throated voice with the musical accent.

But she had no time to think about it because his

mouth had found hers, and he was quieting any further observations. She wondered for the briefest of seconds if that was the reason. Or was there another?

And then she didn't care.

The second time he made love to her, his movements were slow and tantalizing until she ached with wanting him again. Of course, she knew now she would always want him, want that fierce urgency that counterpointed moments of extreme tenderness and wonder. As always, she couldn't predict anything about him. She wondered if she ever would, or even wanted to.

He titillated and tormented her with his hands and mouth, and then slowly, ever so slowly, he entered her again, moving in slow deliberate strokes until she thought she would go mad with wanting, until the world swirled with such speed that she thought she would be swept from the universe. And then the shattering explosion rocked every fiber of her being with rolling waves of ecstasy, with a passion she never dreamed existed.

His body shuddered, and then he rolled over, bringing her with him, and she felt a warm, wonderful lassitude that cosseted and enveloped them like a thick feather comforter on a cold winter night.

She heard his heartbeat and felt his breath against her cheek and nothing in her life had ever seemed so natural, so right, so . . . meant to be.

She kissed him. With all the love and yearning and wonder he produced in her, she kissed him. Softly, slowly, deliberately, and she heard his sudden harsh breathing.

"Don't," he said almost as if he was in pain. "Don't think . . ."

Her tongue licked the tiny lines that fanned from

his eyes, that crinkled when he squinted against the sun. "Don't . . . what?"

"Think that there is more . . . than . . ."

He was struggling with words. He never struggled with words. That thought fastened in her mind because she knew what he was going to say. The knowledge of his difficulty in saying it softened the blow she knew was coming.

She waited, but he didn't continue. Instead, he moved away, and started to dress. He had to turn around to do so, and she saw faint ridges on his back, and a jagged scar on his side near his back. She wondered how her hands had missed it.

Rhys appeared unaware of her scrutiny as, very efficiently, he pulled on his shirt. A sheen of sweat almost immediately stuck his clothes to him, and she watched as he rolled up the shirt sleeves. Reluctantly, she reached for her own clothes. She could have stayed here forever.

She'd barely slipped the camisole over her head when he was there, fully dressed, his eyes unexpectedly clear, his expression surprisingly sheepish. His hands helped her with the riding habit, then expertly fastened her buttons. When he was through, he hesitated, then one of his hands went up to her hair, his fingers brushing it back. "You have lovely hair," he said. "Bloody hell, but I don't want to let it go."

It was the first real compliment he'd given her. "Thank you," she said solemnly.

He stood there for a moment, as if he didn't know what to say. "I didn't mean for . . . this to happen," he said finally.

"I know you didn't," she replied. *But I did.* She wanted to say the words, but she couldn't. Besides, he knew. She knew he knew. Just as he knew everything.

"We'd better go." But he didn't move. She looked too pretty, standing there on the hill with a breeze blowing through slightly tangled hair.

"Yes," she agreed, but neither did she move. She couldn't. Her legs had lost their ability to walk. She wanted to stay on this hill, where she used to come to dream, where now she knew she would always come to remember.

He shook his head slowly as if wondering at both of their sanities. He reached out and took her hand and he felt her fingers curl around his. Bloody hell. Almost roughly he pulled her to the horses and helped her mount. "I'll ride back with you. You shouldn't be out here alone."

Susannah shrugged. "I've always ridden by myself." She looked at the rifle she was carrying. "I can also shoot."

He grinned suddenly. "I remember." And he did remember the coolness with which she shot the man who tried to take their wagon. But she had aimed for the leg, where Rhys would have aimed for the heart. It was a distinct difference, and one that could matter in a crisis.

He didn't wait for a reply but strode to his own stallion, who was feeling every bit of his own maleness. Rhys sympathized. A few strokes on the horse's neck and it quieted. He would require a strong hand, however, and Rhys was not displeased at the notion. He needed something to take his mind from what had just happened. He needed time to put it into perspective. He needed time away from her. But he wasn't going to allow her to return alone. Not after what had happened here a few days ago. Wes was a bloody fool for allowing her to venture out alone—an even bigger fool for not suspecting what might happen.

He moved his horse next to Susannah's. "Why don't you sell Land's End?" he said suddenly. "It's too much for you and . . . Wes."

Her back went rigid. "I've been running it for four years."

"But you've never had this kind of trouble before?"

"We've had some."

"Sell, Susannah."

Her back went even stiffer. "It's not what Mark would have wanted. That's why—"

"Why what?"

But she hesitated. Her wide violet eyes looked suddenly wounded, almost mortally so. Her husband. Was it because she was thinking of Mark Fallon, gentleman? Was she wishing that it were he, not Rhys, who had introduced her to the pleasures of lovemaking? And why did the thought make him ache so? He had gotten what he wanted.

Bloody hell, he would soon be gone, anyway. It would be the best thing for her. And him. So why did he feel so infernally empty at the thought? This morning was . . . interesting, certainly interesting and even, well, remarkable. But nothing more than that.

He swore again. He hated arguing with himself. He hadn't done that in years, not since he subjugated his conscience. The last thing he needed now was to revive it.

"What is your brother doing?" he asked, surprised that Wes had allowed Susannah to ride alone, especially after the raid, not to speak of Carr's own aversion to Rhys.

"Surviving too much drink last night."

Rhys's lips twisted into a frown. "He's not going to be much help, you realize."

Susannah turned on him. "He'll be fine. It's just . . . coming home and finding the ranch, his—our home gone."

Rhys's silence said more than words. And he disliked himself for it. He should be giving her tender words, not additional worry. But he had to. He couldn't allow her to think this morning was more than it was, that it meant he would stay, that it meant he cared. He couldn't allow that at all.

He felt her gaze on him, that serious, determined,

yet vulnerable gaze that carved canyons in his heart. It amazed him the way she never asked for anything, not assurances, not promises, not hope. He wished she did.

And then her eyes turned back to the trail and they rode in silence until they came within sight of the Land's End ranch house. There was a group of mounted men in front of the porch, and Rhys saw Wes come out of the door. Even from here, he could see the belligerent, angry stance.

"Dear God," Susannah whispered. "The Martins." Before Rhys could react, she had kicked her mare into a gallop and was racing toward the house.

Rhys swore. Again. And followed.

Chapter 14

"Get off our land."

"Pretty strong words for a one-legged Yank . . .
'specially when we're here to do you a favor."

Wes glared at the five men, wishing he'd brought
out a gun with him. But the noise had surprised him
as he sipped a glass of whiskey. He had hoped it
would clear his head, but it had the opposite affect,
one he should have expected.

"Yeah," said one of the men. "We heard you was
home. Why don't you go north where you belong?"

Wes fought unsuccessfully to control his rage as he
replied, "And what were you doing during the war,
Hardy, except thieving and murdering?" Maybe, he
noted in quick passing, he *did* have some emotions
left.

The man went for his gun, but the rider next to
him raised his hand to stop him. His eyes went around
the ranch, stopping momentarily to study three men
at the corral who had stopped working to watch, and
then at the two riders galloping toward them. "We
don't want any trouble, Carr," he said in a silky smooth
voice. "We just want to talk to Miz Susannah. We
heard she was back. Heard the bad news about Mark.
Sure am sorry about that." The gleam in his eye belied
the sentiment.

He turned around as Susannah, followed by Rhys, reined up to them.

"What do you want here, Lowell?" Susannah said.

The speaker, the oldest of the men, smiled ingratiatingly. "We heard Mark had died. We came to express our sympathy." He turned to Rhys, his gaze instantly going to his waist and obviously noting the absence of a gun belt. The man's eyes weighed, judged, and obviously found Rhys unimportant. He turned back to Susannah. "I also wanted to tell you how sorry we were to hear about your old ranch. Lightning or some such, I guess. As neighbors, we came to make an offer to help out."

"I'm listening," Susannah said calmly, unemotionally, but Rhys saw the fire in those violet eyes. He had seen it there before.

"I'll buy both ranches. Pay you a damn good price." He beamed at her. "You can go live in Austin real good."

"What do you consider a good price?"

"Well, considering the debts these places have, I think five thousand is real generous."

Susannah laughed. "Our stock is worth more than that."

"You sure about that, Miz Susannah?"

"Even after those you've rustled, Lowell." Her voice was low and deadly now. "And as for lightning, I guess I know who made it."

Rhys had reluctantly admired Susannah almost from the first moment he had met her, but never so much as now. None of the wistful girl he'd been with earlier showed. There was a core of steel where softness had been. He sat back in the saddle, looking as harmless as he could, and enjoyed the startled, confused look on the face of the man who had obviously expected her to accept.

"'You ain't got any proof of that, Miz Susannah."

"Mrs. Fallon to you," she said sharply. "And we will get proof. In the meantime, get off our land."

"You just think about it, *Mrs.* Fallon. The offer is good for a week. You think about it real good. How are you and this ... cripple gonna manage?"

Susannah looked at Rhys, and so did the man who was speaking. "Who are you?" he asked.

Rhys ignored the man and turned to Susannah. "I thought you said there weren't many savages left in the colonies," he said in his haughtiest manner, his eyes flickering over the three men contemptuously.

Anger flashed in the eyes of the three Martins. It was easy to tell they were brothers. They had the same fleshy features, the same cold, pale blue eyes. Rhys had seen more attractive snakes, but he fought to keep his face bland.

"A foreigner," one of the Martins said with a sneer.

"A dandy," another scorned, as if brushing away a mettlesome fly, and despite his worn clothes, Rhys suddenly did look like a dandy, Susannah thought. Perhaps it was the supercilious expression on his face, or the way he was holding his body. He looked like anything but the dangerous man she knew he could be. She still wondered why, while at the same time observing what a magnificent actor he was. And then another unwelcome thought wound its way in her mind. How much acting had he been doing in the past few hours? She wiped it away impatiently. *Concentrate on the Martins.*

Her hand unconsciously went to the stock of the rifle she always carried. She knew the Martins, even if Rhys didn't, and they wouldn't be above shooting an unarmed man. But Rhys looked comfortably unaware that he had insulted about the lowest, meanest sons of bitches in Texas.

But the oldest of the brothers had turned to her. "You better teach your visitor some manners, particularly if he don't wear a gun. Ain't safe out here without a gun."

Rhys gave him a blinding smile. "I thought I was exploring a *civilized* country."

"Exploring," another Martin guffawed. "He's exploring."

But the main spokesman ignored his brother's sneer. "You saying we aren't civilized?"

"You're wearing guns," Rhys observed as he grimaced in distaste. "Only barbarians carry weapons, now." From the corner of his eye, he noted that Wes had slipped into the ranch house and had returned with a shotgun while the Martins had focused all their attention on the newcomer. It took all his concentration to perfect his role, even as his mind was computing how long it would take to reach the knife strapped just above his ankle. One long stretch and a toss.

He'd decided on this tactic as he followed Susannah on the gallop up to the house. The five men were heavily armed, the men left in the corral area were no more than boys, and he had quickly observed that Wes was not armed. He knew he was very good at the useless English dandy role. God knew he had seen enough of them in London. He knew just how far he could push, how far he could goad to distract the visitors and give Wes a chance to get a weapon. At least, he usually knew how far he could go. Now he wondered, as the men looked at him as if he were a bug they would enjoy squashing.

"You heard my sister." The men looked back toward the porch, at Wes standing on one crutch while balancing the shotgun in his hand. "Get off our land."

The diversion gave Susannah time to unstrap her own rifle from the saddle and point it at the spokesman. "You heard my brother, Lowell."

"One week," the man said. "I'll give you one

week." He gave Rhys a malevolent look. "And you better make tracks out of here. I don't like foreigners."

"I'm devastated," Rhys replied with somewhat of a gentle grin which prompted a twinkle in Susannah's eyes. It quickly disappeared, however, as her fingers seemed to tighten on the trigger.

Lowell Martin gave her a long stare, then nodded to the other four men. They turned their horses and trotted away.

Wes watched as they disappeared down the dusty road, and then lowered the shotgun and leaned against the wall of the house as Rhys dismounted and helped Susannah dismount.

She hurried to Wes, while Rhys followed lazily, prepared for a barrage of questions. He wasn't disappointed.

Wes glared at him. "Where have you been?" His eyes took in Susannah, lingered on a blade of grass in her hair and the sudden flush on her cheeks.

"Exploring," Rhys said with a mocking, satisfied look he knew was going to madden Wes. But he didn't like the smell of liquor on the man's breath, nor the way Wes had evidently been taken by surprise. "While you were drinking, I see."

"What in the hell are you playing at?"

Rhys knew exactly what he meant. Susannah. But he pretended otherwise. "Oh, that little performance. Giving you some time to do what you bloody hell should have been doing. Looking out for this place." Despite the lightness of his tone, the undercurrent was sharp, like a razor's edge.

Wes glared at him before his eyes dropped. A hand went up and rubbed his unshaved jaw. He looked back up. "You're right, Redding. You're right about that, but I warned you before. Stay away from my sister."

"And what are you going to do if I don't?" Rhys deliberately goaded him.

"I'll kill you."

"You don't have the guts anymore." Rhys turned around and saw Susannah's now ashen face, eyes that begged him to stop. He was suddenly angry, very angry, with her, with himself. By saying nothing, she was denying this morning. Denying those hours. Denying him. It was clear she was ashamed of those moments this morning. Well, why not?

He abruptly turned and strode over to the horse, mounting without using the stirrups. Without looking back, he spurred his mount into a gallop.

Rhys rested on his mount, his right leg hooked over the front of the saddle. He was still using the cavalry saddle, rather than the heavier ranch saddles with the horn in front.

The river was below him. He had followed the Martins for a distance, making sure they were indeed headed away, and then he had turned back toward the river.

He didn't understand the anger boiling up inside him. And he sure as bloody hell didn't like it. Anger destroyed his cool detachment. Anger meant mistakes. Anger accomplished nothing. He'd learned that long ago. And he also knew it was unreasonable. What had he expected, anyway? That she declare to the world that she had slept with him?

He was *never* unreasonable. Never, until now, dammit. But all his long-tamed emotions were exploding now, like a bottle of wine whose fermentation had gone awry. One ingredient too many had been thrown in the process.

Susannah.

The ever-changing Susannah. The feisty Susannah. The tender Susannah. The passionate Susannah. Damn her!

He had planned to go to Austin tomorrow, to see about getting his funds. He had not really planned beyond that. But the Martins today changed that. Leaving Susannah and Wes Carr now would be like leaving newborn kittens outside a wolf's den. He knew he couldn't leave Susannah to fight them alone, and fight she would. Nor, he knew, could he leave Wes Carr to their dubious mercy.

Why, he didn't know. He had traveled with Nathan. Fought with him. Adventured with him. Learned from him. But he'd never felt one ounce of obligation toward him. He had never even liked him, although he had admired the man's total lack of conscience. They had been convenient to each other. Nothing more—even after many years. He had always known Nathan wouldn't hesitate to kill him if it was profitable. Rhys had always made sure it wasn't profitable.

So why after two months did he feel responsible for a man who obviously disliked everything he was?

He dismounted and walked to the water's edge, picked up a stone and skipped it across the water as he watched little circles form in the river, widen, and then disappear.

A week. They probably had a week before any more trouble. He would go to Austin as planned, and make arrangements for some money to be transferred. Perhaps stay a day or two. Even try a woman. Get Susannah out of his system. Lust. That's all it was. He had simply been too long without a woman.

And Wes Carr? Bloody hell, but that damnable wound must have included a crack in the man's brain, to be drinking now.

Rhys reassured himself. A few days away from the whole bloody crew would reestablish his basic set of principles: Never get involved, never be weak enough to care for someone else, and finally, always be on guard against both calamitous foibles.

That's all he needed. A couple of days.

· · ·

Susannah knew he was gone even before she was told. It was as if a grayness had draped the sun.

She didn't know what time he had returned the night before, or when he had eaten. But Miguel said he'd left before dawn this morning, and asked the route to Austin.

He didn't say whether he would return.

She wasn't sure he would this time.

She hadn't missed that flare of anger and something else in his eyes yesterday afternoon. A kind of disappointment. In her.

Perhaps she should have said something to Wes, insisted that Rhys stay in the house, defended the man she'd been with. But Wes's self-confidence still seemed so fragile. She was afraid openly defying him would send him back to the bottle.

Erin! She wondered whether Erin had heard they were back. The Martins had certainly heard, and word spread rapidly among the families along the Colorado River. She had seen Erin over the past years, had reported to her about Wes, as much as she knew anyway. And Erin was still waiting, despite a family bitterly opposed to any match between her and the man they considered a turncoat. Susannah was only too aware that Wes's letters to Erin had been intercepted by her family until she, Susannah, had delivered them in person in secret meeting places.

But she knew Wes had no intention of going through with an engagement that was made before the war, before Erin's family learned he was going with the North, before Wes had lost his leg. She also was aware that Wes still loved the fiery redheaded daughter of the largest plantation owner in the county. She had seen it in the pain in his eyes during the days in the hospital, whenever she mentioned Erin's name.

Now that his small legacy—the small ranch house, along with most of the cattle—was gone, Wes would be even more convinced than before that he no longer had anything to offer Erin.

Susannah suspected that Erin and her family would also be in financial straits. Much of their wealth had been tied up in slaves and cotton. They had not been able to get much of the cotton to market in the past years, and now slavery would be a thing of the past. The MacDougal family might well be ruined now, and also fodder for the ambitious Martins.

Susannah had been barely tolerated by Erin's parents; she had been saved from complete ostracism by her marriage to Mark, but still branded by her relationship to Wes. She knew Mr. MacDougal remained a rabid secessionist and Confederate, along with his son-in-law, Sam, who helped him operate what was left of the plantation. Sean MacDougal's only son, Erin's brother, had been killed at Glorieta Pass with Mark's brother. Now, there were only two daughters remaining: Heather, who had married Sam Harris, and Erin.

Erin, despite all the pressure Sean and Mary MacDougal had placed on her, had absolutely refused any courtship offers during the past four years, insisting that her engagement to Wesley Carr was still valid and, if she couldn't have Wes, she wouldn't have anyone.

They were a fine pair, she and Wes, Susannah thought. She had been unable to love a man who loved her, and now she loved someone who didn't love her. And Wes . . . he loved and was loved, but he couldn't accept it. Lunatics. They were both lunatics.

She still didn't completely understand how she had fallen so completely in love with her nighthawk, with a man who was such a thorough mystery. A man who obviously wanted no attachments or commitments. A man she wasn't even sure she would see again.

It didn't bear thinking about. She turned her mind, instead, to the problem of the Martins. A week. They might have a week before any more violence. She needed to talk to other families about what had happened in the months she'd been gone. Perhaps now the war was over, they would be willing to band together to fight the Martins.

Wes, thank heavens, had gone out with Jaime this morning to pasture the horses. He had not started drinking again last night, not, at least, that she knew of. He had been unusually subdued this morning after Miguel's visit and hearing that Rhys Redding and what few belongings he had were gone.

She had almost gone with them. She had ridden with the hands for the last three years, but again she thought better of the idea. Even as the thought chafed at her hard-earned independence and authority, nothing was more important than restoring Wes's confidence and sense of worth. So she had watched them ride off, leaving only two men to take care of the remaining stock and protect the house.

She'd prowled through the house restlessly before deciding to visit Erin, and Jacob's Crossing, the small trade center that was optimistically called a town. Hannah needed some supplies, and Susannah needed information—and something to do before she went entirely loco. She would take the buckboard. And her rifle. And a pistol.

And she would banish thoughts of a dark Welshman from her mind. She would!

The MacDougal home needed a coat of paint. It looked much shabbier than four years ago, when the house was the showcase of the county. Fences needed repairing; the cotton fields were only partially planted and nearly empty of workers. The slave cabins looked deserted.

The MacDougals were one of a number of slave-holding families in the county, probably the largest and, until the war, the wealthiest. But like everyone in Texas, they had operated principally on a barter system: Seed bought from a store was repaid in cotton, and so forth. When their slaves heard of the defeats in the south and learned there was safe refuge in Mexico, they started slipping off. Now, there were no hands to bring in the cotton, and thus pay debts. Like Wes and herself, the MacDougals were in danger of losing what they had left.

As she drove up, a figure rose from a stooping position in the vegetable field, and Susannah saw it was Erin. Susannah also recognized Heather and Sam as well as one of the house servants bending over in the field. Erin waved and walked over toward her, pushing back a wet red curl from her face where it had escaped from a sunbonnet. She looked like anything but the well-dressed, laughing girl Wes had known.

But as Erin approached, she smiled wearily. "All but a few of the field hands left when they heard the war was over," she explained. "Papa had to promise an acre of land to those who stayed, but they're not enough to tend even a quarter of the cotton, much less the garden. We're helping as much as we can. Have you heard from Wes?" The sentences almost came as one as her face scrunched up in worry.

"He's home," Susannah said, as she climbed down from the buckboard.

Erin closed her eyes, and Susannah knew it was in grateful prayer. When she opened them again, they were filled with worry. "He's . . . all right? Why didn't he come with you? When can I see him?" Her hand went to her hair, which was straggling from an untidy knot, with a kind of desperation, and Susannah saw blisters on her fingers.

Susannah hesitated. "He was wounded, Erin. Things are a little difficult for him now."

"Wounded? How?"

"His right leg, Erin. He lost it."

"Dear Mother," Erin whispered, then in a stronger voice, "but at least he's alive. I have to see him."

Susannah bit her lip nervously. "I have to warn you, Erin. He thinks . . . that he should let you go, that . . . he can't take care of you." She couldn't use Wes's words. *Cripple.*

"Oh, he does, does he?" Erin said, her voice low and determined. "And me waiting this long!"

Susannah had to grin at the dangerous glint in Erin's eye. Erin had always had a temper. She'd struck a blow at Wes's stomach once, when Wes and Mark had had too much to drink. Susannah had always thought they made a good match, but now she had to make sure Erin wouldn't hurt Wes. "Then it doesn't matter to you?"

"Of course, it matters," Erin said. "But not the way you mean. It matters because I know how much he must be hurting, because I can almost feel it myself. But that doesn't mean I'm going to let him make me a spinster. I told him before the war it was him or no one. And I sure don't intend on that happening. I'll ride back with you."

"Your family?"

"They won't like it, but then they never have," Erin said frankly. "I never felt about the war like they did. I never did like slavery, and I'm glad it's gone," she added defiantly. "Even if I do have to work in the fields." But then her face fell slightly. "I don't even know if we can keep this place. We haven't been able to pay taxes the last two years."

"The Martins are buying up everything, I heard," Susannah said cautiously.

"Whatever they don't steal," Erin said angrily. "They took our last crop of cotton, said they would see it got to a Mexican port. Their men came back empty-handed, said it had been stolen by bandits. Not their responsibility. Now the bank says they've made inquiries about buying the plantation . . ."

"How many others?" Susannah said. She had been fairly isolated the past year. She'd heard rumors from her own men, but the other landowners hadn't approved of her, her family, nor a woman running Mark's ranch.

"I could name a dozen."

"We think Lowell Martin burned down Wes's ranch."

Erin nodded her head. "I heard about that— through closed doors, of course. Papa won't mention Wes's name in my hearing."

"Have there been others?"

Erin nodded. "No proof, but the Embrys' stock was run off, their field trampled. They sold out, ten cents on the dollar, I heard."

"Do you think people will band together?"

"You mean, sort of a vigilante force, like a few years ago?"

Susannah nodded.

"I don't know," Erin said. "Everyone has had so many losses ..."

"Wes—"

"Wes is the last person to propose it," Erin said, her eyes clouding. "There's still a lot of hatred." She didn't have to say that much of it came from her own family. "But Mark ... you went to Virginia to see about Mark?"

"He's dead, Erin. In Virginia."

Erin impulsively hugged her. "I'm so sorry, Sue."

Susannah felt her heart squeeze tight against the expected pain. They had done so much together at one time, Wes and Erin, she and Mark. Dances and barn raisings, picnics and church socials. She struggled to speak. "That's how I found Wes. He was in Libby Prison in Richmond."

"Prison?" Erin's voice was soft. "Oh, Susannah."

"I was lucky to find him."

"And you came all the way across country? By yourselves?"

"We had some help."

Erin looked curious.

"A ... Welshman. He was in prison with Wes. I think he's been good for Wes."

"A Welshman? What was he doing in a Confederate prison?"

"I don't know exactly."

Erin looked even more puzzled, but then her concern for Wes eclipsed her interest in a stranger. "Can we go now?"

"I have to stop at Jacob's Crossing for some supplies. And Wes went out this morning with Jaime. I don't know when he'll be back."

"I don't care," Erin said stubbornly. "I want to be there when he comes."

"You might not get the warmest of welcomes. And he'll probably want to kill me."

"I'll take care of that," Erin said with supreme confidence. "Let me tell Heather I'm going to have dinner with you."

She hurried away before Susannah could say any more, and Susannah saw her arguing with her sister in the field, saw the chin tilt defensively before her friend returned. "Come inside while I change clothes," she said, "I must look terrible."

"Is it wise to delay?" Susannah said.

"No," Erin said with a grin. "But nothing can keep me away from Wes. Not Papa, not Sam, not even God. And I sure don't want Wes to see me like this."

Susannah understood that sentiment only too well. She remembered the times she had looked like a grubby field-worker during the long trip from Virginia to Texas, and how much she had wanted to look pretty for Rhys. But she worried about Sean MacDougal.

"Papa's not here," Erin said conspiratorially, "and I

don't think Sam knows that Wes is back yet. But we best hurry."

The usual house servants weren't around, and Susannah followed Erin upstairs and waited while she washed and then changed from the faded cotton dress into a simple but fetching blue dress, which deepened the blue of her eyes. She brushed her hair and tied it back with a matching blue ribbon and put gloves on her reddened hands. Her cheeks were already flushed with something akin to joy, and her eyes were the color of a summer sky. Susannah only hoped that Wes wouldn't quash the happiness in them.

The changing of clothes had taken only a few moments. Erin was obviously impatient. It had been more than four years since Wes rode away to war. She caught Susannah's hand, and Susannah found herself skipping down the steps like a schoolgirl. She understood Erin's impatience. If only she, Susannah, knew whether Rhys Redding was coming back. If only. If only so many things.

Hannah greeted Erin with a smile. "I've missed you, Miss Erin."

"I hope Wes feels that way," Erin said, showing nervousness for the first time. She had asked a million questions about Wes during the buckboard trip to Jacob's Crossing and then to the ranch. How did he look? How did he feel? Did he say anything about her? Did he say anything about the past four years? Did he plan to rebuild the Carr homestead?

Susannah only wished she knew some of the answers.

"They should be back soon," Hannah said. "Can I get you some lemonade?"

"Lemonade," Susannah sighed. "It's been months."

"I bought these lemons four weeks ago," Hannah said. "I've been saving them for a special occasion.

Don't know of any better time, now you and your brother are home." There was a sudden silence. *There would have been a better time, had Mark returned with them.* The words were unsaid but still seemed to echo in the room.

Erin started to pace and suggested they go outside and wait. Susannah thought that would be a very bad idea indeed, but she didn't say so. She was desperately afraid that Wes would bolt when he saw Erin, something easier to do on horseback than on crutches. She convinced herself that Wes couldn't resist Erin if they were in the same room. Her reluctance must have shown, however, because Erin sat back down.

She tried to make small talk, but it was difficult. Erin kept asking about the trip across country, and the shadow of Rhys Redding seemed to loom over the room. How to talk about the trip, the deserters, the long days and sometimes longer nights without mentioning, and thinking about her nighthawk? And that was altogether too painful.

"Where is he?" Erin said suddenly when a silence fell between them.

"Wes?"

"No, silly. The man who came with you."

Susannah tried to shrug carelessly. "He went to Austin."

"Is he coming back?"

Is he? He had to. "I don't know," she said.

"Tell me about him."

"There's not that much to tell. He's Welsh." Even to Susannah, her words seem to carry a special softness. She hoped Erin didn't hear it.

"I've never met anyone from Wales. Is he very different?"

Dear God, how different he was. How completely different. "A little."

"You aren't saying anything, Sue."

I know. I can't. "There's nothing to tell. He just

wanted to see the West." Susannah looked at Erin and suddenly realized her friend wasn't listening at all. She was just asking questions to mask her nervousness.

"It will be all right," she said in a soft voice.

"Will it?" Erin said. "He can be so stupidly stubborn sometimes. And it's been so long."

Susannah was saved from answering by the sound of hoofbeats coming into the yard. At least, she hoped she was saved. She might have just disturbed another beehive.

Susannah heard the clump of the crutches on the porch and held her breath. She felt Erin's nervousness, and her friend reached for Susannah's arm and clutched it tightly. Despite her outward calm, Erin was obviously desperately afraid.

Susannah knew that fear, that uncertainty. She had been feeling it all day. She had felt it for days, weeks. It had to do with caring about someone you weren't sure cared about you. She couldn't think about the word love. She just couldn't. Susannah forced her thoughts back to this moment.

The door opened, and Wes came in. His clothes were dusty, his forehead wet with sweat, his dark hair plastered against his head now he'd taken off his hat. He looked terribly tired on the crutches, as if he was holding on to them for dear life.

His eyes went directly to Erin, as if some unknown force had directed them there. He straightened, as much as he could, and his face went white, his dark blue eyes turning as frosty as ice reflecting a dark blue evening sky.

His voice, when it came, was grating.

"What in the hell are you doing here?"

Chapter 15

Rhys tried. He honestly tried. He visited each of the saloons. He eyed the women there with a knowing look that invoked any number of fluttering eyelashes, simmering expressions, and open invitations.

He tried to think their eagerness flattering, though he knew it was part of their business. Still, their seductive attempts seemed to be more ardent on his behalf than on others'.

Some of the attraction, he knew, could be his clothes. His first stop in town was a haberdashery, though he was surprised to find one in this young capital of Texas. It felt bloody good to be in decent clothing again, one luxury he'd always enjoyed. He liked the feel of good cloth on his back and a tailored fit. He liked the contrast of fine black broadcloth against the soft linen of a shirt. He used, as payment, some of the gold coins he had found on the deserters in the Carolinas.

He had no scruples about doing so. When his own funds came in, he would replace the money and give it to Susannah and Carr. In the meantime, respectable clothes were as much a necessity as the horse he had stolen. He needed to look the part of a wealthy Englishman to convince a banker to go to all the trouble of tranferring funds, and perhaps risk an advance.

And he could be bloody imposing when he wished. He was very good at aping the arrogance of an earl or baron. He was even better at looking down his nose at recalcitrant tradesmen.

Armed with a bath, a fresh shave and haircut, and a new set of clothes, he located the largest bank in town. A clerk's glance at the tall, distinguished-looking figure with the disdainful features gave him immediate access to the middle-aged banker. He had to use his real name, but at this distance there shouldn't be any connection between him and an escaped blockade runner who'd killed a Union officer in Virginia.

The bank manager, a Josiah Baker, had been more than eager to help, particularly when Rhys introduced himself as Lord Rhys Redding and named the amount he wanted transferred. "Are you staying in our area, Lord—?"

"Mr. Redding," Rhys said condescendingly. "I don't want anyone to know of the title."

"Mr. Redding," the banker agreed readily, greedily. "Do you plan to stay in our area?"

"I'm considering it," Rhys said, knowing from experience that the title and prospect of future business would speed cooperation. The man obviously coveted his business, especially such a large sum deposited in his establishment; and he, like so many Americans, seemed awed by a title.

Rhys felt absolutely no compunction at claiming the latter. It was, after all, only a small lie. His father had been a lord, and Rhys had once owned a great estate. Little matter that he'd been a bastard and had won the estate on a bet.

"I hope you will consider our bank then for your future business," Baker said. "We're considered the soundest establishment in Texas. Not many banks are solvent now with the war . . ."

Rhys took a proffered cigar, and sniffed it with some disdain before accepting a light. "That is why I chose to come here. You can expedite this, can you not?"

"Communication and shipping are not yet back to normal," Baker explained. "We don't exactly know what to expect, but I'll do everything possible. Still, it will be eight weeks at least, more like twelve. A ship to England, authorization, and then a return ship."

Rhys took a long draw on the cigar and leaned back carelessly in the chair. Bloody hell, but it tasted good after the past tobaccoless months. "I would like my business kept private," he told Baker.

"Of course, Mr. Redding. We are very protective of our customers." He eyed Rhys carefully as if trying to come to a decision, and then obviously made one. "If you need a small advance . . . ?"

Rhys gave him a glacial stare. "That won't be necessary." Not now, but he'd laid the groundwork for the future if necessary.

"Of course not," the manager hurried to respond. "Where can I reach you when the money arrives?"

"I'm staying at a ranch south of here. I will check with you frequently."

"Of course," the banker said. It was obvious the visitor was not going to say any more about his current residence. The banker chalked it up to the man's request for anonymity and confidentiality. He almost drooled at the prospect. The foreigner must have some kind of big business in mind to want the kind of money he was transferring, and the bank was in need of wealthy customers, now that the war had ruined so many of its old customers. He tried to restrain his eagerness.

"A drink, Mr. Redding?"

Rhys considered. That kind of familiarity would be unheard of in England, but here it might turn to his advantage. He might well need money before his funds arrived. He agreed with a patronizing nod. He was bloody damn good at this, he thought, as the man anxiously pulled out a bottle of whiskey. Rhys knew it was quality stock from its rich dark color.

As the banker poured healthy portions into two glasses, Rhys sat back and enjoyed the cigar, his gaze absorbing everything, the banker's slight nervousness, the stack of papers on the man's desk.

"Any news of the war?" he asked.

"Kirby Smith finally surrendered," the banker said. "Federal troops are expected anytime. I didn't like Abe Lincoln, but it looks like the South is going to pay dearly for his death." He handed the drink to Rhys. "God knows what we can expect. Damned firebrands brought this on us. My sympathies were with Sam Houston . . . a lot of people's in Austin were. I think Texas's decision to secede was what eventually killed him." He took a drink, obviously wondering whether he'd said too much. "But Texas has a great future. A great future."

"To the future," Rhys said as he raised his glass and watched the banker visibly relax.

"The future, Mr. Redding." The banker beamed.

One mission accomplished, Rhys went in search of another kind of fulfillment, or at least momentary oblivion. He did not want to think of Susannah, or the morning he had spent with her, or believe it had been any different from any other romantic encounter. A woman, any kind of woman, would prove that to be so.

And so he had prowled the saloons of Austin, positive that one of the available women would stir him as Susannah had, would prove that nothing in his life had really changed.

But it had. He usually liked blondes, but every blonde he saw left him as cold as a January night in Wales. He put his arm around an abundantly endowed body, only to be reminded of Susannah's lithe one. No matter what he did, nothing in his body responded, certainly not the part which had always risen before to the occasion.

He felt like a bloody damned eunuch.

He had planned to stay a few days, to savor the delights of a city, no matter how rustic. But by midnight, he knew it was useless. He wanted none of the painted women. He wanted none of the obvious charms. He wanted no one—except Susannah.

Rhys left the saloons early. Even sober, he thought disdainfully of himself. He didn't even want to drink, because now he thought of Wes as well. He wasn't going to bury himself in drink. But by God, he sure understood why Wes Carr did it. He felt every bit the cripple that Carr believed himself to be. That's what came of involving yourself in someone else's life.

And now he had bloody damn little choice. Twelve weeks. Twelve bloody damn weeks before his money would arrive. Twelve weeks in which he had to do something about the Martins.

Despite his intention to linger a few days, Rhys decided otherwise as he mounted the steps to his hotel room. Whores were not going to help. A change of scenery was not going to help. Drink was not going to help.

He had to control his own destiny, his own life, just as Carr was going to have to control his. He had to face his own demons and defeat them.

He had to prove to himself that Susannah was nothing but an aberration, a brief interlude that had nothing to do with the real Rhys Redding, with the heartless, soulless Rhys Redding he knew and understood and accepted. And the only way he could do that, he knew, was to show her exactly what he was, in the harshest possible way.

Erin didn't flinch as Wes glared at her after stomping into the room and demanding what in the hell she was doing there.

She gave Wes back as good as she received. "To see that you keep your word," she said.

"Forget it," Wes said. "I give you your freedom."

"I don't want it."

For a moment, Wes's eyes softened, then grew hard again. "I don't want to marry you, Erin. I've outgrown you." The words were purposely cruel, and all three in the room knew it.

Only Susannah felt Erin's pain as her friend's hand dug even further into hers.

"Have you?" Erin challenged softly. "Don't you?"

Wes moved farther inside the house and sat down in one of the large chairs.

"I've changed, Erin. The boy you knew no longer exists."

"Neither does the girl," Erin said. She took off her gloves and showed her hands to Wes. "I've been working in the fields with my sister. I've learned to make my own clothes and to cook. Does that bother you? Do my hands bother you? We've all changed, Wes. We've had to. But one thing hasn't. I've loved you all my life. I'll never love anyone else."

"It's no good, Erin. I have nothing. Not even two legs to be able to build again."

Erin couldn't stand it a moment longer. She rose, went over to his side and sat on the arm of his chair. Her hand loved his face, every plane of it, every curve, every new crease. She leaned down and kissed him, slowly. Very slowly until his lips responded. Hungrily. Even desperately.

"I love you," Erin whispered, when finally their lips parted. "I missed you so much. I prayed and prayed you would come home." She felt tears well behind her eyes, but they weren't for him. They were for all the years and days and minutes they had lost.

"It's no good," Wes said. "I can't tie you to a . . . cripple."

"I already am tied to you," she said. "Don't you know that yet?"

"Your family—"

"Didn't change the way I felt before, and certainly won't now," she said.

"We have another war on our hands. I don't want you involved."

"Papa's involved, too, The Martins and their ... friends ... want his land, too."

"Dammit, Erin. It won't work. I don't have anything left. I have to start all over again, and I don't know whether I can."

"As for starting over, we're all going to have to do that, my family included. And you can do anything you want to do."

Her lips nuzzled boldly at his, and he wanted to take them. He wanted that more than anything in his life, but he couldn't. He couldn't do that to her. He couldn't do it to himself.

"Except walk on two legs, or help a colt foal, or brand cattle, or so many other things I took for granted." Including making love. How could he make love to her now? How could he wrap his legs around her as he had once dreamed of doing? He looked around for Susannah, for help, but she had disappeared. He felt Erin's hand trail down his face, and he closed his eyes. It had been so long, so very long since he had touched her. He had tried to wipe her from his mind, ever since the amputation, but it had never quite worked. She had been there too long, for four years. He had thought of her during the long lonesome nights, during the battles when he had tried to keep alive for her, during the endless marches and the waiting, always the waiting.

She had always been so full of life, her eyes dancing with fun and teasing and love. She'd made his heart jump just by entering the room, had banished a bad mood by smiling. But she was accustomed to the best things in life, to servants and money, and he didn't even have a house now to bring her to.

And he didn't think he could bear to let her see the ugly stump, the wound that still drained on occasion, that still kept him awake at night with sensations in parts of him that were no longer there. He couldn't ask her to share the nights with all their nightmares, the nights when he thrashed hopelessly against memories.

"Go home, Erin," he said flatly.

"Sue invited me for dinner."

"Then have dinner with her," he said rudely. "I'll eat in the bunkhouse."

"Damn you, Wes. We're engaged."

"I'm breaking it."

"You can't. You still love me."

"No," he denied.

Erin leaned over, her lips touching his, lightly at first and then with a need that had been building for four years. She felt his resistance at first, but then his mouth gave way, meeting hers with a violence that spoke of his own need and frustration.

She felt his arms go around her, arms that were still strong and protective and wonderful. She knew when the blaze started deep within him, the blaze that had always been between them since they'd first touched as man and woman. It had been so hard to wait, to keep from satisfying the craving between them, but she had always known someday they would marry. That had made his absence bearable.

Now the blaze was alive again, strong and bright, brighter than ever, because she had come so close to losing him, because she'd had four years of waiting and praying, of crying herself to sleep because of loneliness.

Now he was here, and she was not going to let him go. She felt her own desperation reflect in him. His lips clung to hers with sudden fierce urgency, and she

sensed the coiled tension in his body, saw the taut line
of his face as he tried, but failed, at restraint.

"I love you," she whispered into his mouth, and
heard his agonized groan. Any doubt that she might
have had about his own feelings disappeared then. She
knew she could conquer that foolish feeling of nobility
he apparently had about marrying her. She had never
let anything stand in the way of loving him. She
wouldn't now.

Wes pulled her tightly against him, unable to do
otherwise at the moment. He had waited so long that
now he couldn't stop, not with the warm contact of her
body with his, or the sweet fragrance of her hair, or its
silky feel against his skin.

He wanted to hold her forever now that he had her
here, and for the briefest of seconds he allowed himself a fleeting hope, the possibility that somehow . . .

With that very fragile thought hanging between
them, he reveled in her closeness and moved his
mouth to hers again, bruising her with the violence of
a kiss that grew in intensity. His tongue found its way
into her mouth, probing.

It was all there for the asking. She leaned into his
arms and responded in ways she'd never responded
before, casting aside that very thin veneer of ladylike
conduct her mother had drilled into her all her life.
He needed her. She knew it. If only he would, could,
accept that. Accept her. Accept that together they
could do anything!

She had slid down from the arm of the chair to the
edge of the seat. Almost unconsciously she slipped
over to his lap, leaning her body into his, unaware that
her movement jammed the stump of his right leg
against the leg of the chair. He couldn't stop the agonized gasp that came from his mouth, and she moved
swiftly off, her face mirroring his pain as she realized
what had happened.

"Oh, Wes," she whispered, her body trembling

with the need that had sprung between them in those minutes, and now with the knowledge she had caused him pain. "What can I do?"

"Go home," he said with a rasp in his voice. "Just get the hell away from me."

"No." Her blue eyes were determined as she stared at the beloved features. They were as she remembered: strong, even features made even more striking by suffering, by the lines etched around his eyes and mouth. His eyes were a dark blue, and they had changed more than a little. She remembered them as being lighter, always full of adventure and mischief. But now they brooded, just as his mouth had changed from when it had easily laughed to the now grim set. He was right. He had changed. But then so had she. She had grown in these past four years of waiting. She had learned what was important. And that was Wesley Carr.

"Please." He was almost begging, and it broke her heart. Wes Carr had never begged in his life. Her resolve crumbled as she realized she probably wouldn't accomplish any more here today. She knew the leg was still paining him from the way he sat so stiffly, as if the slightest move would bring on additional waves of suffering.

"All right," she said. "For now. Just for now. But I've waited for you these four years, Colonel Carr, and I have no intention of being jilted now." Before he could say anything, she leaned down and very, very carefully kissed him. A long yearning, loving kiss that made it very clear she meant each and every word she'd said.

And before he could protest, she gracefully slipped from the room.

Rhys stared at the ranch house a long time before spurring his mount toward it. Rings of smoke rose from the chimney fireplace, and it looked inviting.

He remembered Ridgely, the great estate he had won in a series of wagers. The manor house had been six times the size of the home before him, but it certainly had little warmth. He'd grown to hate the house, perhaps because it had blood on it, the blood of the man who had committed suicide when Rhys had assumed ownership. He had sat in that lonely derelict of a place, thinking that perhaps it might win him acceptance in the circles he thought to invade. But it hadn't. He hadn't the skill or interest to run it, and the fields had grown ragged and bare, and the tenants sullen and lazy. He had been relieved, truth be told, to turn it over to the rightful owner.

Land's End looked like a real home. Another man's home. Mark Fallon's home. Just as Susannah had been Fallon's wife.

Rhys had been a pretender once. He didn't fancy doing it again.

Twelve weeks. Twelve weeks to solve her problem with the Martins. Twelve weeks until he could do anything, or go anywhere, he wanted.

Twelve weeks with Susannah! He couldn't let her know he was staying at her ranch for her sake. He didn't want to appear a hero in her eyes, when he was anything but.

He would do his best to be a royal ass.

And his best was very, very good.

He looked down at his clothes. He had bought two more shirts and another pair of tailored trousers. He had grown used to good clothes in the past few years, and he also knew it suited his new image as a dandy or, as the westerners apparently said, a tenderfoot. He sort of liked the idea of goading Wes, who knew better, who knew a few of his talents.

But he would stay away from Susannah. She was very, very dangerous to his plans. The fact that he had gone to bed alone last night was testament to that fact.

After an evening of ogling, he found every woman a pale imitation of the one who had so aroused him two days ago. He just couldn't bring himself to take one to bed.

Bloody hell. It was going to be an intolerable twelve weeks.

Susannah saw Rhys coming. She had been looking out the windows all day, although she knew it was unlikely he would return this soon—if he returned at all. Austin was nearly fifty miles away.

But pleasure filled her at the sight. He rode so well, so easily, as if he had been born to the saddle. As if he really were an English lord.

It really didn't matter what he was, only that he filled her heart, and that she felt safe with him. Especially after her latest confrontation with Wes. Just the reminder made her wince.

He had stumbled in late this afternoon and had gone straight to his room. And to a bottle, she suspected, just as he had last night after Erin's departure. He had refused any food, called her a traitor for her part in bringing Erin here, and firmly closed the door behind him. He was gone before breakfast this morning.

At least, Wes *was* working. She was grateful for that. But instead of being exhausted, he'd apparently remained awake much of the night. She could hear the clump, clump of the crutches into the wee hours of morning.

Poor Erin, whom he'd sent away yesterday. But at least Erin knew what she was facing. She had known Wes since childhood and was absolutely convinced that she could reach him again, that he would eventually accept the loss of his leg and get on with his life. With her.

Susannah knew nothing at all about the man she thought she loved. Not where he came from, or where he had learned such deadly skills, or where he planned on going. She knew Wes loved Erin, and that was what maintained Erin's hope, but she, Susannah, certainly had no such confidence about her nighthawk. He was just as likely to take what he wanted, as a bird consumed its prey, and fly away, as he was to stay and make himself a part of this ranch. More likely, in fact. Much more likely.

Still, he *had* returned!

She went out on the porch. It was twilight, and his horse was lathered, but he looked relaxed. And extraordinarily striking in a white shirt, black trousers, and black broadcloth coat. Striking and distant. His cheeks were just a little darkened by the shadow of a beard, but other than that his dark eyes appeared anything but tired. They were as bright, alert, and wary as ever.

"Mrs. Fallon," he greeted her with that distant mockery he used with such effectiveness. She even wondered briefly whether they had spent that glorious time together.

"We didn't expect you back this soon," she ventured cautiously.

"But you did expect me back." It was more a statement than a question. And it discomforted her for some odd reason, perhaps because he always knew what she was thinking.

"I was hoping."

"Your brother?"

She suddenly grinned. "Was he hoping you would return? Or how is he doing?"

He dismounted in one long lazy movement. "I know the answer to the first. So I suppose the second."

"Don't be so sure about that first question," Susannah said. She knew Wesley realized they needed

Rhys Redding. He just wasn't going to admit it. But she couldn't think much about Wes at the moment. Rhys was too close, even if he was five feet away.

He looked irresistible. But then, she admitted to herself, he always did, to her. Whether in a dusty cotton shirt with its sleeves rolled up, or now, impeccably dressed and appearing cool and rakishly elegant even in the late afternoon heat. He looked as if he had just stepped out of an English drawing room. Or she supposed he did, she amended, since she had no experience with English drawing rooms. The thought gave her a painful twinge. She knew so little about *his* world.

"No more trouble?"

She shook her head, unable to take her gaze from this new Rhys. Yet there had already been so many of them. A dozen people under one skin. The only thing that remained the same was that tall rangy build that disguised so much strength. The voice, the speech, even the dark eyes changed at the slightest whim.

"You look different," she finally managed, feeling ridiculously inadequate and foolish.

He shrugged. "I still have some money from the deserters. I like good clothes, particularly ones that fit."

Was that why he went to Austin? Just to find clothes? Or something else? The thoughts pounded at Susannah's brain. And her heart.

And the money. She felt a momentary disappointment in him. She and Wes needed every dollar they could get. Yet, it *was* Rhys's. Unquestionably. She and Wes would be dead, or worse, if it hadn't been for his quite deadly assistance. But the fact that he had gone off and obviously spent a large portion of the money without discussing it first hurt. The action once again proclaimed his separateness from them, his unwillingness to become a partner with them. And he obviously didn't believe any more explanation was necessary. Well, it wasn't.

Was it?

He was watching her with wary amusement, and she knew he was just begging for a reason to leave. His expression held the usual challenge he always threw at her and Wes: *Take me as I am, or I'll get the hell out of here.*

It was galling, and yet she wondered whether that wasn't part of his attraction. And, God help her, the attraction was stronger than ever. She was practically vibrating with need, her entire body aching with it, her nerve ends sizzling so loud she thought he must hear them. Waves radiated through the air, those now familiar flashes of pure want that were like a magnet between them.

He was feeling them, too. She knew from the puzzled comprehension that flared so fleetingly in his eyes before he controlled it, and the subsequent wry smile she had come to love. And suspect.

"It must have been a long ride," she said finally. "And supper is about ready. Will you eat with me?"

The amusement came back into his eyes. "I thought your brother had banished me to the bunkhouse."

"It's my house," she said defensively.

"I hadn't noticed," he drawled, this time in the Texas accent that he had somehow perfected. It was disconcerting. So was his new dare. A dare for her to defy Wes. And not only in the matter of dinner.

He stepped closer, and she felt herself trembling with his nearness, the yearning to run into his arms and feel that hard body against hers again. The air radiated with that hunger, her body evolving into a heated mass of desire. She looked up into his eyes, and, for one of the few times, saw emotion roil in them. He stepped toward her. "Do you really think

that's a good idea?" The words were practically a tiger's purr. Ominously soft. Deceptively gentle.

"No," she answered. "But I don't care."

"Big brother will." The voice was taunting, but still
a question of sorts.

"Wes . . . has gone upstairs. I don't think he'll be
down for supper." She heard the suggestive whisper in
her voice, and she was surprised at how adept she had
become at . . . seduction. But her forwardness did not
seem wrong at all. Not with him. Not with her nighthawk.

His eyes bored into her, those dark hooded eyes
that were such an enigma. Yet she knew he felt the
same overwhelming attraction that she did, or he
wouldn't be here, standing so still before her, tension
now so evident in the stiff set of his body.

He didn't want to be here. She knew that. There
was a frustration in him she could almost touch, a kind
of bewildered acknowledgment that for once he didn't
have absolute control over his actions. He didn't like it
one bit, but neither, she realized, could he seem to do
anything about it.

The sudden instinctive knowledge cheered her and
sent new waves of heat curling inside her, along with
a certain pleasure she dared not show. So she waited,
aware she couldn't push.

He suddenly nodded. "I have to wash up first."

Susannah kept the small victory from her face as
she turned, trying also to keep the skip in her step
contained, but failing as miserably as he had just failed
in refusing her.

Chapter 16

The large room seemed very, very small and very, very close.

At least, it did to Susannah. Hannah had served the meal and retreated into the kitchen area, as if fully aware of the vibrating tensions in the room. The table where they ate was at the side of the large living area.

Wes, as Susannah had expected, declined to come to dinner. She had not told him they had a guest, much less who it was. Her brother had been in a morose, belligerent mood since Erin's visit, and Susannah did not particularly want his glowering presence at the table.

There was nothing special to eat tonight: just a plate of stew from the huge caldron that also fed the hands, along with freshly baked bread and newly churned butter. To Rhys, it was a banquet after Libby Prison and the weeks in the saddle, although he had indulged himself in an expensive meal in Austin. He wondered whether it was Susannah's company that added spice to this meal.

Her violet eyes were sparkling with devilment, as if she knew she had lured him here against his will. She was beguiling when she had that look in her eyes, when the little lines of worry were eased. Beguiling and enchanting. And so very, very touchable.

It was all he could do to keep his hands on the utensils, eating slowly to occupy his mind with something other than deep, teasing eyes and soft skin and the faint scent of flowers. And even though the food was good, it was all he could do to eat when another part of his anatomy was so bloody damned hungry.

To ease some of the tension, he reintroduced a subject calculated to cool himself off. "You never did say how your brother was?" It was a question.

Susannah hesitated, a frown burrowing between her eyes, and Rhys knew something was wrong. He suspected she was torn between loyalty to her brother and the need to talk about what was happening to him. Rhys already knew. He'd seen it before, the slow dissolution due to drink. Wes had a better reason than most, but that didn't help Susannah.

"What is it?" he coaxed.

"Yesterday, Wes saw the girl he was going to marry before the war."

"And she decided she didn't want him anymore," Rhys guessed. With two exceptions, one sitting across from him, he'd never had much faith in women.

Susannah shook her head. "You haven't met Erin. No, she wants him as much as ever."

Rhys began to understand. The damned bloody fool. Rhys had always believed in taking what was offered. The only reason he was hesitating even a little now about taking Susannah again was for his own sake. He didn't want to get involved any more than he already was. He didn't want to be responsible for anyone.

He certainly didn't want any responsibility for damned stiff-necked Wes Carr. Yet Susannah was looking at him with a kind of pleading hope in her eyes that tore at his insides.

"And he doesn't want her?" he asked, deliberately misunderstanding.

Susannah looked at him through suddenly narrowed eyes, as if she suspected he was playing games again. "Of course, he does. They've always been in love." She consciously ignored his amused look, the look that denied the existence of love.

"What's the problem, then?"

"His leg, of course," she said impatiently, only too aware that he understood far more than he was indicating.

"If he would get over that damned self-pity," Rhys said, suddenly annoyed with himself for giving even the slightest damn, "he could do anything he wanted. I knew someone in England, a retired soldier who'd lost a leg. There wasn't anything he couldn't do." It was a lie. He didn't know anyone like that at all, but Susannah's eyes had misted in a way that always did weakening things to him.

"How?"

Rhys hurriedly improvised. "He had this special leg built. He didn't even need crutches."

Susannah's eyes cleared, and her lower lip trembled in a way that made him want to nibble it. "Do you think we can find someone to make one?"

Bloody hell. What had he gotten himself into? Still, it couldn't be too difficult. His mind started working on the possibilities. Just as he had a talent for picking up dialects and languages, he also had knack for improvising when necessary, a talent of particular value in Africa.

"Perhaps," he said cautiously, wishing he hadn't brought up the subject of Carr after all—until he saw the smile on her face, the look that said he, Rhys Redding—scoundrel, thief, bastard—could do anything.

If only she knew.

He turned back to his food, but it had suddenly turned to sawdust. He had somehow committed himself again, and to a bloody damned fool he didn't even like.

Susannah saw him do as he did so many times, almost will a distance between them, and she searched frantically for another subject. "The Martins are trying to take land from other families, too."

He looked up, but this time he didn't meet her eyes. He had found that to be too dangerous. "Oh?"

"Half the families in this county," she said. "They buy up the bank notes, and then something happens— fields trampled, livestock disappearing, hands killed—so they can't be paid back."

No! He knew what she was trying to do. Draw him into a lake of quicksand. He didn't care about anyone else. He sure as hell didn't care about people who had apparently turned their backs on Susannah because of her brother. He tried chewing again, but the food was worse than sawdust. Bitter now.

"So many of the leaders, those with influence were killed during the war," she said. "More than two-thirds of the men in this county went to war, and many of their companies were nearly wiped out. There's no one left to fight the land-grabbers."

"Why was your . . . husband so far east?"

"His was one of the companies sent to Shiloh. He caught the attention of a general who used him as a scout, and he just got passed along as most of the fighting moved east."

"And Wes?"

"That's the ironic part. He didn't want to fight his friends and neighbors, so he went east to volunteer. They might well have faced each other, Mark and Wes. I think that's one of the things that's bothering Wes. All of us grew up together. Mark and Wes were really close, almost like brothers. Mark was the only one other than Erin who stood up for Wes when he decided to fight for the North, the only one who defended my father who argued against secession. We owed him a lot."

That's why she'd married him. He suddenly realized that. She hadn't said she loved her husband the other afternoon, only that he had been her best friend. And now ... she said she'd *owed* him. Not loved. Owed. Now it made sense, that innocence he never quite understood. He remembered something else she'd said. *It's not what Mark would have wanted,* she'd replied when he asked why she didn't sell out.

She was every bit as bloody noble and honorable as her brother. Hell-bent stubborn in both qualities. He'd given her credit for more sense, especially after the way she had lied their way through Confederate lines. But although this facet of her character rather distressed him, the newly discovered understanding of her marriage, for some reason, did not.

But she seemed oblivious to his thoughts. She was back to making a point he didn't want to hear. "The sheriff isn't doing anything. Erin says everyone thinks the Martins are paying him off. There's talk of vigilantes, but there's no one strong enough to pull people together."

Rhys didn't like the way she was looking at him. He didn't like it at all. He yawned as if in boredom. "They'll find someone," he said, dismissing her implication, "if they care enough." Rhys hesitated a moment, then added carelessly, "Maybe your brother ..."

"He fought for the Yanks. No one will listen to him now."

"Then that's their loss," he said. "Why should you worry?"

Susannah bit her lip. "They're my neighbors."

"Don't sound much like neighbors to me," he retorted.

"Rhys ... ?"

"No," he said flatly.

She gave him that searching look that always made him feel she saw things that weren't there.

"In any event," he said, "why should they listen to

me? I'm British, and ... little but a foppish adventurer."

"Not always." She grinned impishly. "Although you can do foppish well."

He wished he had never used that bloody Texas accent. "They would never listen to a stranger."

"I wonder," she pondered out loud. "There's something about you . . ."

"That makes people detest me," he finished, remembering Wes's attitude.

"How long are you going to stay?" Susannah asked, suddenly changing tactics.

"Depends on how old the bunkhouse gets."

"You can move in here anytime you want."

His eyes opened in pretended horror. "And have everyone talk?"

"Not with Wes here."

"Ah, our other problem."

"He'll come around."

"I doubt it." Not until hell grew as bloody cold as a Welsh January, and he wasn't planning on staying that long.

He pushed the plate aside and stood, stretching as he did so. It had been a very long day in the saddle. It had been a long day, period. Too much time to think. Thinking, he'd decided long ago, was hazardous to one's well-being. Much better to stick to instinct, and his instinct told him to run like hell.

Still, he wished she didn't look so damned wistful and soft. And she wasn't that soft, he reminded himself. She had traveled as well as any man, had run this ranch alone for years. *Don't forget that.*

And she wants something now.

Problem was, so did he, but he was afraid their needs didn't completely coincide. Not in all things, anyway.

"You're still welcome to stay in the house," she said. "We have another room."

"Not yours?" He was brutally frank now. He even made himself leer a bit. It wasn't at all difficult.

He saw the sudden confusion in her face, the wound he had purposely inflicted in the coarse invitation.

"Is ... that what it would take for you to stay?"

The soft voice, laced with determination, was like a blow to his stomach. She would openly become his mistress, even in front of her brother. He remembered another proposal in England months ago. Christ, he didn't want to think another woman would consider she had to sacrifice herself in exchange for his assistance. It was too bloody damn wounding to the ego.

"No, Mrs. Fallon. It is not. I'll stay until I'm ready to go. In that time, I'll do what I can to help you with the Martins. You. Not your neighbors. Not Wes. I don't give a bloody damn about any of them." He started to turn, suddenly angry with himself and with her. Her, because of her attempt to involve him in even more lives; himself, because he wanted her so badly at the moment, he was about to agree to almost anything. Almost.

Her hand touched his arm. "I'm sorry," she said. "I didn't mean to push you into something you don't want to do."

"Yes, you did," he retorted, but he smiled wryly, taking any sting out of his words.

"I'll walk out with you."

"Don't think I can find my way?"

"I'm afraid you will keep going."

"Not right away. I promised you a wooden leg."

They were out the door now, into the night. Lights shone from the bunkhouse and the ranch buildings, and overhead a part moon decorated a dark blue sky. A horse neighed and another answered, and there was the nightly chirping of a grasshopper. A silent figure, rifle in hand, sat like a stone sentinel on the fence that bordered the road into the ranch.

A cool breeze ruffled the few trees in the yard, and the bull, King Arthur, pawed at the ground in the corral. Despite his physical weariness from a sleepless night and the long ride today, Rhys was restless . . . as he always seemed to be around her. He was afraid if he stopped moving, he would grab her and hold her tight, kiss those soft inviting lips. . . .

Bloody Christ, he felt his manhood harden with the thought, with the closeness of her presence. Why in the hell couldn't it have obliged last night? Why only for Susannah Fallon, of all women?

He felt her hand on his shirt. He had taken off the jacket, holding it over his shoulder. And now her touch penetrated the cloth and sent hot shocks through his body. He wanted her even more than he had yesterday. It scared the bloody hell out of him at how much.

"Thank you for coming back," she said.

"I had no place else to go."

"I . . . missed you."

"Don't do that, Mrs. Fallon," he warned, although he knew he was actually warning himself. He could scarcely think, now, of a day without her, without that smile that vacillated between uncertainty and delight, that teased and invited.

"Will you ever tell me more about yourself?"

"There's not much to tell."

She gave him a disbelieving look. "The way you pick up dialects and accents . . ."

He shrugged.

"And glare at people."

He raised one eyebrow in question.

"You practically scared that deserter out of his mind back in Virginia," she said with a slight grin. "And even me sometimes when you're angry."

The other eyebrow went up, causing a frown to furrow between them. "It doesn't seem to have bothered you."

"Only on behalf of others," she said. "It's difficult to be afraid of someone who has saved your life."

"I'll have to try harder," he said with the slightest of grins breaking the austere countenance. Susannah felt her heart pound faster. He looked, at the moment, almost accessible again, as he had on her hill. She leaned into him, loving the strength of his body, remembering exactly how hard it could be.

"Ah, Mrs. Fallon, you mustn't do that."

"Why?" she asked innocently.

His head turned down toward her. His eyes had grown accustomed to the darkness, but he couldn't really see the depth of her eyes. He could just remember the passion that had shone in them two days earlier when he'd . . .

He shook his head to rid it of the memory. "You were asking me about my dreadful past." The mockery was back in his voice.

"Was it dreadful?"

"Oh, quite. Much too dreadful for the ears of a lady," he replied in his best upper-class British accent.

She put her finger to his mouth. It was so sensual, so incredibly enticing. She ran the finger along its edges, in the crevices bracketing it. "I haven't been a lady for a long time."

"You will always be a lady." For once the mockery was gone, and he surprised himself as much as her with the honest sincerity in his voice.

"Even . . . the other afternoon?"

"Especially then."

He wanted to grab that finger between his teeth and nibble on it. He wanted to nibble on all of her.

"Rhys . . ."

He turned away. "Hummmm?"

"Don't turn away from me again."

He gave her the raffish smile. "I thought you were afraid of sharing a room with me."

"Not afraid of you, afraid of the way you proposed it." She hesitated. "Cruelly," she added.

He turned back to her then. "I have a cruel streak, Mrs. Fallon. Don't you know that, yet?"

"I think you want me to believe that," she replied. "I think you were trying to scare me off for my own sake."

"I never do anything for someone else's sake."

"You told me you did once."

"To my everlasting sorrow," he said. "It taught me a lesson. I'm more careful these days."

"You've done a great deal for Wes and me," she argued.

"For my own reasons."

"And what are those reasons?" she asked. "Oh, I know in the beginning you wanted to get out of Libby, but then . . . you had many chances to leave."

He shrugged. "I didn't have any place else to go."

Susannah looked up at him doubtfully. "I'll never believe that's the full reason."

He shrugged. "Believe what you wish."

"Come stay in the house," she offered again.

He touched her face, his fingers tracing patterns on her skin in light, teasing strokes. "You don't really want that, Mrs. Fallon. And I might just have to fight your brother."

"I don't want you to leave here, to leave Texas."

"I won't. Not for a while."

"You left me minutes ago . . . you traveled a thousand miles away. Back to England?"

"No," he said honestly. He hadn't done that, wasn't able to do that, not when she was so close. He had only been trying, quite unsuccessfully, to back away from the chaotic feelings she was causing in him.

"Will you go back there? To England?"

"I don't know."

It was one of the few times she'd heard an indecisive statement from him.

"What is it like in England?"

He relaxed slightly. "Cold. A great deal of rain. Fog. England's very green, vividly green, perhaps because of all the rain. It's more . . . golden here. Like Africa."

"Africa?"

"I spent a number of years there," he said almost absently, not as if he were dropping a diamond of information at all, she thought. She grabbed that scrap of information for the treasure it was.

Africa. Exotic and foreign. Perhaps that explained some of the mystery about him, a certain quality that set him apart from everyone else.

"What . . . were you doing in Africa?" she asked, unable to keep her curiosity to herself. It was at fever pitch, as every part of her was.

Perhaps because of the night, and the attraction that so sparked between them, the sudden closeness she felt and oddly enough knew that he did too, he gave her a wry, searching look and started to speak.

"I was a mercenary, Mrs. Fallon," he explained, emphasizing the "Mrs." again with a maddening smile. "I accompanied settlers into the interior." He didn't say what else he'd done.

Susannah was fascinated, even more intrigued than before, which was considerably. Africa, she wondered again. A word in a geography book. There were so many puzzles about Rhys Redding, and this tidbit only added to them, rather than providing any solutions. His accent and speech proclaimed him well educated. He had said he was the son of a lord, although so derisively, she hadn't known whether to take him seriously. How did a man like that become a mercenary in a faraway country like Africa? And then come to be in a Confederate prison? A wager, he'd said. But that explained very little.

"Is that why you know guns so well?" she asked. "And ride so well?"

He nodded. "In some ways, Texas reminds me of the southern part of Africa, the rolling hills, the plains. Areas so vast, you could ride for days without seeing a human being."

"You said you . . . accompanied settlers?" *More*, she thought greedily. *Tell me more.*

"I traveled with a land company seeking to settle a southern part of the country." He shrugged. "I was guide, hunter, guard." *Gambler, opportunist. Treasure hunter.*

Her hand found his, and she entwined her fingers in his. "What is Africa like?"

"That's like asking what America is like," he replied. "Africa is the second largest continent and has much in common with your country. Rich forests, plains like these, vast deserts."

"And who immigrated there?"

He shrugged again. "People who always think the rainbow is just within reach but never find it, so they keep moving. The adventurers, or would-be adventurers, who buy land but don't know how to use it." There was a great deal of cynicism in his words. "And the idealists and missionaries. They go there to build a new society, convert the natives who don't want to be converted, and force their customs on people whose values often surpass theirs."

"And you? Where do you fit?"

"Ah, there you have me, love. I don't fit anyplace."

There was the slightest chagrin in the words, so slight she almost missed it. "Tell me about the animals," she urged before he grew quiet again.

"Ah, now they are spectacular," he said, a light coming into those dark eyes. "The animals are Africa's richness. Huge herds of them. Gazelles, antelope, giraffes. Zebras. Prides of lions. And flamingos. Birds of every description and color. I *do* miss those."

Susannah's fingers tightened around his. She wished she had been there with him, to see those ga-

zelles, antelope and flamingos. She wanted to see his
eyes light and his mouth smile. She felt a greater
closeness to him now than at any previous time, even
that afternoon on the hill, because tonight he was sharing something of himself with her. She didn't know
why. She just knew she wanted these minutes to go on
and on and on. There was an intensity in him, and she
was drawn to it like a magnet. But then she was always drawn to him, to that elusive demon in him that
both frightened and beckoned.

"You loved it, didn't you?"

"Perhaps. I didn't realize it then. I just thought of
England, of returning. Now, I really don't know why. I
suppose I was like those people chasing that rainbow,
only to find it dissipate as they approach it." There
was a painful honesty about him she had never seen
before, a momentary glimpse into a soul he usually
kept securely barred from intrusion.

He leaned against the corral post and gave her a
crooked smile. "So never depend on rainbows, love.
They are very unreliable."

"But well worth looking at and enjoying," she said.

"From a distance ... if you realize a rainbow is
nothing but a refraction of the sun, an illusion. Turn
away for a moment and it's gone."

"Like you?"

"No one's ever called me a rainbow before," he
said with a grimace.

Susannah cocked her head slightly. "No. You're
much too substantial for that."

"Ah, Susannah. I'm not substantial at all. I'm someone you made up. An illusion, just like that rainbow."

"You don't feel like an illusion."

No, he didn't. He felt very much like a man. A very
aroused man as he looked at her. Her dark hair was
tied back with a ribbon, and her face was tipped upward toward him, the expression expectant and chal-

lenging. Bloody hell, what had happened to his willpower?

It certainly wasn't around at the moment. He bent his head and she stretched up until her lips met his with mutual longing, mutual need. The two emotions floated between them, the yearning so strong that the air around them seemed to sing with it. His arms went around her, gathering her against him with a sudden turbulent possessiveness. He hurt with wanting to touch every part of her, to run his fingers along her back and watch her tense with that passion she'd so openly expressed two days ago. He felt an intense burning in his loins, a need he was beginning to think began and ended with her. Would it ever be thus? Even when he left?

The very thought brought desperation to his kiss, a wild uncontrolled thing that shook him to the core.

If only there was privacy, but there wasn't. He . . . cared too much to take her inside the house, despite his earlier lewd suggestion. He didn't particularly care about what Wes thought, but he found he did care about causing her pain. And he knew a fight with her brother would do that.

God help him if he was becoming magnanimous. He hated what she was doing to him, washing away layers and layers of protective plate so he didn't even know who or what he was anymore.

He untangled himself gently but firmly, his eyes avoiding hers. "It's been a very long day."

"Will you have breakfast with us in the morning?"

"I don't think that's wise, love."

"Why?"

"Do I have to explain?"

"Only if you don't feel as I do."

His brows furrowed together with interest. "And how is that?"

She tried to describe what was indescribable. "Hungry," she finally said. "But not exactly for food."

He choked, her comment spurring a very distinct hunger of his own. "You can be very ... forthright, you know."

"I know. and that's very peculiar. I used to be the model of propriety. Well, almost," she amended.

He grinned, and the amusement reached his eyes this time. "A model of propriety? Traveling across country. Shooting people. Wearing trousers. Propriety, my love, has never seemed your long suit."

Susannah's heart flipped several times at the warm, intimate way he said "love." Almost as if he meant it. But before she could explore his meaning, he stepped away.

"Good night, Mrs. Fallon," he said, but there was no sarcasm this time, only a husky warmth that made her glow as he strode across to the bunkhouse.

He slowed as he opened the door, shuddering at the sound of regular snoring that came from within. Bloody Christ, he could be in her bed tonight.

What had he done? He hoped to hell nobility wasn't catching. God help him if it was!

He had the depressing, sneaking suspicion it might be, and that it was a damned lonely business.

Wes looked out the window from his darkened room. He preferred it that way now. It suited his dark mood.

He watched as Rhys Redding took his sister in his arms, and the way she responded to him, the way the two silhouettes became one. He closed his eyes against the sight, trying to think it was anger that chilled him to his bones, but he knew it wasn't. It was his own emptiness, his own envy. His own desperate loneliness.

How he had wanted to do that to Erin, to just hold her in his arms, to surrender to the softness of her. To use that sweetness to wipe away the pain and nightmares and memories.

He swallowed, and tasted the bitter aftermath of the whiskey he had been drinking. He tasted more: disgust at himself, at what he was becoming.

Redding was moving away from Susannah now, and Wes felt a momentary relief. He had not missed the attraction between the two; damn, he would have to be blind and deaf as well as crippled.

Crippled. He still had times when he forgot that. When he first woke up in the morning and felt the missing leg tingle. And then it was like learning the news all over again. Every morning of his life, he was told by his own body that he was no longer whole.

And so he had said little to Susannah. He knew they needed Redding, and it galled him as nothing before in his life. He couldn't protect his own, and he had to hide behind an adventurer, or worse.

He turned away from the window and looked at the bottle on the table. He wanted another drink. God, how much he wanted the oblivion it temporarily gave him.

His jaw tightened. Not tonight. Maybe if he could get through tonight without another drink, perhaps he could get through tomorrow without any. He had to. For Susannah's sake, if not his own. He couldn't leave her alone anymore with Redding.

Chapter 17

"Bill and the wagon are late."

Ordinarily, the news wouldn't be jarring, but Wes and Susannah stared at each other over the supper they'd just started. Bill Morris had gone into town at noon for supplies.

Wes struggled up. "Get a group of men together," he told Jaime. "I'll go with you."

Susannah felt sick, a premonition settling in her heart like a stone. Bill was another young hand, and usually reliable. He had been known to take a drink at the saloon in town, but he wouldn't do it now, not when he knew how worried they would be.

Susannah ached to go with her brother, but he had been taking more and more responsibility, and she didn't want to do anything to slow the inch-by-inch progress of his confidence.

Dear Lord, she hated to sit and watch him go, to watch things happening on the ranch and not be a part of it, but she felt she had to do it for Wes. Learning he could still lead and contribute was absolutely vital to getting well and eventually striking out on his own.

And Rhys. He had kept his distance these last days, ever since that kiss at the corral. She didn't know where he was now, and that hurt. She wanted him here. She wanted his assurance. She wanted him to go with Wes to make sure there would be no trouble. But she could ask that of neither man. She felt so darn helpless, caught between her need to do something, and her need to protect and nurture.

She swallowed, stifling both protests and suggestions as Wes hobbled to the gun rack and selected a rifle. She'd almost allowed herself, in the calm of the past three weeks, to hope that the Martins would leave them alone. She should have known better.

Susannah and Wes had expected violence of some type immediately after their week was up, but nothing happened. Susannah was reminded of the sword of Damocles, hanging by a hair above them all. And she thought now that Lowell Martin had probably planned it that way.

Guards had been doubled as the horses grazed, and a double contingent of men surrounded the ranch at night. It meant that the hands were working seventeen, eighteen hours a day, and tempers were frayed.

She often wondered what they thought about Rhys Redding, whether they ever considered him any more than a tenderfoot and a guest of the owner. None of them had posed any questions, but merely accepted his presence, if not him personally.

Susannah had noticed they avoided him. He was different. And he seemed satisfied to remain that way. While he wasn't unfriendly, neither was he in any way approachable beyond the barest civilities. A "good day" rather than a "morning." He also avoided ranch work, disappearing often during the day, although he did take guard duty on some of the nights. And then he would stand out there alone, a silent, solitary figure who no one was quite sure would be of any use in a real fight.

After their talk at the corral, he had thoroughly avoided her, tipping his hat when he saw her and giving her that mocking, half-twisted smile that no one else could ever duplicate, and walking on. To the deep misery of a now awakened body and a yearning heart, he was as elusive now as he had been on the trail, following his own path, whatever that might be. He never came to the house at mealtime, and usually returned to the ranch late, going directly to the bunkhouse.

Even if Rhys hadn't avoided her of his own accord, Wes had made it clear in the past weeks that he was taking on a new brotherly protectiveness. He seemed determined not to leave her and Rhys alone. Her brother even went back to eating dinner with her, taking a walk with her at night, devising any scheme he could to keep Susannah in sight.

Unfortunately, she thought bitterly, the protectiveness that she had once tried to stir was no longer needed. Rhys Redding apparently had little interest.

The thought was devastating. And now, as she watched Wes move carefully toward the door, and apprehension flooded her, she wanted Rhys and she had no idea where he was. She knew only that he had ridden out early that morning.

The need for him pounded inside her. She wanted that natural competence, the assurance that everything would be all right, that Bill was alive and that Wes wouldn't run into trouble. She wanted him to confirm she should not go, that she needed to give Wes more time.

She wanted *him* so badly she wanted to curl up with the pain of that wanting.

And she wondered whether she would ever stop wanting him.

Wes saddled up with five other men. They found the wagon halfway from the crossroads. It was empty, the horses gone, the man dead, crushed under the wagon. A visit to the sheriff provided no help.

"Must have been an accident," the lawman said. "Don't see no bullets."

Wes struggled to control his anger. "Don't see no supplies either," he mocked.

The sheriff gave him a long, hard look. "Look, you ain't none too popular 'round here. I can rightly see how some folks might think they have a right to take whatever they find."

"Are you going to do anything?"

"Oh, I'll ask 'round, all right. But don't expect nothing."

Wes barely contained his frustration. Well, he'd been warned, and now he knew. The sheriff was obviously in the Martins' pay. "I'll take care of it myself," he grated out.

The sheriff eyed him contemptuously. "A one-legged Yank?" Those were the same words the Martins had used, and Wes felt the same kind of growing helplessness. It was also direct proof in his mind that the Martins and the sheriff had talked, and recently. He wanted to strike out, wipe that smug look off the man's face, but he couldn't even do that. He'd fall flat on his face. He gritted his teeth and mounted, spurring his horse into a gallop, hearing laughter ring in his ears.

Rhys returned two hours after Wes had left. When he heard the news, he came to the house to wait with her, his mouth grim and his back stiff.

"Do you want me to go after them?" he asked.

She made the most difficult decision she ever would. "No," she said. Wes, she knew, would never forgive her if she sent Rhys Redding to nursemaid him. Her brother had made a decision, one she'd been longing for him to make, to take charge, and she couldn't second-guess him now.

Still the waiting was excruciating. Rhys very carefully sat on the other side of the room, his eyes and his person keeping a distinct distance. It was as if those few moments of intimacy at the corral had never happened.

She offered him something to eat, and was surprised when he accepted. He ate as he did everything, with a lazy surface indifference which belied the wary intensity of his eyes.

He set out to charm Hannah, as if it were an exercise of some kind, and did so extremely well although Hannah was usually quite cautious about people. He asked about her family, ferreting out details and stories even Susannah had never heard.

And Susannah suddenly realized she was relaxing slightly as she listened to the sudden passion in the housekeeper's voice. She looked over at Rhys and met his eyes, which instantly shuttered but not before she saw the smoldering heat there. It ignited the already glowing embers in her, and she knew he was not nearly as indifferent to her as he appeared.

If she hadn't been so worried about Wes, she might have done something about it. But even as she wondered over it, she heard hoofbeats and ran to the door. All six men who had left were returning. She whirled around, a grin on her face, right into Rhys's arms.

They opened automatically, and she felt his heat against her body, the brief tightness of his arms, before he quickly moved away as if stung. She turned and saw Wes's thunderous expression as he moved up the steps.

She looked back at Rhys. The mocking smile was back in place as he regarded Wes. "You missed a bloody damn good dinner," he said easily. "Find your missing rider?"

Wes glared at him. "He's dead."

The grin left Rhys's face. "Do you know . . . ?"

"I know, but can't prove anything. The sheriff says being a Yank I can expect such hostilities."

"It's started then," Rhys said in a coldly impersonal voice.

"It's started," Wes confirmed with a new hard edge to his voice.

Wes, Susannah, and Jaime decided that night that no hand would go out alone again, nor would Susannah make any more of her lone visits to Erin's or to the old homestead.

The exception, Susannah knew, was Rhys, who she knew would follow no one's directives. As if to make that clear, he had left abruptly last night, just after Wes's return.

But to her surprise, he saddled with the other hands in the morning as they took the horses out to pasture. Susannah was there to watch them ride away, her heart thudding as it always did when she saw him.

Rhys saw her at the door. She was wearing a blue dress, one he knew would deepen those violet eyes if he were close enough to see them. He could see them well enough in his mind.

Devil take it, but he wished he could will them away, as he had willed away so many other things in his lifetime. But she had snaked her way into every part of him, and no matter how he tried, or what distance he had put between them, he couldn't seem to extricate himself. He'd halfway hoped, as days went by without trouble, that perhaps the threat had been exaggerated, that he wouldn't be needed and he could depart without leaving unfinished business behind. Unfinished business. That's all it was. Not conscience, or loyalty, or any such nonsense. It was just that he hated loose ends. They offended him.

So he had decided to ride along this morning. He needed the distraction of others. How many times in the past few days had he started for the ranch house? How many times had he wanted to climb in the window he knew was her bedroom? How many times had he imagined kissing her throat, her breasts? How many times had he thought about burying himself in her again?

He couldn't afford such folly. He'd thought once he'd had her, the overpowering attraction would disappear. But it hadn't. It had grown even stronger, more compelling. It dominated nearly every waking moment, and some of his sleeping ones. He woke in a sweat, his manhood stiff and wanting, and he had to use every ounce of self-control he'd ever developed to maintain a distance.

Not to do so was disaster. For her. For him. There could be no future for them. He wasn't the marrying kind—even if she wanted him after knowing his background, his history as a whore's bastard and a self-made scoundrel. If he succumbed to his need, he would leave even more ashes in his wake, and he couldn't do that to her. Or even to himself. He'd never had trouble living with himself before; he didn't want to start now.

To direct his baser instincts into something productive, he turned all his attention to the land they were riding. He'd already explored much of it; now he would become even more familiar with every foot of the ranch, the pastures, the boundaries.

And places of concealment! A man never knew when he might need them. He said nothing to the others, keeping aloof as he always did, his gaze always moving, searching, taking in every tree and hill and crevice. Roads. Distances. Landmarks.

He enjoyed the ride, despite his disturbing obsession with Susannah Fallon. It was an unusually fine day: a bright sun, eggshell-fragile clouds drifting lazily across a vividly blue sky. It reminded him of the uncomplicated days in Africa. Of the pure physical delight of riding . . . of feeling the sun on a gemlike day.

If only his mind wasn't crowded with so many distractions. Pretty dark-haired distractions. Responsibility distractions. Bloody Christ, he hated responsibility.

Always had. It limited one, limited freedom, limited choices.

Problem was, and this was most troubling of all, he couldn't particularly think of any choice he wanted, other then staying here. But he had no home here. He knew that. No more than any other place. Pure lunacy to even think differently.

He watched as Jaime and Wes hobbled the horses and stationed the pickets around the herd. Jaime had tried to be pleasant but Wes had, as usual, mostly ignored him.

Rhys wondered whether Wes had seen the embrace a fortnight ago. That ought to give him something to think about next time he tried blackmail. Rhys also noticed with some satisfaction that Wes did not smell of whiskey this morning, and his face didn't have that bloated red look that it had frequently had during the first few days after they had reached Texas.

But he quickly grew bored with the lack of action and, around noon, he gave Wes a taunting salute and pressed his mount into a gallop. He turned west toward a part of the ranch he hadn't fully explored yet. He knew Wes would worry about his whereabouts, and whether he was circling back to the ranch. He knew it, and he dismissed it from his mind. Wes could bloody damn well think what he wanted.

He wondered about the Martins as, once out of sight of the others, he slowed his pace. Yesterday's killing had been the first strike of a rattler. There would be others. He wished to hell he knew more about them.

His hand went back to the rifle on his saddle. He still didn't wear a gun belt as every man on the ranch, including Wes, did. He had worn one in Africa with a familiarity that he was afraid would reveal too much about him. There was always an aura a man had, when he wore a gun, that said more than words about how well he used it. A natural familiarity. He didn't want anyone to sense his yet. That knowledge might be too useful to Susannah's enemies.

Susannah. Why did his thoughts always turn to Susannah? A woman had never before remained in his thoughts more than a few hours, a week at most if she was very, very good at certain activities. He usually got bored quickly.

He had known Susannah months now and his fascination with her, his desire for her, had surprisingly grown even stronger, day by day, until he was almost consumed by it. He had never loved anyone as he had the other day, with that kind of slow, deliberate tenderness he hadn't known he possessed. His own physical pleasure had never been greater, had never encompassed him so entirely.

Just remembering made his body tense, his loins rigid and heated, and he shook his head to clear it, to concentrate instead on more deadly things. Or, he thought wryly, less dangerous things.

He spurred his horse into a faster pace, trying to outrun his thoughts. He was a long way from Wes and the other Fallon hands, more than a hour's distance, he guessed as he crested a hill and saw oncoming riders.

If he hadn't been so preoccupied with Susannah, he would probably have sensed their approach sooner. But he had been, and he didn't. He considered alternatives for the briefest of seconds, his mind quickly flipping through them, weighing each. What would the Rhys Redding he was trying to portray now do? Run, or stay and meet them with the arrogance he'd shown a few days ago? Bloody hell, it had been that lapse in attention, those thoughts of Susannah, that had made him careless.

Devil take it. He knew better!

There were at least twelve, maybe more. They were coming fast. He evaluated his weapons: a rifle and a knife tucked in his boot, and decided on wisdom. He turned around and dug his heels in the side of his horse.

He would have made it, if his horse's hoof hadn't found a rabbit hole. The animal went plunging down on its side. Rhys had just enough time to throw himself clear and rise, when he was surrounded by the riders, two of them with guns pointed at him.

The leader, he noted, was Hardy Martin, brother of the pack leader who had visited Susannah's ranch. Rhys forced himself to stand easily next to the thrashing horse, whose leg was obviously broken. He eyed the rifle, still in the holster.

"The loudmouthed tenderfoot," Hardy Martin sneered. "Cain't ride, either, I see."

"The barbarian," Rhys replied, unable to keep from taunting the man. He stepped toward the horse, and the rifle, stopping only when a shot rang out, raising dust at his feet.

"Surely even a barbarian," he said, "would allow me to end the suffering of an animal." His voice again had the condescension of an English lord. Christ, he had known enough of that and had even grudgingly admired it at times.

Hardy looked at one of his men. "Take care of it."

The man leveled his rifle and a shot silenced the horse. Rhys knew a deep regret, even grief. The horse had carried him a long way, and he'd always liked animals better than people. Another mark against the Martins.

If he ever got a chance to do anything about it. Looking at Hardy Martin, he doubted it. His glance went again to the rifle, pinned now under the dead horse. He swore to himself while his mouth bent into a smile. "And what can I do for you ... gentlemen?"

Hardy Martin growled. "It's time someone taught you some manners."

"You, for instance?" Rhys asked, lifting his eyebrows in bewilderment. He doubted whether he was going to get out of this, anyway, and he was damned if they would see him grovel. Even the worst of Englishmen, he thought with the Welshman's disdain, wouldn't do that with this scum.

Hardy looked at one of his men. "No horse. Guess he'll have to walk."

Another nodded. "I'll help him." Rhys watched warily as the man took a rope from his saddle and whirled it. Rhys ducked and it fell on the ground, and then there was another, and another.

Until one settled around him and quickly tightened around his body before his hands could tear it off. He tried to reach for the knife in his boot but he was thrown off his feet by a tug on the rope, and then the men were trotting away, dragging him behind.

He had landed on his back, and he rolled over, trying to raise his body from the ground with his hands as he was dragged over dirt and rocks. He felt blood running down his arms as his clothes ripped, and a sharp pain as his hand scraped over a pointed rock. He was bouncing like a sack of potatoes, his body hitting the ground in awkward ways, bruising and cutting.

Suddenly the horses stopped, and Hardy rode up to him, eying him with no little satisfaction as Rhys slowly, painfully, got to his feet.

Hardy looked over at his men, sneering. "Let's see how tenderfooted he really is," he said to one of his men, who then got down and walked over to Rhys. A jerk of the rope pulled him to the ground again, and the man on foot jerked off Rhys's boots, and the knife came tumbling out.

"Hey, boys, look at this. You think he can really use it?"

"Hell no," Hardy said. "Must be for whittling or some such. Tie his hands and get him on his feet."

Rhys saw the man put the knife in his belt after cutting a length from the rope which had been dragging him. Bloody Christ, he hurt. But his fury was greater than his hurt, than his caution.

The man, thinking Rhys's spirit was broken by the dragging, leaned down and reached for his hands. It was a mistake. Rhys forgot about his plans to remain the innocuous Englishman. He forgot about everything but getting even. In a movement so fast no one could stop him he grabbed the knife and plunged it into this tormentor, pushing him into a horse which then stumbled, throwing its rider to the ground. Rhys grabbed that man's neck and started to pull back, just as he had the army major months ago, when hands started to grab him from several directions.

"Don't kill him," he heard someone yell, "not yet," and then he sensed danger from behind. As he started to turn, he saw a pistol coming down on his head. He tried to duck, but too many hands were holding him, and it caught the side of his head. Everything dissolved into darkness.

He woke when water splashed on his face. He tried to move but he couldn't. His hands had been tied tightly behind him, and a rope encircled his neck like a hangman's noose. His shirt had been pulled or torn off, and his feet were bare.

"Got more spirit than I thought," Hardy said, sitting up in his saddle and looking down, as he loosely held the end of the rope which encircled Rhys's neck. "Might take a while to make you whimper." He grinned at the thought.

He turned away toward another man, who was replacing his canteen on his saddle. A body lay across it. "You got Hooper tied down?"

The man nodded.

"Let's go then. I have an idea for a little fun. There's a right fine tree I have in mind." He turned back to Rhys. "Don't mind walking, do you?"

Rhys was silent, trying to bottle his rage. He had acted too soon before. He had been careless twice to-

day. He simply stood, his back straight, knowing he
was bleeding from a dozen cuts already.

Hardy shrugged and spurred his horse into a slow
trot, not looking back to see whether Rhys could keep
up.

Rhys saw the slack in the rope begin to tighten. He
was thirsty. Dear God, he was thirsty. But his legs began to move, his feet touching as lightly as he could
make them over the hot dried earth and rocks. He had
to keep slack in the rope, or his neck would be broken. And he wasn't ready to die. Not yet.

He had one hell of a score to settle now. And he
wasn't going to die until he did exactly that.

Susannah! He tried to think of Susannah. Not the
pain. Not the thirst. Not the exhaustion. But
Susannah's violet eyes and her smile, the fresh smell of
her hair.

Keep the rope slack, he kept warning himself, but
it was getting more and more difficult. The hemp
scratched his throat, tightening when he stumbled, but
now Hardy slowed, as if he wanted to make sure he
didn't kill his victim too soon. He was walking his
horse, but Rhys was tired, his feet now a bloody mess
from the rocks under his feet, and he was stumbling
more often. The rope collar was in a slipknot; tightening when pulled, but loosening only slightly when
slack, stopped by a large double knot positioned just
below the loop.

He didn't know how far he'd walked when they finally stopped beneath a large cottonwood tree. Hardy
threw his end of the rope over a branch and tied it
around the base of the tree. Rhys had to remain standing or he would strangle himself to death. There was
some slack but not much. He waited for what was
coming. He found out soon enough.

Hardy nodded to one of the men who took a whip
from his saddle. "Let's watch the tenderfoot dance,"

he said. "And beg a bit. Ask our forgiveness for his big mouth."

"And for Hooper," one of the men said.

"Yeah, maybe he'll hang himself."

The whip snaked out, raising dust around Rhys's feet, and Rhys knew it was intended to make him flinch, to move against the rope. He forced himself to remain still.

"Wanna start begging now?" Martin asked. "Wanna talk about our manners again?"

Rhys had never begged in his life. He wasn't going to start now. "Somewhat lower than a snake's," he said contemptuously.

Hardy nodded to the man, and the whip snaked out, cutting across his arms and chest, laying the skin open. Rhys closed his eyes against the pain. The whip had missed his barely healed wound. He might not be so lucky next time. And he couldn't move. Not with the rope around his neck.

The whip sang out again, and he braced himself. He couldn't fall. He couldn't. But how much could he take before doing so? This time the whip caught his back. And then again.

Years flashed back. So many years. When another whip had wound through the air, had made him feel less than human, less than a horse or a dog. He couldn't do anything then. But now, now was a different story. If he survived.

He forced himself to look at Hardy. The man had a puzzled look on his face. So did the man wielding the whip. It was obvious they didn't understand why he wasn't begging, why he wasn't dancing around at the end of his rope, trying to avoid the whip. That was, he realized, what they wanted, what they thought they would entertain themselves with. But he'd known the whip would reach him anyway, and he was damned if he would give them any satisfaction, or pleasure.

It was also obvious that a few more blows would render him unconscious. He was barely standing, his body dripping blood. The rope was already tight around his neck since he was sagging slightly.

There was a consultation. And he realized they were discussing his fate. He heard some of the words. "You know Lowell ain't going to like it—not without his say-so."

"The other looked like an accident."

Hardy's voice seemed to reject the advice. "He seen us."

"He also killed Hooper," another man said. "If he says anything, we could say we found him on Hooper's horse. Produce Hooper's body. Then he would hang, legal-like."

"Yeah," Hardy started to agree. "In the meantime . . . let people see what we do to them that gets in the way."

"If he makes it back . . ."

The eyes turned back to Rhys, studying him.

Hardy hesitated. "Arrogant bastard . . . don't look so almighty superior now."

"What happens if he don't make it?" one man said.

Another shrugged. "Who knows who may have done it. He's a foreigner staying with a Yank lover."

Rhys forced himself to remain upright as his fate was being discussed with such cavalier indifference. The rope was tight now around his neck, his entire body on fire.

Hardy suddenly grinned. "We'll give 'im a fighting chance. See if he can make it back." He took a knife and cut the rope at the base of the tree, and Rhys fell to his knees, knowing that would have happened in any event.

Hardy came over. "That's what happens when you try to steal one of my horses," he said. "Caught him red-handed, didn't I, boys? Right after his own got killed. Foreigners jest don't have no respect for our laws."

Hardy stared hard at Rhys. "Go to the law, and I'll tell them I caught you stealing. That you were riding Hooper's horse, only we couldn't find him. 'Cause you being a foreigner and all, I didn't hang you, just taught you a little ole lesson. But the law might wonder what happened to old Hooper, and we'll jest do our duty and help the sheriff find him."

He turned to the man wielding the whip. "I think another lesson is in order. We don't like foreigners in Texas. 'Specially uppity ones."

The whip unfurled again and struck, the rawhide running over the earlier cuts, crisscrossing them in rivers of agony.

"Git out of Texas," Hardy said, "or next time I *will* hang you." He laughed. "*If* you make it back like that. It's another long walk. A real long walk."

Rhys forced himself to remain in the half-kneeling position until he heard the sound of hoofbeats disappear in the distance. And then he crumpled flat on the ground, his blood mixing with dirt and grass, his labored breathing blowing little wisps of dust into the air.

Chapter 18

"Dammit, boy, I said I was in a hurry."

A very young Rhys struggled to get the saddle on the moving bay horse, but his usual soothing touch wasn't working. The bay was almost frantic, and Rhys saw the whip scars on its hide, and he understood the horse's skittishness. He wished that he, like the horse, could kick out at his tormentors.

But instead he kept his mouth shut, knowing that any response would earn him a back hand or worse. He tried to throw the saddle over the horse's back, but he was small, only ten, and the horse lunged against the stall, nearly crushing him.

The owner of the horse impatiently moved to the stall, jerking the horse's mouth cruelly. He lifted the whip in his hand and struck the horse, and Rhys tried to dart out of the stall.

The whip suddenly hit his back, tearing through the thin fabric of the too small shirt. Rhys felt the pain, then the blood start running.

"Ye lazy little bastard," the man said, and Rhys, weak from hunger and a sickness that wouldn't go away in the cold damp of the barn where he slept, struck back. In a sudden unexpected action, born of impotent rage and hopelessness, he struck back, knocking the whip from the man's hand and skittering away.

*But he wasn't fast enough. The man's hand came out
and grabbed what was left of his shirt. The whip came
down, again and again. Rhys tried to roll into a ball,
just as he did against so many things, against hunger
and loneliness, against the vast dark fear that never entirely left him.*

He kept hearing the man's word. Bastard.

*Like his mother's words. "Ye be a lord's son, not
that he wanted ye." His mother's words, beat again
into his consciousness as the whip tore into his back.
He remembered each one. "You should have died."*

*Red clouded his eyes, and he fought unconscious-
ness, afraid he wouldn't wake again. Instead, he steeled
himself inside, forever shunting away any softness still
left there and making a pledge. When he was bigger, no
one, absolutely no one, would ever touch him again.
No one would ever call him bastard again. No one
would . . .*

No one. He struggled up from where he lay. No
one, he thought, would touch him and live. He had to
get back. He had to get back to Land's End. And then
. . . he would make someone pay.

And pay big.

It was Wes who found him.

He and one of Miguel's sons were bringing a string
of horses back to the corral late in the afternoon, when
he saw buzzards circling above in the distance. Wes
didn't really know why he decided to check; it could
well have been a small animal, but then too much had
been happening lately. He handed the lead rope to his
companion and spurred his horse toward the carrion.

Wes saw it was a man before he knew his identity.
But then he saw the black hair, and instinctively knew
it was Rhys Redding. As he drew close, he swore. If it
hadn't been for the hair, he wondered if he would even
recognize the body. It was covered with dirt and sweat

and blood, the skin flayed and the face cut and bruised. He saw the tracks in the sand, obviously Rhys's, obviously staggering, and he wondered how far Redding had come like this.

Was he even alive?

Wes dismounted, taking his canteen, and signaled to Miguel's son to approach. When the young man saw Rhys, he made the sign of the cross. "Is he alive, señor?"

Wes bent on his remaining knee and balanced himself with the other half leg. A rope was around Redding's neck, and Wes took a knife, cutting it away. He felt for the pulse in Redding's throat, and relaxed slightly when he found one. He tensed again, though, as he noted the raw red ring around Rhys's neck.

He looked at the bruises, the torn pants. Rhys's hands were tied in back of him. Wes quickly cut through those ropes, too. "I'd say he's been dragged, and whipped. Christ knows what else. Bastards," he said, almost spitting out the words. He didn't like Redding, but he wouldn't wish this on his worst enemy, except perhaps on the men who did this. Redding was here because of Wes, because of his threats, and because of his sister. "Goddamn them," he said. And then he thought of Susannah, and his throat went dry.

Wes thought about taking him someplace else, but there wasn't any other place. He knew he wasn't welcome in any home in the county. And Redding needed a doctor. Badly.

He poured some water on Redding's face and was rewarded as the man slowly opened his eyes and stared at him a moment, before his lips bent into the usual wry smile. "I'd rather drink that, than . . . have you drown me," he said, each word said in a harsh almost gasping tone which spoke, more than his words, of his thirst.

Wes couldn't help a slight smile. Nothing had changed Redding's caustic personality, at least. He helped lift Redding's head and held the canteen to his lips, letting the water drip into his mouth. He saw the throat gulp greedily, and again he cursed under his breath. "I take it you're going to live," he finally said.

Rhys's dark eyes fixed on him. "So I can get those bloody bastards," he said.

Regardless of Rhys Redding's current condition, Wes knew he was damned glad it was the Martins the Welshman hated. He suspected they had made a bad mistake leaving Redding alive. The look on his face was different from any Wes had seen; it reflected a cold implacable fury that created shivers even down his own back. He had thought the Welshman's expression, when confronting the thieves months back had been daunting; it had been downright friendly compared to this silent, soul-deep rage. Wes knew his war, his and Susannah's, had now become Rhys Redding's war, and for the briefest of moments he pitied the Martins.

"Lowell Martin?" he asked,

"The sniveling brother," Rhys said.

"Should I call the sheriff?"

Rhys shook his head. "It's my business now!" The words were a low rumbling promise. He moved, and his body seemed to shiver with pain.

Redding stilled, apparently, it appeared to Wes, to adapt to the pain, and then his expression eased slightly. "As you said, the sheriff is probably on their payroll. Martin said . . . if I went to the law, he and his men would say they found me on a stolen horse, that they were only . . . teaching me a lesson. And then they would 'discover' the body of the man who . . . had been riding that horse."

Wes thought he knew what was coming. "What did happen to him?"

"I killed him," Rhys said emotionlessly.

"And they left you alive?"

"An object lesson, I believe," Rhys said. "And I'm

... not sure they really thought I *would* get back. If you hadn't come along ..."

"I saw the buzzards ..."

Rhys closed his eyes. "I don't know how far I came. It was an old cotton tree ... a hanging tree."

"Christ," Wes said. "That's at least three miles away. How the hell did you—?" He looked down at the man sprawled on the dirt. He had apparently walked, or crawled, three miles on feet that were butchered, with his hands tied, and a back which must be sheer agony.

But now was no time to talk, and Wes knew it. Those cuts needed cleaning and tending. "Can you get up?" he asked.

Rhys opened his eyes again, his eyes almost blank now. But he nodded.

"Take Jesus's horse. He can ride bareback on one of the string. He'll help you mount."

Rhys nodded again. He looked down at his chest, at the matted blood. "Your shirt," he said.

Wes looked confused.

"Your ... shirt. I don't ... want to ... scare Susannah. My back ... I think it's even worse."

"She'll have to see it."

Rhys shook his head. "No. You ... or Hannah. Swear it."

Wes shook his head. "She nursed you in the hospital. I don't—"

"You don't have to understand. Your word ... she won't see my back?"

Wes finally nodded his head. He didn't know whether it would be possible, but he now realized Redding wouldn't move unless he promised. Wes knew Susannah too well. She would try to take over immediately. Damnation.

"Say it."

"I swear," Wes said, exasperated now. Yet it was the

first time Redding had ever asked anything of him. It was unnerving.

Wes got up on his crutches and leaned down, offering his hand while Jesus did the same. The Mexican was seventeen and slim, but he had a lean strength. Redding took Wes's instead, and Wes again felt a small bit of satisfaction as he provided the strength and balance Redding needed—even on the damned crutches.

Redding swayed for a moment, and Wes saw the lips press tightly together, watched a muscle twitch in his throat, and knew the pain must be enormous. He didn't think he had ever before seen such willpower . . . three miles, for God's sake. "Your shirt . . ." Redding repeated.

Redding was standing on his own now, though swaying slightly.

Wes took off his shirt and handed it to Redding. "That blood's going to go right through it."

"It's mostly dried," Redding said as he shrugged the shirt on carefully.

Wes knew the pain must be agonizing. He looked at Jesus. "Go to town for the doctor."

The Mexican nodded, but hesitated for just a moment. "You can manage the horses . . . and the señor?"

Wes nodded. "Once we get Señor Redding on a horse, he'll be all right." He looked at Redding, who nodded.

The Mexican looked dubious, but he went over to his mount and held it as Rhys hobbled over to it. Jesus made his hands into a cup and leaned down, waiting for Rhys to put his left foot in it.

Rhys took the saddle horn, grateful for it now, put one of his bloody feet into Jesus's hands, and painfully rose into the saddle, discarding the stirrups.

"You will be all right, señor?"

No. But he would survive as he'd survived other times. He nodded. "Thank you," he said, as he looked down at the Mexican's bloody hands.

"It is nothing, señor. I will bring a doctor."

Rhys forced a smile. "Be careful."

"They killed my brother. I am always careful, but I will avenge him someday."

"We both will, Jesus," Rhys said softly. "We both will."

Rhys fought to stay in the saddle. The saddle horn he had so disdained earlier helped him do it, and he clung to it as a leech clings to its victim. He wasn't sure he had told Wes and Jesus the truth. He wasn't sure at all that he could make it.

He had survived on pure hate thus far. He had wanted to give up so many times, but something in him would not give Hardy Martin that satisfaction.

He tried desperately to fasten on something. Not Susannah now. Not the pity he knew he would see on her face, not the horror if she saw the whip marks. Especially if she saw the old ones. They were faint now, very faint, but they could still be seen. One woman he'd slept with had felt them, and asked about them. Since then he had either kept his shirt on when he made love or kept his back turned away. He'd done that with Susannah the other day.

There was something so ... demeaning, so ... shaming about a whipping, about that rope around his neck. He swallowed, still feeling the choking sensation, the humiliation of being led behind the horse like an animal. The anger kept him conscious, as his mind debated different forms of punishment. He would ruin the Martins. He would humiliate them as he had been.

Susannah's war had become his.

Susannah paced the floor restlessly. She thought she might go mad with the waiting.

She had hoped Rhys Redding would return before

supper. And Wes was also late. The others had returned an hour ago, and they said Wes was on the way.

Where were they?

She wished she had gone with them this morning, but she was so determined that Wes take responsibility. But it gnawed at her, this sense of helplessness, this need to be doing something.

And Rhys? How she had hungered to see him today, as she did every day. But each day that hunger grew stronger, more powerful. Her occasional glimpses merely whetted that need.

He'd evidently had his meal with the hands this morning, and she'd just barely had a glimpse of him riding off with Wes and Jaime. She wondered if he'd changed his mind about working the ranch, but then one of the hands came back and said Rhys had left the others about noon.

Just thinking about him hurt. Every inch of her ached for him, to be with him. To her soul, it hurt. She cared so desperately about him, and in so many ways. Her elusive nighthawk.

"Riders coming in!"

She heard the call, and she strode over to the door and threw it open.

Two men and a string of horses. She recognized Wes holding the horses. The other man—

Dear heaven, it was Rhys. She saw his dark hair, but little else was recognizable. Not his horse, nor his seat on the horse. He was barely holding on to the saddle horn, his shoulders slumped, and . . .

She saw the blood then, and the bruises on his face. His feet weren't in the stirrups but hanging down, bare and terrible looking.

Her heart clenched. Her fingers turned into fists for a moment, and then she ran to him. "Rhys!"

He barely looked at her. Wes called to her, "Go get some help."

"What happened?" she said, unable to take her eyes from Rhys.

"I'll tell you later. For God's sake, get Miguel or Jaime to take him upstairs."

She didn't have to. She was suddenly surrounded by men, and Wes was giving orders as he once had. But she barely noticed that. She noticed little except all the bruises and cuts on her nighthawk, the paleness of the usually tanned face, the pressed lips which she knew from experience meant extreme pain.

"Oh, Rhys," she said, her heart in her stomach. She reached out to touch him, but he flinched away. She quickly withdrew her hand.

His eyes focused on her then. With difficulty, she could tell. "I'm all right," he said. He swung his leg over the saddle and slid off, wincing slightly as his feet touched the ground.

Jaime was there, and he put his arm around Rhys. Rhys straightened, tensed. Bloody Christ, but he hurt. But Jaime didn't know about his back. Not yet. No one did, except the Mexican lad and Wes, and for some reason he trusted both Jesus and Wes not to say anything.

So he bit back the agony and said nothing as the man's arm pressed against the cuts.

"The second bedroom on the right," Susannah told Jaime, and started to hurry after them.

"Sue!"

She turned as she heard Wes's voice.

"Stay here," he said.

"But—"

"If you care anything about him, you'll stay here," Wes added.

"No," she said.

"It's what he wants, dammit."

That stopped her. "What happened?"

"Hardy Martin."

"His feet—"

"I don't know all of it," Wes said, "but he's had a hell of a time, and he doesn't want to talk about it now."

"I . . . can help."

"Jesus went for the doctor." The words were curt and he didn't add that was Redding's choice. He didn't have to. Her face flushed red and the violet eyes filled with tears.

"What do *you* care about him?" Her question was unexpectedly sharp, but also full of hurt.

Wes wished he hadn't given his word to Redding, but he had. And he understood Redding's demand. Dammit, but he understood. He understood better than most men could.

"For him, personally, I don't; for a . . . man staying here on our—your—property, I care one hell of a lot. Call it a violation of our hospitality or whatever you will. And I'll abide by his wishes."

Part of Susannah's mind noted Wes's newfound decisiveness and determination, but the other part, the larger part, focused only on Rhys, the way he looked, dear God, and how much she wanted to help him.

If you care anything about him, you'll stay here. Her heart was breaking for him, for her wounded nighthawk. But she cared, dear God in heaven, how much she cared.

Wes turned to Hannah, who had been hovering anxiously nearby. "Get some hot water and plenty of towels. And the salve. And whiskey. Plenty of whiskey." He clumped away on the crutches toward the room where Rhys had been taken. Susannah bit hard on her lip, tasting blood where she'd done so, and then hurried after Hannah. If nothing else, she could help boil water and gather towels. Perhaps some bandages.

Her eyes now nearly blinded by tears, Susannah filled the pots as Hannah put wood in the stove. This was her fault. She had continued to urge and entice

Rhys to stay when he hadn't wanted to. She and Wes. They were both responsible for this.

How much more could his body take? The terrible wound that had put him in Libby Prison, the subsequent infection, and now this. And she didn't even know how bad it was. That was the worst. She didn't know what had happened, whether he'd been shot. She knew how cruel Hardy Martin could be. Once, when she was in school, she and Mark had found him torturing a dog. Mark had attacked Hardy, beaten him in front of a number of classmates who'd gathered at her screams. He had never forgiven Mark that. Nor her.

Lowell was more sophisticated than his brother, more cunning, but just as wicked. The Martins had been nothing before the war, and she had watched as they profited by it. And the more they'd profited, the greedier they'd become.

The water was boiling now . . . too hot. She moved it aside and placed another pan on the oven, quickly warming the water, and then she carried both to the bedroom door, followed by Hannah, who held towels, salve, and a bottle of whiskey.

Susannah heard voices inside, but they were too low to understand. She knocked and the door opened. Jaime took the pots of water, and then the other items. Susannah could see Wes's back, but his body shielded the bed from view. "How is he?" she whispered.

Jaime's young face was hard, his jaw set, and his eyes angry. "He'll be all right," he said. "Send the doctor in, as soon as he gets here."

"Isn't . . . there anything I can do?"

His face softened as he shook his head. "I don't think so, Miss Susannah. Well, maybe there is. Is there a nightshirt around . . . Mark's or his father's?"

Something to do. Susannah nodded. "I'll find one."

She directed Hannah to stay on the porch and await the doctor. She went to the room she'd shared with Mark, that one night so long ago. She had not touched his things since she'd returned. She didn't even know what was there. She closed her eyes against the welling behind them, that ache of grief that made her head feel like hot lead. Was she a Jonah? Everyone she loved seem to be . . . destroyed. Her father. Mark. Wes. Now Rhys. She had to send him away. If he got well, she had to! Tell him he was no longer of use.

Despair, grief, emptiness, fear gripped her in tandem. Despair and emptiness for her. Grief and fear for Rhys.

A nightshirt! So little to do for him! She finally found one. Linen. Light. But she couldn't imagine him in a nightshirt. Not that hard, lean, beautiful body.

What did they do to him?

She swallowed hard, then closed the trunk she'd been riffling through and took the garment to Rhys's room, handing it through a door barely cracked open, wanting to hurl herself past the barriers and see him.

"Some more," she heard Wes say inside, soothingly. So unlike his gruff voice of late. "A few more sips." There was a gentleness in her brother's voice she hadn't heard since before the war. A soft persuasion.

"Bloody hell, I don't want—" Rhys's voice was somehow different, harsh now without the aristocratic tone to it, more of a . . . what? She couldn't put her finger on a description. It was just . . . different.

"I'll be damned if I'll clean those damn cuts unless you drink more whiskey," Wes said with a firmness that would usually have warmed Susannah's heart, but now that heart was too uncertain, too afraid.

And then Jaime shut the door again. Against intrusion. Against her intrusion.

She leaned against the wall, feeling the outsider, feeling lost and lonely. And then she straightened. She realized she was feeling sorry for herself as well as Rhys. He wouldn't appreciate either of those emotions.

Susannah set her jaw, firmly locked back the tears, and went to join Hannah to wait for the doctor.

Rhys bit back the groans. The whiskey had helped—the whiskey he hadn't wanted. He knew from the look in Wes's eyes that Susannah's brother knew exactly why he hadn't wanted it. He hadn't wanted to become dependent, as Wes had been well on his way to becoming.

Wes, his face flushed and even a bit chagrined with the knowledge, had still insisted. "We don't have anything else," he said, and "I'll be damned if I'll clean those cuts unless you do."

So Rhys had taken a few sips, and then a few more. He tried not to tense as Wes's hand soaked a towel in the hot water and then slowly started to clean his back, where the worst slices were.

Wes and Jaime had packed pillows around him so as little of the torn skin as possible touched anything, but some did, and every movement was pure agony. He concentrated on that pain, every second of it, every burning instant. He wanted to remember it when he went after Hardy Martin.

"Christ," Jaime said, "I wish Doc Campbell would get here."

"No more than I," Wes said, although their patient said nothing. His face was blank, as if he had willed away any feeling.

Wes eased the cloth along the ridges caked with dirt. He noticed some very old scars, but he didn't say anything. He just knew his respect for Rhys Redding was growing. He thought he would probably be yelling like a baby if someone was doing this to him. It didn't make him like the Welshman, but he sure as hell admired him. He still couldn't figure out how the man had walked so far.

He finally finished. There was nothing more he

could do to help the back wounds. He wasn't about ready to pour alcohol on them, not without the doctor here. "Can you turn over?" he said.

Redding sat up awkwardly. "I don't think I want to try it."

"That's good enough," Wes said, as he leaned over and started rinsing Redding's chest. "Why don't you go back to England?" he asked suddenly.

"I thought you wanted me to stay . . . badly enough to blackmail me."

"I was wrong. It's our battle."

"Not any longer," his patient said through gritted teeth.

Wes watched a muscle flex in Redding's cheek as he started cleaning yet another cut. "I'm sorry," he said suddenly, surprising even himself. "I—we shouldn't have asked you to fight our battles."

Rhys glanced up at him, met his direct gaze. "Don't be. I probably would have died if you hadn't come by."

Wes grinned. "I don't think so. You're too damned stubborn to die, and . . . too damn mean as well."

Rhys's gaze met his, and this time there was no amusement in it. "I came pretty bloody close," he said slowly. "Too close."

Wes's hand stilled. And his eyebrow raised, just as Rhys's had on occasion.

"Is that amusing?" Rhys asked with irritation.

"Only that you finally admit you may be human."

Rhys glared at him.

"Why weren't you wearing a gun?"

"A misjudgment," Rhys said. "I found out long ago not to let my enemies know my . . . capabilities. Usually, I compensate for that. Unfortunately, I was distracted."

"I don't think I want to ask you why."

"Don't," Rhys said. "But it's a mistake I won't make again."

Wes's smile disappeared, but his touch remained light.

He was almost through when the knock came at the door, and it was opened to admit an older man with a black bag. He took one look at Rhys's bruised and torn torso. "The Martins?"

Wes nodded.

The man walked over to Rhys's side and held out his hand. "Dr. Campbell. From the looks of you, I think you're damned lucky to be alive."

"A miscalculation on their part," Rhys said.

The doctor didn't comment. His hands touched the torn skin on Rhys's chest and then his back, his breath catching as he did so.

"I'm going to have to stitch some of those, or you're going to have some godawful scars." His gaze fell to the newly healed wound Rhys had received in Virginia. "Looks like you lead a mighty interesting life, Mr.—"

"Redding," Wes interceded quickly, his eyes meeting Rhys's dark gaze. "He's a guest here."

The doctor shook his head. "Things just aren't the same anymore. Been busier than I've ever been. Suspect most of the cause are those Martin boys."

"No one's doing anything about them?" Wes asked.

"Not too many folks strong enough left," the doctor said. He mentioned a dozen men who had died, all once friends of Wes or Wes's father. "Everyone's scared now." He looked over at Wes and then down at his missing leg. "I'm glad you're back, Wes. We need you."

Wes gave him a sardonic look. "The Yank?" The words were bitter, deriding himself.

"Give 'im time."

"I don't know if we have time."

The doctor eyed him carefully. "Doesn't sound like the Wes Carr I knew. Nothing stopped him, then." He changed the subject. "There's an anxious young lady outside. Why don't you two go outside and talk to her while I take care of Mr. Redding?"

Wes looked at Rhys, who nodded. "Just tell her I'm all right."

The doctor waited until Wes and Jaime left, and then he fastened all his attention on Rhys. "Are you?"

Rhys raised a dark bushy eyebrow in question.

"All right?"

"Hell, no."

The doctor smiled. "Then let's get to work."

Dr. Campbell left two hours later, after accepting a cup of coffee from Susannah, who searched his face for any kind of news.

"He's going to be in a lot of pain, and he needs a lot of rest, though I would guess right now you might have to tie him down. Damndest constitution I've ever seen."

Susannah wanted to scream. No one, not her brother or Jaime, would tell her what had happened.

"What exactly," she asked the doctor, "are his injuries?"

"Cuts, bruises, general mishandling," Campbell said. "Nothing that time won't cure. Interesting man. Where's he from?"

"Wales," Wes said, and Susannah glared at him, realizing there was a conspiracy to keep the conversation away from Rhys's injuries. But then, all that was really important was that her nighthawk would live.

"Can I see him?"

The doctor shook his head. "I gave him something to sleep. He didn't want to take it until I told him rest was the only way he'd get his strength back. Don't you go disturbing him, now."

When he left, Susannah turned on Wes. "What happened to him?"

Wes gave her an abbreviated story. "Hardy Martin

and some men surprised him. Dragged him behind a horse. He's damned lucky to be alive. I don't think Hardy really intended that, but he was too much of a coward to finish it himself. If Redding had been found dead on the prairie or in the hills, anyone could be blamed.

"But if he lived . . ."

"Hardy believes he's a harmless tenderfoot. He threatened to charge him with horse stealing and murder if Redding survived and said anything."

"We've got to make Rhys leave," Susannah said.

Wes shook his head. "I don't know why you brought him along in the beginning."

Susannah hesitated. "Remember, when we were kids, when I brought that hawk home?"

Wes's eyes narrowed. "It died."

"I know," she said softly. "But Rhys reminded me a little of the hawk in the hospital. Wild and free . . . and so badly hurt. Yet defiant. I thought maybe . . ."

"You could save this one," he finished for her. "I seem to remember that hawk bit you."

Susannah winced. He would remember that. "Anyway, we have to make him go now. He's been hurt enough."

Wes's gaze never left her eyes. "There's no way in hell you can do that now, sister mine."

"But—"

"Ask him to leave the ranch, and he'd only go someplace else around here. He wants Hardy Martin and by God, he'll get him."

Susannah looked at him with tear-glazed eyes. "What have we done, Wes?"

"Unleashed your hawk, Sue."

Clad in a linen nightshirt made bulky by bandages, Rhys squirmed slightly on his stomach. He had taken only a sip of the opiate the doctor had left. He didn't want his mind befuddled.

He had memorized everything the doctor said as he worked on his cuts, sewing up two wounds on his back. Rhys had asked about the Martins, about every family who'd had unexplained mishaps, about Martin's wealth and how he used it, about the sheriff.

The doctor had rambled on, apparently trying to keep his patient occupied as he sewed up the whip-lashes and applied salve to the other wounds caused by the dragging. When he finished bandaging Rhys's feet, he sighed heavily. "You won't be able to walk for at least a week."

Rhys merely stared at him with eyes that he knew unsettled the doctor. There were no other prognostica-tions about his rate of recovery.

But he had information he needed, that he was stacking in orderly piles in his mind. Ten families, lo-cated along the river or along creeks running into the river, were holding out against the Martins. Six others had folded, selling away their land.

Ten families!

The question was how to bring them together.

He remembered Susannah's words the other night. They needed a leader. They wouldn't follow Wes. They probably wouldn't follow anyone associated with him. The wounds from the war were still too deep.

How then?

He recalled what Susannah had called him the other day. A hawk. A nighthawk.

Thoughts tumbled over each other in their eager-ness to be heard. A leader. Perhaps he could conjure one up. Perhaps someone they didn't know but could grow to trust.

Rhys knew he could probably take the Martins alone. One by one. But now he didn't want to do that. He didn't want any trouble placed on Susannah. Any suspicion.

And his desire went even deeper than that, less philanthropic. He wanted the Martins to suffer, to see everything slip away without knowing how or why. And then ... then would come the time to finish it.

The nighthawk. It had a nice ring to it. Like the names of the English highwaymen of years past. It seemed rather appropriate.

Unable to sleep because of the agonizing pain, he lay awake, making plans.

And he smiled, a smile that had no amusement in it at all.

Chapter 19

Her heart in her throat, Susannah took coffee and food into Rhys the next morning. No one who looked into her eyes tried to stop her.

As usual, he surprised her. She hadn't known what to expect, perhaps a half-dead Rhys Redding, but although his face was battered and his hands in dismal shape, his dark, onyx eyes were glittering and alive. They were, as always, difficult to read, but she would swear she saw anticipation in them.

His powers of recovery had always astounded her, but never more than now. He was like a weed plant in the garden. The more you tried to destroy it, uproot or stomp it, the faster it seemed to regenerate.

She had to smile at the analogy. This was one weed that she wanted. The thought sent shudders through her body, a dart of desire flaming through her like an arrow.

Rhys looked puzzled at her expression, even as his gaze settled on her tray. He looked strange in a white nightshirt. Incongruous. The white linen contrasted with the darkness of his hair, his eyes, the deep tan of his skin and now the dark stubble that covered his cheeks. She suspected the nightclothes were probably the first he'd ever worn, though she didn't know where that idea had developed. But it was there. And the hot, dizzying feelings propagated.

"I was just thinking," she said, "that you are indestructible. I expected to see you half-dead."

His twisted half-smile was amused, much to her surprise. "It would take more than that little coward."

She moved over to him and set the tray down on his lap, and she couldn't help but put her fingers to his swollen bruised cheek. "He did well enough."

"Not by half, my love," Rhys said lightly. "I was once a street kid in London. Your God doesn't make them tougher than that."

Street kid in London. Another little gem dropped. And again, it created more confusion in her mind. Son of a lord. Street kid in London. Africa. Blockade runner. None of it made any sense. She wondered if he'd meant to reveal that tidbit of information, and then she knew he had, as she looked into his eyes. He never said anything he hadn't thought out. At least, hardly ever. He had meant to say exactly those words, and now he waited for her reaction.

She didn't disappoint him. She cocked her head and grinned at him. "A street kid in London, a mercenary in Africa. What else, Major Redding?" She couldn't keep the teasing note from her voice.

"Certainly not a major," he said.

"No," she agreed softly, her hand gently caressing his face. "Nothing as ordinary as that."

Now his expression changed, looked momentarily uncertain, as if he'd not expected that particular answer.

"No questions?"

She smiled. "I discovered long ago that you're going to tell me exactly what you want to tell me."

His hand, which was raw and cut and blistered, reached up and took her hand, turning it over and looking at it, at the calluses there, probably from riding, at the strength which could also be so gentle as it had when it brushed his face. "You're an extraordinary woman, Mrs. Fallon."

"You're pretty unique yourself." She grinned. "The doctor said anyone else would be dead. I expected a near corpse, and I find you almost totally resurrected."

"Not totally," he said. "A few days perhaps."

"The doctor said a few weeks."

Rhys merely raised one of those eyebrows that made him look perpetually amused.

"And then what?" she asked, holding her breath.

"And then I'll do what you've wanted . . . take care of your problem, everyone's problem."

She shook her head, the smile gone now, and her eyes pleading. "I don't want that anymore."

"What do you want?"

"For you to be safe. I don't want you to be hurt anymore, particularly for me. Neither does Wes."

He looked questioningly at that last comment, then shrugged. "It's not for you, anymore," he said, surprising her that he even admitted that once his actions might have been headed in that direction.

"What are you going to do?"

But his little revelations had come to an end, and she knew it. His hand played with her much smaller one, then unexpectedly he brought it to his lips and kissed it in a gesture at once so unexpectedly cavalier and achingly gentle, she could only stare at him. His gaze met hers, and for the first time she saw something hurting and wounded in them for the briefest of seconds.

"Thank you for caring, my love," he said in a low but light tone. The obviously intended self-mockery in the words didn't work, not with that brief flash of vulnerability, and she sensed there were more words unsaid. But she couldn't believe what immediately flashed into her mind. *No one has done that before.* Of course, they would have. Many people must have cared for her nighthawk. How could they not?

How could they not, when everything inside her ached for him, shared his hurt and his pain? And loved so desperately that she was afraid to show it?

But what few seconds of intimacy there had been were gone, the opportunity vanished. He had surrendered her hand and was now drinking coffee and eating.

"Rhys?"

His gaze moved up, and any feelings that she might have imagined were gone. "What are you going to do?"

"Go to Austin again," he said. "As soon as I can. Probably in two days."

"That's not what I meant."

"You are better off not knowing," Rhys said.

"And Wes?"

"Wes, too."

"Are you coming back to the ranch?"

His eyes were blacker than ever, more impenetrable. "I don't know yet."

She tightened her hands into fists. She had a terrible sense of dread, of disaster. He couldn't fight the Martins, and all their men, alone. But that, she knew, was exactly what he intended. "Leave Texas."

"After everything you and your brother did to get me here?"

"Please."

"No." The denial was so flat it screamed at her.

There was nothing else for her to say. "Do you need water? Or me to shave you?"

His hand went up and felt his cheek. He grimaced, then smiled dryly. "I'm afraid that would be a torture of a different kind."

Her gaze went down to the sheet covering the lower part of his torso. Even with that, and the nightshirt, his arousal was evident.

Susannah forced her eyes upward again, trying to

ignore her own responding body. "Isn't there anything I can do?"

"Tell me everything about the people here, everything the Martins have done. Dr. Campbell told me some. I want more. As much information as you can give me."

"Why?"

He looked at her stonily again.

"Erin," she said, understanding once more that he was not going to explain himself.

"Erin?"

"Wes's girl. My friend. She knows everyone."

He looked surprised. "Don't you?"

She hesitated. "I've . . . lost touch with some."

His obsidian eyes studied her. "It hurts you, doesn't it?" he said suddenly, his mouth grim.

She imitated his casual shrug. "It doesn't matter."

He nodded, but she knew he didn't believe her. She wished she believed it. But the ostracism was a sore wound. She'd always liked people, had enjoyed them, each in his or her own way. These last four years had been lonely.

"Can you get her over here?"

"Easily," Susannah said. "I'm surprised, in fact, that she wasn't here earlier."

"Two nights from now," he said.

She eyed him dubiously, her gaze going over his face, his hands, and then farther down. She still didn't know the extent of his injuries; she only knew how he looked yesterday coming in, the uncharacteristic droop of his shoulders, the raw soles of his feet, the battered face that looked even worse today, now that the bruises had all turned multicolored.

"Will you do it?" he asked.

She nodded. Of course she would. If he asked her to walk on fire she'd probably do it. A humbling realization. But true.

He took another sip of coffee and moved slightly,

very carefully, too carefully. So carefully her heart almost broke.

He looked up and caught her expression. "Tell me everything you know," he demanded.

And she did.

Hours later, he was alone again. It was late afternoon and he got to his feet. He hated the bloody nightshirt, but it shielded his back. Still, he felt like an idiot in it. He always slept nude, and he hated the confinement of any kind of clothes when they weren't necessary. He tested his feet. Christ, they hurt.

He looked through the window at the activity outside. Another day. It had been more than twenty-four hours since he'd encountered Martin yesterday.

So much had changed in those twenty-four hours.

When Susannah had begged him to leave, when she had said Wes agreed, he'd felt a weakness inside that momentarily tore down every bit of armor he had.

No one, not Lauren Bradley, nor Adrian Cabot, who had probably come as close to being a friend as he'd ever had—even in the brief time they'd known each other—had ever thought of him first. It was a new thought, a new emotion, a new . . . burden.

Susannah? Susannah, he partly understood. She was probably the most . . . Bloody Christ, he didn't know what she was most. Loyal? Sympathetic? Giving? Never really having come in contact with the above, he wasn't sure.

But Wes Carr? He didn't understand that at all. He hadn't been surprised at his rescue by Carr; the damn idiot would rescue any soul lunatic enough to get himself in the position Rhys had been in, but the man's understanding, his unexpected gentleness when he'd started cleaning his wounds, had startled Rhys to the core. And then his plea that he leave—now that really was beyond understanding.

Unless he thought Rhys was going to be more trouble than help. That was a thought, Rhys rationalized cynically as he mostly did. That must be it.

It didn't matter. Wes couldn't be connected with what he was planning. Wes was too identifiable with his missing leg. And probably much too honorable for some of the tactics Rhys planned to use.

A bit of safecracking, perhaps. Some robbery here and there. Some rustling in kind. Rhys knew he had skills no one, especially not Wes or Susannah, would ever suspect.

Through the window, he saw Susannah moving toward the corral, her dark hair pulled back into a careless knot as she spoke to one of the cowhands. Her dress was simple, and yet he didn't think he'd ever seen anyone quite as lovely. He swallowed, remembering how she had looked at him, even with his day-old beard. As if . . .

As if he could start over again, and be everything she wanted him to be. But by the end of this battle, she would probably run screaming at the sight of him. No. Susannah wouldn't do that. But those beautiful violet eyes might well regard him with fear. He would be gone before he saw that. Long gone. Why did the thought hurt so bloody damn much?

Susannah didn't have to invite Erin. Her friend showed up the next day in a buckboard after going to the crossroads for supplies and hearing something about trouble at the Fallon place. No one knew exactly what. No one was talking except in whispers.

And she had other news, too. Federal troops had arrived. Some folks had seen Lowell Hardy talk to the captain in charge.

Rhys, completely bored with the bed and the room, had made his cautious way into the main room, wearing nothing on his feet but the bandages. It still hurt like bloody hell, and his feet were too swollen for any of the boots Susannah had given him to try: her dead husband's, his brother's, and her father-in-law's. Rhys felt like a damned vulture, although he'd worn dead men's clothes before. But there was something different about this. More personal. He didn't like it. And he'd hated the damned nightshirt. At least he was wearing one of his own shirts now, after wrapping a cloth around his back wounds so they wouldn't stain his very limited wardrobe.

To say he was out of sorts was an understatement. Even Susannah had been tiptoeing around him all day. When he appeared in the doorway, she said something about the doctor's orders, and he glared, that all too familiar glare that said keep away, a very long distance away.

She didn't do that, but neither did she suggest he return to bed.

Susannah really didn't know what to do with him. He was restless, even though she knew from the tense look on his face that he was still in a great deal of pain.

He asked about Wes, and grunted when told he'd gone out with Jaime. He ate breakfast and thanked Hannah graciously enough, but when his gaze turned to Susannah his eyes were as shuttered as they had ever been.

Only when he rose from the table, and seemed to sway a moment, did he show any weakness, and then he walked cautiously to a chair and, again, very carefully leaned back.

Susannah, who had at first been pleased that he'd joined her, soon found he was in no mood for small talk. He had milked her of all knowledge of the community the day before and now he appeared indifferent to her, lost in his own thoughts, his own plans, which he obviously had no intention of sharing.

He asked for some paper, and she watched him sketch something, but she didn't know what. His fist crumpled the first effort, and he tried again. Finally, he seemed satisfied.

She went in and helped Hannah with the cooking chores. Some of the men would be back for the midday meal. Food would be taken to the others by pack horse. She halfway thought about going along.

But then Erin came, obviously looking for Wes. She was prettily dressed, and Susannah almost immediately knew that any excuse to come would have sufficed. Susannah had heard the familiar call, "Riders coming," and she had gone out on the porch, half expecting to see the Martins again. Rhys had tensed in the chair, and risen too, this time tucking a gun in his belt underneath his shirt and placing a rifle just inside the door. Susannah watched Erin's eyes widen at the sight of Rhys next to her, and she understood why. Rhys was two inches taller than Wes's own substantial height, and his dark Welsh features were distinct, even as discolored and swollen as they now were.

"Erin," she said, realizing they had not met before, that Rhys had always been off somewhere before, "this is Rhys Redding. He's the man who accompanied us from Virginia. Rhys, this is Erin MacDougal, my best friend." Only friend, she almost added, but didn't.

She didn't know what to expect of Rhys, but he turned the full force of his charm on Erin, bowing low and taking her hand, bringing it to his lips.

Erin cast a quick glance at Susannah, who merely smiled and shrugged.

"My pleasure, Miss MacDougal," Rhys said, ignoring Erin's avid, fascinated, even horrified gaze as she registered his face and all the bruises coloring it.

"Should I ask what happened?"

Susannah looked heavenward.

"A small disagreement, Miss MacDougal," Rhys said easily with a charming smile, even on battered lips. Susannah wanted to murder him, maybe even do

worse than the Martins had, after the icy treatment
she'd received most of the day.

Rhys's British upper-class accent was back firmly
in place. He was the dandy again, completely charming, completely innocuous in his bandaged feet. The
chameleon had returned.

Erin looked around. "Wes?"

Susannah smiled conspiratorially at her. "He's out
working with the horses."

"I came . . . to let you know federal troops have arrived. There's a small contingent at Jacob's Crossing."
She looked over at Rhys. "And there were whispers of
some kind of trouble here."

Rhys shrugged. "A difference of opinion over my
nationality, it seems," he said, almost indifferently.
"Breaking in a . . .tenderfoot, I think they called it."

Erin's eyes narrowed in concern and sympathy, and
Susannah had to smile. Erin had always had a soft
heart, but Rhys probably needed it less than most.

Susannah left them and sent one of the few remaining hands after Wes, saying there was news he
should hear. Federal troops. She didn't know whether
that was good or bad news, whether they were here to
protect or plunder.

Erin was inside the house with Rhys when
Susannah returned, and she felt a cold jolt watching
them together, Rhys wrapping his easy charm around
the other woman like a gentleman placing a coat
around a lady. But he was no gentleman. He'd told her
often enough, hadn't he?

Susannah scolded herself. She'd seen enough of
Rhys Redding to know he must have a purpose. But it
hurt, seeing him so attentive to another woman. Remember yesterday, she told herself. When he'd kissed
her hand with such . . . tenderness.

But had that been just an act, too? He was so
damned good at it, she didn't know. She wondered
whether she would ever know.

Rhys was asking Erin about her family, and in minutes he had the complete story about the stolen cotton last fall. Susannah was astounded at how much Erin was saying, even figures about the loss, the value of the cotton, the prospective buyers. Susannah didn't know why he wanted to know every detail, nor why Erin was providing them so readily, but he was extracting the most personal of details. The size of the mortgage on the plantation, the threats of the Martins.

And yet he was doing it in such a way that Susannah was sure Erin wasn't aware of his conscious intention to discover what he wanted to know, or even how much she was saying. Erin's eyes were almost glazed with that magic Susannah knew Rhys could invoke when he so wished with the easy twist of his mouth, the intensity of his eyes. And when he was through, he leaned back, one hand going over the side of the chair with the indifference of a dilettante.

But Wes had already seen the two heads close together—Erin's and Rhys's. Susannah had been so fascinated with the performance she hadn't heard Wes's approach until his voice, angry and barely controlled, come from the direction of the door.

"What a cozy scene!"

Jealousy fairly radiated in his voice and Susannah understood it only too well. She also felt a stab of satisfaction at Wes's proprietary tone toward Erin.

Erin's face, which had been so serious in its concentration, suddenly lit at the sight of him despite the disapproving tone, while Rhys virtually beamed with that supercilious smile that so irritated Wes. Susannah had to hold back a smile.

Wes glared at him and then at Susannah. "You sent for me?"

She nodded. "Erin said federal troops have headquartered in Austin and now there's a unit in Jacob's Crossing. They've assumed all civil authority."

Wes stumped over to the large sprawling sofa and

sat, but his gaze didn't leave Erin, and he couldn't quite hide the wistful gleam in his eyes. "What do all my neighbors think about that?" he asked in a wary tone.

Erin's eyes met his. "They hate it."

Wes sighed. "Probably won't improve my popularity. I'll have to ride over there. Talk to them about my disappearance from Libby Prison." He shot a quick look at his sister. "God knows how I'll explain it."

Erin's eyes grew wide as she tried to make sense of the words, and she looked from Susannah to Wes to Rhys, who was lounging as if he didn't have a care in the world.

"Lowell Martin was seen talking to the captain in charge," Erin offered.

"Captain? Do you remember his name?"

Erin shook her head.

Wes looked over at Rhys. "This might change things. The army might take a hand."

For a moment the hawk's eyes were back, piercing and dangerous as they fixed Wes in their sights, but the flash of emotion was so quick Susannah doubted whether Erin saw it. Her whole concentration was on Wes.

"No," Rhys said simply. Then he stood lazily. "Time for my afternoon nap, I believe," he said in a bored voice. "Miss MacDougal," he acknowledged. "So good to make your acquaintance."

He walked out of the room as if his torn feet were as whole as ever, with an arrogance Susannah thought only he could effect.

Chapter 20

Wes's mouth was dry as he watched Erin.

After Rhys had made his somewhat spectacular exit, Susannah pleaded dinner as an excuse and disappeared into the kitchen area. Wes suspected a conspiracy of some sort in the making, but then he dismissed it. Redding didn't care enough about anything to go to the trouble.

Except, perhaps, revenge. And that worried Wes. He had no idea what Rhys Redding was capable of, yet he suspected it was a great deal. He would prefer to let the army take care of lawlessness, but Redding had made it very clear that he would not.

But all those scattered thoughts fled his mind as he looked at Erin and saw the soft smile on her face, the gentle yearning that reached inside and grabbed his heart. He needed that softness. He needed her laughter. Her natural joy in life. He didn't even want to think when he'd laughed last, or even smiled with any meaning.

And now there was a lump the size of a boulder in his throat. He'd learned in the past week that he *could* do things he'd never expected to be able to do again, that he wasn't completely useless, but still . . . neither was he whole.

"Thank you for coming with the news," he said stiffly. "I don't think anyone else would."

"Your hands would have learned soon enough," she said, her eyes intent on his face, on every expression that flitted over it. "It was really just an excuse, you know." She gave him the impish smile that he always thought the leprechauns must have bestowed upon her. She was so completely guileless, which was why he had always trusted her. Why he had always loved her.

And now her heart was in her eyes, in her face, and it was asking questions he didn't have answers for. He had more confidence in himself now, but was it enough?

He had lost not only a part of his body, but any standing he'd had in the community. He was a pariah, and he would make her a pariah too.

No, he couldn't ask her to share what was left of his life. Not yet. Especially not until this thing with the Martins was settled. Not until he felt certain he could protect her, and what was his.

Perhaps then. It was the first hope he'd really felt, and something in his face must have revealed it, for she slipped over to the sofa when he sat, and moved down next to him, taking his hand and holding it tight.

"I've missed you, Wes. Knowing you're here. It was bad enough when you were thousands of miles away, but now . . . it's torture. I keep making excuses to come, and then I worry you'll hate me for doing that."

Wes buried his head in her hair. "I could never hate you, Imp," he said, sliding into his pet name for her. "It's just . . . I have things to work out."

Erin wanted to say so much. She wanted to say she didn't care about his leg, but that, she knew, wouldn't help now. She'd always been able to sense things about him; she'd probably even known he was going to join the Yank army before he did. She'd seen his struggle with himself, and made herself be silent, although it was difficult. But she had loved him all her life, since she and Susannah were children, and he and Mark had taken the role of protectors. The day he asked her to marry him had been the happiest in her life; the day he left for war the saddest.

And now he was back. Austere instead of carefree. Bitter instead of happy. Wary where once he'd plunged into anything. He was different. Yet the same. And she loved him even more for the suffering which had creased his face and made his eyes so still and solemn. She both loved and hated his sense of honor, his unwavering loyalty to those he loved.

How could she convince him that only he could make her happy, that only he, one leg or not, could make her own life worthy of the name?

"What did you think about our guest?" he asked suddenly, and Erin had to think a moment before answering. She knew he was trying to divert her attention, and yet there was a curious insistence in the question. And then she recalled the curtness in Wes's face when he had entered the room.

"He's . . . charming."

"Charming?" he echoed with something close to an explosion.

Erin's usually straightforward nature took note. Could that be jealousy? She liked it. She liked it very much. So much for his declaration a few days ago that he had outgrown her.

She nodded. "In fact," she said, "he's fascinating. I've never met anyone from England before. Much less Wales."

Wes's eyes narrowed and he looked as if he'd swallowed a varmint. "Fascinating?" he asked.

"You keep repeating me," she complained, barely able to keep a twinkle of mischief from her voice. "I hope he's going to stay a bit longer."

"You hope . . . ?"

A lock of Wes's dark blond hair fell over his forehead, and his eyebrows had drew together. He looked thunderous, and as if he had more life than any time since he'd returned from war. His eyes, unlike Susannah's, were a bright blue, although they had seemed dull days ago. Now they had a fire Erin recognized. She felt a fire herself, burning bright inside.

She loved his indignation, his ... outrage, which said more than anything he still cared.

She nodded seriously, knowing she probably shouldn't do this, but anything, anything that would knock him out of that lethargy, that despair she'd seen the other night was worth his momentary discomfort. She'd really been rather disconcerted by Susannah's visitor, as if something was not quite right but she couldn't put her finger on it. She knew Susannah was smitten. There was no hiding that fact, but despite the man's charm there was something about him that made her uneasy.

"Stay away from him," Wes suddenly ordered.

"Why?" she asked. "He's your guest."

"He's not a guest," he denied, despite the fact that the man had acted quite at home as he sauntered toward a bedroom for his "afternoon nap."

"What is he?" she asked, wide-eyed, fascinated by all the clouds now in Wes's face.

Christ. How to answer that? Wes had no answer. None that made any sense. He didn't know exactly how the Welshman had wended his way into their lives so completely, had him, for God's sake, tending the man so sympathetically.

"A hand," he finally said.

Erin's face showed her doubts. No one had ever acted less like a cowhand than the lazily charming Welshman. It was quite astounding, she thought, how interested he had seemed in her for a while, only to let that interest completely drop so suddenly.

"Is he going to be staying?"

A muscle flexed in Wes's throat. "I don't know."

That seemed another rather odd statement, but she let it go. He looked so angry, so full of spit and vinegar, as her father would say. She found herself leaning closer to him, and closer, until their lips met, and then she forgot all about the odd visitor as Wes's arms went around her and she felt his violence turn to an aching tenderness.

Susannah started to come into the room and stopped. Erin was finally in Wes's arms. She quickly turned around and retreated back into what was now the modern kitchen. It had a water pump inside, and a cookstove; the old cooking area, a tiny room reached by a breezeway, had been abandoned except as a storehouse. She had thought the kitchen the height of luxury when she first saw it, and even now she had moments of wonder about it.

But that was of such small concern. She would happily live in the meanest of places with Rhys, but she knew that would never happen. He never allowed anyone to get that close. But Wes . . . perhaps there was some hope after all, and that delighted her heart.

She helped Hannah with supper. She hoped that Erin would stay, that Wes would ask her, that they would announce a wedding. The temperature in the kitchen rose as her thoughts quite naturally went then to Rhys, and it wasn't all from the stove. Susannah went to the door and looked out.

The late afternoon sun was bright, and she saw a string of horses coming in. Then she saw Rhys. He was standing in the shadows at the far corner of the barn, away from the other activity. He appeared deep in conversation with Jesus. How had he gotten outside? She hadn't heard anyone other than Wes and Erin in the living area; she hadn't heard even the door, which creaked and groaned from its stoutness. And he shouldn't be out there; he should still be in bed, resting, keeping off those torn feet of his.

As usual regarding Rhys, she argued with herself. The mothering, nurturing self wanted to run out and scold; the woman part, which was growing more and more to understand him, knew he would disdain any such admonitions. She knew instinctively that her strongest hold on him was no hold at all.

So she merely watched, wondering why, when he had avoided most contact with other workers, he appeared so engrossed with Jesus. He usually did that only when he wanted something from someone.

She considered that thought very carefully. On the surface, it was horrifying that she could so love a man like that. Or it would be if she hadn't seen other sides of him, of momentary gentleness and compassion that were—true—rare, but must come from some place that could be nurtured.

Again, she ran over the information she had. So little. A sentence dropped here, a cannonball there. The only consistent thread was his aloneness. He had never mentioned another person, other than the woman with whom he'd wagered. He had obviously always been on his own, a loner who knew nothing else.

Who wanted nothing else?

She wasn't sure. There had been seconds, such fleeting seconds, when she'd glimpsed something else in him, but then he'd controlled that, just as he controlled everything. She saw him move away from Jesus, the same grace in his movement despite his injuries, the same jaunty arrogance that placed him apart. And her heart swelled with want and love and the need to give. Such a need to give.

And take, she admitted honestly. She wanted to feel his body next to her again, to feel him become a part of her. She wanted to feel him throbbing inside her, and the mere thought pushed her body to running rivers of heat. The core of her hungered as it never had before because now it knew . . . of the incredible sensations. . . .

"Oh, Rhys," she breathed, as she saw him move behind the house, and she suddenly realized he must have exited his room by the window. Why?

Why so many things?

Dear God in heaven, why?

Rhys tried again to pull on a pair of boots. Bloody Christ, but his feet hurt. But he managed to get them inside the largest boots Susannah had given him to try.

He was going to Austin again, tomorrow. There were certain things he needed, that he could come by only there. A horse without a brand for one. Some more clothes. A few tools. He had a list in his head, and he was already impatient.

Jesus had been able to provide the one missing step in his plan. The boy's eagerness for revenge had supplied a name, an introduction. It was all Rhys needed, and he knew Jesus would be silent about his request, even to his father. He'd sworn because, Rhys had explained, any lapse might endanger everyone on the ranch. But it went deeper than that. Rhys knew the boy—no, Jesus was obviously a man now, even at seventeen—had said nothing about Rhys's injuries, nor the extent of them. Therefore, Rhys trusted him as he trusted few others; he had already proved himself.

Rhys knew, however, he would have to keep Jesus from any deeper involvement. He did not want the boy hurt.

So Rhys tried walking in the boots which pressured the still swollen feet. Tolerable. And as he walked, accustoming himself to the discomfort, he did as he often did, thought of other things to allay it. His one defense.

At least it used to be.

But now his thoughts were always of Susannah, and how much he wanted her. It was that obsession that had made him so curt with her this morning when what he had really wanted to do was carry her off to bed and, despite his wounds, bury himself in her.

His stiff, wanting manhood had been as painful as his back. He had never wanted a woman as he wanted her. Especially this morning when her violet eyes were so filled with a yearning of her own. Every time he looked at her, he became tense and hard ... and needing. He'd never needed anyone before. Never in his life. Now was certainly not the time to begin. He didn't need distractions like that.

Watching Wes and the girl, Erin, hadn't helped. He'd been amused at first at Wes's initial anger, and the way it had defused at the sight of the girl's face, which had lit like a church candle when she'd seen him. And then, he'd never seen such calf eyes before as they gazed at each other. He hoped to bloody hell he'd never do that.

So why didn't the bloody ache in this groin go away?

Rhys did consent to have supper with them that night, with Wes and Erin and Susannah, though he wasn't quite sure why. Amusement, he told himself. Instead, he'd felt an odd sort of emptiness as he'd looked at Wes and Erin.

It was obvious that Wes was still being stubbornly proud, but the girl was obviously wearing him down. One of Susannah's riders had been sent to tell the MacDougals that Erin was staying and would be escorted safely home.

Rhys liked her. The admission astounded him, but he did. She didn't see the empty pants leg when she looked at Wes, and there was something rather fine about that. Not noble—he hated noble—but real. He thought Wes a fool for not taking her when obviously he wanted to.

So why didn't he take Susannah? He looked up and found her gaze on him. That stiffness he'd suffered this morning—the aching, wanting, demanding call of the most sensitive part of him—took over his body. He knew it must have reflected in his eyes because her eyes suddenly glittered with a fire he knew came from deep inside her. There was a hunger there as deep as his own, an acknowledged need. He felt shudders of want rack his body and he struggled to control them.

They were almost finished with the meal when the call came that riders were coming in.

Both Wes and Rhys rose immediately, Wes moving quickly to pick up a rifle. He had become adept at that now. Rhys also found a rifle in the gun rack, as did Susannah, and the three approached the door together, Susannah opening it.

Erin was right behind him and she identified the rider first. "Sam!" she said.

Susannah looked toward Rhys. "Erin's brother-in-law."

Wes leaned his gun against the wall and limped out on his crutches, Erin beside him.

"Sam?" he asked cautiously. Sam Harris had been one of his bitterest critics when Wes joined the Union.

Harris ignored him, and directed his gaze to Erin. "Your father . . . he was shot this afternoon."

Erin's face paled. "Is he . . . ?"

Sam Harris nodded, his face stiff with anger and grief. "He wanted to try a newly broken horse. . . . We tried to get him to take someone with him, but he wouldn't. Slow him down, he said."

"Who?"

Sam's gaze turned to Wes, who had spoken. He hesitated, as if unwilling to speak to him, then said curtly. "No witnesses . . . as usual. He was late in coming home so we went to look for him. We found him shot. The horse was gone."

"Was it branded?" Wes had put one crutch against the door and had put an arm around Erin, balancing himself on the other crutch and holding her tight. Her face was pale, her eyes still disbelieving.

"No," Harris said bitterly. "We've been so god-damned shorthanded—" He snapped his mouth shut and looked at Erin. "I'll escort you home. Your mother needs you."

"I'll go with her," Wes said.

"No!"

Wes just stared at him. "The war's over, Sam. Erin needs all of us now." His voice was strong and sure, as he felt Erin's trembling body next to his. She *did* need him now, more than he needed his pride.

"I want him to come," Erin said in a low voice. "Please, Sam."

"Your father . . ." His words dropped away. And nothing that had been said previously brought the reality home quite as surely. Her father wasn't there now to protest. Erin bit back her tears, but her hand held tightly to Wes's arm.

Sam's face turned even more grim, but he shrugged helplessly. "Do as you will."

"I'll go, too," Susannah said.

But Wes turned to her, and shook his head. "I don't know when I'll be back. I think probably one of us is as much as the MacDougals can stomach." It was a hurtful but frank assessment. It was his place, and damn if he wasn't going to be there, but at the same time he didn't want to test Sam's bare tolerance. He shot a look at Rhys, but he didn't really worry about leaving him alone with Susannah, not with his injuries. And he would provide some protection.

Susannah hesitated, still thinking she should go. She hugged Erin. "You'll let me know if you need me, if there's anything I can do?"

Erin nodded almost blindly as she clung to Wes.

And then Wes was helping her into the wagon and climbing up next to her, grim determination written all over his face. He snapped the reins and the horses moved out down the road.

Susannah was alone with Rhys. They had gone inside, and suddenly they were standing there together, the emotion of the past few moments welling in Susannah's eyes. And then she was in his arms.

"Will it never stop?" she cried out. "The killing?"

He held her tight against him, disregarding the pressure against his chest.

Without even seeming to try, their lips met, melded and melted, becoming one. He leaned down and picked her up and carried her into his bedroom, his strength seemingly undiminished by his recent injuries.

There was little tentativeness this time. Only the impatience and open need of two people who had restrained themselves too long, who had wanted and lusted after each other, who had watched and yearned, who had curbed themselves so tightly that now there was no reining in the passion.

It was fierce and burning and totally wanton.

He took off her clothes with little regard to their stitching. She undid his trousers with no attempt to save the buttons. She started to unbutton his shirt, but his hand stilled her, and she stopped, her own fingers dropping to his hips and then to his aroused manhood. She did what she not done before, run her fingers over the skin, feeling it growing so taut she wondered how it contained itself.

It didn't.

He lowered her onto the bed, and stationed himself above her, his torso balancing on his hands so that he imprisoned her on both sides. It was a prison of her own dreams, her own desire.

She cherished every possessive move he made.

His arousal teased her for a moment, setting her afire, inciting all her sense to fever pitch. She felt a craving so strong she thought she'd die unless it was satisfied. Now!

Her hands entwined in his hair. Her body arched up, meeting his, and he plunged inside, no long teasing, but taking, demanding, plundering, and she loved it. She relished it. She exalted in it. She treasured it.

All her fear for him, her pain for his pain, even her new grief for Erin responded in a way that grabbed for life, for renewal, for something alive and splendid and caring.

She met his rhythm with a rhythm of her own, one every bit as imperious. She looked up into his eyes and for a moment they were naked. Raw. Hungry. So much hunger. She slowed her movements suddenly, her belly going in circular movements like a slow dance, taunting while loving, inviting while demanding, the tension, the lovely abrasion spiraling between them as tremors started from small quakes, and increased voraciously into major ones, rocking her, sending her into unknown spheres of sensation, each more titillating, more delicious than the former until she thought she would burst with wanting the ultimate.

Fire raced along her blood, her nerves, as he convulsed, and spasms sent new waves of satisfaction flooding her. His body rippled in hers, along hers, all the strength she loved caressing her body. "Susannah," he gasped, as his body quivered along with her own. "My God, Susannah . . ."

But she couldn't speak at all. She could only issue little whimpering sounds as his arms clasped around her and together their bodies felt the continuing, satisfying aftershocks of something so wonderful it had no name.

Chapter 21

Susannah stood next to Wes at the small private cemetery on the MacDougal plantation as Sean MacDougal was laid to rest.

Erin and her sister stood pale-faced, along with their sobbing mother. House servants attended with them along with a number of women and children from neighboring farms and plantations. There was a conspicuous absence of men, which made Susannah realize once more how many had been killed during the four years of war. The Martins were rapidly adding to that tally.

"Dust to dust," recited the preacher.

But there was so much more to life than that, Susannah thought with her newfound knowledge. So much living to do. Had Sean MacDougal experienced it all? She hoped so. Her hand reached out and clutched Wes's. She knew how much he wanted to be next to Erin, but Erin had been maneuvered between her sister and mother, obviously out of reach of the renegade Wes Carr. She suffered for Wes, perhaps now even more than in the past. Because now she was suffering her own particular torment.

He had left three mornings earlier, the morning after they had made love.

She had reached for him, just as she had reached

several times during the night, but this time he had been gone.

She closed her eyes, as the preacher's voice intoned on.

Why, how, could she still feel him inside her, filling her? She shivered in the hot sun and felt Wes's hand on her. She shook her head, trying to concentrate on words, not dreams, not images.

Rhys. Where did he go? Would there ever be a good-bye? A tender kiss after such tempestuous love-making? The words a woman wanted to hear after a night such as they had spent?

The only thing she knew was he would return. She didn't know when. She knew, however, he would be back. She knew that with every fiber of her being.

But it was almost like loving a phantom, loving Rhys Redding.

The words were said now, flowers thrown on the coffin, and Susannah clasped Erin's hands. Sam, who had assumed the role of authority, started ushering people toward the house. Susannah noted he seemed to have an extra word for the few men there, for everyone but Wes, who had been studiously ignored. A few in the crowd had acknowledged his presence by a bare nod, but there had been no more cordiality than that from one-time friends.

She hurt for him, for the tight-lipped mask he wore to hide the pain of continued rejection. She slid her fingers over his, fastened tightly to the bar of his crutch, and he looked down and smiled grimly. "I'm sorry I've also made you ... unacceptable," he said.

"You're worth dozens of them," she said fiercely, and then Erin came up, obviously defying her mother.

"Yes," she said, standing up on her tiptoes and giving him a public kiss. "You certainly are. Thank you for coming."

Wes's eyes bore into hers. "Will you be all right? Should I stay?"

She shook her head. "Not now. Mother's too upset. I'll come by tomorrow."

Wes nodded as he watched her rejoin her mother and sister, and Susannah noticed how white his hands were where they clasped the crutches. "She'll be all right," she whispered. "She's stronger than she looks."

"I know," Wes said. "I'm beginning to learn that."

Susannah glanced up. But Wes's face was inscrutable now. They walked slowly back to the buckboard as others watched in condemning silence.

Dressed entirely in black and leading a dark bay horse whose color became nearly black at night, Rhys approached the Martin ranch.

He had watched the two-story house for two nights now, approaching as evening darkened the skies on these nearly moonless nights. Only the slightest slice shed illumination, and that merely made the shadows more impenetrable.

He tried to dismiss any thought of Susannah, although his body still ached for her. It was three nights since they had joined, and he still felt remnants of the rapture he'd experienced and hungered for again.

But he had accomplished much in those days. During his trip to Austin, he had taken Josiah Baker, the banker, up on his offer of an advance, insisting on leaving with him a "family heirloom," one of the pieces he'd taken from the bandits in Virginia. He had hoarded those jewels for such an occasion, despite Susannah and Wes's preference that they be sent to someone in authority in that state to see that they were properly returned. They were too useful at the moment.

With the proceeds, he had visited several carpenters and blacksmiths, showing them a tentative design for a wooden limb and asking for suggestions. He finally chose one of each, asking them to work together.

He would return to see the result, he'd said, leaving a tidy sum for inspirational purposes.

He also purchased some tools, new clothes, two pairs of boots, and the horse he now rode, keeping his regular mount at the stable of a family called Diaz. Ramon Diaz, recommended by young Jesus, had been helped once in retaining his contested land title by Susannah's father, and he was pleased to return the favor. When Rhys, using all his charm, explained he was helping Wes and Susannah fight off land-grabbers, Diaz offered any help he could, including stabling a horse and keeping some of Rhys's gear. Diaz asked few questions after Jesus had simply nodded his head in endorsement.

Rhys had arranged it all with his usual precision, meeting Jesus on his trip back from Austin and then going to the small Diaz farm some twenty miles west of Susannah's ranch. The Diaz holding was too small and inconsequential for the Martins' attention. It was obvious he barely scratched out a living for himself, his wife, and three daughters. The land itself was dry, a deep well providing the only water.

Rhys had taken up temporary residence in the small tumbledown stable, riding out as it became dark, he and his horse mere shadows in the dark evening. He had heard the Martins often rode out at night, and thus he'd taken up a position in swamplike bottomland alongside the river, and watched and waited, using a spyglass he'd found in an Austin general store.

There was nothing unusual the first night—a lot of activity around the ranch house, but no large movement of men leaving the ranch. So he settled against a tree on this second night. And waited.

Rhys could be very patient when he had a goal. He liked the night, especially the clarity of one like this. So little moon, but an excess of stars as if one had reached down and taken a handful of silver dust and thrown it up into the sky. One sparkled more than most. Like Susannah, he thought fleetingly before dismissing it as a poet's fancy. If there was one thing he was not, it was a poet.

Particularly tonight. He had more nefarious chores in mind tonight.

His hand went up to the bandanna around his neck. Like his other clothes tonight, it was solid black. It matched the inky ebony of the broad-brimmed hat he wore, fastened by a black leather thong beneath his chin, and the practical black cotton shirt and trousers he wore, right down to the black boots. He grinned at the affectation of the outfit, yet it would serve a purpose.

Rhys Redding meant to make the Nighthawk into a legend, a legend that would serve as a rallying point for the beleaguered ranchers and strike fear into the Martins. And to do that, he knew he needed to create a new identity, one that would never be associated with Wes or Susannah, or with the eccentric Englishman they were sheltering.

The Nighthawk would be a Texan, a Texan with a Texan's accent, he had decided during that long day after his beating. He could easily kill Hardy Martin, but there would still be two additional brothers, and he didn't want Susannah and Wes to pay for his actions. It would be much better, he knew, if the whole community was involved, and no one person could be blamed; the only way to do that, he knew, was to give them a rallying cry. A hero.

So he would be a hero, after all. For a very brief time, he hoped. The idea was almost laughable. But it was also workable, and now his main goal was to make the Martins pay. Pay slowly and painfully as they watched their plans fall apart.

For that, he could be a hero. Of sorts.

And enjoy the irony of it.

He put the spyglass to his eye again, and squinted. Men were moving now, saddling up. He relaxed against the tree. How many would be leaving? he wondered.

He watched as lights went out in the ranch house windows. All of them. He knew that Lowell Martin was married, which presumably meant a wife inside. Hopefully, she would be asleep in one of the upstairs bedrooms.

Rhys felt a jolt of anticipation, of a familiar excitement when danger was near. An owl screeched to his left, and frogs were croaking a melody of their own. He reveled in the night sounds, feeling at one with them and yet apart. He liked that feeling, being alone, responsible only to himself.

The horsemen beyond started out at a fast pace, and Rhys forced himself to remain still. There must be sentries, guards of some sort.

He gave himself nearly a half hour before he moved forward. His horse was already tied in the thickets, and his black clothes melded into the night. He knew he was just another shadow. His feet were still hurting from the forced march of a week ago, yet he ignored the discomfort, moving rapidly now through the pasture leading up to the house.

He settled down in tall grass and looked around again. There were guards. Two that he could see, one at the entrance of a barn and another on the porch of the house. Neither looked alert. One was sitting, leaning the chair back against the barn door; the other was smoking near the house, a rifle resting nearby.

Which should he take first?

He decided on the one at the house. He could slip up on the porch that wound around the house and quiet the man. Perhaps he wouldn't even have to do anything with the second man.

He slithered through the grass to the side of the porch. He then took off the boots, his stocking feet moving soundlessly on the wooden boards. He was wearing a gun belt now, one he'd purchased in Austin, also black, also deadly looking. The gun itself was a Colt, one of the best there was, the storekeeper had bragged.

Rhys took it out now, twining his fingers around the barrel. He moved soundlessly behind the man who was looking out toward the drive, to where the others had disappeared. Rhys raised the gun, and it came down hard on the side of the man's head. Rhys broke his fall, easing him to the ground.

He then considered his options. Should he go after the second man and chance an outcry? There might still be others around. Or should he go on in, hoping the man at the barn noticed nothing unusual?

Rhys instantly decided on the latter option. He placed the guard against a pillar of the porch, as if he were sitting there. He was alive, but he would be out for a while—and have a bloody sore head in the morning.

Rhys opened the door, and allowed his eyes to grow accustomed to the dark. He struck a match, sheltering the light in his fingers so the glare went only where he wanted. He was looking for a desk. Or a safe. He was looking for the notes the Martins had purchased from various creditors.

He felt urgency, but not enough to make his movements wasteful. He didn't see anything in the main room, and he moved on to the next door, opening into what must be an office. Both a desk piled high with papers and a safe furnished the room.

The match started to burn his fingers and he blew it out, making his way to the desk. Once there, he lit another match and quickly opened the top drawer, riffling quietly through the papers, seeking anything that looked like deeds. Nothing.

He turned to the safe. Bloody hell, but it had been a long time since he'd tried to open a safe. It was another skill Nathan had taught him, and one of the reasons Nathan had had to leave London. But Rhys had never actually tried it by himself; he had drawn the line at actually breaking into a safe. He hadn't needed to, since his talent at cards earned him more than enough money and with much less risk. Still, he had never been averse to picking up new skills and so he had learned, using an old safe in a Victoria warehouse to practice on.

Now he concentrated, remembering everything Nathan had told him. *Place your ear next to the lock, listen for the clicks, feel for a certain hesitation.* Rhys didn't need the matches now. He did everything by touch, and his eyes were growing accustomed to the dark, and adapting to it.

Nothing happened. No clicks. No hesitation. He tried to remember how it had felt. He and Nathan had bunked in the warehouse, along with goods readied for a caravan into the interior. They had been hired as guards. It was like sending wolves to guard the sheep, but Nathan and Rhys had landed in Africa with bloody little money.

There had been nothing in the safe, but Nathan amused himself by teaching Rhys how to open it, and then again on another owned by a merchant who had tried to cheat them. They had simply taken their due wages. Nathan would have taken more, but Rhys demurred. The man wouldn't come after them for the sum they took; they would be marked men if they took more.

Enough. Enough of the past. Bloody hell, but time was running out. And then he heard the clicks, and his fingers felt the rhythm of the lock. Three more times and it opened.

Rhys lit another match then and peered inside. Stacks of money. Stacks of paper. He took out a sheath of them. The deeds. The flame burned his fingers again. He lit another match. A bill of sale. Why would a bill of sale be there? And then he grinned as he made out the words. Cotton. There it was, bloody hell. The MacDougals' cotton. The man must be crazy to keep it, but then he seemed to be a packrat, if his desk and safe were any indication.

The fire burned his fingers again. Another match. This would have to be the last. He needed to go before the unconscious man outside woke, or before his companion wondered about his stillness. Rhys also listened for any movement upstairs.

The light flashed on the bill of sale. The total sale had been $25,000. He looked back at the stack of federal greenbacks, extracted exactly $25,000, and grabbed the stack of deeds and the bill of sale. He reached in his pocket, took out a drawing of a hawk, and placed it where the deeds had been. He then closed the safe.

The office was at the back of the house. He went to a window, opened it, and slipped outside. He quietly made his way to where he'd left his boots, picked them up, and moved swiftly down the hill to the woods where he'd left his horse. Just as he reached it, he heard a yell, and then a gunshot.

He untied the reins from the tree and mounted easily, still holding the boots. He urged his horse into a gentle lope, as he heard additional yells coming from the house on the hill.

Erin and her sister had finally managed to get their mother into bed. The last drunken guest had finally left the wake, an old-fashioned Irish affair, just as Sean MacDougal would have wanted. The drink flowed easily, the food would have supplied the Confederate Army for several days, and the guests were loud if not merry.

She went to the door, looking out over the clear sky, wishing with all her heart Wes was here with her.

He had been so tight-lipped at the burial, so ostracized. Even in her own hurt, she'd felt his.

Erin heard the sound of hoofbeats, and wondered whether one of the guests had lost his way home. Fear suddenly struck her as she thought of her father. No one was safe anymore, not even on their own land. She looked toward the sound, wishing she had a weapon with her.

Sam came out, and he was prepared. He held a rifle in his hand, just as a rider seemed to appear out of nowhere. The rider blended in with the darkness so perfectly that only the sound of his horse had given him away.

Sam leveled the rifle, and the rider slowed, raising his arms to show peaceful intentions. But there was something in one of them, a leather bag. He came right to the door. "Miss Erin," he said in the soft, slow drawl of Texas. He ignored Sam and Sam's gun.

"A present," the rider said as he leaned down and handed it to Erin. "I hope it helps on this day of grief."

The rider's hat was pulled down, protecting his eyes, and a mask covered the lower part of his face, but in some odd, silent way he conveyed he was no threat.

Sam stepped closer. "Who are you?"

"A friend," the man said softly. "One willing to fight the Martins. Tell the others."

"But—"

The rider controlled his skittish horse with a light affectionate stroke. "Don't go to the sheriff. This is private business. The bill of sale came from the Martins' safe, but they can't do anything, not without admitting their theft."

There was a note of amusement in his voice. "There should be more than enough to pay your debt to them."

The words made no sense to either Erin or Sam.

"Who . . . ?" Erin started to echo Sam, but now there was only emptiness where the horse had stood, and the sound of hoofbeats growing fainter.

"I'll be goddamned," Sam said as he eyed the leather pouch much as a man regarded a snake.

They went inside together, and in the light of an oil lamp looked inside the pouch. Money came tumbling out, a lot of money. And then an official-looking document, along with still another paper containing a drawing of a hawk. Erin took the drawing; Sam took the bill of sale, his face growing red as he noted the date and the number of bales of cotton. It was indeed the MacDougal consignment. He counted the money. "My God," he said. "Twenty-five thousand dollars."

Erin could only hold the drawing and stare at him in befuddlement. "But . . . who . . . ?

Sam slowly shook his head. "I don't know, Erin. Nothing about him was familiar."

"He has to be someone we know. Otherwise—"

"How would he know about the cotton? Why would he care?"

Erin met his stare. "And why did he say to tell the others?"

The news spread among the ranchers and planters like wildfire. The hawk who'd arrived at night. He was almost instantly dubbed the Nighthawk.

He had looked like a hawk, Sam had said, as well as presenting his calling card. He had been as dark and lean as one, as elusive.

Who was he? What did he want? How did he get the money and papers? From the Martins' safe, he'd said, but how was that possible?

The sheriff heard the rumors and visited the MacDougals, who just shook their heads as if they didn't know what he was talking about. The lawman left, his face flushed with rage.

So, reported a man at the Western Union Office, was Lowell Martin's face when he marched into the small office to order a new safe from Austin.

Chapter 22

Susannah heard about the Nighthawk two days after
Sean MacDougal's funeral.

Erin had finally made it over to the ranch. She
apologized that she hadn't made it the day before, as
promised, but the night visit of the stranger had
thrown the MacDougal plantation into an uproar.
There had been a visit from the sheriff, and a fresh
flow of tears from her mother over the fact that Sean
MacDougal hadn't lived to see justice done.

Rumors had been passed around, and an unending
string of men visited the ranch, closeting themselves
with Sam as they tried to determine who the man was,
and what he wanted.

Susannah listened in silence as Erin described the
black-clad man, the contents of the pouch he'd delivered to her, the vow to return. "No one can guess who
he is," she concluded.

Where was he now?

Susannah had to clench her fists. She had not seen
Rhys for days, not since that night he'd made love to
her. She had not seen him, or heard from him.

It hurt beyond imagining that she was hearing
now, from someone else.

Where was he?

The question kept ringing in her head. Why hadn't he come back? Had he been hurt again?

Wes rode in then, summoned by Susannah, and he listened intently as Erin repeated the same story. The news was common knowledge now, but the Fallon ranch was still so shunned that no one had ridden in with the information, and they were so shorthanded, no one had had contact with hands from the other ranches.

"A black horse?" Wes asked, trying to understand. He had not seen Rhys Redding since Sean MacDougal's death. Where in the hell would he get a black horse? But it had to be Redding. His mouth twisted at the thought. A Texas twang, a black horse, a superb rider. A phantom. And he'd thought perhaps Redding had given up on them, had taken his advice and ridden out. Wes thought he used to be a hell of a lot better at judging men, but then Redding had been an enigma right from the beginning.

"Nearly black," Erin replied, looking a little puzzled at Wes's frown.

Wes cursed to himself. It was like Redding to take off on his own. No word. No explanation. Certainly no discussion of what he planned to do. Christ, a holdup man, a bandit.

Still, as he listened to Erin repeat the man's words, he couldn't help but consider the poetic justice of it. *The bill of sale came from the Martins' safe, but they can't do anything, not without admitting their theft.*

He recalled the threat made to Redding days earlier. If he said anything about the whipping, he would be charged with horse theft, perhaps even murder. How neatly the threat had been turned around.

Still . . . safecracking?

He saw Susannah's eyes on him, a twinkle in them, almost as though she understood every thought going through his mind. Perhaps because they had also gone through hers.

But the discussion now was back to the identity of the masked stranger. Susannah and Wes played the game, weighing different possibilities even while wondering what Rhys Redding was up to now. And why he hadn't returned to the ranch.

"Sam's invited most of the involved ranchers to a meeting tomorrow night to discuss the Martins—and the man who calls himself the Hawk," Erin said, her eyes on Wes. She knew he would hear of the meeting in any event, and she wanted to prepare him.

His eyes darkened. "But not me. Is it because I fought for the North, or because I have one leg?" He laughed bitterly. "At least no one can accuse me of being your hawk."

Erin's mouth dropped open at the thought. There was no one along the Colorado with more integrity than Wes Carr. And yet . . . there was something in his eyes that seemed to say more than his words were saying.

But for the life of her she couldn't imagine what. The horseman did have two legs. She'd seen that much. And Wes Carr was simply too blindly honest to ever wear a mask. It was one of the things she loved best about him, even when he went off to fight for the Union.

She sighed. "It'll take time, Wes, before they forgive your siding with the Union. Men were hanged a few miles from here for their northern sympathies. Germans from the San Antonio area." She shook her head. "They're so proud of their own loyalties, I don't understand how they can be so unforgiving of loyalties of others."

He shrugged. "I realized that when I came home, but I'd hoped . . . Hell, I don't know what I hoped."

There was a sudden silence, a pall that dropped over them like a shroud.

"I'm going into Jacob's Crossing tomorrow to talk to the army. I imagine that will make things worse,"

Wes said finally. "But tell Sam that if they . . . need any help, I'll do what I can."

She nodded. She tore her gaze away from his, unable to bear the desolation there.

"Is Mr. Redding still here?"

Somewhere. The word radiated between Wes and Susannah.

Wes nodded grimly.

"Is he better?"

Wes's eyes cut over to Susannah, who smiled. "Much better, I think."

"There's some soup in the buckboard for him."

Wes glared and started to say something, but Susannah interrupted. "He'll be very grateful."

"I'd better go. I promised to be back before supper," Erin said, obviously reluctant to do so. Susannah hurriedly excused herself and went out on the porch, which overlooked the river. If she had any idea where he'd gone, her nighthawk, she would saddle up and go after him.

She thought about him all dressed in black. She'd seen him that way before, but then in formal, civilized clothes, not as Erin had described him. He had been devastating then with his lean dark looks. She tried to imagine him as Erin had described—dressed in a black shirt, a deadly-looking gun belt, snug black trousers. Well, perhaps Erin hadn't mentioned snug, but Susannah pictured them that way. His trousers were always snug as they hugged those long, muscular legs. The image sent shivers snaking up and down her spine, coiling the nerves in the pit of her womanhood. She didn't even question for a moment that he was the mysterious "hawk." It fitted him so perfectly. But why hadn't he returned to the ranch, if he was back in the area?

She hadn't missed Wes's moment of censure, when Erin had mentioned the safe, but even then there had been an understanding of sorts there. And she also knew why Rhys had not discussed his plans with Wes. Wes could be rather . . . rigid about such things.

So had she been at one time. But those days were gone. They were fighting for their lives now, and she knew there was no one she'd rather have at her side.

Rhys, where are you?

He rode in later that evening.

Susannah had picked at her food, and Wes didn't eat at all. Susannah didn't know what he and Erin had discussed after she'd left, but her brother's lips were grim, and the lines around his eyes even deeper.

Wes retired after checking the pickets around the ranch, leaving Susannah alone in the room. Hannah had already gone to her room, being a firm believer in "early to bed, and early to rise."

Susannah heard the now familiar warning of "riders" and she felt her stomach start to twist. Instinct, which was so strong where he was concerned, told her the rider was Rhys. She put down a book she was trying to read and went to the door.

A solitary figure rode in on a chestnut horse. She noticed that right away. No black horse. No dark bay. A chestnut. The same one he had taken. He was dressed as he had been days ago when he'd come from Austin, black broadcloth coat, fancy trousers. No gun belt, but a rifle was tucked into the saddle. His head was bare, his face tan, his eyes as dark and unfathomable as ever.

She waited on the porch as he rode to the barn, past the armed sentries, and dismounted. She knew he saw her, but he didn't acknowledge it. Instead, he took the horse inside the barn.

Susannah couldn't help herself. Her feet inexorably carried her over there. She hesitated just inside, watching him as he took off the coat and laid it carefully on the side of one of the stalls, rolled up his sleeves, and started unsaddling his mount.

She walked over to his side, watching his back tense as if he were about to receive a blow of some kind. She didn't understand why. But then she never completely understood anything about him, merely accepted, because she had to accept. No, because she *wanted* to accept.

"I was worried about you," she finally said after a tense silence.

He started to say something and then stopped, giving her a wry smile. Then it broadened into an abashed grin that so lightened and changed his face that she had to grab onto a stall divider to keep her legs from failing her. This was the Rhys she so rarely saw, and yet made his place in her heart so poignantly alive. The glimpse of a boy through the cynical shell.

"I was going to say there is no need to worry, but I've given you some, haven't I?" he said with that hint of amusement that was so effectively turned back on himself. "It seems you, or your brother, are constantly nursing me for some reason or another."

His hands easily lifted the saddle from the horse's back and balanced it over the wall of the stall, not far from Susannah's hands. Hands she feared were trembling from their need to touch him, to reassure herself he was here, whole. His gaze met hers for a moment, and they seemed even darker than usual, the ebony piercing her like daggers, reaching into her without giving anything in return, without revealing what she knew her own eyes were revealing: the need that was radiating between them again, that heated the air between their bodies with such intensity she thought she would explode in flames.

But still his eyes said nothing.

His body did. He couldn't control that as well as he could his eyes. His hand had curled into a fist, and his back had gone rigid. Her eyes lowered. His pants were stretched tight over his growing desire.

His gaze had followed hers, and now his lips twisted into a smile again, this time a dangerous smile without amusement as he reached for her, pulling her roughly into his embrace, his lips plundering hers, so hungry she thought they might devour her.

A lovely thought.

She relished the hunger in the embrace, the angry surrender she knew he abhorred but couldn't prevent. She knew suddenly why he hadn't returned before.

His body cried out with need his face didn't show. Oh, Rhys, she thought as her arms tightened around him. She wanted to scream at him that it was all right to show emotion, to love and want love, but he seemed to resent that need so much he'd purposely stayed away.

She hung onto him, her body clinging to his, grateful that the barn was empty, that the sentries were outside. She felt him grow hard against her, even as his lips and tongue made their own kind of love, wild and turbulent. Untamed. Always untamed. Like him.

She felt his muscles ripple in reaction to her touch as her fingers played with the back of his neck. No, not played. They were too intense for that. They seduced, demanding with their wandering pressure, and she felt him tremble with the resulting spasms. She was learning a great deal of seduction. Peculiar how naturally it came.

She smiled through his kiss, and he felt it. He drew back and watched her expression with a bemused expression. "Are you laughing, madam?" he said stiffly, though there was a current of laughter in his own voice.

"I was giggling happily," she defended herself.

His mouth twitched. "I've been accused of many things, but causing giggles is not one of them," he said sternly, although his eyes gleamed, the blankness filled.

"Your frown is gone," she observed irreverently.

"You have a way of doing that, Miz Susannah," he said, "despite my best intentions."

"Why?"

"Why, what?" He was holding her, looking down at her face with interest.

"Why is your best intention to frown?"

"To scare away little girls."

"I'm not a little girl."

His mouth grew grim again. "No, Susannah, you're not. You're not that. But I'm no good for you."

"Is that why you stayed away?"

"Partly."

"The other part?"

"I made you a promise."

Susannah thought of their conversations. What promise? He usually avoided them like the plague. Her eyes asked the question.

But instead of answering, his fingers touched her lips, which she knew were trembling, and then they spread their magic over her face with a touch so wondering that it incited her even more than the barely contained violence of a few moments ago.

Gentle. So gentle. So much more gentle than the wildly needful kiss of seconds earlier. So much contrast, each shade speaking of a different part of him, revealing another piece that he tried to keep to himself. She heard his groan, low and harsh, and knew that he realized his tightly woven cloak was coming unraveled.

She put her hand to his face for a moment, holding it against the slightly bristled cheek, enjoying the roughness, the slight abrasion that pricked and tickled rather than hurt. She loved him so, that mouth that twisted to hide his emotions, the eyes trained to keep at bay any sign of weakness. He hated that, those moments of weakness, and yet here he was, allowing and enduring her search into him.

"I wasn't going to come back here," he said in a low, intense voice.

"Because you're the Hawk?" she said.

He looked at her through hooded eyes, just like the bird of prey she'd mentioned. "You've heard."

"Oh, yes," she said softly.

He didn't bother to deny anything. He knew her too well.

"And your brother?"

She nodded. "Erin came over to tell us."

"To tell you, or to see him?"

She grinned. "Both."

"I hope . . . he's coming to his senses."

"That's a strange observation, coming from you."

"Hummmmm," he said, his hands moving down to her breasts. "Might improve his disposition."

She glanced up and met his eyes. "What improves yours?"

"You do," he said. "Unfortunately."

"And you don't want it improved?"

His mouth went down to the hollow in her neck. "Not particularly," he said in a muffled voice that she barely understood.

She wanted to say she very much liked the way it had improved, but then his mouth moved upward, his tongue leaving a blazing trail from her neck to her lips, and blocked any more questions.

And she didn't want to ask any more. But first . . .

She steeled herself and then ducked from his arms, almost skipping to the door and bolting it from the inside. She then returned, an impish grin on her face.

An inviting grin.

A seductive grin.

He didn't need it.

Heat had already enclosed them, wrapping them together as their mouths closed on each other franti-

cally. The talk was gone now, the light teasing that hid
so many currents underneath. Those currents had
swollen, like those in a storm-tossed sea, and they
rushed between them in ever-growing fury.

He picked her up, grabbing a blanket as he did so,
and he carried her over to the floor, disregarding a
stack of hay. He knew how bloody damned uncomfortable that was, and he didn't want any diversion. Not
now.

He managed to lay the blanket down while still
holding her, and then set her down, falling next to her
with a grace she'd come to expect. His hands were already busy unbuttoning his trousers.

She watched avidly as her interior seemed to vi-
brate with expectation, her blood like a boiling tide,
her nerve ends twitching in need. He was so beautiful
as he slipped off his boots and then trousers and
kneeled next to her. His shirt still hung over his chest,
and she longed to see him entirely naked as she had
on the hill. But as his hands now busied themselves
with her shirt and long skirt, she cared only for the
feel of his hands against her skin. They could be so
gentle. So efficient. So caressing.

It was the only time he gave her any of himself,
when the glint in his eyes gentled and the sardonic
twist of his lips changed into something fine and inviting.

She didn't think what might happen if someone
tried to enter. She didn't care. She had been so alone
without him, so afraid for him, so empty.

But now as he lowered himself on her, she felt her
heart would explode with pleasure, just touching him,
being with him, knowing he wanted her as much as
she wanted him.

He nibbled. Nibbled everywhere, moving from her
neck to her shoulder . . . down to her breast to where
her nipple hardened and waves of feeling, of beautiful
expectant torment washed through her, arching her

body as his manhood pressed against her legs, teasing and taunting, ready for the exact moment to plunge inside.

"Oh, Rhys," she whispered. Or was it a whimper? She only knew how vibrant and alive she felt, that every part of her body seemed to have been waiting for this.

His mouth came down on hers just as his body did, wiping from her mind every coherent thought. She just felt. She felt and she loved. With everything in her, she loved him.

Her body arched toward him as he plunged in, his hips bucking as her body closed around him. Her legs went around his, seeking to bring him deeper and deeper, to unify their bodies so completely he could never deny it. Pleasure, sheer exquisite widening circles of sensation, flooded her, making her even more responsive, her movements making music with his, a silent, sensuous song that was heard only in her heart. And his, she hoped. She prayed.

And his.

And then she didn't think any more about music or sound because she was whirling in a world of ultimate feelings and emotions. Sublime and magnificent. And then when she thought she could stand no more, the world exploded in a burst of heat and shuddering reactions, each one bringing its own flavor of pleasure, its own unique quivering sensation, each one to be savored before the assault of the next one.

Motion and reactions slowed to ripples of satisfaction, and that was perhaps the most wonderful of all, because he lay there on her, connected in the most intimate way, each feeling the other's tremors, the internal quivering that played against each other so pleasurably.

He rolled over so she was on top, his weight not bearing on her, and he held her close to him, closer than he ever had when they weren't in the process of making love.

His eyes were not hooded now. They were virtually smoldering with passion. One could almost explode in fire looking at them, she thought.

And did. All over again.

The second time was slower, more creative. She hadn't known how creative two people could be. She hoped he hadn't either, but she knew that was a fool's dream. He guided with unerring skill, his lips sucking at her breasts as she felt him grow hard again within her. And then his hands cradled her buttocks, settling her firmly on his hips, his hands rocking her until she understood, and then she was riding him, riding the shaft that filled her with a brimming ecstasy that was unlike any before. He was moving now too, his hips arching rhythmically, and she felt the oddest sense of power, as if she were the aggressor, a much desired aggressor. She felt her body take more and more of him. Dear heaven, how could anything feel so good, so . . . immensely wonderful.

Susannah looked down at him, at the smile that played around his lips, the most sensuously beautiful smile she'd ever seen. She put a finger to it, tracing it as if to hold it there forever. She swallowed at how much it lit his face, how much it changed it into something close to contentment, even to happiness.

But then his movements grew more fevered and so did hers, and all she knew was a soaring flight upward, a thrust that blinded her to everything but the most exquisite fulfillment which rushed through her body and sapped any power to reason.

They lay there sated for several moments. Susannah knew she should be thoroughly ashamed of herself. She had just acted like the—the most wanton of women.

But she couldn't be ashamed. Not with him. She didn't think she would ever be ashamed of being with him.

What if there was a child?

The thought wriggled seductively inside her. She wouldn't regret that, either. There was something to be said about ostracism, she thought with a smile. You could then do almost anything you wanted. It was probably worse, right now in Texas, to be a Yankee sympathizer than a husbandless mother.

A boy with raven black hair and ebony eyes, but one who smiled. Who chuckled and laughed. Who loved without reservation.

Suddenly, the thought exploded back on her.

"Susannah?"

She forced a smile.

"Oh, Susannah," he said with a defeated sigh. "You make me want to have principles, and then you destroy them."

He looked so disgusted with himself that her smile turned real.

"*I* make *you* want to have principles?"

"Bloody hell, I'm afraid so," he said, chagrined. "I'm not very experienced with them. My first was not to seduce you. You can see how successful I am."

She leaned down and kissed him. "I think I like you just as you are."

Rhys grinned wickedly. "So much then for principles. But I do think we ought to consider ... discretion."

"I don't think we're very good at that, either," she said.

He looked around the barn, and thought of the men outside. And winced.

He lifted her off him. Reluctantly, she thought. Very, very reluctantly. She wanted to say something, something possessive, something he would loathe. So she satisfied herself with a mere, "I'm glad you're back."

He grumped.

She watched him pull on his trousers, then his boots. His linen shirt was wrinkled and stuck to his skin.

Susannah felt too lazy to do anything. And she didn't want him to go. No matter what anyone thought.

He returned to her side and shook his head. Her dark hair had escaped the bow and had settled around her shoulders in tumbling curls. Her face was flushed and her lips ripe and swollen. Her violet eyes would light the sky all by themselves.

She was infinitely kissable. And other things. And he'd never wanted anything so much in his life—to keep. The thought shocked him. Horrified him. The last thing in the world she needed was someone like him.

Why had he come back?

Because he couldn't stay away. He'd tried, bloody hell, how he'd tried. He'd had the Diaz ranch from which to operate, but he told himself he needed more information, the kind of information he could get only here.

Lie. And he didn't usually lie to himself. His whole body tensed. Because he'd been thinking of her, he'd allowed himself to be taken the other day. Because of his bloody carelessness. And now, he was lying to himself.

He wished like hell she didn't look at him like that, with that wistful fulfillment on her face, that bloody determination. He leaned down and handed her her clothes, and she took them reluctantly. She took her time, and every moment was seductive to him. He wanted to take her to bed for the next ten years. The problem was he wanted to wake up with her, too. And there was no bloody solution to that one.

"Are you going out again," she said, "as the hawk?"

He shrugged.

"There's a meeting tomorrow night . . . to discuss him, and Mr. MacDougal's murder."

He grinned, the old half grin that said nothing. "You can find out what they say?"

She nodded. "Erin will tell us."

"I wonder if the Martins know about it," he said.

Susannah looked at him quizzically. "Why?"

"If they do, I'll give you odds they'll be up to some mischief of their own. To prove a point."

She frowned. "They might be expecting you, now."

"They might."

"Rhys . . . ?"

She was completely dressed now, and he took a finger and pulled a stray piece of hay from her hair. His hand hesitated just a moment before moving away. "Yes?" he replied, his attention still occupied with how fine her hair felt, how silky and soft. How lovely she smelled.

She hesitated. "You will be careful?"

It felt strange being worried about. It also felt . . . very good. He nodded, but he felt a nerve jerking in his face. He didn't want to go. "I'll go on out before you."

She nodded. She wanted more.

He pulled on his broadcloth coat, ran a finger through his dark hair and, without another word, left.

Chapter 23

Wes was in a very foul mood the next morning. Susannah wasn't quite sure why. She hoped he hadn't seen her go into the barn last night with Rhys, but then she discarded the idea.

He would have been banging on the doors if he had.

And she doubted whether anyone would say much to him about it, if indeed anyone had noticed. There had been two sentries on duty, but they looked out away from the ranch, and a closed barn door was not unusual. And she knew their main loyalty, after four years of her running the ranch, was still to her.

Still, Wes was glowering at her.

"Heard Redding came in last night," he said, and she realized he had already been out to the corral this morning.

She nodded.

Wes's eyes narrowed, especially when he noticed that she was dressed in the pants she'd worn on their trip west. His eyebrows went up.

"I'm tired of sitting and waiting," she said defensively. *Especially after last night.* She couldn't just sit and read, or sew and bake.

"You shouldn't be riding with the men," he insisted.

Susannah's temper snapped. "What do you think I've been doing for the past four years when you and Mark were gone? I've had to run this ranch."

His face clouded. "Stan . . . and Miguel?"

She slowly released a long breath. It was time he understood. She was no longer just a little sister to be protected. "Stan was wonderful. So is Miguel, and now Jaime. But . . . I needed to know what was going on. I had to know the basics of ranching, if anything happened to them. I had to know how it felt to run cattle, to brand, if I was ever to understand what to expect of the men."

Wes stared at her, almost uncomprehending. He'd been so involved in his own misery throughout the trip home that he hadn't even thought about how competent she was on a horse, and with a gun. He hadn't thought about anything but himself.

And now knowledge was pounding at him. "Then . . . why . . ." But he didn't have to go on. She hadn't needed him. He'd been more a liability than anything. She had stayed here, playing little sister to the hilt, to give him pride. He hadn't done it on his own. He felt the old frustrated fury boil up inside.

He stood, holding to the table. "Dammit. I'm not an object of charity."

Susannah stood too, suddenly very angry. She had spent the past night thinking about Rhys, how he had distanced himself again last night when they parted. She had tried to do what was best for both men, to suffocate what was best in her, to smother all the independence and competence she'd earned in the past four years. She had given to each of them as freely as she could, and still Rhys Redding walked away, and her brother resented the one gift she'd tried to give him.

In a moment's realization she saw she had gone back to being an eighteen-year-old, trying to please everyone. That was why she had married, why she had stifled so much of herself. Four years on her own, four years of making her own decisions, had given her enough confidence and strength to make her way to Richmond alone, and to return here, but somewhere along the way she'd tumbled backward, perhaps because Wes had taken her back to the past. Or perhaps because she'd fallen so deeply in love with Rhys and had been afraid to lose him. But how could you lose something you never really had?

Maybe she'd lost herself because of both reasons. Well, no more. Not for anyone.

"I didn't ask you to be one," she said. "I just wanted you to pull your own weight, to do what I knew you could do. I'm sorry you resent that." She started toward the door, and turned around. "You think it was easy for me to watch you try to destroy yourself during those first days here? You think it was easy for me to sit here and wait . . . to see whether you—and Rhys—returned each time you went out? Damn you, Wes. Damn men and their stupid pride . . . and arrogance."

She flung open the door and noticed Rhys standing there, as if he were about to knock. There was a wrapped package in his arms.

But she merely glowered at him and went past, striding toward the corral. A horse was already saddled, a man about ready to step into the stirrup.

"I'll take him, Kenny."

"Miss Susannah?" He was young, like the others, too young to have served in the war, and he had a puppy-dog adoration for her.

She gave him a blinding smile, one that hid the turmoil fighting in her head. She suddenly realized how Rhys managed it. It was really quite easy with the proper incentive. She hated herself for it.

But she took the reins and vaulted easily into the saddle. She dug her heels into the side of the horse, and they raced down the road.

• • •

The two men inside stared at each other in astonishment.

Rhys had watched her leave, galloping off on her own, and he knew he should go after her. He remembered what had happened to him when his mind had been elsewhere, and he had the distinct feeling now that her mind was not on caution.

He turned to Wes, whose face was pale. "What in the bloody hell—?"

Wes turned his frustration on Rhys. "What are you doing back here?"

"Bringing you this," Rhys said, still confused. "I was in Austin."

"You were safecracking," Wes accused.

Rhys gave him that twisted, enigmatic smile, although his mind was with Susannah. "That, too. Do you object?"

"I object to you," Wes said bitterly.

Rhys remembered Susannah's glower. He shrugged. "So do a lot of people, but I don't think we should debate that now. I don't like Susannah riding out there alone."

He saw the struggle on Wes's face, concern mixed with the urge to strike out. What had happened here? He put down the package he was holding. "You might try this when you have a chance. In the meantime I'm going after her."

Wes glowered, a look very much like Susannah's just seconds ago, but he picked up his crutches. "I'll go with you," he said.

Rhys shrugged. "As you wish." He turned, without waiting for Wes's slower pace, and strode to the barn, quickly saddling the stallion he usually rode now. He was aware of Wes's entrance into the barn, aware of eyes boring into his back. He ignored them as he mounted the horse, refusing to wait for Wes as he galloped from the barn, following the direction Susannah had taken.

His first thought was her father's ranch, the hill, the small cemetery, the wildflowers. He would always think of those flowers when he thought of her.

He didn't know why he felt the kind of fear he did, the cold sickening feeling that something was very wrong. He didn't know what had happened between her and Wes, but her own look toward him had told him something was very wrong there, too.

He didn't have to search his mind far to find it. He knew he had been abrupt in leaving her last night, but he just hadn't known . . . what to say.

He wouldn't make promises he couldn't keep, say words he didn't mean. Not to her. And he'd been so bloody angry at himself. He didn't understand why he couldn't keep away from her, why he kept coming back when he knew—knew, dammit—how much he was hurting her. Hurting himself.

The cold, hard truth was he was no good for her, never would be. He had lied and cheated his whole life, had never had a friend or known how to keep one, had never stayed one place long enough to have a home. He had never shared anything with anyone, never trusted anyone, and he doubted whether he could begin now. She would discover these things about him, and they would kill that light in her eyes.

He knew he couldn't stand that. He didn't intend to bind her to a man like himself, a man without scruples or honor, when she had so much of both. He thought of last night. Bloody hell, but he'd already corrupted her. She wasn't a lightskirt, but she didn't know how to give a little. She had to give everything.

He didn't know what to do with everything.

Rhys wondered at the ache in his heart at that knowledge about himself. He suddenly wanted everything. That was why he hadn't been able to stay away.

He'd never felt that kind of tenderness or love or loyalty before, and it was as irresistible to him as honey to a bear, or the apple to Adam. No matter how hard he'd tried, he couldn't keep away.

What if there was a babe?

The thought was as piercing to his soul as a knife to the belly. The women he'd bedded before had little concern about that aspect of a physical mating. Either they were careful, or were married and could pass the child off, or were whores who had their own way of taking care of things. Like his mother.

Brat. Why didn't you die like the others. His mother's words. Every time he had gotten in the way. He'd learned quickly to scoot away, to hide in the shadows. And shadows had become a way of life.

He felt a tightness in his chest. And for a moment, he could barely breathe. A baby. That looked like Susannah. They were both dark, Susannah and himself, only his eyes were nearly black where hers were that incredible soft violet.

Rhys closed his eyes against the pain of the thought, against the sudden inexplicable yearning that shot through his heart. He ruthlessly tried to shove the feeling away, as he had banished the physical pain of days earlier through sheer willpower.

Only this was worse, much worse. The other, he knew, was temporary. That had made it tolerable.

The thought of her alone in the hills terrorized by the Martins made his skin crawl. He'd never worried about anyone before, and it was a fearsome thing.

Susannah, he whispered in the air, hearing the name on his tongue and knowing it was indelibly in his mind forevermore. He wanted her safe. And he wanted her touch. And he wanted her beside him, and under him and over him. He wanted her in a way he never thought he would want anyone.

The only solution, he knew, was to finish the business here as soon as possible, and be on his way.

Be on his way. . . .
It was an unbearably lonely thought.

Susannah slowed the horse. Foam was dripping alongside its mouth, and she felt its sides heaving. She ran her hand along its neck as a form of apology.

She had avoided her old home. Too many memories. She didn't want any more memories.

But they were here too, here alongside the river where she'd found the hawk. The other hawk that wasn't meant to be tamed.

She had allowed herself to believe that . . .

Believe what?

That Rhys could be captured and tethered? Like the sporting birds in England? She had seen that wildness roil in those eyes on two occasions—in Virginia and again after his encounter with the Martins. She had felt it in his restlessness on the trail and again here, the way he could never content himself with staying still. He was always wandering, always disappearing as if he feared lighting for even a fraction of time, as if he was afraid of being trapped and shackled.

Even in those tenderest of moments, when his hands gentled and his eyes softened, there was an inherent violence in him, the hint of cynicism in his face.

She dismounted, grateful that she wasn't on a sidesaddle. She had conformed to that, too, for both Wes and Rhys. She had become something she wasn't, hadn't been for years. And that pretense hadn't helped anything at all.

Wes appeared more discouraged than ever. And Rhys? She was foolish to think a dress and sidesaddle would make a difference.

She looked around. She was at least twelve miles from the ranch, probably on the Ables' property. It was difficult to tell, since no one had fences. The Martins were across the river from here.

The Ables, like Erin's family, had raised cotton and had been slave owners. And like the MacDougals, they were struggling to exist after four years of war. They had been luckier than most; two of their three sons had made it safely through the war. But their wealth was gone.

Lives had changed, worsened, for so many of them, except for the Martins. Her thoughts turned to them, to the three brothers she'd known all her life.

She'd felt sorry for them, except for Hardy, who'd always been a bully. The other two, Lowell and Cate, had always kept to themselves, self-conscious in their outgrown clothes and obvious lack of mothering. They didn't always come to school, and sometimes, when they did, they were covered with bruises she suspected came from their father. The father was hung, when Lowell was fourteen and Hardy twelve, as a horse thief.

And then the war came, and practically every man in the area enlisted. Lowell, who was the brightest and best looking of the three, obtained a job in the general store, and when the owner died the widow kept him on to run it. His appearance improved, possibly through the help of the widow, who married him a year later. The prices at the store went up, and the next year he bought the ranch of a widow whose husband had been killed in the war and who wanted to return to her family's home back east. There were no other buyers, not with the South so close to defeat, and Lowell apparently purchased it for practically nothing. He then moved his brothers there, and his greed for land grew.

Because so many families had credit at the store, he knew everyone's business; he knew who was in trouble and who wasn't, and he used that information to buy cheaply, to purchase notes from the now defunct bank. If a family refused to sell, hard luck suddenly struck. Workers disappeared. Livestock wandered away. Piece by piece, he had assembled a giant tract of land, and now only ten families stood in the way of his controlling a very large section of the river and the bordering land.

And in the doing, Lowell had painted himself with a veneer of respectability.

Susannah stared across the river at the land he now owned. He badly wanted the land on which she now stood, and the Ables, too, had suffered raids on their livestock. Their barn mysteriously burned one night, destroying cotton they had stored, along with two horses.

That was before James and Andy Able had returned home, tired, thin, and, like so many others, bewildered about their change in fortunes. They now worked daylight to nightfall to turn their fields to uses other than cotton, which demanded labor they no longer had.

The war had created so much misery, she thought. Why did the Martins have to compound it?

She was standing by a clump of cottonwoods that lined the steep banks of the river. She couldn't see the Ables' house from here; unlike others, it was set well away from the river. Some cattle, longhorns, had wandered down to the water, and were drinking contentedly.

Susannah knew from Erin that some of the ranchers, even plantation families, were thinking about combining what cattle they had, rounding up additional wild cattle, and driving them northeast to Kansas City where they had heard there were buyers, or even north to the Colorado mining towns. It would mean badly needed cash. But it also meant leaving their families again, and they couldn't do that with the unsettled conditions.

She led the horse, now that he had cooled, to the water, allowing him to drink slowly. She would walk him back, although it would make her very late. Wes would worry.

Hell's bells. She had worried about him, about them all, she thought defiantly.

She pulled at the horse, and led him back to the trees where there was better footing, not the muddy, sliding ooze caused by animals watering. She'd just mounted when she saw riders across the water. She moved further into the trees, seeking their leafy protection, as she watched eight riders come to the opposite edge of the river. Her stomach tensed as she watched one of them pull out a rifle, then another, and take aim at the placid cattle watering fifty feet downstream.

Susannah heard the shot, saw one go down, and felt sick inside. It was wanton slaughter for no reason at all. She heard the sudden bawling of a downed animal, and she reached for her rifle, even knowing that it was a mistake.

She was one against many, and the river was shallow now. But she couldn't watch, even as the remaining cattle began to scatter, several splashing panicky into the water. There was laughter from the other side.

She aimed the rifle at the hat of one of the firing men, and squeezed the trigger. The hat went flying off. She heard loud swearing above the bawling of the cattle, and then the movement of horses as the riders searched out the opposite bank for the gun. She moved a short distance and fired again, this time toward a spot in front of one of the horses.

Loud arguing drifted across, and she knew they were debating the wisdom of crossing. She started to inch her horse backward through the trees. There was a yell. She heard another shot, felt pain as a bullet grazed her arm, and turned the horse. She would make a run for it.

Susannah heard the splash of horses across the river, then another shot, from her side of the river. She hesitated and looked back. A man was floundering in the river; two others were reaching down for him. She looked around and saw a lone man on a chestnut, a rifle held easily in his arms as he took aim again.

Rhys! How had he found her? How did he know where she'd gone? Yet, she wasn't surprised.

And then there was another rider behind him. "Wes," she cried out.

His rifle, too, was out and he aimed at the men who were now turning back again across the river, the wounded man riding double behind one of them.

Shots from both Rhys's and Wes's rifles speeded their departure. But just as they disappeared over the far bank, they heard additional horses.

Two men, one still wearing Confederate trousers, reined up, regarding Wes, Susannah, and Rhys with hostile faces.

But Rhys had moved over to her side, his eyes on the blood that was soaking her blouse. She followed his gaze and looked down, amazed at how red the cloth was. She'd known instantly it hadn't been a serious wound; she could still use the arm, and her hand and fingers also seemed to work. After the first initial sting, she hadn't really felt much pain, perhaps because of how quickly events had followed each other. The glimpse of Rhys and then Wes and now the Able brothers.

Rhys slipped from his horse and held out his arms to her, catching her as she obediently did as he silently ordered. Wes, too, had dismounted and was hobbling toward her, ignoring the newcomers.

Rhys ripped the sleeve of her shirt and used it to

wipe away the blood, his hands unbelievably gentle, his eyes dark and glittering with anger. He looked toward Wes. "Flesh wound, apparently just creased her." He tore a strip of the blouse and tied it tightly above the wound to stop the bleeding.

He and Wes then turned to the riders. Wes leaned on one of his crutches, his blue eyes wary. "James, Andy," he acknowledged.

The younger one's expression lightened slightly, and he nodded. He dismounted and went over to Susannah. "What happened?"

Susannah started to move forward, but Rhys placed a hand on her shoulder, restraining her. "Riders from the other side; they started shooting your cattle." She nodded toward the riverbank.

The other rider had dismounted now. He walked toward them stiffly, avoiding meeting Wes's gaze. "Susannah," he said. "Hell, they're going after women now. I'll take you back to the house. Get that tended properly." He turned to Rhys, who stood several inches taller than he. "You that tenderfoot I heard about? You don't hold a rifle like one."

Susannah looked from one to the other. Despite James Able's offer, there was no friendliness in his voice, not like when they'd been schoolmates together.

Rhys shrugged. "I know how to use a rifle," he said in an English accent tinged with obvious disdain for his questioner.

The man's face flushed slightly. "Heard Hardy and some of his boys messed you up a bit."

Rhys shrugged indifferently. "Exaggerated, I expect—"

Susannah interrupted. "James, this is Rhys Redding. Rhys, James Able. And Andy Able."

They heard a plaintive bawling from the river, and James and Andy strode in that direction. Susannah heard the sound of a shot, then another.

Rhys spun around. Wes moved closer to Susannah.

And then James and his brother returned. Andy stopped and looked down. "I had to kill two of the wounded cattle." His face was gaunt, his lips tight. "Damn butchers. There was no need . . ."

He turned back to Susannah. "I take it you saved the others. Thank you." His gaze then turned to Wes and down to the missing leg. "I heard about that," he said softly. "I'm damned sorry, Wes."

Wes stilled. He hated being reminded of his lost leg, yet it was the first sincere gesture he'd had since arriving home, the first acceptance from men he'd once called friends. He nodded, wanting to say something about the third Able brother, who'd been killed, but he held his words, not sure whether they might revive the hostility.

Even James's mouth had relaxed slightly, but he stood stiffly, unwilling to make the same concession as his brother. Instead, he looked down at Susannah. "We'll take you to the house."

She looked down at her arm. The bleeding had slowed. It hurt now, a consistent burning pain. But she didn't want to go to the Able house, not where she knew she and Wes would normally be unwelcome. She wanted to go home. She wanted to feel Rhys's hands on her, not the reluctant ones of people who had turned their backs on her and Wes.

"Thank you," she said slowly, "but I'll be fine. I'd rather go back to our ranch."

Andy's face flushed with quick comprehension. "Susannah . . ." he started, and then stopped as he saw her face. He stepped back. "If there's anything we can do . . ."

Wes shook his head as Rhys helped Susannah onto her horse. Rhys waited until he was sure she was steady and then looked over at the two Ables, his eyes contemptuous as they studied them, obviously finding them wanting. As even James grew uncomfortable, Rhys unpinned them from his gaze and moved to his own horse. Rhys swung up lazily on his mount and followed Susannah and Wes as the brother and sister spurred their horses into a slow trot.

Chapter 24

Susannah tried to dismiss the pain in her arm. It was so little compared to what both Wes and Rhys had suffered. If they could endure much more severe injuries with tight-lipped stoicism, so could she.

She glanced to her side, to Wes's stiff body. And behind her. She wished she hadn't. For a man who seldom showed emotion, Rhys was showing it now. Stark anger. Disapproval. And something else she couldn't fathom.

She felt sick inside. She had known him for months, and she had seen him make only two mistakes, once when Hardy Martin had taken him, and seconds ago when he revealed much more than he intended to the Able brothers.

She couldn't forget that unforgiving stare he had given them. He was anything then but the harmless Englishman he'd wanted to portray. Still . . . no one could guess his gift for dialects. No one would suspect he was the Nighthawk.

Susannah looked behind her again. Rhys's face was grim. She didn't even want to guess at his thoughts.

She'd been a fool. She knew it. She shouldn't have ridden out by herself. And then she shouldn't have fired that shot. If Rhys and Wes hadn't come . . .

But she hadn't been surprised when Rhys appeared. Part of her had come to expect him when she needed help. He'd become her reluctant guardian angel.

She didn't want an angel. She wanted him, the flesh and blood man.

She looked over at Wes. "How did you find me?"

"I didn't," he said. "Redding did."

Susannah's expression questioned further, and Wes continued somewhat reluctantly, as if it were difficult to admit he'd needed help, particularly Redding's. "I caught up with him at our place. It was obvious you hadn't been there. We backtracked and he found your tracks." Wes shrugged. "Don't ask me how. But he picked them up, and then we heard the shots." He was silent for a moment. "I'm sorry, Sue, for this morning. I . . . needed to strike out at something and you . . . were the easiest target."

"Give Erin a chance, Wes."

"She deserves more than I can give her."

Susannah shook her head in disgust. "Why do men always think they can make that decision? Isn't it her right to know what she wants? Not yours?"

"I can't—"

"Of course you can. You have King Arthur—he's a fine bull and can sire a wonderful new strain of cattle. Miguel and his sons would do anything for you. You have Papa's land, and you have his dream."

"And what dream do you have?" he asked quietly.

Susannah didn't dare look back. "I want Mark's ranch to survive."

"And?"

"Don't ask, Wes," she said, forcing herself not to look back.

His eyes narrowed, but he didn't say any more on the long way back.

•   •   •

Both Rhys and Wes were barred from Susannah's room by a protective Hannah, and they both paced the floor of the main living area as she went in and out with hot water, alcohol, and bandages.

At least, Rhys paced.

Wes clumped. He felt a tearing guilt as he remembered every bitter word this morning. But he'd felt the need to strike out, and his sister had been the easiest target, the most vulnerable target. God, what was happening to him?

If only the pain would go away. If only the sense of helplessness would fade. But he knew that was no excuse. Others had suffered more than he during the past four years. Mark had died, for God's sake. Mark and Mark's brother. And here he sat, feeling sorry for himself and chasing his sister out into danger.

He looked over at Rhys, his nemesis, and saw another face creased by guilt. He didn't want to know what kind of guilt. He had his own to manage.

"Is the Nighthawk going to ride again tonight?" Wes asked, already knowing the answer. He knew Redding that well by now.

Rhys didn't answer, but his face became enigmatic again.

"Why?" Wes asked. "Why the masquerade?"

Rhys thought about ignoring the question, but he couldn't dismiss the worry lines etched deep into Wes's face, the pain of helplessness.

"I don't want it to rebound on you or Susannah," he said quietly, without the usual mockery.

"But why leave a signature?"

Rhys stopped his pacing and went to the window, staring out.

"Redding?"

Rhys turned.

"A game?"

The mocking light came back into Rhys's face. "You can say that. A jolly good game."

Wes sat down in a chair wearily. "I would have accepted that a few days ago. Not now."

"I don't give a bloody damn what you accept," Rhys said.

Wes's eyes met his. "A rallying point. That's it, isn't it?"

Rhys shrugged. "Think what you want."

"Dammit, man, do you always have to be so prickly?"

Rhys raised an eyebrow, and red flooded Wes's face. But still the Texan persevered. "What do you plan?"

"Kind for kind," Rhys said. "They shot Susannah." He let Wes guess the rest.

"One of the Martins?"

Rhys shrugged.

"I want to go with you."

Rhys shook his head. "No."

"I can still shoot, dammit."

"And your horse has a brand. So do you." Rhys's eyes went down to Wes's missing leg. "You think any of your so-called neighbors will join if you're involved?" He was deliberately cruel. "And I can't leave here until I know . . ."

Wes felt his entire body tense. It seemed even his missing foot twitched. Redding didn't have to finish the sentence. *Until I know Susannah is safe.*

It was difficult to think of Redding gone now. He was like a chronic disease, Wes thought dryly. A condition you got used to and lived with. And, after a while, wouldn't know how to live without. And Susannah . . . dear God, Susannah?

The sooner Redding was gone, the better.

"It's time I pulled my own weight," Wes said stubbornly.

Rhys regarded him thoughtfully, then looked toward the package he'd brought this morning. It had been forgotten in Susannah's headlong flight. He wasn't sure how Wes would accept it, but perhaps he had an incentive.

Rhys went to where he had laid it and carried the wrapped bundle to Wes's side. "Susannah asked me to get this for her," he said with a challenging look.

Wes looked down, and then started to unwrap the bundle, his hands slowing as he realized what it contained. It was a piece of wood, a light wood, carved in the shape of a leg and a foot. The foot had a kind of spring attaching it to the limb. The top had been carved in such a way that his stump would fit into it, and a leather halter had been designed to hold it to the upper part of his leg.

Rhys shrugged. "It may not work, or might need adjustments. It was designed by a carpenter and blacksmith in Austin. Easy enough to correct."

Wes eyed it with an appreciation Rhys hadn't expected. He looked up. "No more brand?"

Rhys gave him a level stare. It was obvious how much Wes wanted to participate in Rhys's war now that his sister had almost been killed. No more brand meant no easy identification of a one-legged rider. "Perhaps not."

"Then I'll go with you next time . . ." Wes hated begging.

"The leg may not work."

Wes suspected it would, since Rhys had something to do with it. He'd always admired Rhys's competence even as it had irritated him. "If it does?"

"There's still the problem of your horse and *its* brand."

"That's easy enough to cover," Wes said, a gleam of light coming into eyes. "Some dried mud can correct that."

Rhys hesitated. He was used to working alone. He didn't like feeling responsible for someone else. Wes was a liability, yet Rhys knew if he were to leave Texas, Wes had to have the confidence to take over.

"You were going to visit the military in town?"

Was nodded. He had almost forgotten in his concern over Susannah, but it was something that had to be done.

"Go and see them," Rhys suggested, "and get used to that leg . . . and then . . ."

"Will you hold off tonight?"

"No."

"Redding!"

"This is personal." Rhys's voice was curt. Uncompromising.

"You don't think it's personal for me, too?"

"I don't know if you have the stomach for it."

"After four years of war?"

"That's it, Carr. That was war."

"So is this," Wes said, his voice tight. "The Martins have gone over the line."

"I remember those thieves in Virginia. You didn't like the idea of killing."

"Is that what you have in mind?"

Rhys's gaze met his. "If I have to."

"And if you don't?"

"Kind for kind," he said softly. "A bullet in the arm."

"And Hardy . . . if you see him?"

"Now that's a different case," Rhys said softly, his voice almost a purr as if he were contemplating a particularly tasty meal. "But I can accept kind for kind there, too."

"If the army will help . . . ?"

"From what I've heard, they won't. No more than your sheriff has."

"I have to try."

"You do," Rhys said. "I don't."

"Don't go tonight. Wait."

"No," Rhys said.

To Rhys's surprise, Wes surrendered. He shrugged. "I can't stop you."

"No," Rhys said again, and he turned around and walked out the door.

Wes waited impatiently on the porch of a home confiscated by the military. A widow still lived in one of the upstairs rooms, but the rest of the house had apparently been taken by a Captain Harry Osborn.

A new U. S. flag flew on a staff attached to the house. Wes knew that General Gordon Granger of the Union Army had landed in Texas in June and proclaimed that the authority of the United States over Texas was restored, that all acts of the Confederacy were null and void, and that the slaves were freed. Wes also knew, from Erin, that military rule had been declared and that army tribunals had replaced the civil courts. Making things worse, he knew, were rumors that many of the occupation troops were Negro, a red flag to Texans who had never before been defeated. Men who made gestures of resistance, or who appeared in public in remnants of gray uniforms, were being arrested.

A sergeant answered the knock on the door, and told Wes that Captain Osborn was currently occupied, and he would have to wait his turn outside. Wes tucked his crutches under one arm and leaned against a pillar, watching the other occupants of the crossroads community avoid the house like the plague, often crossing the street rather than walk in front of it.

His stomach tightened.

The door opened, and Lowell Martin came out, a smile on his face and a cigar between his teeth, until he caught sight of Wes. The smile disappeared and two fingers retrieved the cigar from his mouth.

"Carr," Lowell said. "Coming to see my friend, Captain Osborn?" His tone was sneering.

Was felt his fingers wanting to strangle. Instead they stayed on the crutches. He had tried Redding's device, and it had worked for a few steps. There was pain—he suspected there would always be pain—but he could live with that. But for this trip into town, he had pinned the leg of his trousers back.

"Stay away from my ranch, Lowell."

"Heard you had some trouble. Too bad about that. That tenderfoot left Texas yet?"

Wes ignored the question. "Did you hear my sister was shot today?"

Genuine shock flitted across his face. "No . . . who?"

"Some of your men, I understand. Rein in your mad dogs, Lowell, or I'll do it for you."

"You and who else? That tenderfoot guest of yours? I hear no one else will have anything to do with you. And don't forget that payment due on your place."

Wes had learned something from Rhys Redding. He didn't let his anger show. He merely stared at Lowell as if he were a snake's belly. He hoped he was as good at it as Redding, but he doubted it.

Lowell shrugged. "It won't do any good telling the captain any lies, Carr. He knows the truth about who's loyal and who isn't."

"You've never been loyal to anything in your life."

"Of course I have. None of us went out and fought secessionist battles. Didn't have no brothers-in-law that did either."

Wes decided on another tack. "Heard rumors you lost a few papers the other night." He grinned, the same kind of Redding grin that he had hated.

The satisfied smirk faded from Lowell's face. His pale blue eyes stared into Wes's face, as if to extract any knowledge he might have.

"Excuse me," Wes said. He stumped by him, and without waiting to be invited in, opened the door and entered the military headquarters.

An overweight officer stood up. "What the devil?" He stopped when he saw Wes's missing leg. "You must be Carr."

"Colonel Wesley Carr, U.S. Army," Wes said coolly. The officer had all the earmarks of one who had not seen combat. His uniform would have been immaculate on someone whose build was more suited for it. But now it simply looked sloppy strained against a bulging stomach. "You are?"

"Captain Osborn. You're out of uniform."

"Haven't had one in months. Rebs weren't very particular about preserving it."

"You were a Reb prisoner?"

"Libby. Escaped just before the surrender."

"I hear your brother-in-law was a Reb hero." There was a bluster about the officer, an air of defensiveness that suddenly warned Wes. This was not the man to report that he had . . . taken his own leave from the army.

"You heard right," Wes replied frostily.

"They warned me you would favor the Rebs . . . because of your sister."

"And where did you fight, Captain?" His condescension made the other man flush.

"I served in Washington."

"It figures," Wes said contemptuously. "What brought you out here? Thought it was safe? Or that you could take a little for yourself?"

The man turned an even brighter red. "You have no call to say that. I'm responsible for law and order now, and I have friends in Washington. Don't interfere."

But Wes went on. "I want to know what you plan to do about the lawlessness in this area."

"Those rebels, you mean?"

"I mean Lowell Martin and his brothers."

The captain's eyes narrowed. "They're the only Union men around. Lowell Martin has been very helpful."

"They're cowards who are Union men only because it's profitable."

The captain puffed up. "I don't believe you. You just want to save that Reb's ranch for your sister. He told me all about you."

"How much is Lowell paying you?"

"You can't—"

"I can damn well do anything I want," Wes said. "I fought four years for that right."

"I can arrest you—"

"You can try," Wes said. "Christ," he added in disgust. "I need air." Without another word, he turned around and left.

Rhys counted the guards. There was a number of them tonight. And a great deal more alert than in the past.

In fact, the Martin ranch was ringed by them.

That was no problem. He could take them one by one. But that wouldn't give him what he wanted: one of the Martin brothers.

Kind for kind. An eye for an eye. And he wanted his eye tonight. He wanted it before Wes Carr interfered.

He wasn't exactly sure, however, how to get to one of the Martins. It might mean going back into the house, and he wasn't sure he wanted to do that.

A diversion of some kind, however, might bring them out.

He tried to judge the time. It had to be around two or three in the morning. He'd had to ride to the Diaz farm, change clothes and mounts, and then make his way here. The last few miles were cautious. He had no intention of placing himself back into the tender hands of the Martin brothers.

A diversion. His mind rapidly thumbed through possibilities. Cattle. That was his best bet. Stampede whatever was available. Hopefully they would lose more than the Able brothers had earlier today. He liked the idea. He wouldn't mind taking off with a few himself.

He wondered whether they were branded. Branding, he understood, was just now coming to Texas. Cattle had not been valuable until the last year, and therefore had not been worth the trouble of branding. It had been different with horses, which were valuable indeed. And then he thought of the stolen MacDougal horse, the one Erin's father had died for. He wondered whether it was in the Martin stable.

But that would have to wait. One of the Martins tonight. They had to learn that whatever they did, they would get back in like measure. That might insert a card of caution in their deck.

Rhys left his horse behind, staked out alongside the river. His feet were nearly healed now, and his movement was fast and stealthy.

He found one guard shadowed in the tree, given away by the cigarette he smoked. Rhys took him from the back. A quick stroke to the side of the neck, and then he gagged and tied the man securely. He downed two more before he reached a fenced pasture. One man sat on a fence, a rifle cradled in his hands.

The moon was a trifle brighter tonight, a slice of pie rather than a sliver. Lacelike clouds slid between it and the earth, briefly extinguishing what faint light it gave. Rhys waited until a cloud glided across its beacon, and then he struck, moving quickly among the shadows, his hand pulling the sentry down and hitting him so quickly and accurately that there was merely a surprised grunt.

He opened the gate, grateful for the sudden stomping of the cattle that had obscured the brief cry. He looked around. A horse, unsaddled but bridled, was tied to a nearby fence. He took out a picture of a hawk and stuffed it in the guard's pocket. He then made for the bridled horse, leaving the gate open. A few cattle started to ramble out. He vaulted to the back of the horse, and then fired the gun over the cattle. There was a bawling protest, then panic, and the cattle started thrashing toward the gate, and running. He leaned down, close to the horse's back, almost invisible in the darkness, and watched the lights go on at the main house. Two men in long johns came out, both holding rifles, and he recognized Lowell, then the third brother, Cate, whom he'd seen at Susannah's ranch when he'd first arrived weeks ago.

Men were shouting, running, trying to get out of the way of the moving, frightened cattle. Some ran for the barn, and one came toward his horse, not yet seeing the body on its back.

He could shoot Lowell now. He almost did, but—something stopped him. And then the younger man next to Lowell saw Rhys, and started to raise his gun. Rhys fired, and he saw the man grab his shoulder and start to fall.

Rhys kicked the side of the horse, and it spurted into a gallop. There were other yells. Gunfire. But he was low on the horse's neck, guiding it entirely by his legs. He knew exactly where to go, through the unguarded area he had created earlier by knocking out the sentries.

"Don't let him get away, dammit," someone yelled, and he thought it must be Lowell, from the air of angry authority. A bullet whizzed just over his back, and he stretched out even lower, whispering words of encouragement to a frightened horse that needed few of them.

They reached the woods, and he slowed his mount, guiding the horse to where his own waited. Slipping off the borrowed mount, he grabbed the reins of the bay. He slapped the back of the horse he'd just dismounted, and listened to its hoofs pounding against the earth as it fled whatever terror was behind it. Rhys mounted the bay and sent him into the river, hearing shouts in the distance. They were going after the horse he'd just released.

Rhys reached the other bank, and allowed the bay to stretch into an unhurried trot, pleased to note, when looking back, that a few maverick cattle had followed him across to the Able property.

Perhaps young Andy Able might get some cattle back, after all.

Chapter 25

Wes heard the results the next day. Knowing that Rhys most likely had taken some kind of action, Wes sent Jaime into town to pick up whatever information he could. At the one saloon, Jaime listened to some Martin cowhands, who'd dropped in for a drink after coming into Jacob's Crossing for ammunition.

"Like a phantom, he was," one man said as he gulped the contents of a shot glass and asked for another. "Never did see him. But he got Cate right through the shoulder."

"Remming got fired," said another, wanting to share the attention of a bartender and hoping for a free drink that way. "The boss found him on the ground with a note stuffed in his pocket. Don't know what it said, but the boss sure was angry. Talking to that military commander right now."

"Cain't figger it. Who . . . ?"

"Has to be one of the ranchers."

"Heard tell they wuz all in a meeting, trying to figger it themselves."

"They didn't stay very late," came the voice of the helpful bartender. "They met in one of my back rooms. Left early."

"Leaves jest 'bout anyone in the whole goddamn territory," one of the Martin hands said disgustedly.

"I'm thinkin' 'bout leaving myself. Didn't sign on to fight ghosts. Been to the house twice ... and no one seen him. Just those goddamn notes."

A man apparently keeping watch outside came in. "Boss is leaving the captain's office."

The men hurriedly paid up and made for the door. Jaime, who had been sitting in a corner, his back to the bar, rose and moved over to the long plain bar. "Another beer," he said.

"Ain't seen you in here for a while," the barkeep said.

"Don't much like the company."

The barkeep shrugged. He was also the owner of the small establishment which was the center of activity, had been for twenty years. "Me, either. The war sure has changed things." He hesitated. "Heard Wes came into town yesterday."

Jaime nodded warily.

"Went to see the new ... Yank officer. Didn't look none too happy when he came out."

"Wes don't like what's going on any better than the other folks," Jaime said. "The Martins are after him, too."

The bartender nodded his head. "Time the war ended for good."

"Folks around here don't seem that charitable."

"Andy spoke up for him last night—said he should be included in their meetings."

"And the others?"

The bartender shook his head sadly. "Not yet ... but they'll come around."

"When everyone's dead or chased off," Jaime said bitterly. "Don't they know they need to stand together?"

"They know ... but—damn, Jaime, you know how high feelings are ... and that bluebelly captain ain't helping none."

Jaime nodded. "I know. Wasn't too happy myself

'bout working for Wes Carr, but I owed Mark and Susannah. I'll tell you this, though, with that one leg of his he works harder than any of us, and I've seen how much pain he has. Yank or not, you got to respect that."

Jaime tossed a coin down on the bar, and left.

Wes eyed Rhys warily. "What now?"

Wes stayed at the ranch after Jaime had made his report and returned to join the other men guarding the pastured horses. After last night, he hesitated to leave Susannah alone. He wasn't altogether sure who he feared might threaten his sister more, the Martins or Rhys Redding, Nor was he sure that Susannah would stay put herself. If he hadn't been so damned wrapped up in himself, he knew, he would have noticed her restlessness, would have recognized that she was bottled explosive.

But he had ignored the changes in her, the new self-reliance and confidence he had seen in Richmond and the trip west. He had ignored so many things because of his self-absorption, and he knew it was time to leave his shell and take a much better look around him. He just wasn't sure, however, that his baby sister, no matter how much she'd grown, was a match for the Welshman.

And so he greeted Rhys, who rode up late in the afternoon, with a great deal of reservation. He wished he wasn't halfway beginning to—

No, he would never like Rhys Redding. The man had no principles, not at all. But he did have a good many other attributes, some of which Wes was reluctantly coming to appreciate.

Still, he hadn't liked the sunrise smile with which Susannah had greeted Redding, the obvious spontaneous delight that lit her face every time she saw him.

But then her first words defused him.

"Wes showed me the . . . leg you brought," she said, her eyes thanking Rhys.

Rhys looked over at Wes, who busied himself cleaning his gun. "Will it work?"

Wes nodded. "I need to work on it a bit, but . . . yes, I think so." A muscle vibrated in his throat as he struggled to say just two words. "Thank you."

Rhys looked even more uncomfortable than Wes, and Wes started to grin. "Gratitude is a hell of a burden, isn't it?" he said.

"Wouldn't know anything about it," Rhys answered with just the slightest of answering smiles on his lips.

"Don't suppose you would," Wes commented, and turned the subject adroitly away. "Had yourself a time last night, I heard."

And then they sat down, and exchanged information: what really happened at Martin's ranch, and Jaime's report. Rhys looked up at Susannah, who had sat down with them, listening avidly.

"Do you have some coffee?" he asked.

"I'll boil some," she said, pleased to do something for him after his efforts on behalf of Wes. She was even willing to overlook, for the moment, an obvious attempt to exempt her from talk the men considered dangerous, or unfit, for her ears. Well, she had plans of her own in that regard.

As soon as she left, Wes looked at him. "What now?" he said.

Rhys picked up the saddlebags he had brought inside with him, and took out a sheaf of papers. "I picked these up the other night."

Wes shuffled through them. His father had been a lawyer and Wes had toyed with the idea of following that profession, even studying with him some, before deciding he wanted to be a full-time rancher. But he'd picked up, and retained, some rudimentary knowledge.

"You didn't get these last night?"

"No," Rhys said cheerfully.

"When did you decide to show them to me?"

"Yesterday."

"Why not earlier?"

"I didn't want you to go honorable on me. Try to give them back or some bloody fool thing."

"And now?"

"I see a little promise."

Wes was sure it wasn't a compliment, yet he couldn't hold back another smile. Rhys Redding could seduce the angel Gabriel to do the devil's bidding, given long enough. And make him like it. Or at least justify it.

Redding's gaze remained on him. "What can we do with them?"

Wes chuckled. "I thought you had that all figured out."

Rhys shrugged. "I'm not familiar with your legal procedures. I thought you might have some ideas."

Wes stared thoughtfully at the documents in front of him. "I'm not sure, either. These deeds won't help anyone. They belong to people already forced out. Besides, there would be copies of them in Austin. But the notes . . ." His eyes twinkled, becoming warmer than Rhys had ever seen them. Rhys now saw a glimpse of the man that Wes had once been, and he understood Susannah's protectiveness. "Unless there are live witnesses who will testify, I don't know how he can prove them. And the only witness I see is the damned crooked banker who sold them to Martin. He disappeared months ago after selling out everyone. Christ, Martin must be livid."

Wes was flipping through the notes now, looking at the names. "Mark's note isn't in there," he said. "Neither is the MacDougals'. Here's one for the Ables, signed over by the bank. Damn Elias for selling them all out."

"The banker?"

Wes nodded. "Elias apparently sold the Martins every note he had. He also stole the town's money before disappearing a few months later."

"Does Lowell Martin have another office?"

"In town," Wes said. "But they'll be waiting for you now. Let's just wait, see what happens."

"After one more ride by the Hawk," Rhys said. "To deliver these notes to the people involved."

"Stirring the pot some more?"

Rhys simply raised an eyebrow. "Want to come?" he invited.

Wes grinned. "Why not, now that I have two legs."

Susannah finally found Rhys alone later that afternoon. He and her brother had been huddling together nearly all day, and while part of her had been pleased at their apparent newfound cooperation, another part felt left out.

She hadn't been able to contain the unbridled joy she felt on seeing Rhys when he appeared at the door earlier. She had been desperately worried about him, only too aware that he had been bent on some kind of vengeance the night before. She didn't know whether it was the pain in her arm or the worry that kept her awake all night, but something had.

Her anger of yesterday had disappeared in the stark anguish in the eyes of both Rhys and her brother after the shooting, in the tenderness with which Rhys had held her and carried her inside the house, obviously reluctant to leave her in Hannah's care . . .

And it further dissipated today when she saw the quick concern in his eyes before he so carefully dropped that curtain on them again.

He had looked smoothly elegant, even in the working clothes he'd worn, the dark brows framing those eyes which so fleetingly ran a gamut of emotions.

He frowned then, suddenly. "Should you be up?"

She smiled. She remembered her resolve of yesterday. She wasn't going to hide who she was, the strength she knew she now had. "Look who's asking. I had a mere scrape, whereas you—"

He'd started to scowl at her, but then Wes came in and the two men bent their heads in cooperation. Susannah didn't know whether they meant to leave her out, but that was the net effect.

She was infernally tired of being left behind. This time, she decided, she was going along. Even if it required manipulation of the tawdriest kind.

Susannah finally coaxed Wes to join his men, assuring him that she was feeling well and in no need of protection. The Martins wouldn't dare strike during the day. She watched him talk to Rhys for a moment at the corral and ride off, obviously satisfied that Rhys was also leaving.

Susannah waited until Rhys had saddled up and ridden out down the road. Sending Jesus, Miguel's son, on an errand, she then saddled her own horse, disregarding the pain in her shoulder, and followed Rhys far enough so that she knew he would never let her return on her own. And then she caught up with him.

He glared at her. "What are you doing out here alone?"

"I'm not alone," she countered.

"Bloody hell, Susannah, this isn't a game." His eyes blazed, and Susannah relished this unfamiliar chink in his usual armor.

"I thought you liked games," she said innocently. "That's what you do, you said."

If looks could blister, she would be covered with them. For a moment. And then the frown smoothed

out, and his lips twisted in that little indecipherable
half-smile of his.

"All right," he surrendered. "Where then do you
think you're going?"

"Wherever you are."

His eyebrows furrowed together again, and he
glowered, even though he was afraid it didn't work any
longer. "You can't."

"Yes, I can," she said simply. "You can't leave me
out, you and Wes. I'm part of this, even more than you
two. And if I have to, I'll follow you, wherever you go.
You can't send me out of the room, like I'm a child."

He moved restlessly on his horse, obviously at a
loss. It was one of the few times she had seen him that
way. He looked at her wryly. "You are definitely not a
child, Susannah."

"Then tell me where you're going."

"It would be better if you didn't know."

"Why?"

For the life of him, he couldn't think of one solitary
reason, other than his own natural, well-honed inclination to keep everything to himself. It had cost him to
confide even in Wes, which was necessary, for he really hadn't known what to do with the papers he'd liberated from the Martins' safe. He didn't know how to
trust, or how to share any part of himself. It was like
self-betrayal, a violation of rules he'd established for
himself long ago.

Still . . . there was a reason for keeping her from
wandering out alone.

Rhys wanted to take her somewhere private, someplace where they could be alone again. She was beautiful in the afternoon sun, the dark hair gleaming in
the bright rays. Her wide violet eyes were challenging
instead of soft and that, as usual, fired him more than
helplessness ever had. This was the part of her he admired so much, that sent the sparks raging between
them. The dueling, the abrasion, the stimulation. She

was dressed in pants again today, and they fit snugly on the slender but softly rounded body. But he knew how strong it was, how responsive. He felt the heat ignite in him, the abrasion of cloth as his trousers stretched tight against his expanding manhood. He cursed himself for the inability to control himself, as he'd always controlled himself in the past.

But he didn't have time now, and he murmured an unfamiliar prayer of thanks for that fact. He had already done her enough injury.

Rhys also knew he couldn't allow her to follow him. It was too dangerous, and he knew she would unless he gave her a good reason. For once, he decided on the truth.

"I'm riding to the Diaz farm," he said. "That's where I've b̶ ̶ ̶aying at times. They're keeping my horse and clo̶ ̶"

"The Nighthawk," she said. "Then you're going out again tonight."

"With your brother," he said. "I found a few documents some of your neighbors might want back. It'll be quite safe," he said, thinking to reassure her about Wes.

Her eyes softened. "Thank you for that, and for—"

He nodded, cutting off her words. "He'll be all right, you know."

"Thanks to you."

"I didn't have anything to do with it," he replied curtly.

Susannah decided not to press the issue. She had another instead. "Can I go with you tonight?"

"No."

"Why?"

"Someone might get careless and decide to shoot before thinking."

"That could happen to you, too."

He grinned, the old self-mocking smile she re-

membered so well. "I have more lives than a cat. I
doubt if you do."

"You've already used up too many."

His smiled vanished. "Then let me give you another reason, Mrs. Fallon. I seem to get careless when
you're around. I imagine your brother would, too. Do
you want to risk that?"

"No," she said, realizing he knew the one argument
that would dissuade her. As much as it would pain her
to remain behind, she knew she couldn't take a chance
of endangering them. "When will you be back?"

"Tomorrow." Her eyes met his, asking questions
she couldn't ask. Would he really?

He nodded.

"Rhys?"

He looked at her.

"Be careful."

For a moment, his gaze seemed unable to leave
hers. She saw a muscle jerk in his cheek. His voice
was rough when he finally answered. "I'm always
careful."

"Not always," she countered, but before he could
answer, she turned her horse and started back for the
ranch, knowing that he would follow until she was
safe.

Rhys met Wes at the prearranged meeting place,
the cemetery where Wes's father was buried. Wes, too,
was dressed in black, having hunted through all of
Mark's and Mark's family's clothes to find what he
needed. His clothes were mismatched, unlike Rhys's,
and his black hat was floppy instead of broad-
brimmed, but they would serve their purpose, especially in the dark early morning sky.

Wes wondered what in the hell he was doing, skulk-
ing around at night. It was so unlike his nature, which
was to get angry and openly fight his battles. But he un-

derstood Redding's purpose, and even his reasoning—the need to bring the families here together again—and he was willing to give it a try. He knew that alone, particularly if Redding left, he stood damn little chance of besting the Martins.

Still, it galled him, being sucked in like this. He had waited to attach the leg until he reached the cemetery. He had tried it again this afternoon in his room. The first minutes, even the first hour, were tolerable, and then the pain increased rapidly. He was already working in his mind ways to improve it, a better molding for the stump, a padding, and an improved sheath to hold it more securely to the upper part of his leg. If it worked better, it could be a boon to so many more like him. Even as painful as it was, it promised a liberation that was irresistible. He knew he owed that to Redding, too.

Redding was already at the old homestead, relaxed in the saddle on a dark bay horse. Wes wondered briefly how he'd obtained it, and then decided he didn't want to know.

Redding was a daunting figure, framed against the night sky like some mythical creature. He sat the horse as though he were part of the damn beast, as well as any Texan, and that was saying a great deal. Wes wished like hell he understood the man better, but Rhys Redding defied any ordinary description: good, bad, evil, righteous, honorable, dishonorable—classifications usually pinned on a man. He seemed a little of all of them.

And whenever Wes thought he understood just a little, the man confounded him again, like bringing that damn leg. Even with its deficiencies, it had taken a great deal of thought, ingenuity, and ... money to produce.

Damn. Just bloody damn, he thought, unconsciously using Rhys's favorite oath. The man was like a sorcerer, not only to Susannah, but even now to him.

Here he was, in the wee hours of the morning, dressed like a goddamn fool ready to play Robin Hood. He suddenly grinned at himself, and he felt a streak of exhilaration roll through him, as he'd felt during the first heady days of the war when it all seemed a noble adventure rather than the nightmare of death and pain it became.

He rode over to the cemetery and dismounted, taking his crutches from the special straps Redding had designed and laying them next to the grave of his father. He took the artificial leg he'd wrapped in a blanket and tied behind the saddle, and fitted it to the remaining part of his leg. The foot had already been encased in a boot which matched the one on his good leg. He used the stone marker to stand, and then reach for the saddle, as he looked down. Two legs, by God.

Wes put his good left foot into the stirrup and cautiously swung back up into the saddle. The wood weighed on what remained of his right leg and scraped the back of the horse, but still he made it. The exhilaration spread.

He tightened his knees against his horse, and rode to where Rhys waited.

There was a peculiar comradeship in riding the night. Wes identified the homes of families who were affected by the notes Rhys had stolen. The two men took turns delivering them. A shout first, identifying himself as friend, then, as a door opened, a package landed on the porch as the messenger rode off.

Like pranks when he was a boy, Wes thought, but this was deadly serious with lives and futures involved. Still, he felt alive again. Very, very alive.

Within several hours, however, he was rigid with pain from the weight of the stump, and only iron determination allowed him to continue. Rhys followed him back to the cemetery, where Wes removed the leg, reattached the crutches to the saddle, and re-mounted.

Wes rode on alone, only once looking back at the man sitting astride his horse under the great oak tree Wes remembered so well.

Rhys watched until Wes disappeared down the road, wishing he rode alongside him home toward Susannah. But it was too risky now. He had to take the horse, and his clothes, back to the Diaz ranch. Wes would have to manage on his own.

His respect for Wes had increased during the night. The Texan had been tireless and uncomplaining, despite the pain Rhys knew he'd endured, that was etched on his face.

So many things were disrupting his usually orderly mind. He had actually started to care for some other people. Even for stiff-necked Wes Carr, and that was terrifying as little else in his life had been.

Not to mention the constant, burning need for the man's sister. Now that could be explained, if it weren't for the feelings he had in other parts of his body regarding her. Something akin to pure pleasure, for instance, when he merely saw her. His unprecedented lack of control when he was with her. The tenderness that punched a hole in his heart when he touched her.

He recalled her face this morning when she greeted him with such delight. He'd never been welcomed that way before, so unreservedly. Her eyes sparkled, her soft skin glowed, and her mouth curved into that delicious smile that made him want to make a meal of it. Bloody hell, but he'd felt as if someone had kicked him in the stomach.

All were alien feelings and, therefore, to be distrusted.

A few more weeks, and his funds from England should be here. In a few more days, he hoped, the Nighthawk could unite the ranchers. His aim was to build trust in the Nighthawk and then reveal Wes Carr as that man. It was why he had been so abnormally careful to insist on kind for kind, not to shoot Cate until the man had aimed at him, not to take more money than was owed the MacDougals. He hadn't wanted to overtax the so-called law, or Wes's morality.

Wes, he was sure, didn't yet know his own final role in Rhys's grand scheme.

And then he, Rhys, would go, and leave behind this particular venture into the quicksand world of benevolence.

Lowell Martin slammed the ledger book down on his desk. He looked over at the sheriff, the sheriff who no longer had any authority.

"Who in the hell could it be?"

The sheriff shrugged. Again, rumors had flooded the town. The black-clad man who called himself the Nighthawk had been seen again last night at various ranches along the river. No one was saying anything, but where there had once been worried frowns, there were now open grins.

And the descriptions differed, almost as if it *was* a phantom. He rode a bay horse; no, a black one; no, a chestnut. He was tall, short, medium.

"It's one of those who came back," Lowell said. "Didn't start until after the war."

"'Didn't start until Wes Carr came home," the sheriff said.

"Couldn't be him. Carr just has one leg. People would know him.

"What about the Englishman?"

Lowell shook his head. "Doesn't even carry a gun. Besides, I have a man at the MacDougal place. Heard Sam say the man had a Texas accent."

"What about one of the Able brothers?"

Lowell shrugged. "The timing isn't right. Why would they wait until now? And getting into my safe was no easy matter. No cowboy could do that. What I can't figure out is what he wants. Why he wears a mask."

"Maybe they know you have spies at the ranches."

"They can't know that."

"What about the military?"

"I've convinced that captain they're nothing but Confederate renegades. That and a few dollars put him on our side."

"Why not offer a larger reward?" the sheriff said. "People now are mighty short of money."

Lowell's face brightened. He was firmly convinced that everyone was basically a thief. He nodded. "I'll talk to that Union captain tomorrow."

After the sheriff left, Lowell gazed down at his desk at the MacDougal note. He had taken it from the safe in his office in town today. He didn't know why he had kept it separate from the others, that one and Mark Fallon's, but he had.

No. That wasn't true. He knew exactly why. He swallowed as he thought of the girl, of the one person who had never looked down on him, who had treated him like a human being when everyone else treated him like dirt.

He had wanted her for years, but she'd had eyes for only one man. He'd hated the man for that.

His hand went up to his mustache. He was not a bad-looking man. He had his wife, Louise, to thank for that, as well as other things. She had taught him how to dress, how to groom himself. He was perhaps a little heavy; all the Martins were, now that they had as much food on the table as they wanted. It went back, he was sure, to the days when they had little, if any at all.

But all and all, he thought he'd turned into a fine-looking man, an impressive man, who could influence important people. Not like his brothers.

He thought of them. Cate . . . well, Cate was an

empty shell. Not very bright, but he could do what he was told. Now Hardy . . . he could ruin everything. He had that mean streak that warped his judgment. Yet they were his brothers, the only family he had, and he believed in family loyalty, no matter what you got.

And Louise? He tried hard to be civil to her, but it was more and more difficult. She was ten years older than he, and she looked every moment of it. Haggard and overweight. Always nagging for something else. She had made it possible for him to become rich, to become powerful, but he needed something else.

He needed the girl.

Chapter 26

Susannah accompanied Wes the next day on the normal ranch duties.

If she couldn't ride with Rhys and Wes at night, she would at least resume more of a role in running the ranch, particularly now that Wes realized how much she had done in working the ranch during the war years.

Wes was obviously tired this morning, but she didn't ask questions, and he didn't volunteer answers. He had returned safely and so, apparently, had Rhys, although she hadn't seen him this morning. That was all that was important. Wes glanced at her riding attire—trousers—and noted that she was again riding astride, but refrained from saying anything. There was a truce on that matter, a growing tolerance between them.

He surprised her when, at midday, he rode up to her, his expression set and determined. "I've been thinking," he said. "Perhaps it's time to think about rebuilding at . . . our old ranch."

She had been eating a hard biscuit, and her mouth stopped in midswallow. She managed to choke down the rest. "And Erin?"

Wes hesitated. "I don't . . . know. I don't think she really realizes . . ."

"I think she realizes very well," Susannah said. She bit her lip, then plunged into the touchy subject. "If she could put up with your disposition for the past month, she could certainly put up with something as . . ." she searched for the words, "merely inconvenient as your leg."

Wes leaned back in the saddle and grimaced. "I've been that bad?"

"Worse," she confirmed. "Blind, too, if you don't realize what you're throwing away."

"It isn't just the leg, Sue. I have nothing to offer . . . not until this battle with the Martins is over. Even then, I'll have to start all over again."

Susannah sighed. "Most people will."

Wes hesitated. "And you?"

"What do you mean?"

"Redding," Wes said bluntly.

She shrugged, trying to hide her own fears. "He'll be leaving."

"You're in love with him, aren't you?"

She thought about denying it. But why? She had accused him of avoiding the truth. "Yes," she said softly. "That's why I get so angry with you. You can do something about Erin. I can't do anything about Rhys. He's a loner . . . an adventurer. He doesn't want any attachments. He's made that clear."

"Don't be so sure of that, Sister Sue," he said with a slight grin. "I've seen him look at you, too."

She shook her head. "He'll leave."

"Hummmm," he said, doubt remaining in his voice. He'd never expected Redding to stay this long. Neither, Wes knew, had Redding. Something was holding him, and Wes was sure it wasn't any sense of obligation.

He looked at his sister, and realized how very much she'd grown up in the past four years. In some ways, he admitted honestly, more than he had. She had learned to accept, where he hadn't. He wondered if that was good or bad.

But instead of saying any more, he turned his horse around and galloped back to his men. He was the last one to give advice. They both had their own personal battles to fight, and he knew that each of them would have to do it alone.

"Wanted" posters went up the next day. Everywhere. They covered the entire Colorado river area below Austin. The charge was attempted murder on the person of Cate Martin. The description was somewhat wanting itself, however: "Wears black clothing, rides dark or chestnut horse."

Signed by U. S. Captain Harry Osborn, the posters offered one thousand dollars for the apprehension of the "outlaw" who called himself the Nighthawk.

Rhys smiled to himself as he saw the first one. How better to earn the trust of the wary ranchers than be posted by their hated enemy?

Neither Susannah nor Wes shared his appreciation when he showed up later that afternoon, joining them where they had taken the horses. He looked uncommonly cool and elegant while Susannah felt sweaty and dirty. She wondered exactly how he managed that.

She hadn't seen him in two days, and he would have looked wonderful no matter what he wore. She felt her hands tremble slightly on the reins. His hair ruffled in the breeze, a dark undisciplined lock falling on his forehead, and his eyes, when they focused on hers, were heated. Yet everything about him looked relaxed.

He rode to Wes and took a paper from his pocket, passing it to her brother. She rode over and took it from Wes. A "Wanted" poster.

She looked at Wes, who frowned. "This means every bounty hunter in Texas will descend on us."

Rhys shrugged. "No one knows anything."

Susannah saw Wes's worried frown, and something of his disquiet transferred to her. "But if you . . ."

Rhys shook his head. "No one has any idea where the Nighthawk comes from, or when he'll strike. These should bring the ranchers even closer together."

He looked so infernally relaxed, so confident, that Susannah banished that moment of apprehension. Already, she knew from Erin that the ranchers would protect the Nighthawk. They didn't know who he was, but they all suspected he was one of them, and they would protect him to the death because of that.

Wes voiced his fears. He had come to expect little of his neighbors. "I'm not sure about that. Everyone needs money."

"Then we will make sure no one discovers who the Nighthawk is."

Wes hesitated. "When will he ride again?"

"I don't know," Rhys said. "It depends on what happens next. Whether the Martins do more than this." He let the poster drift to the ground.

Susannah wished he didn't look so . . . darn irresistible on a horse, but then, unfortunately, he looked that way walking, standing . . .

Lying down. Next to her.

She felt desire snake up and down her spine. She wondered if it would always be thus. But then, she wouldn't know.

Rhys made his way over to her. "Susannah," he said, his voice lingering over her name as if he'd missed her as much as she missed him, his eyes roving over her as if she were a particularly tasty morsel.

Two days. And it seemed like two years.

His eyes were no longer roving but devouring. She felt an answering hunger assault every nerve in her body.

But it was also enough, at the moment, just to see him, to have him safe. And with her.

She knew she couldn't stay here, astride a horse, staring at him like a dew-eyed schoolgirl. She glanced at Wes, then back at Rhys. "Will you have supper with us tonight?"

He hesitated.

Susannah saw his hand move slightly. A slight trembling, just like hers. She wondered whether he also felt the quaking inside, the first tremors of that volcano of feelings he always awakened in her. She looked at Wes again. "We can invite Erin . . . find out what people are saying about the posters," she added hastily.

Wes gave her a disgusted look, and Susannah cringed at how transparent she obviously was. Her excuse for inviting Erin was obviously that: an excuse.

"I think it's a good idea," Rhys said.

Wes and Susannah looked at him. It was the first time since they had met him that he seemed amenable to any kind of social event.

"Normal curiosity about the Nighthawk," Rhys added cynically, dispelling any doubts that this was anything but another of his usual Machiavellian moves. "We should express some, you know. Like everyone else."

"I'll go back and tell Hannah," Susannah said. "Then ride over to Erin's."

"Not alone," Wes warned.

"I'll go with her," Rhys said. "I've had enough horse herding for a day."

"You've had five minutes," Wes said pointedly.

Rhys gave him that twisted mocking grin. "As I said, I've had enough for the day." He looked at Susannah. "Ready?"

Susannah glanced at Wes, remembering their ambivalent conversation this morning. And then she remembered her own vow to herself. She was important, too, and at this moment she would take as much of Rhys as she could. She nodded.

Susannah wasn't sure she knew what to say to him after that wanton evening in the barn, and she pressed her horse into a trot which precluded talk. Rhys kept pace, trying neither to hurry nor to slow her speed. She occasionally stole a glance, but his face was neutral again, that rare unlikely warmth cloaked in a mask of indifference.

When they reached the ranch, he dismounted to help her down, his hands catching her easily. Then the mask slipped, and he held her a fraction too long as his eyes appeared to catch fire deep within, a glow bringing them to life so brilliantly she caught her breath.

Rhys swallowed deeply, and Susannah realized he wasn't nearly as indifferent as he tried to pretend. She remembered Wes's words this morning. *I've seen his look at you, too.* Susannah couldn't imagine his being that transparent, particularly with Wes, but . . .

But. But was the big word. Rhys wasn't like Wes. He didn't hunger for hearth and home and family as she knew Wes did. She'd never met anyone so satisfied to be an outsider, a loner. Who, in fact, made an art of it. Who refused in any way to surrender even one small piece of himself, or his independence.

And then he had placed her on the ground, and turned back to the horses, and Susannah turned to face him. "I'd better use the sidesaddle to ride to Erin's."

He raised an eyebrow at her return to conventionality, but said nothing.

She started to explain that it would be easier for Erin, but then decided against it. *He* didn't explain anything. *She* didn't have to explain anything. She turned and hurried into the house, stopping only a moment to tell Hannah there would be at least three for supper, perhaps four.

Susannah hurriedly washed, brushed her hair, tying it back with a blue ribbon, and changed into the blue riding dress that always seemed to deepen her eyes. She glanced in the mirror, winced at the tanned skin, and bit her lips to make them redder. She cocked her head, wondering at the reflection for the briefest of seconds, what there might be in it for a man like Rhys Redding who had probably had his choice of fashionable ladies in London.

So little. Her face was not fashionable at all: her chin too determined, her hair too curly and unmanageable, her eyes, though vivid, an unusual color that often defied description. She was anything but porcelain-colored perfection, the blond-and-blue-eyed preference in England and Europe if *Godey's Lady's Book* was any indication.

And her dress. It was faded and long out of fashion, if it ever had been in, although it was certainly an improvement over the man's trousers she'd been wearing. She sighed. Wes was seeing things that weren't there. She was . . . convenient for Rhys Redding. No more than that.

Having established that fact in her mind, she pulled her riding boots on and went back out, mentally, practically, armed against Rhys's undeniable attraction.

He had already changed saddles on her mare, and was waiting, standing languidly against the rail post. Susannah tried to steel herself from the usual elation at seeing him, even if only a few minutes had passed. How could he keep his face so still, and emotionless, when she knew she was as transparent as a window? She noted his glance sweeping over her and she wondered if it was an appreciative glance or an amused one. Her hand touched his as he reached to help her, and it burned down to the bone and through it. Her eyes flew up to his, and suddenly she knew what Wes meant. They were no longer jaded and amused, but darkly, intensely personal, desire evident in depths he seldom allowed to show. And emotion. Dear God, the emotion. Like river rapids, his eyes were swirling with it. Desire, need, something more. Memories flickered through them, hot powerful memories—and she knew exactly which ones. Her body vibrated with the knowledge, with her own sudden, uncontrollable need.

She watched him clench his teeth in uncharacteristic frustration. A muscle flicked in his cheek and for a moment his hand tightened against hers so strongly she thought he might break it. But she said nothing as she watched his face try to regain the control he was so very good at. His hand lessened its grasp slightly, as if he suddenly realized he was hurting her, and that knowledge seemed to break the hold of the inexplicable moment.

He released a long breath and looked down at her hand, drained white by his hold. "I'm sorry, Miz Susannah," he said in that mocking Texas drawl that always startled her when he affected it. So different from that usual clipped brevity of expression, yet so very natural. She would have sworn, had she heard it for the first time, that he had been raised in Texas. The chameleon again. "That dress should be outlawed."

She wanted to scoff. The dress was nothing at all, unfortunately. But amid her own sudden sexually intense fog, she felt pleasure at his words.

And then he was lifting her into the saddle so effortlessly she might well have been a sack of feathers. And this time his eyes refused to meet hers. For the first time, she realized, he was avoiding a challenge.

Susannah felt the waves of tension radiate among the four of them at dinner that night, as much between Wes and Erin as between Rhys and herself. It made for a conversationally stiff meal, dominated by a verbal discussion of what the Martins would do, and a nonverbal one of what each of the two couples wanted to do.

The ranchers, according to the spoken discussion, were emboldened by the Nighthawk. Released from the immediate threat of foreclosure by the theft of the notes, they had decided to proceed with plans to band together, round up stray cattle, and drive them north to raise enough money to get started again. They would pool their resources, some staying home to take care of one another's families. No one knew who the Nighthawk was, but they were firmly convinced it was one of their own number. They were ready to defend themselves now that one man had defied the Martins. The lassitude and discouragement which had lingered from the loss of so many of them, and finally from defeat in war, were replaced by determination. One man's refusal to submit had flamed the lingering embers of courage that lay within each one of them.

Erin had been equally as determined. She reached over and touched Wes frequently and the contact, Susannah guessed, was every bit as potent as that between herself and Rhys. What was wrong with men, anyway? Stubborn. Intractable. Always sure they knew what was best, when they didn't know anything at all.

But Wes, still unsure of his future, refused to discuss renewing the betrothal of five years ago, although his eyes seldom left Erin's face . . . Erin, who had once more defied her family to come tonight. She'd made it quite clear to Sam, her brother-in-law, that he had no say over her and would have to tie her to a chair to prevent her from joining her friends for dinner.

And Rhys—well, on the surface he was entertaining and roguish, although Susannah knew if Erin hadn't been so intent on Wes her friend would have seen beneath Rhys's studied layered charm. There was an intensity burning in him tonight, like the center of a flame so hot it was in danger of burning itself out. Susannah felt its scorching heat, the flicker of the flame touching her.

And then he left them abruptly, saying he had guard duty, and Wes and Erin were so involved with each other, they noticed little and said nothing. When Wes took Erin home an hour later, Rhys Redding was no place to be found.

A week went by, and then another. Calm before a storm, Susannah thought.

Although she was anything but calm. Her body was already a storm, a roiling, tempestuous hurricane.

For a man who proclaimed he didn't like nobility, Rhys Redding seemed the epitome of exactly that. He was now staying at the ranch, available in case of trouble, but he had kept his distance from her, ever since the ride to Erin MacDougal's and the uncomfortable intimate dinner that night.

A pattern was forming, one she didn't like at all. Susannah always felt Rhys was near, but she seldom saw him. And she thought she knew why. He was still planning to leave, and he didn't want to hurt her. Like Wes didn't want to hurt Erin. But neither man realized, she thought sadly, how very much they were both already doing that.

She didn't even think it odd that Rhys Redding, who had so despised Wes in the beginning, seemed to become more and more like him, and Wes, who'd had an equal disdain for Rhys, was, since that night they had gone riding together, becoming more like him. Rhys appeared to be appropriating some of Wes's rock-solid integrity, and Wes was taking on Rhys's more pragmatic view of the world. She wasn't sure she liked either change.

All she could do was watch and wait with the others, her days full of longing and her nights ... so lonely, particularly when she sometimes went to the window and saw a solitary figure leaning against a post and knew it was Rhys. But she also knew that if she

went to him, he would be gone. He had become a
shadow, a phantom, again.

Two weeks after the dinner, the Martins made their
move through the U. S. military captain. Each of the
ten families received notice of failure to pay taxes for
the previous year; the sum was triple that of past
years. Unless the money was paid immediately, their
property would be forfeit and presented for auction.
No one needed to tell them who the principal bidder
would be.

They had ten days to pay. Susannah knew there
was no way. Five hundred dollars was a fortune. And
they didn't have time to sell any of their horses, not
and receive any kind of decent price for them. Wes received a bill for two hundred dollars for the land his
father had left him.

A total of seven hundred dollars. It might as well
be a million, Susannah thought.

So the Nighthawk's efforts had been in vain. The
notes may have been difficult for Lowell Martin to
verify and enforce, but now he had another means of
getting what he wanted.

Supper was quiet between Wes and herself. Rhys
disappeared shortly after an army corporal had delivered the demand for money. When Susannah asked
Wes about their guest's whereabouts, he shrugged.
"He doesn't confide in me."

Susannah pushed the nagging worry away, along
with the growing resentment she felt. They needed
Rhys now. *She* needed him. For moral support. For the
endless ingenuity he seemed to manage when everything looked bleak.

"We can sell some horses," she suggested, even
knowing they could never raise enough. Something
was better than nothing, better than sitting back and
allowing the Martins to buy land that had been in

their family for so long, that had so many years of hope and labor and love invested in it. "Perhaps we can get enough to pay your taxes."

"No," he said abruptly. "I won't take any more from you, for God's sake." He hesitated. "The jewels we took from those deserters . . . ?"

Susannah bit her lip. "Rhys still has them." Or did he? She remembered the new clothes, the unexplained horse he kept at the Diaz farm. She did not want to lose faith in Rhys now. He'd always been there when she and Wes needed him. Always. She wasn't going to doubt him now.

And he'd had as much right to them as she and Wes, if not more. They would be dead if Rhys hadn't interfered. Still . . .

Her eyes met Wes's, and his too were clouded. She tried to remember what jewelry there had been. Not that much, probably, she comforted herself. No more than a couple hundred dollars worth, not today when everyone was selling off family jewels and heirlooms . . .

Neither of them ate much. Wes went out to relieve one of the guards around the barn. Susannah followed him out to the corral and sat up on the railing next to one of the posts.

King Arthur was stomping his feet in protest of the invasion. Poor King Arthur. They had not had time to find him a harem yet. The horses had come first. But she understood his tension, his impatience.

She was ready to explode with her own.

Rhys felt as if his nerves were crawling with fire ants. He'd never known that the need for a woman could be like this. No, not simply a woman. One woman. One woman with velvet eyes and skin like silk, and a touch that would gentle the wildest of beasts. And he felt every inch that beast now. Bad-tempered and jumpy.

He patted his saddlebags. The Austin banker had been horrified when Rhys said he wanted five thousand dollars in cash.

"Cash?" he'd exclaimed. "We've heard there's a bandit down that way—a man who calls himself the Nighthawk."

Rhys had merely arched his eyebrows. "What an uncivilized name."

"Mr. Redding—" Josiah Baker had started, but something in his visitor's eyes stopped him. A sudden hardness he'd not seen there before. He dropped back in his chair, wiping his brow. He wanted to do nothing to alienate this eccentric Englishman whose bank draft had resulted in a very large deposit just four days earlier. Even after this withdrawal, there was a great deal of money left. The English banker, who'd sent twenty thousand dollars to a Galveston bank which, in turn, sent Baker a draft, had practically slobbered in his note, saying he was so pleased to hear that Mr. Redding was alive and well.

The last, Rhys thought, was somewhat debatable. Here he was preparing to give away thousands of dollars. There was something very distinctly unwell about that. A disease named Susannah.

A disease he apparently had no vaccination against. A disease he couldn't fight. He could only hope to outrun it. Bloody Christ. Giving away money. He flinched at the thought. Oh, well, he had every intention of finding a way of getting it back.

He absolved himself of sentimentality by picturing Hardy and Lowell Martin when they learned their latest scheme had backfired. He had made his own little visit to a higher military authority in Austin, a man introduced by Josiah Baker. Colonel A. D. Sanford had heard him out, even looked interested when Rhys wondered aloud whether the Martins had also been taxed on all their newly acquired property, considering they had such a strong friendship with the captain there.

He'd been asked to inquire, Rhys lied, by a northern officer, a hero who had lost his leg at Libby Prison, and who was still too ill to travel this far. It was a miracle the man had survived a gallant escape from Libby Prison through southern lines, Rhys added, saying nothing about his own role in that particular endeavor. He was merely, he related, a concerned friend of the family.

The officer, a veteran of the war himself, was impressed. He obviously had little confidence in his junior officer stationed at Jacob's Crossing.

Rhys was smugly pleased he'd not lost his persuasiveness, the ability to so neatly twist the truth to conform with his own aims. The bloody devil knew he'd reformed as much as he intended. The fact that he had restrained from touching Susannah these last two weeks dishonored his lifelong belief in taking whatever pleasures were within reach. But he'd looked at those clear violet eyes and realized he couldn't take away her self-respect, not any more than he had.

At least, he would leave her a ranch intact, and hopefully a brother who could take care of himself. His one gift. A small one for the days of brightness she'd given him, for the hours of tenderness he'd always remember, the moments of making him feel like someone to be trusted and even . . . admired.

Bloody Christ, he would be crying in his beer next. He set his jaw and spurred his horse into a trot. The Nighthawk was riding again tonight.

Chapter 27

Two days, Susannah thought miserably as she washed
for supper. Two days since she'd last seen Rhys, since
he'd ridden off after hearing about the taxes. There
had been no word.

She couldn't help but feel a measure of betrayal.
He had done it before, of course, just disappeared
only to return with some card up his sleeve.

But as close as she and Wes were to losing everything, she needed more than speculation and hope.

Much more.

And she knew that Rhys Redding probably didn't
have more to give.

She wasn't sure how much longer she could take
the violent emotions swinging back and forth—the uncertainty, aching loneliness, and sickening fear that he
wouldn't return, and then that wild, uncontrolled elation when he did. He had become the center of her
world, even more than the ranch, and that world kept
spinning out of control.

"Rider." The familiar call drew her from the bedroom and out to the porch where Wes was standing,
watching as Andy Able approached on horseback.

Disappointment and then apprehension racked
Susannah as she glanced quickly at Wes and noted the
familiar wary expression. It was the first time that

someone other than Erin and Sam, seeking his sister-in-law the night Erin's father was killed, had stopped by since Wes arrived home.

Susannah felt a quickening of her heartbeat as she wondered about the purpose of Andy's visit. What had happened now? It had to be important for him to come by the home of the outcasts, she thought with some bitterness. She had hurt for herself long ago. Now she simply hurt for Wes.

Wes hesitated, then invited Andy down from his horse, adding a somewhat curt invitation for a drink. To his surprise, and to Susannah's, their visitor accepted.

Andy still wore Confederate trousers, a violation of decrees announced by the new military authority. He could go to jail for that offense, but then many of the jails would be filled. It seemed at least one-fourth of the male population of Texas wore pieces of Confederate clothing, out of either necessity or defiance.

Susannah poured each man a healthy portion of whiskey and herself a glass of sherry. Andy glanced her way as if hesitant to speak in her presence.

Wes smiled grimly. "She's run this place for the last four years, both of our places. Anything you have to say, she has a right to hear."

Andy flushed. "I know," he said. "I'm sorry, Susannah." He took another gulp of his drink. "You must have heard of the man called the Nighthawk."

Wes nodded.

"You wouldn't have any idea who he is?"

Wes stiffened.

Andy took another long swallow and shrugged helplessly. "We can't ... dammit ..." He looked at Susannah and flushed again. "Begging your pardon, Susannah." He started again. "We can't figure it. But he came by again last night."

Wes stiffened even further, and Susannah's eyes grew larger, but Andy was too uncomfortable to notice.

"He . . . left money. Enough to pay our taxes. Some—the Thorntons, the Kellens, Oley Olsen—saw him, or at least heard something. When they went to investigate, he was gone. There was only a leather pouch with money—greenbacks, and a picture of a hawk."

Wes couldn't hide his astonishment. Neither could Susannah. "Money?" she said oddly.

Texas pride struggled with practicality in Andy. "We . . . none of us—well, we hate to be indebted, but we don't know how to return it, and . . ."

"So you decided to use it for the purpose intended," Wes said wryly.

Andy's face turned red. "You wouldn't . . . know anything about it?"

Wes laughed bitterly. "Did you take a vote and the loser got to ask that question?"

Andy's face grew even redder. "I guess you have a right to say that, but no, I—I volunteered."

"Why?" Wes's voice was frank.

"Maybe it *is* time to put the war behind us. Someone, God knows who, is apparently fighting our battles. I don't know why, but we do want to thank him and try to pay him back someday."

"Why come here?"

"We're going to every ranch and farm in the area and asking the same question," Andy said. "We hope eventually someone will come forward."

Susannah saw Wes relax slightly.

"And we know you've been having problems, too," Andy said awkwardly. "That Englishman being roughed up . . . taxes." He hesitated a moment, as if he'd just thought of something. "Say, where is that Englishman?"

"Went to Austin for a few days," Wes said. "I don't think Texas hospitality has impressed him."

Andy squirmed slightly. "Well, I'd better be getting along. I have a few more stops—"

"Are you still planning to take the cattle north?"

Andy sat back down. "Yep."

Wes hesitated. "I don't suppose . . . you want an ex-Yank along?"

Susannah knew how much that question cost him. She twisted her fingers together. *Please, God. . . .*

Andy's glance fell down to Wes's missing leg.

"I've been herding horses here," Wes said. "I get along. And I came all the way across country by horseback." The words were spoken matter-of-factly, but again Susannah knew how much he was hurting. Wes used to be one of the best riders and ropers in the county. Now, he was close to begging.

Andy suddenly smiled. "I'll do what I can, Wes." He hesitated. "I can't promise anything—"

Wes rose with his crutches. "I know," he said, "but thanks."

Andy nodded to Susannah. "Susannah, I'm glad to see your arm is all right." He hesitated a moment, then held out his hand to Wes. "Welcome back."

Wes's lips broke into a slight smile, and he took the proffered hand, balancing himself on one crutch. Susannah felt a film of tears cloud her eyes. She followed Andy to the door.

"Thank you," she said, her tone heartfelt.

"I'm sorry, Susannah. I'm sorry about everything."

"Maybe it's coming to an end . . . all the hate."

"Maybe," Andy said, but his voice was doubtful. "I really will do what I can." He hesitated again. "Has the Nighthawk come by here?"

Susannah shook her head.

"Can you pay the taxes?"

"I don't know," she said bleakly. She didn't understand what was going on—what Rhys was doing, or where the money had come from, and why he hadn't returned. She didn't understand anything.

Andy stood awkwardly. "There was a little extra. All of us. Not much. But I would share ours."

She bit her lip to keep from crying. Four years of

being alone, of fighting alone, and now this offer. She couldn't speak. She merely nodded in acknowledgment of the gesture, neither refusing nor accepting. It was something she had to discuss with Wes, and she doubted whether his pride would allow it. Or hers. Not after the last four years. Not even if she was taking Rhys Redding's money. Or especially because she might be.

Dear God ... where did it come from? And why hadn't he returned to the ranch?

"Just say the word," Andy said, his face reddening again as he obviously read her first thoughts. He turned away quickly, mounted, and spurred his horse into a trot.

Wes and Susannah went inside, Wes dropping down into a chair. They stared at each other.

"I don't believe it," he said.

"Where is he?" she added.

Wes ignored that question, but posed one himself. "What game is he playing now?"

"Where did he get the money?"

"Those jewels?"

"They wouldn't bring that kind of money," she said.

"Damn," Wes said.

"And why everyone but us?"

"Maybe he hasn't gotten to us, yet," Wes said dryly. "Or knows I won't take it."

"A bank?"

"Not unless he robbed one."

Her eyes widened as she realized her brother was perfectly serious.

"He broke into a safe, didn't he?" Wes said. "It takes some specialized knowledge to do that."

Susannah had a very sick feeling in her stomach. "But he didn't take money, just those deeds and—"

"We really don't know what he took," Wes said, watching Susannah start to rise, then sit again.

"But he wouldn't."

"Wouldn't I?" Rhys Redding was standing in the opening of the door. They hadn't heard his approach, nor had there been a warning, since the hands felt he belonged at Land's End. There would be no alarm at his approach.

He was dressed in the black suit she'd seen him wear the first time he returned from Austin. His hair was windblown, a hank of hair falling over his forehead as if to give the lie to the rest of his elegant self. He was lounging against the doorjamb, apparently very interested in the conversation.

"Redding," Wes exploded.

Rhys sauntered into the living area and arched an eyebrow in that maddening, condescending way he favored when he wanted to enrage Wes.

Susannah stood absolutely still, fighting her own emotions. Relief, at first, at seeing him, followed by the familiar thrill she always felt. And then, an inexplicable anger. Anger that apparently had been building, anger born of frustration and fear and worry. Anger at the arrogance she'd always accepted until now. Anger at his aloof independence, which she'd tried to understand until now. Anger at herself for caring about someone who just kept disappearing, and showing up again with no explanations. Anger at caring so much when he obviously cared so little. She didn't know whether she was angrier at herself or at him after the past weeks of living in a netherworld of uncertainty.

She was very, very angry.

He had been popping in and out of her life like a jack-in-the-box. He had been playing his games, just as he had told her he would, but that didn't make them more palatable.

She felt the volcano inside her build, the volcano that had been dormant on the surface but seething at the core. She wanted to tear off that mask he wore. She wanted to rip away the armor and see whether the man she sometimes thought she saw was really there, or whether she had simply imagined it all. Had she built him into something he wasn't, would never be? He had accused her of that. And now, apparently, he was trying to prove it.

In trying to rip off the mask, she might well find there was no mask at all, that he really was no more than a gamesman, a renegade with no loyalties at all . . . and no interest in her beyond the obvious.

She glared at him. She had run the ranches for four years, she had traveled to Richmond, had engineered a prison escape, had, thus far, survived every attempt by the Martins to take her land. She had been in control of herself and her life, and she had been so proud of it, and now she was in control of nothing, particularly her own feelings.

And then something in his eyes changed as he watched her, the hardness melting into something like regret or chagrin. His hand moved up, as if to reach for her, but he was too far away and it dropped to his side. For one of the few times since she'd known him, he looked uncertain.

"I didn't rob a bank," he said simply, making an explanation he had never made before.

Wes was staring at him, from him to Susannah and back again.

"The Martins?"

He shook his head. "I had some money of my own in England. I sent for it when we first arrived. It just got here a few days ago."

"From England? Yours?" Wes was now as open-mouthed as Susannah. The idea of Rhys Redding giving away his own money to strangers was more than his mind could comprehend. "But why?"

Rhys shrugged in a gesture that was dearly, infuriatingly familiar. "To frustrate the Martins," he explained simply.

"My God," Wes uttered, even more startled that Rhys had explained than at the explanation itself, as incredible as it was. "Giving away money to frustrate someone?"

"I plan on getting it back," Rhys said, "one way or another." But his eyes were on Susannah, not Wes. And they were suddenly wary.

Susannah clenched her teeth. None of his rare explanations meant anything at the moment. She only felt a deep aching hurt that ran so deep she could hardly bear it. And betrayal. Both by him and herself.

She had never known much about him, only the few droplets he'd allowed, and now she realized again how meager they had been, even after all the intimacy she thought they'd shared. The fact that she had accepted so little only compounded her anger. She had been so smitten with him, so afraid to do, or say, anything that might cause him to leave or make him feel a responsibility she knew he didn't want, that she had abrogated every responsibility she had to herself. She had allowed him to drop in and out of her life, making decisions on his own that vitally affected her, without the slightest protest.

And now, after two days of misery and uncertainty, he simply appeared again as if he'd returned after a ten-minute absence, and dispensed astonishing news as if discussing the weather. He talked about large sums of money as if they were nothing at all, and she realized that every one of her conceptions of him was wrong. How he must have laughed when she offered him a job!

A street kid in London. A mercenary in Africa. How much was true? Probably none of it. But it had certainly worked in fascinating her. She felt sick inside.

He undoubtedly thought she and Wes would accept his money as they had, albeit Wes reluctantly, everything else. Susannah realized she had never known him at all, nor he her.

Watching him now, as stunned understanding spread across his face, she knew she loved him as much as she ever had. Her body reacted in the same trembling ways, but this time she wasn't going to let them take over, or she would lose herself forever.

"This was our problem," she said, forcing the words out in harsh tones to keep the tears back. "Our property, our home. It might have been nice to be consulted just a little about your plans."

He stood there, watching, his eyes hooded again, but his stance was no longer lazy, more like coiled for a blow. He didn't say anything. Just waited.

"And the money for *our* taxes—an act of charity on your way out, a dab of largess after an interesting game?"

He started to shake his head, the expression on his face unfathomable as he obviously comprehended the direction of her thoughts.

She swallowed, the tears burning behind her eyes. "Or a present for services rendered?" she said.

"No," he said simply, the dark sun-bronzed skin of his face appearing to pale as a muscle throbbed against his cheek. She wanted to go to him. She wanted to take that face in her hands. It took everything in her not to.

"I just thought . . ." He hesitated. He had never justified anything before in his life. He didn't even know how. He'd done as he had always done, concentrated on an objective without thinking about anyone else. He'd never thought about anyone else before. Bloody hell, there had never *been* anyone else before to consider.

But she interrupted before he could really try. "You. *You* thought. *You* did."

"Susannah—"

"Do you know how you make me feel?" she asked suddenly, her voice breaking now. "How useless, how unimportant, how ... usable? We didn't know if you were alive or dead, whether you were coming back ..."

Her heart was breaking, crumbling into small pieces. She had been telling herself for two days he might not come back. She had tried desperately not to care. But she had grieved. Just as she had grieved before, dying a little every time he disappeared. She whirled around. He wouldn't see her cry. He wouldn't. That would be the ultimate self-betrayal.

She sought the door through the film that fogged her eyes. She felt dead, as if she had just destroyed the thing that had kept her alive. But part of her kept going, as her throat clogged with lumps and the back of her head pounded with pressure.

She had to get away from him. From the anger. The despair. The knowledge that she had betrayed everything she was to pursue a phantom, even when she knew it was nothing more than illusion. Like the rainbow. Well, he'd warned her.

As she had the other day, she sought speed, to run away from the images and memories. Rhys's horse was there, tied to the rail post. Without thinking, she mounted it. She would find some place. A haven. A place to cry out six months' worth of tears. A place ... no one could find her.

She heard her name being called behind her. There was anxiety in his deep rich voice, even fear, and she ignored it, kicking her heels into the horse and sending it off in a cloud of dust.

Rhys turned to Wes, who had struggled to his feet.

"She can't go out there alone—not today. The Martins will know what happened last night. That their newest hand went bust."

Wes glared at Rhys. Then the expression softened

as he saw the clenched jaw, the worry in the man's eyes. "You really care, don't you?"

Rhys didn't reply. He couldn't. He didn't know how to say yes, particularly when she'd just made her feelings clear. She detested him. And why not? He didn't even know how to do something decent. And he cringed inwardly as he suddenly realized exactly how she'd felt. "Usable," she'd said. Had he really made her feel that way when, in his own way, he had been trying to protect her by keeping away? Or had he been trying to protect himself?

Wes wasn't feeling very proud of himself, either. He had complained and whined and pitied himself until even he was sick of his own company. He didn't really know how Susannah had borne either of them: Redding's arrogance and his own self-absorption.

"She won't go to the old place," he said thoughtfully. "She'll know we will look there. She might go to Erin's."

"I'll go east along the river," Redding said.

"I'll go to Erin's," Wes announced.

But neither of them found her. Erin rode with Wes as they checked several other ranches. Sam had agreed to ask their remaining hands to search. A stop by the Ables also proved fruitless, but they too offered to join a search.

And then it was dark, and it was useless to continue. Erin returned to Land's End with Wes, wanting to be there if there was any news or if Susannah returned. She also didn't want Wes to be alone.

Rhys rode in an hour later to see whether Wes had had any luck. If she didn't return by morning, Rhys said, they would pay a visit to the Martins. He was all for going now, but Wes stopped him. No sense in alerting them that Susannah was out alone.

Coolness and objectivity had always been among

Rhys's few virtues, particularly when something important was at stake. But he had neither now. He paced the house, then the barn. He rubbed down the horse he'd ridden. He had to do something.

He didn't know when it actually occurred to him that this was exactly what Susannah had been doing ever since he met her. Flashes skipped through his mind. Her gentleness when she nursed him, her determination when she shot the man trying to take their dilapidated wagon, the steadiness when one of the deserters held her, her insistence that Wes take charge even when he'd seen the longing, even desperation, in her own eyes to take control herself.

Susannah was not the type of woman to stay home and wait. He'd known it, and that was one of the reasons, he also knew, that she was so appealing. Her courage and independence had been as heady wine to him. Yet he and Wes had both, in their own ways, stifled that independence, Wes by needing to prove his worth and he, Rhys, by fearing any kind of reins on his freedom.

He felt as if a horse had kicked him in the stomach. Love. He had avoided that word all his life. He'd convinced himself he hadn't needed it, that it would weaken him, but now he knew those rationalizations were not valid. He had simply believed himself unlovable. And so he had shut Susannah out, time and time again, so he wouldn't be dealt the blow he was sure would come.

Instead, he had dealt it to himself.

He started to saddle his horse again. He couldn't stay here. He had to at least look.

And then he heard the call, "Miss Susannah. It's Miss Susannah."

He looked out the door of the barn. Her back straight, Susannah rode first to the house, and he saw Wes and Erin come out on the porch to greet her, and then she turned toward the barn on the chestnut horse he'd claimed as his own. He went further into the barn, waiting for her, knowing she would come in herself to unsaddle the mount. She always did.

Rhys watched from the shadows as she rode inside, and then he moved to her side, disregarding her attempt to slide down herself. He caught her instead and held her tightly for a moment, reliving for brief moments the fear he had felt at the possibility of losing her.

She started to pull away, but he wouldn't let her. And then she didn't try again because her body, willingly or not, melded into his and her mouth came up automatically to meet his.

The kiss was tentative at first, then violent with the need that was always between them. It was like a grass fire, he thought, an African grass fire torched by lightning, which nothing on God's earth could quench.

He felt himself tremble with the fear that still remained in him for her, and he removed his lips from hers and buried them in the softness of her hair. They moved to her face, and he tasted the saltiness of dried tears and, if he'd never despised himself before, he did so now.

"I'm sorry," he said for the first time in his life.

Her eyes widened at his words, and impaled him with a sadness he knew he would never forget.

He hesitated, then said in a harsh voice. "I had no right . . . I've just . . . always done what . . . I thought had to be done. There was never anyone before . . ."

Never anyone. It seemed an incredibly sad admission to Susannah, and the last remaining anger seeped away, but not the realization that Rhys Redding would always be a law unto himself. She had fought that battle with herself all afternoon on a lonely hill.

She reached out her hand to touch his face, the hard angles and lines that would always be there, carved by circumstances and events she would probably never know.

She wanted to surrender again, to take whatever he would give her, but she couldn't, not this time, not and remain the person she wanted to be. The person she had been.

Susannah met his gaze. "You're slicing me in little pieces." The words echoed with pain in the barn. Rhys closed his eyes against them, but they still hovered in the air.

But Susannah wasn't through. "I love you, Rhys. I love you, and I don't know if I can survive loving you."

She felt his body shudder next to hers. "You can't love me," he said finally and absolutely, as if even the concept were the most impossible thing in the world.

"Why?"

Because there's nothing to love, he wanted to yell at her, so loud that she would understand. But he stood silent instead, hurting in a way completely new to him.

She took his hand and ran her fingers over it as if somehow it could tell her what she wanted to know, and then very gently she led him over to where they had loved the other night. To her surprise, he didn't protest, and when she looked up at his eyes they radiated a kind of pain she'd never seen there before.

"Why?" she said again, insistently.

His jaw stiffened. Perhaps now was the time, the time he'd known was coming, the time to tell the truth, the time to see distaste replace the tenderness on her face. Did he even know the truth any longer?

Still holding his hand, she slid to the floor, forcing him to do the same unless he tore his hand from hers, and he didn't want to do that, not yet. It was too warm, too gentle. She wasn't just touching his fingers, she was reaching in and touching the core of him, and after his hours of anxiety about her, he couldn't let her go. Not yet. That would come soon enough. In minutes, perhaps.

The horses stamped restlessly in the stall, and

Susannah knew she should attend to her mount, but nothing was more important than this moment. Rhys had opened a small portal, one she might be able to creep through. She knew her brother would keep others away. Wes had said Rhys was in the barn, that he had been worried, and she had asked Wes for some time alone with Rhys. Her brother had looked at Erin, saw her nod, and had reluctantly agreed.

Now Susannah traced patterns on his hand, sensing the indecision in him, the unnatural stillness in the energy-driven body. "Why?" she asked again. "Why can't I love you?"

He stiffened even more, but he didn't draw away as she half expected. "I told you that I was the son of a lord. That may or may not be true. My mother told me that, but I don't think she knew. She was a . . . prostitute, you see, in a small dirty inn in Wales." His voice was harsh, agonizingly honest. "She used to tell me over and over again how she tried to rid herself of me before I was born . . . I was a devil, she said, of devil's seed; that was why I lived."

Susannah felt sick. She didn't know someone could hurt inside like this. The bewilderment of a small boy reverberated in his harsh tones, in spite of how matter-of-fact he tried to keep them.

But she was afraid to show anything, afraid he would reject it as he rejected any sign of pity, or compassion, or even caring. She was beginning to understand why.

Rhys hesitated. He'd half expected her to move away at his confession. Many women would at that revelation about his pedigree, or lack of it. When she didn't, when her fingers kept playing a tune of love on his hands, making his whole body hum along with it, he continued, trying to make her understand why she couldn't love someone like him, why it was impossible. And also why he did the things he did, the way he did. Alone.

"She died when I was seven," he said flatly. "I didn't mourn. I was even relieved. No more slaps or hits or screaming. The innkeeper kept me on as little more than a slave, tending horses, cleaning up the taproom, delivering food and drink to couples too busy to come down . . ." He didn't have to elaborate. Her eyes told him he didn't. So wide, so sad. So incredibly sad. He didn't want them to be sad for him. That wasn't what he'd meant to do. He'd meant to warn her, to make her realize he was no good for her.

"Once," he said, "I didn't move fast enough for one of the guests, a lord. He used his whip on me, and I said never again, never again would anyone touch me and live. And they didn't—until Hardy the other day . . . You see, love," he said with some of the old mockery, "my generosity to your neighbors really didn't have anything to do with you, or Wes. It's my vengeance, mine alone."

But Susannah didn't hear that. She was still with that little boy. How did the son of a prostitute learn the manners he had, the speech, the obvious education? "What happened to that boy?" she asked.

"He ran away and became a thief," Rhys said in a measured voice. "The streets of London can be a fine school. You steal or starve. So I stole. I was a very good pickpocket, a shill for crooked gambling, anything for a pence. You didn't make friends, because if you did, your throat might be cut for what little you had when you least expected it. There is no loyalty among cutthroats, no matter what you might hear," he said dryly. "You quickly learn to trust no one."

"And . . . Africa . . ."

"Ah, Africa," he said in the lazy amused voice he had used so much when they first met. Another part of his armor, she thought. "I learned to hone my skills in Africa. Hunting. Cheating. How to become a more sophisticated thief. I had a good teacher, a man named

Nathan. Now he *was* a lord, or at least the son of one, before he was disowned after stealing from his father."

"Your friend?"

"Friend?" Rhys laughed, but as in the beginning, when Susannah had first met him, there was no amusement in it. "Oh, no, never that. As I told you, cutthroats have no friends, and Nathan was one of the best of the former. But he recognized a certain talent in me, and used it. He became my teacher, and because it was important that we present a good front, he taught me manners, speech, how to read, the ways of the gentry, along with a number of ways to swindle. I was an excellent pupil with a natural aptitude for deception. I had a gift for languages, for dialects, that stunned Nathan, but he quickly learned how to use that too. I could become anyone, anything, he wanted. A chameleon who could change at will, a creature without substance, only camouflage.

"That's all I am, pretty Susannah," he said with that tone that masked every emotion, every feeling, although Susannah felt the radiating tension in him. "No hero, no white knight. A simple thief."

Despite all the ache inside her at his emotionless recital, she suddenly had to smile at the word "simple."

He looked slightly stunned, even a bit insulted.

"It's just that . . ." she horrified herself by starting to giggle, realizing as she did, it was reaction to the powerful emotions that were running through her. If she didn't giggle, she would cry, and that was one thing that would make him flee again. "Just . . . that there is . . . nothing . . . *simple* about you."

Rhys started to frown, dragging his eyebrows together in that forbidding way he sometimes had, but then his mouth twitched slightly. He worked feverishly to keep it from spreading. Susannah never reacted as he expected, to anything. Never had, in fact, and he wondered for a moment why he thought she might now. Perhaps she still didn't understand the scope of his dismal character.

"There's more," he said sternly.

He watched as she tried to compose herself. He found his free hand, the one she was not holding, drawing her close, much closer than he intended. Don't, he told himself, but he couldn't help it. She was so irresistible, with her expression swinging from emotion to emotion, her mouth trying to keep from chuckling at its own joke, her hair falling over his arm in silky waves that he wanted to bury his cheek against.

Bloody hell, he wanted to be everything she had believed him to be.

But nothing had changed. He was still poison for someone like her, and something of that belief must have reflected in his eyes, because she suddenly stopped smiling and looked up at him with the accepting intensity of a puppy who suddenly believed it had found a loving master. It was terribly disconcerting.

He tried, however. "After some eight years, we'd accumulated a great deal of money, and I was thinking about returning to England, although I knew Nathan never could. Perhaps that was even why. Nathan was taking more and more risks, almost as if he was courting death."

Rhys hesitated. "Bloody hell, I don't know why I wanted to return, except to prove something. Nathan was angry because I was leaving, and he went off on a treasure hunt; someone had claimed to have found diamonds. He made it back to Victoria, just before I left. He had a diamond with him, one of the finest I'd ever seen. He also had a raging fever. He died four days later.

"I never did find out where he'd gotten the diamond. It was his last joke, his revenge, because I was leaving. He wanted me to know he'd found a diamond field, that it was there waiting, but I would never know where. He somehow made it back . . . just for that."

Rhys shrugged. "It didn't matter. Not in the way he thought it would. I had enough to return to England, and the diamond made me very wealthy indeed." His voice was mocking again. "You see, I had never forgotten my father, and all those years I thought that someday . . . someday, I would find my rightful place. But society didn't see it that way. I could never buy my way in with mercenary money, nor conform with aped manners. The ton saw right through them, so I decided to make them pay for that insult. I was always a damnably good gambler, even when I didn't cheat, and so many of the young lords were not. I won myself an estate, never mind that the man who lost it later took a gun to his head and killed himself."

All her giggles were gone now. Susannah felt the taut emotion in him, heard, even if he didn't, the need and yearning for an acceptance he had never known. She knew now why he had never confided in her or Wes about his plans; he'd never been able to trust another human being in his life, and he didn't know how to change. She cried for him inside, for the man who had always been so alone, who had so obviously hungered for somewhere to belong.

And yet, despite the way he had lived, he still had a reservoir of decency in him; she knew that as well as she knew anything. No matter how he decried his reasons for coming with them, he could have left at any time, could have deserted them. Instead, he had helped give life back to Wes, had given them his constant, unswerving protection. She had seen his gentleness with her, with animals, even in his roughness with Wes. There was so much hidden beneath that hard, bitter exterior.

Her hand moved up to his face, her fingers followed the grim lines around those hooded eyes, down to the lips that were now firmly clamped together as he waited for her censure.

She leaned up and kissed that mouth, teasing it into relaxing, into gentling. As it started to surrender, she moved slightly away. "I love you, Rhys Redding," she said softly. "I'll always love you."

"You can't."

"You keep assuming what I can and can't do," she said. "What I should and shouldn't know."

"But—"

"I can't change what is, Rhys. Neither can you."

His jaw worked slightly. "I can't ever give you what you need," he said raggedly. "I don't know . . . how to love someone."

"I think you do," she said slowly, "or you wouldn't be telling me this."

"Susannah—"

But she stopped any more words, any more denials, with her own mouth, and the grass fire roared through both of them, unstoppable, unquenchable.

And they both knew now it wouldn't burn itself out.

Chapter 28

Susannah couldn't sleep that night. Her mind kept hearing Rhys's words, each painful one of them spoken with such harsh reality that she doubted none of them.

She understood Rhys better than she had before, which obviously had not been much at all. But she realized she could probably never understand him completely; the forces that drove him were ones she simply couldn't comprehend.

Until the war, she had always felt safe, even in a land that could be so unforgiving. Her father and brother had always protected her, and then Mark. Even during the war, she knew she had their love, if not their presence. She had never felt an absence of love.

It had been that love that enabled her to grow, the deep inner knowledge that others loved her and trusted her and believed in her, and it had been that fountain that led her to do what she had done: to keep the ranches going, to go to Richmond, to bring Wes back, to fight those who would rip the beloved heritage from her.

Rhys Redding had never had the gift of someone else's trust or caring, not even, apparently, of friendship. He'd never had anyone but himself. She wanted to cry for that boy, for the man, but the grief for him was too deep for simple tears, too scorching to extinguish in such a way.

So was the grief for herself, because she wondered whether it was too late for him to ever surrender the world of aloneness he had built for himself, that apparent belief that total self-reliance was his only road to survival, and that any personal attachment was doomed to disaster.

Understanding wasn't a solution. It only made her comprehend the enormity of the problem. It amazed her to discover he thought he wasn't good enough for her, while she'd felt, deep in her soul, he couldn't love a Texas girl in trousers when he'd probably his choice of beauties in England.

But this new revelation frightened her even more than her old belief. She knew her brother's blind stubbornness in that regard, the fact that he wouldn't, couldn't, accept the fact that Erin loved him for what he was, despite that he had only one leg.

Why were men so impossibly stupid?

Susannah still felt the power of Rhys's lips on hers. So hungry, so wanting. But they had not made love last night, although both their bodies had obviously disagreed with the decision Rhys made. It certainly hadn't been hers, even though she knew that many eyes were on the barn, unlike several nights ago when they'd made love, oblivious to the world and believing the world oblivious to them.

After that long, painful kiss, Rhys untangled himself, gave her a crooked smile, and said he had better take her home. She didn't want that, but all his shields were back in place, his face erased of any emotion. Only the muscle that twitched in his throat showed the cost of his restraint. Or, she wondered, was it regret that he had said so much?

And then she discarded the latter thought. No matter the strain, Rhys Redding never said anything he didn't intend. He had meant to scare her away, perhaps even to remind himself of the barriers between them. They weren't barriers to her, but she knew now how strong and impenetrable they were to him. If only she could make him believe they were less than paper, flimsy and without substance. Only his belief made them strong.

Susannah believed one thing, however. He wouldn't disappear again, not as he had, not after that remorse he'd felt, not now that he knew how she felt. Not without telling her.

That, at least, had changed.

Wes did not say anything when she walked in later, but merely looked at her flushed face and announced he would take Erin home. And tell the other ranchers that Susannah was safe.

She nodded and went to her room, wishing that Rhys was with her.

But then she had much to think about. She could be just as Machiavellian as he as long as she knew the rules of the game. And she was beginning to learn them.

Lowell Martin spent the morning watching one rancher after another pay his taxes. They lined up in front of the tax office, their faces wreathed with smiles. There was a celebration at the one saloon.

Gossip told him where the money had come from, gossip and his spies at some of the ranches. The Nighthawk again.

Damn, where did that infernal varmint get the money? And why would he give it away? Unless he was trying to create some kind of legend. Like Robin Hood, or some such nonsense.

It didn't make sense. And Lowell Martin didn't like things that didn't make sense. He also knew that legends were dangerous. He had used fear to drive people out. He knew that hope could make them stay and fight.

He'd planned everything so carefully. And when the notes had disappeared, he played his other card: urging the military occupation forces to collect past due taxes. He wanted this valley. He wanted to take from all those who'd looked down on him and his family when he was a boy, who'd snickered when he'd married, who had laughed at his ambitions.

They didn't laugh now. He had more than any of them. But it wasn't enough. He wanted to rub their faces in his success. He wanted them to come to him and beg, while he coldly refused any mercy. He had planned to own the valley.

And he would have. He would have become the most important man south of Austin—if it were not for the Nighthawk.

Who was he?

His spies knew nothing. The ranchers were as mystified, apparently, as he himself. Sam? The Ables? His mind ran through the names again and again. Still, nothing really made sense. None of them had the kind of money necessary to pay all the taxes. And all taxes had been paid except for Susannah Fallon's and Wes Carr's.

But then, they were considered outcasts now. Just as he had been.

His fist clenched on top of the desk. Every move he'd made had been checkmated since the Nighthawk had appeared. Lowell had to discover the identity of the Nighthawk, had to get rid of him, for the rest of his plan to succeed.

But how?

He remembered when his brother had been shot— right after Susannah Fallon. The note: "Kind for kind." The masked man evidently felt some particular . . . protection for women.

Perhaps that was it. A trap. Baited by a woman.

And he knew exactly which one. He doubted whether the ranchers would go to the U.S. Army for help. They certainly, and rightfully, didn't trust the captain here. And the sheriff, hell, Lowell owned the man several times over.

Lowell would suggest that his wife stay at their house in town, her old house, because she would be safer there after two intrusions here by the Nighthawk. And then he would bring *her*, his bait, back here. And wait for the Nighthawk.

He didn't even think twice that he might have another motive, an even more personal one.

He called his brothers in.

Erin MacDougal gave a light clucking to the horses pulling her old buggy. It was a practical vehicle, not like the fancy carriage the family often used before the war. Now that carriage seemed . . . farcical in light of the poverty they all suffered.

She smiled to herself as she thought of Wes Carr, the hours they had shared anxiously awaiting Susannah's return. He had paced on his one leg and crutches, and then had sat next to her, clutching her hand, holding her as he once had.

He had kissed her, a kiss born of anxiety and worry, the need to be comforted. Sharing. She had seen the love in his eyes, the need, and for the first time since he'd returned, he'd given into it, had reached for her with a desperation that echoed her own.

And then when Susannah had returned, he had turned to Erin again, sharing his elation, even surrendering to her unspoken suggestion that he leave Sue and the English stranger alone. She had known that was what Sue wanted, just as she had wanted Wes.

She hugged the next memory, when they had gone inside and he had balanced himself against the wall, his arms going around her and bringing her to him, whispering, "Thank you for being here," just as his lips closed on hers.

She loved him so. She loved the dark blue eyes, and the unruly light brown hair now made bright by the sun. She loved the strength in his face, and the character that had driven him to go his own way during the war, to defy his neighbors for his belief. She loved the way he coped now, finding his own way of coming back, without ever compromising.

The only thing she didn't like was his stubbornness in believing that his missing leg somehow made him unfit for her. She couldn't seem to convince him that she didn't care a fig whether he had two legs or one. He was still Wes Carr, the finest, most wonderful man she had ever known. She still grew warm and fuzzy with his kisses, and still wanted to explore the deeper mysteries of man and woman with him. His missing leg was a badge of honor to her, nothing more, except for the pain she knew it caused him.

Lost in her thoughts, in the memory of his smile last night, she didn't hear the approaching sound of hoofbeats. She was going into town with several baskets of eggs to sell to the general store, and perhaps on the way back she would stop at Susannah's ranch. She had been driving herself into town every week, since everyone at the plantation had so much work to do. There was no need to worry. There had been no incidents on this road, and she had a rifle with her.

But then she heard the sound, and something inside her mind rang with alarm. She looked behind. A man dressed all in black was moving up on her. He was riding a black horse, and in his hand—dear God, in his hand was a pistol, and in that moment she knew he was going to shoot. She whipped the reins on the back of the horse, asking them to run for her, and they did. The sound of a shot came, and the horses bolted forward even faster, and she lost control. The carriage wobbled on its wheels, careening back and forth on the road as the horses raced out of control, and then she felt it overturning, and she went spinning out, tumbling over and over again.

The note arrived at the MacDougal plantation near sunset.

"We have Miss MacDougal. We will exchange her for the outlaw who calls himself the Nighthawk." It then gave directions to an abandoned shack in the middle of the hill country and directed the Nighthawk to appear at sunset the next day. *"If anyone other than the Nighthawk comes, we will kill her,"* the note continued.

As with Susannah's disappearance, men spread out from the MacDougal ranch with the news. Sam himself rode to inform Wes.

Wes was at supper with his sister, and the Englishman, Redding. Sam barely gave him notice now, but handed the note to Wes. No matter what he himself thought of Wes Carr, Sam knew how Erin felt about him, and not even his own dislike could break his sense of obligation to his sister-in-law.

Wes read the note and passed it to the Englishman, whose jaw tightened perceptibly. Wes's own fist tightened on the table. "I know that shack. There's no way to approach without being seen."

Sam nodded. "I know. I considered calling the other men together and storming it, but—"

"She might be killed," Wes finished for him, a muscle throbbing in his throat.

Sam nodded. "We found her overturned buggy. The horses were gone."

Wes sent a quick glance over to Rhys, as Sam hesitated, then continued, "Do you have any idea at all who this ... Nighthawk is?"

Wes shook his head, avoiding Sam's eyes. "No, but

from what I've heard of him . . . he'll exchange himself for her."

Sam's face creased with indecision. "We couldn't ask that, not after everything he's already done. The Martins will surely kill him. They can't afford—"

Wes had another proposal. "Or one of us could pretend to be the Nighthawk," he said slowly. He looked at Susannah, whose face was white beneath the light tan.

Sam nodded. "I've thought about that." He hesitated a moment, then added grimly, "There's . . . a meeting at noon tomorrow. My place." He swallowed hard. "If you want to come . . ." He left the half-invitation hanging in the air as Wes nodded.

The three of them waited to speak until they heard the departing sound of Sam's horse. The pain lines in Wes's face were etched even deeper, his blue eyes bleak. "If anything . . ."

It was Rhys who answered, his usually melodic deep voice harsh. "It won't," he said, making it clear he planned to meet the terms.

"No," Wes said sharply. "I'll go. She's my . . . girl."

Rhys looked meaningfully toward the area of Wes's missing leg. "I have a chance. You don't," he said brutally. "It's my game, not yours. I set everything in motion. I'll finish it."

"You can't. Not by yourself."

"Do you believe they will kill her?"

Wes nodded. He wasn't sure about Lowell, but he wouldn't take a chance on Hardy. If Hardy was any place around at sunset, and something went wrong, Wes didn't doubt for a moment the middle Martin brother would kill Erin. And take pleasure in it.

"Then let me take care of it. I have a few tricks of my own." Rhys's face hardened. "If I have to tie you down, you're not going. I want your word."

Wes buried his face in his hands, trying desperately to think, trying not to give in to total despair. He had never run away from a fight, particularly when someone he loved was in danger. But part of him knew Rhys was right. Wes knew he didn't have the speed or agility that might be required to save Erin. And despite himself, he did have a peculiar faith in Rhys Redding.

"Go to the meeting, Wes," Rhys said, using his Christian name for the first time. "You can do more there—"

"As a cripple, you mean," Wes said bitterly.

"No," Rhys said. "That's not what I meant. And you're only a cripple if you allow yourself to be." He stood, his dark hawk eyes raking over Wes and then gentling as they moved to Susannah's pale face.

"Where is this cabin? I want to take a look at it."

Wes stood, using the table to balance himself. "I can do that, at least," he said. "Take you to it."

"If you do as I say," Rhys said, and Wes reluctantly nodded.

"I'll go, too," Susannah said.

"No," both men said at once. It was the first time Susannah had ever heard them in harmony, and she felt her anger rise again.

"Why?"

Rhys went over to her, and looked down, his eyes cautious. "Because someone should be here in case anyone comes by with more news," he said logically. "And three people riding at night are more noticeable than two—or one," he added, making it clear he would drop Wes off somewhere along the way. His hand went up and touched her cheek. "I don't doubt your ability or courage . . . it's just that you'll be more help here." He grinned. "I'll bring Wes back safe."

"You *will* come back?" she asked. "Tonight?" She knew how dangerous tomorrow would be. She couldn't bear the thought of not seeing him again before then.

A muscle moved in his cheek. "I'll come back," he

promised, realizing as he did so that it was probably
the first promise he'd made to someone else that he
fully intended to keep.

Lowell watched the slender form in the large bed.
She looked so small, the auburn hair spread across the
white sheet in disarray. He could have killed his
brother when the men came in, carrying the unconscious girl.

His orders had been specific. Hardy was to dress
in black and threaten the girl, and then his men were
to come along and "save" her from the outlaw. She
would be brought to his ranch to recuperate; a drink
would be laced with a sedative that would keep her
asleep until the Nighthawk was killed.

When she awoke, she would be grateful to him,
and the death of the Nighthawk would be blamed on
bounty hunters, who used the girl's disappearance to
apprehend him. He planned to explain that the note
he'd sent to her family must have "gotten lost."

He didn't care if none of the ranchers believed
him. The sheriff would, despite his diminished authority, and so would Captain Osborn. And perhaps even
Erin, in light of his "kindness." Perhaps, she would
even see, in this house, that he could have made her
a fine husband—perhaps still could, if he could get rid
of his wife.

He had certainly not meant to have her hurt, not
like this. He almost called the doctor, but that would
ruin all his plans. He would wait, see if she woke in
the next hours. In the meantime, Hardy was at the
cabin with twenty of his men. The Nighthawk
wouldn't escape them this time.

Wes took Rhys most of the way to the old abandoned shack, deserted years ago when its well dried

up. When they got within a mile, Rhys told Wes to wait with the horses; he would go the rest of the way on foot and look for a way to take the cabin safely without endangering Erin.

Rhys swore at the full moon, so bright as it hung large in a cloudless night. He snaked through the grass quickly for about half a mile, and then he saw the sentries. Every few feet, on treeless hills that apparently had been cleared for farming. Bloody Christ, there must be nearly two dozen of them. He dropped to the ground and crept closer until he saw the top of a shack, smoke coming from the chimney. He didn't dare go further. The men were too close to ambush without giving himself away. And risking Erin MacDougal's life.

He retreated, his mind working out every possibility. There weren't many. The likeliest was his death in exchange for the girl's life.

For the first time he could remember, his life meant something. In the past few weeks, it had been filled with a richness that so bewildered him he kept running from it. He smiled mirthlessly. It was just like his own personal devil to give him something to live for, and then jerk it away as he reached to grab it.

But he had started this, and he wasn't going to allow someone else to pay for his misjudgment. He erred when he hadn't considered that the Martins might retaliate by taking a woman. He'd always paid for his own mistakes. He didn't even stop to think that maybe, just maybe, that thought had a shade of nobility in it.

Susannah was waiting for them when they arrived back. It was almost dawn. Wes, grim and tight-lipped, went to bed, curtly refusing even a small glass of brandy.

Rhys took a glass of whiskey, downed it, and

started for the door. Susannah stopped him. "You really are going tomorrow, aren't you?"

Rhys looked down at her. Her violet eyes, usually so clear and bright, darkened, becoming so deep he knew he could get lost in them. Perhaps he already had. "Please don't," she said, not waiting for an answer. "Don't go."

"What do you suggest?" he said.

"The military . . . the law . . ."

"You know Martin has them in his hands," he said softly. "I told you I play games. And I always finish the ones I begin."

"This isn't a game." She wished she had never heard that word. She remembered the first time he had used it, in the woods, months ago now, when he was trying to frighten her off. Then it intrigued her. Now it terrified her. "If you ride in there alone . . ."

His hand touched her cheek with a tenderness that made her ache. It didn't surprise her anymore, that light touch, which by its own restraint reflected a side within him that gave the lie to that unemotional exterior he tried so hard to preserve. "Ah, Susannah, don't you know I always have another move? I have nine lives, remember. It would take more than a man who kidnaps women to kill me."

"Don't go," she whispered again, her eyes begging him, reaching into the guts of him and tying them into knots. He suddenly knew what real pain was.

He wasn't going to do this. He had vowed he wouldn't. She looked so stricken, so . . . sad. No one had even given a bloody damn before whether he lived or died, and it was achingly painful to realize that someone did now. Bittersweet. But that was too mild a word. He relished the brief, sweet caring while realizing it came too late. Much too late. And Christ, it hurt. He wanted to wrap himself in it, to taste everything he had missed.

Rhys swallowed. It was like seeing a glimpse of heaven before being dropped into hell.

He shouldn't make it worse by kissing her, touching her. Still, he couldn't help himself. His head bent and he kissed her, a long, searching, giving kiss that held a good-bye in it.

But she refused to take it. Her arms went up around his neck, pulling herself to him, her lips locking him to her in another way, in a desperate attempt to meld him to her for eternity. His body strained, and reacted and felt the reckless, urgent need, the powerful yearning that was at once torment and exquisite sweetness. He swallowed, tasting, savoring the gift he knew she was trying to give him, and something inside him swelled with a pleasure so complete that it threatened to consume him, even without another word, another touch.

He was loved. Loved in a way he'd never thought possible, for his own somewhat flawed self. Completely flawed. He held her tight, taking moments that made his entire misspent life worthwhile, that gave all those empty years meaning and value because in some way they had led to this.

He laid his cheek on her hair, that dark hair that always smelled like spring flowers and felt like silk. He was barely aware of moving, of following her lead, of walking into her bedroom and then lying down on the bed with her, moving with her, loving her, giving to her.

Holding her for possibly the last time.

Holding. Loving. A word, an emotion, an act that he now knew was no myth.

The meeting at Sam's house drew forty men. They stood, their eyes angry, their stance defiant. All were determined to do something.

Wes was offered a chair but refused it, standing

against the wall on his crutches. He couldn't sit, not now, not when Rhys Redding had disappeared. The Welshman had been gone when he awoke this morning, and Susannah's eyes had been red, her face drawn.

Wes hadn't asked questions. He didn't have to. He had only to look at Susannah to know how in love she was, how terrified she was for the man who still remained a mystery to him. He'd felt anger toward Redding, but then that anger had leaked from him. Redding was offering his life for the woman Wes loved. And Susannah was a grown woman, who knew the risks.

In fact, he thought as he envisioned Erin in his mind, he admired his sister's courage and love and determination. If only he, Wes, had had that unselfish commitment, then perhaps Erin would be safe with him. His hand tightened around the crutch handle. He would never forgive himself if something happened to her. He hadn't denied Erin out of unselfishness, but out of selfishness and fear. He had been unwilling to risk anything, particularly rejection, while Susannah had been willing to risk everything.

He listened grimly to men who used to be friends as they argued bitterly over what to do. And he couldn't say what needed to be said, that a stranger was planning to give his life for one of them. The Nighthawk's identity wasn't his secret to divulge.

There was something he could do, dammit. And he planned to do it. But first he had to convince these men not to do anything reckless, not to go after the Martins and possibly get Erin killed in the attempt.

"If we attack, Erin could be killed," Sam warned.

"We can't let the Martins get away with this," said another. "It's time to act, by damn."

"But how?"

"Perhaps the Nighthawk . . ." ventured Andy Able.

"We don't even know if the Nighthawk, whoever he is, will get word," another answered impatiently.

"Even if he does, why should he risk his life? Unless he's one of us." For the hundredth time in the past few weeks, gazes traveled from one man to another, seeking to unveil a secret. Who among them . . . ?

The meeting had gone on an hour, and still there was no decision.

Then the call came from one of the black servants who'd remained with the MacDougals. "Rider coming."

They crowded the windows, all but Wes. He knew he couldn't maneuver between the bodies, and he also sensed what was coming. He should have known. Rhys Redding never left loose ends. He wanted to handle this on his own, and he would make sure he did.

But not if Wes could act first.

The thud of a rock was heard on the porch, and he heard the men exchanging words. "It's him."

"The Nighthawk."

"Must be."

"But who?"

"Don't recognize him. Not him or the horse."

One of the men opened the door, retrieved the rock, and untied the message attached to it.

"Do nothing," it said. *"I'll meet the terms of the demand."*

The words were read, and there was silence. "We can't do that," one man said. "We can't let him go in alone."

"Did you notice anything familiar about him?" another man interrupted.

"Only that he's a superb rider," said another.

"I don't understand . . . How did he know about the meeting?"

There was a long silence. How did he know? Word

had been quietly spread among friends and neighbors, every man warned not to say anything, even to wives and ranch hands. They hadn't wanted word to get to the Martins. Again, searching looks passed from man to man. Someone here *had* to know something.

But no one answered the silent query, and the debate continued.

"Now what do we do?"

"*We*," said Wes, "don't do anything."

All the men turned and looked at him, hostility shining in their eyes. "We can't just sit back—"

"She's my fiancée," Wes said sharply, proclaiming that fact now to himself as well as to the others. "I'll go."

There was a sudden silence, all movement suspended, even a shuffling of feet.

Wes continued slowly. "All they want is someone dressed in black. That's all they know."

"They'll kill you," Sam said.

"They can try," Wes said. Then he added grimly, "The Confederate Army tried for four years."

One man looked down at Wes's leg. "Looks like we damn near succeeded." But there was no more hostility in his voice, or in the faces of the other men in the room.

Wes suddenly grinned. "Someone told me 'damn near' doesn't count."

Sam hesitated, the coldness in his eyes warming. "They will know it's not you. The Nighthawk has two legs."

"So do I," Wes said. "I—I've been practicing on a wooden leg. Dressed and on horseback, no one would know. Neither would they know how long I've had it."

"But the Nighthawk—"

"I'll make damn sure I get there before he does," Wes said grimly. "Hopefully, they will release Erin before he gets anyplace close. Some of you can wait down the road for her, and warn him off."

"I don't like it," Sam said. "I don't like anyone walking into a trap like that."

"You don't have to like it," Wes said. "Just stay out of it, at least until Erin's safe." He smiled grimly. "Then you can act like the cavalry if you want. . . . I might even be glad to hear that Reb yell."

But it was unlikely Wes Carr would hear it. They all knew it. Carr would be dead with the first sign of trouble.

Wes didn't wait for more debate. He used his crutches to move to the door before there were any more protests. He didn't want to give them a choice. Besides, of them all, he knew he, as the Yank lover, was the most expendable in their minds. If his experience in the past months was any sign, he didn't think there would be naysayers to that proposition. So why give them a chance to rake over their conscience? "Just don't do anything until Erin's safe," he repeated as he reached the door, opened it, and clumped out.

After Rhys left that morning and Wes a few hours later, Susannah made her own plans. She simply wasn't going to allow Rhys to walk into death. She still felt his tenderness cloak her like a gentle early morning fog. She knew he was saying farewell in the only way he knew, and she wasn't going to have it. She simply wasn't.

She went through every closet in the house, looking for black clothing, finally finding some and sitting down to make a few alterations. She found a knife, and she remembered how Rhys had hid his under his trouser leg. She made herself a band for each leg. She also found the tiny derringer Rhys had given her on the journey from Virginia, and tucked it in the back of her trousers.

Susannah doubted the Martins would kill the Nighthawk on sight. They would want to know about him. When they discovered she was a woman, they might not search her. If she could somehow take one or two of them off guard, hold a gun against them and force them to release Erin . . .

If only she had some luck.

She only knew she couldn't sit and wait any longer. She loved her Nighthawk and, by God, she was going to fight for him.

Sam Harris felt ridiculous. The black pants were too short, but they were the only ones he could find, a pair that once belonged to his father-in-law. The shirt was an old one and barely covered the chest which had expanded in the past months through plain, hard physical work. Work once done by slaves, and now by himself.

The meeting had broken up in disarray, no one able to agree, particularly after Wes Carr had left. The only agreement was that storming that the cabin was not a wise idea. One man's suggestion that they contact the U. S. military authorities met with derision. The captain had already sided with the Martins.

Once the other men had left, Sam went out to water the stock. The more he thought about the situation, the madder he became. Erin was his sister-in-law, his responsibility. No damn Yankee lover was going to take that away. Neither was some mysterious stranger who had offered his family aid when they needed it.

He hadn't gone to war, not because of lack of courage, but because he knew the MacDougal family needed him, and the Confederacy needed the cotton and food he produced. It had galled him to see men ride off, to hear of their deaths, while he was safe at home.

Well, now perhaps he *could* do something. Thanks to the Nighthawk, his family had some security. The least he could do now was assume his rightful responsibility. If he left now, he could reach the cabin before Wes. Or the Nighthawk.

Feeling like a damn fool in the borrowed clothes but better about himself than he had in years, he selected the darkest horse in the corral and mounted.

At last . . . he was going off to his own war.

Andy Able looked disgustedly at his choice of mounts. Not a black among them. He finally selected a bay. He swung his dark-clad leg aboard and started out the barn door when his brother walked in, also dressed in black. They stared at each other, and then grinned.

Andy waited while his brother saddled and mounted a dark gray gelding.

Oley Olsen groaned as he lifted an ancient leg on the back of the dark brown mare that was nearly as old as he was.

Hell, his last hooray. He didn't have anyone left. He'd even considered shooting himself a few days earlier, when he thought he would be forced from this land which he had fought for and which held the grave of his wife. And then a stranger in black had miraculously given him a reprieve.

He didn't have much time left, anyway. His heart was bad, and the doc said he had a year at most. The idea of substituting himself for the Nighthawk had come to him at the meeting, but he didn't say anything for fear someone would laugh, or even physically keep him from going.

He'd fought the Comanche, and he'd fought Santa Ana twice. Those pisspot upstart Martins weren't nothing. He made sure his shotgun, old Bess, was loaded, and he kicked his Sara Jane into a loping trot.

Cal Thornton, whose farm bordered the Mac-Dougal plantation, rummaged around the tack room for a black hat. Any kind of black hat.

He looked down at the watch his father had left him. The watch and the farm. That was all, but he had taken the farm and made it into something to be proud of, until the war came. Like his friends, he had gone off to the march of drums, believing he would be back in a matter of weeks. Instead, months went by and then years.

His baby died, and then his wife. Of loneliness, he believed, not pneumonia as he'd been told. He'd blamed the Yanks, and in his lonely bitterness he'd blamed Wes Carr.

But hours ago, he'd seen courage he had to admire. Carr was the only one among them who'd been ready to sacrifice himself for one of the families which had reviled him, the only one ready to pay back the man who had saved them all.

Cal had made a mistake about Wes Carr. Now he owed a debt. One he planned to pay.

Jesus whipped his horse with the riding crop. The note Señor Redding had given him was safely in his pocket.

All the way to Austin, to the leader of the U. S. soldiers. He wouldn't reach there until afternoon. So late.

He didn't know what the señor was planning, but Jesus sensed it was dangerous. Very dangerous. He dug his heels even deeper into his mount.

Chapter 29

Susannah left the house early, early enough that she wouldn't run into Wes, who was due back anytime. She took her black mare and rode to the old home place, to the cemetery.

She dismounted and walked over to her father's grave, running her fingers over the carved words. "You would have liked him," she murmured. "I know you would. You always saw into people, into their souls. And he has a good one. He just never had anyone to believe in, or who believed in him.

"You would approve, Papa, you would. I can see you now, peering down your glasses at him and asking his intentions. And he wouldn't tell you, but you would know. You would see that gentleness he tries to hide. You would see that strength, and why he hesitates to show any good at all. But it's there. He can't hide it. Not all the time.

"I don't know if this will work, Papa, but I have to try."

Susannah blinked back the tears that had been threatening since she woke up this morning, alone. Only the indentation in the pillow indicated he'd recently left. That and jewelry that lay on the table next to her, the jewelry she recognized from that vividly violent day months ago. It was a gesture of sorts, one that recognized her values, and she relished it.

And she wasn't at all surprised to see money in the other room, enough money to pay the taxes, nothing more, because he would know she and Wes wouldn't take more.

Susannah rose from the dirt, brushing it from the trousers, and tucked her hair under the wide-brimmed black hat she'd found. It was old, and it was too big, but that made it easy to hide the hair she'd pinned up under it.

"I'll be back," she said to the stone, but she knew it was merely bravado. There was a good chance she wouldn't.

"Rider." The call echoed over the hills to the two men sitting in the shack, playing cards. Hardy and Cate looked at each other. "It's early."

"Mebbe it's Lowell," Cate said hopefully.

Hardy shook his head. "They wouldn't be calling out." He picked up the rifle near the door. "Mebbe now we'll find out who's been causing all this trouble."

He opened the door, and watched the black-clad rider come in. "Damn, I didn't think he would do it."

The masked rider reached the cabin. Hardy pointed his gun at him. "Get off. Real easy-like."

The rider slid down, and Hardy stared in surprise. From what he'd heard from their gunhands, the Nighthawk was a monster in size, certainly large and strong enough to down several of them without noise. This man was slender, didn't look strong enough to pluck a willow from the river.

He wasn't wearing any guns, but Hardy looked toward one of several men who had ridden in with the Hawk. "Search him."

One man started to do that, then stopped as his

hands touched the rider's waist. "It's a woman, Hardy, a goddamn woman."

Hardy went up and ripped the mask from the face. "Susannah," he said, then sneered as he added derisively, "Mrs. Susannah Fallon. Shoulda known. Got more guts than the men in her family."

"But how—" started Cate.

"Another rider," a call came. "In black."

Hardy frowned, and then grabbed Susannah's arm. "What in the hell are you trying to pull?"

"Where's Erin?" she interrupted.

"None of your goddamn business," he said, giving the rifle to Cate and taking a pistol, holding it against her head, as another black-clad rider came in, his horse at a slow canter.

"Get down," he ordered the newcomer, and the rider slowly dismounted. "Take off your gun belt," Hardy ordered, and the masked rider did so, his eyes watching Susannah, whose hair had now fallen down around her face.

"*You*," the newcomer said in shock, and Susannah recognized Andy Able.

"What are *you* doing here?" The question came unbidden from her mouth.

"Rider coming in," came a resigned call from the hill above.

Hardy and Cate looked at each other. So did Susannah and Andy.

Hardy swore, but didn't move the gun from Susannah's head as a third man rode in. Susannah didn't even want to guess who this was. She knew from the seat it wasn't Rhys. This Nighthawk was bowed over, and the horse—well, the elderly beast was barely able to make its way up to the cabin.

When, at Hardy's order, he dismounted and demasked himself, Susannah found herself staring at Oley Olsen. Hardy rolled his eyes. "What in the hell are you doing here, old man?"

Oley looked at him indignantly. "You demanded that the Nighthawk come." His eyes suddenly twinkled as he saw the other two black-clad figures. "Seems there's a passel of us."

"Rider." The call echoed through the late afternoon sultriness.

Hardy swore again.

Oley stood his ground and demanded, "Where's Miss Erin?"

Andy moved a step toward the door and threw a hard look at Hardy. "If anything happened to her—"

"Rider." The call came again as two men, both dressed in black, came trotting slowly in.

Susannah recognized one: her brother. The other . . . Dear God, it was Sam Harris.

Wes's horse reached the two Martin brothers, now protected by six of their men, all with their guns drawn but with decidedly confused looks on their faces as if they didn't know whom exactly to aim them at. The Nighthawks had, by common but unspoken consent, separated themselves, standing several feet apart.

"Take off your masks," Hardy said. "Christ," he said. "Every goddamn man and woman in the county is showing up."

Cate looked at him worriedly. "What are we going to do? We can't shoot them all."

Wes dismounted, but Sam Harris stayed astride his horse as he pulled down his mask. Wes limped toward Hardy as he tore his mask off. Hardy stared at him, at the leg in the boot.

"Rider." The call came again, again with a note of resignation. For a moment, all of Hardy's men stared again toward the overgrown road that led to the shack.

Hardy had lost his concentration on seeing Wes's slow but inexorable approach, and his hand lowered slightly, away from Susannah. Just then, Wes attacked, throwing his full weight at Hardy, just as Andy did the same to Cate. Oley, who was standing next to his old horse, grabbed old Bess, and fired at one of the men who was aiming at Wes. Susannah leaned down and pulled the derringer from the back of her belt and aimed it at Hardy, who was trying to scramble up from under her brother. "Tell them to throw down their guns," she ordered.

"Another damn rider," came the persistent call, and Susannah looked at the western sky. The sun was just setting.

A tall man in black, who sat on his horse like a knight of old, was riding in, and behind him rode two more black-clad men. Susannah looked at Wes, who made his way to the cabin door and threw it open. It was empty. "She isn't here," he said.

There was the sound of multiple hoofbeats now, and Susannah looked up. Two additional men in black were riding in, and Martin's men were riding off, the ones who weren't held at gunpoint by the multiplying group of men in black.

There were at least eight Nighthawks at the cabin now, and more were coming in, all cloaked in the legend that had grown after Rhys twice raided the Martin house, easily downing everyone in his wake. Susannah could only guess what Martin's men were thinking. They had obviously been told to allow a man in black to approach and to hold their positions; they had apparently been bewildered as more and more came in. Twenty against one seemed reasonable odds, but now the legend was multiplied, fairly coming out of the air like some kind of magic. Susannah also knew that the Martins had ruled by fear and division. Now that fear was gone, and so was the division between the ranchers, and his men knew it.

Hardy swore as he stood. Held by Susannah's derringer, some erstwhile Nighthawks collected his gun and others; the man felled by Oley's old Bess lay groaning on the ground.

"Cowards," Hardy muttered at his departing men, but he couldn't keep his own hand from shaking.

"Now tell us where Miss Erin is," Wes said, "or I will take great pleasure in doing to you what you did to my guest."

Rhys sat on his dark bay horse and watched. He had timed his arrival for exactly sunset, hoping the last flash of sun might blind his opponents. He had been surprised to see a figure in black ride down the old overgrown road ahead of him, but surmised it was one of Martin's men.

And then he had heard the strangely odd call of "Another damn rider," but it hadn't really penetrated his concentration as he studied the position of each of Martin's men. And as he reached the rise, he saw them, the rather motley group of black-clad men with an assortment of misfitting clothes and dark horses, ranging from the sleekest to the most swaybacked.

His wary eyes caught Susannah's figure. He'd know her anyplace. And then Wes. Sam Harris. Andy Able and his brother. Others he didn't know. He didn't understand at first, and then finally he had to believe his eyes' own evidence. There were at least eight Nighthawks here, maybe more, and more coming behind him, each obviously willing to give his own life to save his. Not even knowing Rhys, or who he was, or why he'd done what he had, they were willing to sacrifice themselves. Including Susannah and Wes.

As he rode toward the shack, Rhys felt as though he'd been kicked in the gut. What he was seeing went against everything he'd ever learned in his thirty-six years of life. All that he'd ever believed.

Rhys saw the gun held on Hardy, and for a moment he regretted that his own revenge was being taken away, but then he saw Susannah's face as she looked at him, the emotion in her eyes as they settled on him. He pulled down the mask, dismounted, and walked over to where the ranchers were holding the Martin brothers and six others.

The other faces also turned that way, wanting to know who the new Nighthawk was. But they had ceased to be surprised as neighbor after neighbor had shown up. The Englishman created little additional interest, only chagrin that they'd all had the same idea and pursued it separately.

Yet there was pride on the faces too, all but Wes's, which was still creased with worry.

"Erin?" Rhys asked.

Wes let go of Hardy, whose hands were now being securely tied behind him. "This little weasel says she's at the Martin ranch."

Andy finished tying Hardy's hands. "Let's go get her."

There was a chorus of nods. They had Martin's brothers now, a basis for trade. The men shoved the brothers on horses and tied the other men hand and foot, leaving them inside the shack.

"We're going over there now," Sam Harris said, his curious eyes on Rhys.

Rhys turned to Susannah, who met his eyes directly. His gaze held hers for several seconds, something flickering deep inside them, then he smiled slowly. "I expect you plan to go," he said.

Susannah nodded. "She's my friend."

"You do a lot of things for your friends."

"So do you," she said, so low Rhys knew no one else could hear it. His hand took her arm. "I've sent Jesus for federal troops in Austin," he said. "I didn't know . . ."

Whether I would still be alive. "In your brother's name," he added.

She raised her eyebrows the way Rhys did so often. "He's not going to like that."

"It's time he made his peace," he said.

"And you, Rhys Redding," she said, "have you made your peace?"

His eyes studied her for a moment. "I don't know if there is such a thing for me."

"I do," she said with a serenity that almost made him believe. Almost.

He didn't answer. He didn't have to. The others were already in the saddles now, the Martin brothers having been hauled up like sacks of potatoes.

Rhys helped Susannah into her saddle, and then vaulted onto his own horse, aware of the stares that settled on him. He ignored them, straightening his back and giving them all his most aristocratically disdainful expression.

Erin woke to the consistent pounding in her head. Her arm hurt, her body ached, but most of all her head felt as though someone were ringing gongs inside. She had a feeling of unfamiliarity. She opened her eyes slowly, somehow dreading what she might find.

Eyes, in a face that might be handsome were it not so fleshy, peered down at her and she instinctively jerked away. And then slowly, very slowly, she forced herself to relax as her gaze met Lowell Martin's.

His light blue eyes, usually passionless, were intense. His hand went out to hers, which was lying on the sheet, and patted it. She resisted the urge to draw it back.

She'd always been a little afraid of him, even as she'd felt sorry for him. She'd tried to make up for her schoolmates' taunts by being kind, but there had always been a kind of sneakiness in him that repelled her. Now his brother, Hardy . . . he had been easy to detest. Cruelty came naturally to him, and she'd always feared him in a way she'd never really feared Lowell. She'd even chalked Hardy up as another reason to feel sympathy for Lowell. One couldn't choose one's family, and Lowell had lived much of his life trying to explain, or get his brother out of trouble.

But now she felt uneasiness, along with the constant aching pain. Why was she here?

"Lowell? What . . . happened?" The words finally made their way out of her wool-fuzzed mouth.

"That . . . outlaw in black attacked you," Lowell said. "Seems he isn't the hero everyone thought. My men came along and chased him off, but your horses spooked."

Erin tried desperately to remember. The black-clad man. The Hawk. The one who had saved them all from so much disaster. She remembered now . . . remembered looking back . . . seeing a man in black riding toward her. Not the Nighthawk. She had seen him that night of her father's wake. Lean and hard. There hadn't been an ounce of fat or extra flesh on him. The man who had chased her buggy . . . he had been bulky.

She shook her head in denial, too foggy to think not to do so. She saw his eyes change, something dangerous glinting in them. "My men saw him," he insisted as his hands fondled hers. The beginning of fear replaced that first uneasiness she'd first felt. "Your wife . . ."

"In town," he said, and the fear spread, although she hoped she'd kept it from her eyes and face.

"Why . . . am I here?"

His hand tightened on hers. "My men brought you here, and then I was afraid to move you. Don't worry, I'll take good care of you."

"Dr. Campbell?"

"He's away from his office."

"My sister . . . does she know?"

"Of course," he said. "We sent a note."

Then why isn't she here? Sam would never leave me in this house, not after Papa . . .

His pale blue eyes didn't quite meet hers. "I've had

some hot milk prepared," he said. "I'll get it. I'm sure your . . . brother-in-law will be here soon."

He disappeared out the door, and Erin tried to sit up. Pain nearly made her black out again. But something was wrong, very wrong. Wes. She wanted Wes. She slid down on the pillow as the door opened, and Lowell walked in, carrying a cup.

He reached over to help her partially sit, and she couldn't help but recoil. She saw several reactions, including hurt, reflect in his face, and then they were replaced by a businesslike expression. "This will make you feel better, Erin."

She started to sip obediently, but it tasted a little strange. If only she could think. But she couldn't, not with her head pounding as it was. She swallowed, and suddenly the milk came back up and splattered over his sleeve, over the bed.

Erin expected him to be angry, but there was only a frightening kind of patience about him. "I'll get some more," he said.

As he disappeared again, she struggled again to rise. She hurt all over, but she was finally able to sit. Then the world went spinning around, and she fell back. It was getting dark in the room. How many hours had she been here? *Wes, where are you? I need you.*

She heard a shout, then another. The sound of horses, many of them. Try. Once more. Try to get up. She stood, holding onto the poster of the bed. *You have to get out of here.* There was something so strange about Lowell. The image of the rider in black came back, the bulky, fleshy form. Hardy! It had been Hardy.

She fell to the floor, images whirling around her. Men in black. Descending on her. Wes . . .

• • •

They'd done it! That was Lowell's first thought as he heard the shouts and hoofbeats. They had the Nighthawk.

He opened the door, not worried about being unarmed. He had taken off his guns to go into Erin's room. He hadn't wanted to frighten her. He wanted her trust.

Expecting to see his own men, he felt his legs almost fold under him as, instead, he saw a dozen men, dressed in black, and his two brothers tied to the saddle horns of their horses.

Most of his own men had been sent out with Hardy and Cate to catch the Hawk. He hadn't wanted anyone around to see Erin, not until he'd decided exactly what to do with her. And now he was alone. Only three men had remained at the ranch as guards, and he saw they had been rounded up, their hands in the air.

He started to step back, into the house, for a gun, but the man in front shook his head threateningly. "Not one foot, Lowell, or you and your brothers will die."

All the black clothes, the black hats, the dark horses had rattled Lowell, nearly blinded him temporarily, but now he identified Wes Carr's voice, the long, solid build of him. Lowell's eyes went to the right leg. It was there!

So Wes Carr had been the Nighthawk all the time.

Lowell blustered. "You're trespassing."

"I want Erin," Wes said in a hard voice.

"She's . . . too ill to move," Lowell said. "My men saved her from . . ." He looked at all the black-dressed men and suddenly understood what had happened. He looked at Wes Carr, the one man the community had abhorred, other than Lowell and his brothers, and saw how the others had gathered around him, accepting his leadership. Lowell's gaze went over the faces of the Able brothers, Sam Harris, Cal Thornton, even Oley Olsen. And the Englishman, who sat tall and languid in the saddle, even more at home in it than the Texans. Suspicion clouded his mind, but then he realized it didn't make any difference now. The one thing he'd known could stop him had occurred: The ranchers had banded together. Vigilantes. An old Texas tradition. He hadn't thought these people had it left in them. And they hadn't, until—the Nighthawk had appeared.

Lowell looked at his brothers, huddled miserably on their horses. Hardy had several cuts, and he was shaking. Lowell shrugged. If anything, he was a pragmatist. He had lost this battle. But he still had a great deal of money, the store, the ranches he'd bought for a song. He could sell his holdings and start someplace else.

He shrugged. "She's in an upstairs bedroom," he said, not even bothering to try to explain. His explanations would have worked with the sheriff, even the Union captain, but not with these cold-eyed men who were more than ready to kill.

Wes dismounted and walked painfully on the wooden leg to the door. Sam Harris started to dismount, but Rhys leaned over and put a restraining hand on his arm, shaking his head. Harris settled back in the saddle.

Wes mounted the steps, using the railing for help. The first room on the right was empty. As he opened the second, he saw Erin crumpled on the floor next to the bed. He limped over to her and sat, reached down and cradled her in his arms.

"Erin," he said. "Erin."

She opened her eyes, the sky blue eyes that put the Texas bluebonnets to shame, and stared at him, her mouth trembling. "I knew you would come," she said, her eyes filling with tears. He leaned down, holding her gently, as if he feared she would break, and kissed her, his own mouth working desperately to keep back his own emotion, the terrible fear that had been building inside him. He felt the wetness on her cheeks, and on his own, and he knew they were coming from both sets of eyes and intermingling.

He took his lips from her mouth and feathered her damp cheeks with kisses. "I love you," he said.

Erin closed her eyes, savoring the sweet words, the barely checked emotion she heard in his voice. She savored them, and some of the pain faded in the wonder of hearing words she'd waited so very long to hear again. She wasn't going to lose this chance, no matter how she felt.

"Will you marry me?" she asked.

He hesitated only a fraction of a second. His hand touched her face. "It seems I must . . . to keep you out of trouble."

"But—" That wasn't what she wanted to hear.

"And," he added, "oh, Lord, how I want you," and then his mouth showed her exactly how much.

What to do with the Martins?

Wes and Susannah, who felt a woman should be along, had left with Erin, to take her home. Wes announced to the others that Rhys Redding would speak for him, and though the Texans eyed Redding dubiously, they had to admit that he too had posed as the Nighthawk to save the real one. They had all silently decided that the Nighthawk must have been Wes Carr, although there were still a few doubts. Wes had been with them, for instance, when the Hawk had made his last ride.

Perhaps, they thought, that rider had been a decoy—even Susannah. Or the Englishman. But apparently no one was going to say and, at this moment, no one was going to push for that information either. They all felt too much guilt.

"We could kill them," the Englishman offered in a

matter-of-fact tone that was chilling. Particularly to the Martins who were sitting there, trussed.

"That's an idea," Andy Able said, his eyes taking in the pale faces of the Martins.

"Or," said Cal Thornton, "they could leave this county and swear never to come back."

"After paying me for my ruined crops," Oley chimed in.

"And our cattle," the other Able brother said.

"MacDougal's horses," offered another.

"They still have the sheriff in their pocket," Rhys said as he leaned comfortably against the wall. "If we let them go, they could deny everything." He had donned his best supercilious smile, but no one seemed to take offense.

"A confession might help," Andy said.

"They could also deny that, say they were forced," Oley contributed.

Sam Harris spoke up. "I have a copy of a bill of sale that shows they stole cotton from my father-in-law. I haven't used it because I didn't want to say how I got it, but ... with the confession ..."

"I still think we should consider hanging them," Rhys countered, his cool, clipped unemotional voice obviously sending tremors down the backs of the three Martins, who were securely tied to chairs as their fate was discussed.

"It's a possibility," Cal Thornton agreed, watching Lowell Martin's face carefully. It was obvious the Martins no longer considered the Englishman inconsequential. He had to grin. The Martins would agree to almost anything after hearing the coldly calculating English voice. He knew he would. Christ, but the man sounded cold-blooded.

Lowell, his hands tied behind him, struggled to keep his voice from shaking. "You can't hang us ..."

Sam Harris looked at Rhys. "Wes said you spoke for him."

"Ah," Rhys said, "that poses a problem . . . a rather severe difference in philosophy between Mr. Carr and myself. I would most certainly vote for hanging. However, my host might frown upon us taking the law into our own hands. If this reprobate agrees to pay what you think he owes . . ."

"I'll sign whatever you want," Lowell said as sweat beaded on his forehead. He knew exactly what had happened to the goddamn Englishman. "And we'll leave Texas," he added hurriedly.

"With no more than your horses," Andy said.

"Damn you," Lowell said, but then he quieted as the Englishman's eyes seemed to slice him up as the whip had sliced Redding. There was an unholy gleam in them.

Andy suddenly took the lead. "It seems we have two choices," he said. "We can turn the Martins over to Mr. Redding here, since he seems to have a stomach for, well, justice. Or Lowell can agree to reparations and a very sudden departure from our community. Should we take a vote?"

The vote came very slowly, each man enjoying the misery of the three men who had almost destroyed the community and their families. The final vote was five to six. "Remember that," Andy told the Martins, "if you ever consider returning. Next time I'll vote the other way. Now for a pen and paper . . ."

Susannah rode by her old home from the Mac-Dougal place later that evening. It was not yet midnight, but she had no fear now of riding alone. She had left Wes and Erin, intending to go straight home, but then she turned her horse at the last minute. She wanted to tell her father what happened. She wanted to stop a moment at the tree where she and Rhys had first made love. She wanted to gather her strength for the battle she knew was coming. Rhys Redding.

The other one was over. Andy Able had stopped by the MacDougals' and reported the final resolution. Lowell Martin had signed a confession to some crimes and agreed to pay the ranchers for their losses. He and his brothers would leave central Texas immediately.

"But MacDougal's murder?" Wes said. "And Stan's?"

"We could never prove it in court," Andy said. "They no longer had Sean's horse. There were never any witnesses. And ... some of us might run into problems, too." He didn't have to mention that someone was the still unknown Nighthawk who had committed a bit of safecracking.

Susannah knew Andy was right, although it didn't seem exactly fair, after all the misery the Martins had caused. Knowing Hardy, however, he would probably get his brothers killed someplace else. While not completely satisfying, that thought provided some consolation.

And she had her brother back. Her home. Her friends. She had seen the way they had looked at Wes, the respect. She knew they thought he was the Nighthawk, and the only way he could deny it was to reveal the real identity of the black-clad Robin Hood. She knew Wes would never do that, either. Not unless Rhys Redding agreed.

And now Rhys had finished everything she and Wes had asked of him. And more. So much more. She felt her stomach tumbling over and over again as she tried to organize arguments for him to stay. Both urgency and delay nagged at her. Urgency that he might leave immediately, delay because she couldn't stand to hear him say it.

She approached the hill where her home had once stood. Her destination was the tree, the tree under which she'd discovered the vein of tenderness in Rhys Redding, where he had first given her a piece of himself.

Susannah heard the faint nicker of a horse. She

held her breath as she topped the hill and saw Rhys's horse, its head arched and alert.

And then she saw him. He was standing under the tree, his form silhouetted against the moon. He was still dressed in black, although his head was bare now, and a breeze ruffled his hair.

Her Nighthawk. She glanced back at his horse. The saddlebags were there, and they looked full. He had been ready to leave.

She dismounted, leaving the mare to nuzzle with his stallion. Rhys had turned and was watching her, his stance wary and unyielding.

"You were leaving without saying good-bye?"

"It's best," he said.

"For whom?"

His hand started up, as if to touch her, then fell. "For you."

"You're doing it again," she said. "Always so sure what's better for other people. What about yourself?"

He shrugged carelessly.

"Then tell me why it would be better for me."

"I told you before. I'm a thief . . . a gambler. A bastard."

"Do you have any idea how many lives you've put back together in the past few months?" she asked.

"Not because I intended it," he said. "I—"

"I know," she interrupted. "You had your own reasons. But somehow they got mixed up in others." She stopped for a moment. "Wes wants you to stay."

He looked at her with guarded eyes. "Why?"

"He seems to like you."

"Impossible."

She nodded. "And he knows I love you."

He flinched at the words. "You can't—"

"I do."

The two simple words were so definite, so sure, that Rhys felt uncertainty for the first time. "Wes can't . . . approve," he said.

"He's the one who told me to hurry . . . before you left." It was only a little lie. Susannah knew Wes would have if he hadn't been so concerned with Erin. The two of them, Susannah and Wes, had a new understanding now.

A sudden gleam came into his eyes. "He doesn't know—"

"Oh, he knows everything, I think," she interrupted. That, at least, was the truth. Susannah had seen it in Wes's eyes, but they had not been censorious.

"Christ, Susannah. I'm no good for you. Can't you see that? I've never stayed anyplace—"

"You've never had a place to stay, a home," she said. "A real home."

A real home. It sounded strange. So strange. But bloody hell, it was alluring. Like that siren call. And possible? Perhaps. For moments back at the shack, when he had watched the Nighthawks descend upon the Martins, and then later when his advice was asked at the Martin ranch, when Andy Able had winked at him as they discussed the Martins' futures, he'd felt a sense of belonging he'd never known. He'd been given respect, and others, including Wes, had offered their lives up for him.

No one had ever done that before, and he'd felt an aching pleasure so deep he'd barely kept it hidden. But it couldn't last. People would discover his true character. That was why he'd decided to leave, after all. That and the fact that he rarely deviated from a course once plotted.

But now . . . he wondered. Susannah knew all about him, and still cared, still wanted him. Wes knew—or suspected—and wished him to stay. And the others . . . well, they had some character problems of their own to work out. In the past few hours, they'd made progress.

Maybe he could, too.

The yearning inside exploded, too great now to be ignored. Or tamped.

"I love you," she said. "I just have to know . . . that you love me. That's all it takes, you know. Three words."

Love. Even more alluring than home. He felt so strange inside, warm and wanting. He wanted her. All of her, all the components of her: the look in her eyes as she gazed at him, the feel of her body against his, the touch of her hand on his as it trembled with the same kind of emotion that was wreaking havoc in him now.

He struggled toward sensibility one last time, only too aware it was a losing cause. "I'm not . . . I don't know anything about love . . ."

She shook her head in frustration, but her eyes softened as she gazed up at him. "Oh, Rhys, you've given me so much of it in the past weeks without even being aware. I've felt it. I just want to hear it."

The words stuck in his throat. A commitment. A promise. He never made promises, not, at least, until he had met Susannah Fallon. He seemed to have made several to her, even if he hadn't meant to keep them at the time. But perhaps he had. Perhaps he had even made her an unspoken one he wasn't even aware of.

And now, looking down at her, at the trust that shone in her eyes, that look that said he was indeed worth every bit of her, he knew he couldn't let this gift go.

Rhys thought about what had brought him here. His one and only good deed, his gift so many months ago to Lauren Bradley and Adrian Cabot. He had often decried it, especially in the weeks immediately following that aberration. Now he was learning that perhaps good deeds had a reward of their own. Perhaps they were not quite as preposterous as he had once thought.

He leaned down, his mouth brushing her cheek

and moving to her ear. "I love you," he whispered, and then, as if he finally understood what he was saying, the words came stronger.

"I love you," he said again, and then swung her up in his arms. The words did have a nice ring to them.

"I love you," he shouted suddenly, and a hawk, that had been resting in a tree, suddenly took flight, calling out its outrage at being disturbed, continuing its scolding as the joyous laughter beneath him faded into an oddly electric silence.

Epilogue

The Nighthawk became a legend along the Colorado River.

No one ever discovered his true identity, but the stories lived on, growing each year.

One day after the confrontation with the Martins, the U.S. military commander in Austin arrived in Jacob's Crossing. He promptly charged the Union captain there with bribery and appointed Wes Carr military commander of the area, since he had such a "fine rapport" with the residents.

It was Wes Carr who eased the transition of the area back into the Union, making sure that the law treated everyone equally. He rebuilt his father's house, and he and his wife, Erin, raised a distinguished new strain of cattle along with four children.

Rhys Redding became a pillar of the community—of sorts. His acerbic observations and occasional high-handedness were forgiven in light of the money he donated for a new school, and then for scholarships for local students to attend college. He was known as an "easy touch" for any hard-luck story, and his skill at gambling was renowned south of Austin. He soon found it difficult to find new players, and set his energies instead on raising some of the finest racing horses in Texas.

The first of his four children was born eleven months after Rhys arrived in Texas, eight months after the wedding of his parents.

It was a boy with black hair and dark eyes who was obviously fighting mad at the disturbance of his heretofore tranquil existence in the womb.

Susannah took one look and exclaimed, "My little Hawk," and Rhys winced. He'd had enough of the hawk business. He'd tried to lay the legend to rest; so had Wes, who would, for most people along the river, always carry that aura with him.

But still, Rhys reached out, and his finger was caught and held tight by tiny fingers. "Fierce," he said. "Like his father."

"I'm naught but a dove these days, my love," he said lazily.

She giggled. "Never that," she said. "What should we name him?"

He sat back and thought. Of everything that had brought him here . . . to the moment of supreme happiness that he never envisioned could exist. He looked at Susannah and thought of the joy she had brought to him, the gift that every minute had been.

"Roarke," he said suddenly.

"Roarke Redding?" She tasted the name on her lips. "Ummmm, I like it."

"It's a Gallic name," he said. "For ruler."

She arched a questioning eyebrow in imitation of her husband.

"You've come to rule my heart," he said, "and I fear *he* might rule both of us."

"Ah, no one rules you, Rhys."

"Hummmm," he said dubiously. But before he could disagree, she leaned up, her lips loving his, and together they went soaring, the hawk and his mate.

A Note
from the Publisher

Many of today's most popular and successful writers of women's fiction began their careers writing short, contemporary romances. Like Nora Roberts, Sandra Brown, and Iris Johansen, the author of this book made her name and honed her craft on what people in the book trade call "category" romance. The category romance—as published by Bantam's LOVESWEPT—is a wonderful and engaging form of short fiction that concentrates on the love story between two modern people. Unlike the old-fashioned, formulaic rich-man-poorwoman romances that dominated the market years ago, today's category romances are contemporary, timely stories, often dealing with the very issues that are important to you. The style is captivating, the love is real, and the passion runs deep. Some LOVESWEPTs are more witty, some more sensual, some are laced with humor, some packed with emotion; but they are all well-written stories of true love by very talented writers that quickly entrance and entertain you for a few hours.

The author of this book has written a brief account of her experience with LOVESWEPT, and invites you *to take a dip into the world of category romance. If you have never read a LOVESWEPT novel, the author and her publisher encourage you to ask for one at your bookstore, and discover a wonderful reading experience.*

A Love Affair with Loveswept

I've always had a tendency to do things backward, more or less the opposite from any reasonable human being.

Most writers in the romance genre begin with short contemporaries, and then continue on with longer books.

Not me!

I had completed ten historicals when a LOVE-SWEPT idea struck me and simply wouldn't go away. The idea of writing about ordinary people with ordinary—and extraordinary—problems in today's world was compelling. And just as challenging as voyages into history where characters are often larger than life.

The idea started with a newsmagazine feature on a teacher in Appalachia and the changes he'd made in the lives of his students and community. I'd always admired teachers and probably would have taught if journalism had not had a slightly stronger tug; this was my opportunity to salute those people who make a real difference in our society . . . and, in doing so, to tell a warm love story about compromise. An added joy was featuring my own animals in this tale.

And after that, after the story of David Farrar, there were others I wanted to write about: bits and pieces of people I'd met, known, and admired. It takes more courage, I believe, to live and love in today's world than it did in the past, and LOVESWEPT gives us a chance to tell these stories.

There is something else about LOVESWEPT. The writing is tighter, faster paced, more immediate than in a longer book. Just as craftspeople seek to expand their skills, a writer, I believe, should never remain static. LOVESWEPTs offer both writer and reader new opportunities to explore today's world and all its complexities and opportunities, in a very readable format.

I shall always love writing historicals, along with longer contemporaries, but LOVESWEPTs . . .

Ah . . . now, they make a tasty dessert.

About the Author

PATRICIA POTTER has become one of the most highly praised writers of historical romance since her impressive debut in 1988, when she won the Maggie Award and a Reviewer's Choice Award from *Romantic Times* for her first novel. She most recently received a 1993 *Romantic Times* Career Achievement Award nomination for Storyteller of the Year and Reviewer's Choice nominations for her novel *Lightning* (Best Civil War Historical Romance), and the hero, Lobo, in *Lawless* (Knight in Shining Silver). She has worked as a newspaper reporter in Atlanta and was president of the Georgia Romance Writers Association from 1988 to 1990.

Don't miss Patricia Potter's next thrilling historical novel,

NOTORIOUS

in which Marsh Canton, the mysterious
black-clad gunfighter from LAWLESS,
faces the biggest challenge of his life—and the most
dangerous threat to his guarded heart.

COMING SOON FROM BANTAM.

Marsh Canton has been a hired gun almost all his life. Now he's nearing forty, and he knows he's pushed his luck to the limit. When he wins a San Francisco saloon in a poker game, it seems a sign. From now on, he'll be Taylor Canton, respectable owner of the Glory Hole—but not if Catalina Hilliard has anything to do about it. Cat's worked very hard to make the Silver Lady the most popular spot in San Francisco, so hell would freeze over before she'd let Canton take away any of her business. She's determined to run him out of town, and once Canton meets the exquisite, untamed beauty, it's a challenge he accepts with relish. The war between them becomes the rage of San Francisco, but even more notorious is the passion that burns between the cold-blooded maverick and the woman who's wrapped her heart with ice.

In the following excerpt, Cat has just walked into The Glory Hole—and the astonishing sight of Canton playing the piano.

Miss Cat," he said as his eyes ran over her dress and shawl. "What a very pleasant surprise to have you visit again. Can't stay away?" His voice was low, and Cat didn't miss the taunt in it.

"I'm just returning your courtesy," she said sweetly. "A special invitation to sit at my table for the opening night of the Can Can." And then, because she realized that there was something about his musical ability he wished to hide, she remarked, "How interesting to discover you have . . . a talent. Are there any more I should know about?"

Something flickered in his eyes—anger, perhaps—before they clouded over as they had before, becoming like mirrors that reflected others but never himself. She wished she could do that. Her eyes could intimidate, but not like his. Never like his.

"Are you sure you want to know, Miss Cat?" Now his voice purred, but not like that of any cat she'd ever known. There was a sensual invitation in it that sent prickly shivers up and down her spine. She felt herself being expertly unclothed, piece by piece, by those damnable eyes. The shivers turned to raw, ragged heat that seemed to claw at her insides.

The air was alive with challenge . . . and that very same heat that had crawled inside her and was making her existence plain hell. It had reached outside her and grabbed him. She saw it plainly in the sudden tightness of his trousers. It was as if they were both caught in incandescent waves that burned and tormented. His dark gray eyes, usually as frigid as an ice-covered lake, were glittering with an internal fire of their own.

A muscle twitched in his cheek, and she took satisfaction in it. He wasn't nearly as indifferent as he wanted to appear. But then, as if through sheer force of will, the muscle quieted and a grim smile came to his lips. "I've forgotten my manners," he said in that natural way that told of breeding.

"Catalina, this is Miss Jenny Davis, who will be entertaining here, and Jenny, this is Catalina Hilliard, our worthy competitor from the Silver Lady."

Jenny flushed and Cat wondered why. She'd seen the quick looks the girl had sent toward Canton, and a bubble of jealousy floated to the surface of her consciousness, even as she tried to disclaim it. Damn the man. Did he have every woman panting after him?

He didn't seem to notice as he turned to the girl. "I'll see you this evening, Jenny. I have some business to discuss with Miss Catalina." It was an abrupt dismissal, but a slight, practiced smile softened the impact, and the girl nodded, though her eyes were curious.

He directed his attention to Cat once more. She wasn't surprised when he took her arm and guided her toward the door. Nor was she capable at the moment of avoiding it without causing a scene and making more of it than it might look to casual observers.

His fingers pressed into her arm in a possessive way, with a fierceness that indicated he wasn't going to let go. "Will you accompany me for a ride?" The question was not a question at all, but an order, and Cat bristled. She thought of pulling away, damn the consequences of a scene, but then he leaned down, his warm breath tickling her ear in a way that dulled her intent and excited . . . combustible parts of herself.

Before she could say no, he whispered, "Of course, you will," as though he heard her unspoken denial. "We have some very important matters to discuss. A certain police captain, for instance."

"I'm not sure what you mean," she said with the composure she'd practiced over the years.

Canton smiled. "You're very good. You would have made one hell of a gunfighter."

She leaped on the words. "Is that what you are, Mr. Canton?"

His smile widened, and Cat realized it was no slip of a tongue on his part. He was offering a slice of temptation, a hint as to what she desperately wanted to know, as part of his invitation. Or order.

"I didn't say that. I merely said that you would have made a good one."

"And why is that?"

"You give very little away, Miss Cat. And then there's a certain ruthlessness."

"You're describing yourself, Mr. Canton."

"I thought we'd gone beyond Mr. Canton." That infernal chuckle was in his voice, that deep sensuousness that was one half invitation, one half challenge and all deadly. Her wayward body felt the craving she heard in his voice, the pure lust that astounded and horrified her.

She summoned every inch of willpower she had and tried to pull away, but his hand was like steel on her arm. "I have to get back."

"Then I'll have to abduct you," he said in a low voice no one else could hear. "I'll try to make it far more pleasant than the one you arranged for me."

"I have no idea what you're talking about."

"Of course, we could discuss it here." They had

reached the door, away from Jenny Davis and customers, but all eyes in the establishment were fixed on them.

Cat lifted her chin. She didn't like the way he called her Cat. No one called her Cat, although a few had tried before she'd fixed them with the look that turned men into bumbling, apologetic fools. She had mastered it to perfection, but it didn't work on this man, seeming only to amuse him, as if he understood all the insecurity and pain that lay behind it, as if he knew it for the fraud it often was.

"We have nothing to discuss," she said coldly, even as she struggled to keep from trembling. All her thoughts were in disarray, and she wasn't sure whether it was because of her rage that he so easily penetrated all her defenses, that he was so adept at personal invasion, or because of that look in his eyes, that pure radiance of physical need that almost burned through her.

Fifteen years. Nearly fifteen years since a man had touched her so intimately. And he was doing it only with his eyes!

And, dear God, she was responding.

She'd thought herself immune from desire, that if she'd ever had any, it had been killed long ago by brutality and shame and utter abhorrence of an act that gave men power and left her little more than a thing to be used. She'd never felt this bubbling, boiling warmth inside, this craving that was more than physical but some kind of deeper hunger.

That's what frightened her most of all.

But she wouldn't show it. She would never show it, and eventually it would fade. She didn't even like Canton, devil take him. She didn't like anything about him. And she would send him back to wherever he came from, tail between his legs, no matter what it took.

But now she had little choice, unless she wished to stand here all afternoon, his hand burning a brand into her. He wasn't going to let her go, and perhaps it was time to lay her cards on the table. She preferred open warfare to guerrilla fighting. She hadn't felt right about the kidnapping and beating, she admitted to herself. She had soothed her somewhat jaded conscience with the fact that, after all, they hadn't achieved the desired result. Even if she did frequently regret that moment of mercy on her part.

She shrugged indifferently and his hand relaxed only slightly, still holding her like a steel manacle as he followed her out the door. He flagged down a carriage for hire and, with those elegant manners that still puzzled her, helped her inside with a grace that would put royalty to shame.

He left her for a moment and spoke to the driver, passing a few bills up to him, then returned and vaulted to the seat next to her. Not across, as she'd had hoped but close ... touching. Hard muscled thigh pushing against her leg; his tanned arm, made visible by the rolled up sleeve, brushing against her much smaller one, the wiry male hair sweeping over her skin with thousands of tiny electrical charges; his scent, a spicy mixture of bay and soap, teasing her senses. Everything about him—the strength and power and raw masculinity that he made no attempt to conceal—made her feel fragile as she'd not felt for years.

But not vulnerable, she told herself. Never vulnerable again. She would fight back, seize control and keep it.

She straightened her back and smiled. A seductive smile. A smile that had entranced men for the last ten years. A practiced smile that knew exactly how far to go. A kind of promise that left doors opened, while permitting retreat. It was a smile that kept men coming to the Silver Lady even as they understood they had no chance of realizing the dream. Hope sprang eternal with that smile. *Perhaps I will be the one.*

Canton raised an eyebrow. "You *are* very good," he said admiringly.

Cat didn't even try to pretend she didn't know what he meant. She shrugged. "It usually works."

"I imagine it does," he said. "Although I doubt if most of the men you . . . use it on have seen the thornier part of you."

"Most don't irritate me as you do."

"Irritate, Miss Cat?"

"Don't call me Cat. My name is Catalina."

"Is it?"

"Is yours really Taylor Canton?"

The last two questions were said softly, dangerously, both of them trying to probe weaknesses, and both recognizing the tactic of the other.

"I would swear to it on a bible," Marsh said, his mouth quirking upward, acknowledging the absurdity of the statement.

"I'm surprised you have one, or know what one is."

"I had a very good upbringing, Miss Cat." He emphasized the last word.

"And then what happened?" The question was caustic.

The sardonic amusement in his eyes faded slightly. "A great deal. And what is your story?"

Dear God, his voice was mesmerizing. An intimate song that said nothing but wanted everything. Deep and provocative. Compelling and irresistible. Almost.

"I had a very poor upbringing," she said. "And then a great deal happened."

For the first time since she'd met him, she saw real humor in his eyes. Not just that cynical amusement as if he were some higher being looking down on a world inhabited by silly children. "You're the first woman I've met with fewer scruples than myself," he said, admiration back in his voice.

She opened her eyes wide. "You have some?"

"As I told you that first night, I don't usually mistreat women."

"Usually?"

"Unless provoked."

"A threat, Mr. Canton?"

"I never threaten, Miss Cat. Neither do I turn down challenges."

"And you usually win?"

"Not usually, Miss Cat. Always." The last word was flat, almost ugly in its surety.

"So do I," she said complacently.

The heat in the closed carriage had escalated. Their voices had lowered into little more than husky whispers. The electricity between them was sparking, hissing, crackling, threatening to ignite. Her gaze couldn't move from his, nor his from hers. His hand moved to her arm, his fingers running up and down it in slow sensuous trails and she felt like a thousand nerve ends being singed. But she wouldn't move, wouldn't give him that satisfaction.

And then the heat was that of the bowels of a volcano. Intense and violent. She wondered very briefly if this was a version of hell. She had just decided it was when he bent toward her, his lips brushing over hers.

And heaven and hell collided.

The kiss had been as inevitable as day following night.

Marsh had known it from the moment he saw her in the Glory Hole.

The only way to get her out of his system was this, and he was deadly determined to accomplish it. He'd thought the fireworks that constantly surrounded them were nothing more than that, a brief flurry of sound and fury, signifying nothing.

He hoped Shakespeare would forgive him for his literary liberties, but the mental diversion helped in reestablishing some kind of equilibrium.

Until his lips touched hers.

He hadn't really known what to expect. Ice that would cool the damned heat burning him inside out. Emptiness that would swallow his unexpected and disturbing need.

But there was no ice. No emptiness.

She was as unwilling a participant as he in the damnable attraction that engulfed them as if it were a hurricane and they were caught in the eye.

The eye that was every bit as dangerous as the wind that swirled around it. And explosive, filled with the hot expectancy of a pending lethal storm.

Her lips, at first reluctant and wary, suddenly yielded, yet she wasn't surrendering, was merely astonished and stunned. A part of him understood that, because he felt the same. He also felt the need to explore, to taste, to test. Even savor the currents of hot pleasure that surged through him as first their lips found common ground, and then their tongues and their hands.

He felt her arms go around him, just as his had wrapped her tightly against him. He felt every movement of her body, every quiver, every stiffening awareness of his own arousal pressed into her. How long had it been since he'd felt this alive? Had he ever felt like this ... even before war and hate and revenge had robbed him of feeling?

A low moan rumbled through his body as, unaccountably, his mouth gentled. He didn't understand where this very odd tenderness came from, where it had been lurking to emerge at this inconvenient time. Still, it was ... pleasant. More than pleasant, even, and some instinct told him it was as new and strange to her as it was to him.

Her mouth opened hesitantly under his lips, greeting him with an unexpected longing that he went through to his core, and his tongue ran knowingly over the sensitive crevices of her mouth. He lifted his head slightly, his gaze moving to her eyes, and he was almost lost in the smoldering green depths of them, even as he sensed the hostility that was still there.

He closed his own eyes against them, against the confused yet heated emotion in them, and his lips hardened. He forced anger. He forced it because he *was* angry, angry that she was stirring things best left alone, angry because he knew he couldn't trust her. She was the woman who had had him beaten, almost shanghaied, who caused his imprisonment in a filthy cage. The gentleness changed to something harsh and bitter. Punishing.

He still felt her response, but now he knew it was unwilling, and took a sudden cruel pleasure in the fact that she was as helpless against this attraction as he was.

His lust reached monumental proportions as he felt the surge of hot heat reach his loins. Christ, he hadn't meant this to happen. He'd wanted to punish her in some way for those two weeks of indignity and pain. He'd wanted to discomfort her, and now he was the one discomfited. He'd recognized her physical reaction to him and he'd wanted to tease and tempt and make her beg for more. But he was the one begging, damn her.

What was happening?

You don't even like her, he told himself.

But his hands wanted to be gentle, and he had to hold himself back. He could not betray this weakness, not to her. She would take that weakness and use it. Just as he would do the same to her.

After the one time in his life he'd lost his self-control, he had spent the rest of his life honing it. He had always been able to distance himself from events, even those he'd participated in as a principal, as if he were standing aside and watching himself do mechanical things.

But he was not standing away now, not any part of him. Every sense was engaged, every nerve ending tingling. The fact that they had been numb for so long only heightened the sensations.

His hands moved to one of her breasts, fondling it through the cloth. Heat radiated through the material, and his fingers moved up to caress her shoulders, then made their way under the material as his lips left her mouth and started nibbling at the soft vulnerable part of her neck. He felt shivers run through her body, almost like spasms. He felt similar spasms rock his body, and his hands became even more invasive. One started to unbutton the blouse in back while the other slipped down further until he found the soft flesh of her breast. It was firm, so firm, the nipple erect in its own excitement.

She suddenly wrenched away with a little cry, staring at him with a kind of horror that stunned him into stillness. For the first time since he'd met her, he saw fear in her eyes. And vulnerability that struck him like a blacksmith's hammer.

He watched her fight for control. He should feel satisfaction, but didn't, only a greater emptiness that he inspired this terror in her, even after she'd responded to him, after she'd been as aware as he of the physical attraction between them.

He watched her with narrowed eyes, wondering if this was some kind of game, even as his intuition told him it was not. No one could quite manage that look of humiliation, the struggle to hide it so gallantly. He half expected an explosion of cries of abuse, of blame, but it didn't come. But then she seldom did the expected; that, he knew, was part of his fascination with her.

Catalina's eyes met his directly. "That was a mistake," she said.

"Your or mine?" His question was cool, as unemotional as her face was now, although his body was still caught in the storm of physical need. It ached unmercifully.

"Mine. I should never have come with you."

"I didn't give you any choice."

"I always have a choice, Mr. Canton."

He leaned back against the seat of the carriage, surveying her with eyes that were ruthless in their prying. "I would suspect that once you didn't." There was no sympathy in the statement, only an observation.

Her eyes went very cold. "You know nothing, Mr. Canton."

"I know you responded to me. I didn't imagine that ... passion. I'm just not sure why you suddenly ..."

"Ah, you're not sure of something. What a surprise."

She was trying to divert him, and he had no intention of letting it happen, not when spasms of want still raked his body.

"The icy Miss Catalina," he said in a silky voice. "Fire and ice. Exactly what are you?"

"Nothing for you."

"That's not what your eyes were telling me minutes ago. You wanted me every bit as much as I wanted you."

"Male arrogance," she said superciliously, though he noticed the slightest tick in her cheek that gave her away. "You're not nearly as ... interesting as you seem to think you are."

He raised an eyebrow. "No?" he asked in a low rumbling voice. "Didn't anyone ever tell you what happens to little girls who lie?"

"Or you what happens to big boys who are arrogant bullies?" she retorted.

He chuckled mirthlessly. "They get shanghaied?"

She didn't blink. "That's a thought."

"I wouldn't try it," he warned softly. "Again."

"If I intended you to be shanghaied, you would be on your way to China," she said.

"Just beaten and jailed, then?"

"Do you always talk in riddles, Mr. Canton?"

He wished she didn't look so damn beautiful when she was angry. A lock of black hair had fallen from the twist that held her tresses back from her face, and it softened her expression.

"We could call a truce, Miss Cat." He hadn't meant to make the offer. She had started this war, and he had lost only one in his life. Actually others had lost that one for him. He'd never surrendered.

"No," she said flatly. "I've worked too hard to build the Silver Lady."

"So the war continues."

She shrugged. "Call it what you will."

"No more ambushes, Miss Cat," he warned quietly.

Her green eyes bored into him. "Who was it who said war was hell?"

His hand touched the soft flesh under her chin, lifting her face until her gaze locked into his. "A northern general, I think. But you don't know the beginning of hell, Miss Cat."

"And you do?" The electricity was there again, darting like heat lightning. Energy pulsed between them. Dare and counterdare. Thrust and counterthrust. Each searching out the other's weaknesses. He moved his fingers along her cheeks, watching as she colored from ivory to rose.

"Don't touch me," she said, jerking away.

"Why, Miss Cat?" He enjoyed using the name, knowing it provoked her, made the green eyes even greener as they glinted pure malice at him. "Does it disturb you? Burn you?"

It did, but Cat wasn't going to admit it. She felt like a rabbit hypnotized by the unblinking stare of a snake. If only her body didn't react to him in such unfamiliar ways. If only she didn't want to reach out and touch him. If only she didn't remember that moment when his lips first met hers, a moment unlike any she'd ever known. Rare and gentle. And she'd responded in a way that was unfathomable to her. But the sweetness was so quickly gone, she told herself that she'd simply imagined it.

He was pure devil.

"I don't like you, Mr. Canton."

"I don't think I asked if you liked me."

"Take me back."

"Not quite yet."

"Just what do you want?"

He leaned back and, without asking her permission, lit a cheroot he'd taken from his shirt pocket. He inhaled deeply, then sent out lazy smoke rings to bounce against the ceiling of the carriage.

"Do you have any idea of what a jail cell is like?" he said after serveral moments of silence.

"No," she said, "but I suspect you do and that you've been in one more than once."

"Only once, Miss Catalina. It wasn't much larger than this carriage, and not nearly as comfortable. I always give back in good measure what I get. I'm making this one exception."

"Another warning?"

"A promise."

She bristled. Catalina hadn't apologized to anyone in a number years. It was a waste. You couldn't take back actions. She knew that better than anyone.

"You don't belong here, Mr. Canton."

He raised an eyebrow. "Where do I belong?" He really wanted to know.

Cat swallowed. There was just the faintest hint of wistfulness in the question. Not enough to invoke sympathy but enough to be intriguing. She remembered again that very brief instant of gentleness. It had to have been her imagination.

"Where did you come from?" It was the first truly personal question she'd posed. She thought he would brush it aside.

He shrugged carelessly, but she saw something flicker in his eyes, something like loss. "A place that no longer exists."

She shouldn't have asked the question. She didn't want to know. The conversation was too personal. She didn't want to like him, or feel the slightest interest. She just wanted him to disappear. She wanted the Silver Lady back like it was. She wanted her life back like it was. No complications. She wanted to be respected. She wanted to be rich. She wanted to ... be safe. Which meant being alone.

Alone. The word had never hurt before. It had always represented Paradise. Why not now?

You can't trust him. You can't trust any man, the voice whispered to her.

"I want to go back," she said suddenly.

"Coward," he accused.

"I just don't like the company."

"But I do, and right now I'm in control."

"I'll have you arrested for kidnapping."

He moved his fingers across the skin of her arms. "Then I might as well make it worthwhile."

The Very Best in Historical Women's Fiction

Rosanne Bittner

_____ 28599-8 EMBERS OF THE HEART $4.50/5.50 in Canada
_____ 28319-7 MONTANA WOMAN $4.99/5.99
_____ 29033-9 IN THE SHADOW OF THE MOUNTAINS $5.50/6.99
_____ 29014-2 SONG OF THE WOLF $4.99/5.99
_____ 29015-0 THUNDER ON THE PLAINS $5.99/6.99

Iris Johansen

_____ 29604-3 THE GOLDEN BARBARIAN $4.99/5.99
_____ 29244-7 REAP THE WIND $4.99/5.99
_____ 29032-0 STORM WINDS $4.99/5.99
_____ 29968-9 THE TIGER PRINCE $5.50/6.50
_____ 28855-5 THE WIND DANCER $4.95/5.95

Susan Johnson

_____ 29125-4 FORBIDDEN $4.99/5.99
_____ 29312-5 SINFUL $4.99/5.99

Teresa Medeiros

_____ 29407-5 HEATHER AND VELVET $4.99/5.99

Patricia Potter

_____ 29071-1 LAWLESS $4.99/ 5.99
_____ 29070-3 LIGHTNING $4.99/ 5.99
_____ 29069-X RAINBOW $4.99/ 5.99

Amanda Quick

_____ 29316-8 RAVISHED $4.99/5.99
_____ 29315-X RECKLESS $5.99/6.99
_____ 29325-7 RENDEZVOUS $4.99/5.99
_____ 28932-2 SCANDAL $4.95/5.95
_____ 28354-5 SEDUCTION $4.99/5.99
_____ 28594-7 SURRENDER $5.99/6.99

Suzanne Robinson

_____ 29574-8 LADY DEFIANT $4.99/5.99
_____ 29430-X LADY GALLANT $4.50/5.50
_____ 29678-7 LADY HELLFIRE $4.99/5.99

Deborah Smith

_____ 28759-1 THE BELOVED WOMAN $4.50/ 5.50